Forgive and Remember

33 Classic Stories About Forgiveness

Rosalyn Falcón Collier, editor

with a foreword by
Marietta Jaeger-Lane

San Antonio, Texas
peace Center

peaceCENTER Books
1443 S. St. Mary's, San Antonio, Texas 78210
210.224.HOPE
www.salsa.net/peace

"Forgiveness liberates the soul. It removes fear. That is why it is such a powerful weapon."

Nelson Mandela
"Invictus" (2009)

On the back cover:
Rembrandt van Rijn, The Return of the Prodigal Son, c. 1662
Peter Paul Rubens, The Reconciliation of Jacob and Esau, c. 1624
Frederic Leighton, The Reconciliation of the Montagues and Capulets, 1854
Ciro Ferri, The Reconciliation of Jacob and Laban, 17th Century

CONTENTS

Preface

Rosalyn Falcón Collier — p. vii

Foreword

Marietta Jaeger-Lane — p. ix

Self

Tajima, Miss Mitford — p. 3
The Heart of John Middleton, Elizabeth Gaskell — p. 9
The Cost of Kindness, Jerome K. Jerome — p. 31
God Sees the Truth, But Waits, Leo Tolstoy — p. 39
Jean Francois, Maurice Baring — p. 47
The Star-Child, Oscar Wilde — p. 53
For Conscience' Sake, Thomas Hardy — p. 69
The Woman Who Tried to Be Good, Edna Ferber — p. 85
Cain's Atonement, Algernon Blackwood — p. 97
The Fiend, F. Scott Fitzgerald, — p. 105

Family

The Parable of the Lost Son, Luke 15: 11-32 — p. 113
The Mirror of Matsuyama, A Story of Old Japan,
    Yei Theodora Ozaki — p. 115
The Christmas Peace, Thomas Nelson Page — p. 127
The Silent Sisters, Israel Zangwill — p. 151
The Hatred of the Queen: A Story of Burma,
    L. Adams Beck — p. 157
A Problem, Anton Chekhov — p. 175
The Requiem, Anton Chekhov — p. 183
A Sister's Confession, Guy de Maupassant — p. 189

The **Reckoning**, Edith Wharton — p. 195
Forgiveness, Guy de Maupassant — p. 215
Joseph and His Brothers, Genesis 42-45 — p. 221

Friends

The **Sexton's Hero**, Elizabeth Gaskell — p. 231
The **Count's Apology**, Robert Barr — p. 241
A Spark Neglected, Leo Tolstoy — p. 259
Forgive and Forget, T S Arthur — p. 273
The **Thing's the Play**, O. Henry — p. 281
Forgive and Forget, Maria Edgeworth — p. 289
The **Penance**, Saki — p. 303
The **Scapegoat**, Erckmann-Chatrian — p. 309
Putting Things Right, Henry Seton Merriman — p. 317
A Jury of Her Peers, Susan Glaspell — p. 321
Forgiveness, Rev Joseph Alden — p. 343
Proclaim Liberty Throughout the Land, Leviticus 45 — p. 347

Afterword

Jerusalem, Naomi Shihab Nye — p. 350

33 "F" Word Films — p. 353

Authors, Stories & Notes — p. 367

FORGIVENESS

"As we are, our hearts are closed, and we cannot place the holy words in our hearts. So we place them on top of our hearts. And there they stay until, one day, the heart breaks, and the words fall in."
Parker Palmer

At the peaceCENTER we have an 'F' word, one that no one wants to talk about in public. About ten years ago we published a book entitled *Walking Jesus' Path of Peace*. After 9/11 several people called us to find out about amending the chapter on forgiving our enemies: surely this could not apply under the present circumstances! We did not revise the chapter and probably lost some fans.

So can you guess what the 'F' word is?

One Good Friday a dozen years ago I had this thought: What if Jesus could not bring himself to say "I forgive you" at that extreme moment on the cross; so instead he stepped out of the way and said "Father, you forgive them, (I can't do it right now) for they know not what they do." That insight has changed how I saw my part, I just have to let go and get out of the way, letting forgiveness come through me.

This is a whole lot easier said than done. How simple it is to tell others to forgive and forget; how difficult it is to budge one iota from holding on to my own resentments and vindication. "All I want is justice (read: retribution) and then I will be satisfied." Forgiveness begins at the home within. Allowing my heart to be broken open in order to be forgiven is an important first step on the sacred journey. Allowing forgiveness to flow through me out to my family and friends is another.

I divided this book of 33 stories into Self, Family and Friends, and added 33 films. This compilation of short stories about the 'F' word has helped me to study the actions of the heart, someone else's not mine, more closely. It is in sifting through the different scenarios, that I find myself remembering past and present situations in my own life still in need of release, needing me to get out of the way of the flow of forgiveness that is everywhere present.

An ancient map that leads us to that home within is the Cretan labyrinth shadowed here. Giving myself permission to find my way through my own personal history while reading or watching each one, has helped me to amplify forgiveness at the center of my life's pilgrimage. I enter the labyrinth burdened with fear, resentments, justifications, jealousies, retributions, fantasies of revenge. When I reach the center if I can open myself to forgiveness, I have felt a movement in my heart as it softens and warms to the flow. While emerging from the center, if I have chosen to release my need to control, I feel myself enveloped and carried along by love, compassion, empathy, reconciliation and remembrance, lightening my load and filling me with peace.

The hardest part is overcoming the fear of stepping into this channel of transformation, because I want to hold on tight and prove that I am right. Yet once I take the initial step it seems less daunting. Allowing myself to imagine a different outcome, brings about fantasies of healing for myself, my family and my friends.

Knowing all of this I'll admit that sometimes I still choose to withhold forgiveness, even or maybe especially, from myself. What am I still afraid of? Let's bring the 'F' word out into the light, into public conversations, into acceptable vocabulary, into my experience, into my heart. What have I got to lose? What have I been missing? Where do I start? When?

By relaxing and entertaining myself with these stories of forgiveness I am learning vicariously how to ask for forgiveness and how to offer it to others. I might even be tempted to forgive myself, to see how it feels; but for now let's just take it one story at a time.

Peace,
Rosalyn Falcón Collier

FOREWORD
Marietta Jaeger-Lane

"Forgive And Remember" is the name of this unique collection of stories, and yet "Forgive and Forget" was the idiom with which I grew up. Even as a child, try as much as I could to be good, the "forget" part was simply unattainable. As an adult, it seemed unimaginable. How does one forget hurtful words, violent actions, unrepentant injustices done to oneself, let alone to loved ones?! Short of developing amnesia, all those events are as much a part of one's history, one's memories, as are the kindnesses, acts of charity, respect and affirmation, and tender demonstrations of love. I did discover that exploring all the aspects and background of the situation or person that called for my forgiveness, enabled understanding and even compassion for the offender. However, because I couldn't forget what the offender did, I was left in a steady state of bemusement and concern for my salvation.

That is, until — my youngest daughter was kidnapped in the middle of the night during a camping trip. Then, forget— "forget!" I couldn't even imagine the possibility of "forgive." Susie was an innocent, defenseless little girl and I had every right to avenge whatever she was enduring. Images of doing violence to the kidnapper, even taking his life with my own hands and a smile on my face, danced tantalizingly through my mind. After all, who wouldn't say I was justified?!

However, the sound-track, deeply instilled in childhood, that still ran loud and strong through my being was "be a good girl." Beyond that, my Christian faith, to which I was committed to live out with integrity and faithfulness, called me to forgive my enemies, in which category the kidnapper certainly belonged. Thus began a wrestling match with God, with me defending my justifiable stance of rage and revenge, and God patiently, gently, but persistently reminding me that forgiveness is healthier than hate, and if I allowed myself to stay in my present state of fury, all that I'd accomplish would be to give the kidnapper control over my state of mind, and make another victim — me. Well, needless to say, it's not too difficult to know that when one wrestles with God, who wins! Knowing I couldn't do it by myself, I promised to work with God to move my heart from fury to forgiveness.

The ensuing year, still not knowing Susie's fate or whereabouts, was the greatest challenge of my life. In all honesty, forgiveness is hard work. It requires daily diligent discipline and control of mind and tongue. Like a recovering addict, most days I had to take it hour by hour — constantly calling myself to what I say I believe: God is crazy about all of us, no matter who we are or what we've ever done. Therefore, in God's eyes, I had to admit that the kidnapper was just as precious as my little girl. He had dignity and worth, just as we all do — not by any merit of our own, but because we all belong to God. I had to think and speak of him with respect and not use derogatory terms which came so easily to mind, given that I had no knowledge of what Susie was having to endure and if I would ever get her returned to me.

Finally, I had to surrender to God's call in Scripture to pray for the kidnapper, which of course, was the last thing I felt like doing. At first, the best I could muster were simple, unsophisticated prayers — just one a day — for trouble-free travel, good hunting or fishing, appropriate weather for whatever he was doing. But, as I made a true effort to be genuinely authentic in whatever I prayed, it became easier and easier to do so and to want him to experience God's providence and provision. I remember hearing long ago that whenever we pray for someone, it's our own heart that gets changed. I experienced that healing reality.

On the first year anniversary that Susie was taken from me — exactly one year to the minute, he said — the kidnapper phoned me in the middle of the night. His intent was to taunt and torment me, get me raging, laugh at me and hang up, leaving me hanging and waiting again. However, to my own amazement, everything that I'd been working and praying for during the past year, came to fruition in me at that moment. All that I had chosen to do and now really wanted to do, happened. My heart was changed from fury to forgiveness, from rage to reconciliation and I felt genuine concern and compassion for the man — no one more surprised at this than me! When I told him that I'd been praying for him and asked what I could do to help him, he broke down and wept. This mentally ill, very violent young man was undone by what God had done in me. Still saying he wanted to exchange Susie for ransom, he remained in conversation for well over an hour. However, in that milieu of calm and forgiveness, the kidnapper inadvertently revealed sufficient information about himself that the FBI were able to identify him. My forgiveness was his undoing.

As he was being arrested, sadly, evidence was found that was concrete proof that my daughter's life had been taken long before, probably two or so weeks after she had been taken from me. Though we'd been searching for her all this time, she was already safely home — Home in the healing, loving arms of God. In all honesty, not the answer I was hoping for, but my spirit had been calmed and I had released my rage and desire for revenge. Because of his confession and other evidence, I know, but cannot bear to dwell upon, all she endured during her captivity. I will never forget any of it.

However, my faith tells me none of that is her reality now. Susie has been set free from her horrific suffering and I have been set free from the ugliness of hate and unforgiveness. My reality is that I am no longer controlled and captured by an event in the past which, whatever I do and however I feel, can never be changed. It is extremely difficult for our hearts and minds to be willing to embrace that truth but I have learned we can do it — with time and care.

I have also learned that we must do it, because, in spite of the old adage, we will never forget what happened, and the only way we can live with those hard memories is to forgive the offender and let go of all those negative feelings. Hatred and unforgiveness are not healthy and they will damage us eventually on every level of our beings. The medical professions are seeing evidence of this phenomenon more and more. There is an old Chinese proverb that states "One who seeks revenge should dig two graves."

Please hear me — I am not advocating forgiveness and then ignoring the responsibilities and appropriate consequences, legal and otherwise, for the offender. I have come to believe that God's idea of justice is restorative — the healing of the wounded human souls of all parties involved, appropriate restitution or service of some kind, reconciliation of relationships if possible. However, we must start with ourselves, learning to forgive, however long and how much effort it takes, and it's worth all the effort it takes.. Forgiveness is a gift to ourselves — of freedom, healing, and the ability to move on with our lives, unchained from the past.

In reading this marvelous collection of stories of forgiveness, I was struck that they were all written long ago, prior to 1923. The ability to forgive is not a new idea, though I think it has always been counter-cultural. However, just as our bodies have the inclination and capacity to heal, so too, do our hearts. Clearly, the characters in these stories demonstrate for us that the principle of forgiveness has long been known to be one of the most life-giving things we can do for ourselves. So, don't forget — forgive and remember!

Marietta Jaeger-Lane
March, 2010

SELF

Tajima
Miss Mitford

Once upon a time, a certain ronin, Tajima Shume by name, an able and well-read man, being on his travels to see the world, went up to Kiyoto by the Tokaido. [The road of the Eastern Sea, the famous highroad leading from Kiyoto to Yedo. The name is also used to indicate the provinces through which it runs.] One day, in the neighborhood of Nagoya, in the province of Owari, he fell in with a wandering priest, with whom he entered into conversation. Finding that they were bound for the same place, they agreed to travel together, beguiling their weary way by pleasant talk on diverse matters; and so by degrees, as they became more intimate, they began to speak without restraint about their private affairs; and the priest, trusting thoroughly in the honour of his companion, told him the object of his journey.

"For some time past," said he, "I have nourished a wish that has engrossed all my thoughts; for I am bent on setting up a molten image in honour of Buddha; with this object I have wandered through various provinces collecting alms, and (who knows by what weary toil?) we have succeeded in amassing two hundred ounces of silver—enough, I trust, to erect a handsome bronze figure."

What says the proverb? "He who bears a jewel in his bosom bears poison." Hardly had the ronin heard these words of the priest than an evil heart arose within him, and he thought to himself, "Man's life, from the womb to the grave, is made up of good and of ill luck. Here am I, nearly forty years old, a wanderer, without a calling, or even a hope of advancement in the world. To be sure, it seems a shame; yet if I could steal the money this priest is boasting about, I could live at ease for the rest of my days;" and so he began

3

casting about how best he might accomplish his purpose. But the priest, far from guessing the drift of his comrade's thoughts, journeyed cheerfully on till they reached the town of Kuana. Here there is an arm of the sea, which is crossed in ferry-boats, that start as soon as some twenty or thirty passengers are gathered together; and in one of these boats the two travellers embarked. About half-way across, the priest was taken with a sudden necessity to go to the side of the boat; and the ronin, following him, tripped him up while no one was looking, and flung him into the sea. When the boatmen and passengers heard the splash, and saw the priest struggling in the water, they were afraid, and made every effort to save him; but the wind was fair, and the boat running swiftly under the bellying sails; so they were soon a few hundred yards off from the drowning man, who sank before the boat could be turned to rescue him.

When he saw this, the ronin feigned the utmost grief and dismay, and said to his fellow-passengers, "This priest, whom we have just lost, was my cousin; he was going to Kiyoto, to visit the shrine of his patron; and as I happened to have business there as well, we settled to travel together. Now, alas! By this misfortune, my cousin is dead, and I am left alone."

He spoke so feelingly, and wept so freely, that the passengers believed his story, and pitied and tried to comfort him. Then the ronin said to the boatmen:

"We ought, by rights, to report this matter to the authorities; but as I am pressed for time, and the business might bring trouble on yourselves as well, perhaps we had better hush it up for the present; I will at once go on to Kiyoto and tell my cousin's patron, besides writing home about it. What think you, gentlemen?" added he, turning to the other travellers.

They, of course, were only too glad to avoid any hindrance to their onward journey, and all with one voice agreed to what the ronin had proposed; and so the matter was settled. When, at length, they reached the shore, they left the boat, and every man went his way; but the ronin, overjoyed in his heart, took the wandering priest's luggage, and, putting it with his own, pursued his journey to Kiyoto.

On reaching the capital, the ronin changed his name from Shume to Tokubei, and, giving up his position as a samurai, turned merchant, and traded with the dead man's money. Fortune favouring his speculations, he began to amass great wealth, and lived at his ease, denying himself nothing; and in course of time he married a wife, who bore him a child.

Thus the days and months wore on, till one fine summer's night, some three years after the priest's death, Tokubei stepped out on the veranda of his house to enjoy the cool air and the beauty of the moonlight. Feeling dull and lonely, he began musing over all kinds of things, when on a sudden the deed of murder and theft, done so long ago, vividly recurred to his memory, and he thought to himself, "Here am I, grown rich and fat on the money I wantonly stole. Since then, all has gone well with me; yet, had I not been poor, I had never turned assassin nor thief. Woe betide me! What a pity it was!" And as he was revolving the matter in his mind, a feeling of remorse came over him, in spite of all he could do. While his conscience thus smote him, he suddenly, to his utter amazement, beheld the faint outline of a man standing near a fir-tree in the garden; on looking more attentively, he perceived that the man's whole body was thin and worn, and the eyes sunken and dim; and in that poor ghost that was before him he recognized the very priest whom he had thrown into the sea at Kuana. Chilled with horror, he looked again, and saw that the priest was smiling in scorn. He would have fled into the house, but the ghost stretched forth its withered arm, and, clutching the back of his neck, scowled at him with a vindictive glare and a hideous ghastliness of mien so unspeakably awful that any ordinary man would have swooned with fear. But Tokubei, tradesman though he was, had once been a soldier, and was not easily matched for daring; so he shook off the ghost, and, leaping into the room for his dirk, laid about him boldly enough; but, strike as he would, the spirit, fading into the air, eluded his blows, and suddenly reappeared only to vanish again; and from that time forth Tokubei knew no rest, and was haunted night and day.

At length, undone by such ceaseless vexation, Tokubei fell ill, and kept muttering, "Oh, misery! misery! the wandering priest is coming to torture me!" Hearing his moans and the disturbance he made, the people in the house fancied he was mad, and called in a physician, who prescribed for him. But neither pill nor potion could cure Tokubei, whose strange frenzy soon became the talk of the whole neighborhood.

Now it chanced that the story reached the ears of a certain wandering priest who lodged in the next street. When he heard the particulars, this priest gravely shook his head as though he knew all about it, and sent a friend to Tokubei's house to say that a wandering priest, dwelling hard by, had heard of his illness, and, were it never so grievous, would undertake to heal it by means of his prayers; and Tokubei's wife, driven half wild by her husband's sickness, lost not a moment in sending for the priest and taking him into the sick man's room.

But no sooner did Tokubei see the priest than he yelled out, "Help! help! Here is the wandering priest come to torment me again. Forgive! Forgive!" and hiding his head under the coverlet, he lay quivering all over. Then the priest turned all present out of the room, put his mouth to the affrighted man's ear, and whispered:

"Three years ago, at the Kuana ferry, you flung me into the water; and well you remember it."

But Tokubei was speechless, and could only quake with fear.

"Happily," continued the priest, "I had learned to swim and to dive as a boy; so I reached the shore, and, after wandering through many provinces, succeeded in setting up a bronze figure to Buddha, thus fulfilling the wish of my heart. On my journey homeward, I took a lodging in the next street, and there heard of your marvellous ailment. Thinking I could divine its cause, I came to see you, and am glad to find I was not mistaken. You have done a hateful deed; but am I not a priest, and have I not forsaken the things of this world, and would it not ill become me to bear malice? Repent, therefore, and abandon your evil ways. To see you do so I should esteem the height of happiness. Be of good cheer, now, and look me in the face, and you will see that I am really a living man, and no vengeful goblin come to torment you."

Seeing he had no ghost to deal with, and overwhelmed by the priest's kindness, Tokubei burst into tears, and answered, "Indeed, indeed, I don't know what to say. In a fit of madness I was tempted to kill and rob you. Fortune befriended me ever after; but the richer I grew, the more keenly I felt how wicked I had been, and the more I foresaw that my victim's vengeance would some day overtake me. Haunted by this thought, I lost my nerve, till one night I beheld your spirit, and from that time fell ill. But how you managed to escape, and are still alive, is more than I can understand."

"A guilty man," said the priest, with a smile, "shudders at the rustling of the wind or the chattering of a stork's beak; a murderer's conscience preys upon his mind till he sees what is not. Poverty drives a man to crimes which he repents of in his wealth. How true is the doctrine of Moshi [Mencius], that the heart of man, pure by nature, is corrupted by circumstances!"

Thus he held forth; and Tokubei, who had long since repented of his crime, implored forgiveness, and gave him a large sum of money, saying, "Half of this is the amount I stole from you three years since; the other half I entreat you to accept as interest, or as a gift."

The priest at first refused the money; but Tokubei insisted on his accepting it, and did all he could to detain him, but in vain; for the priest went on his way, and bestowed the money on the poor and needy. As for Tokubei himself, he soon shook off his disorder, and thenceforward lived at peace with all men, revered both at home and abroad, and ever intent on good and charitable deeds.

The Heart of John Middleton
Elizabeth Gaskell

I was born at Sawley, where the shadow of Pendle Hill falls at sunrise. I suppose Sawley sprang up into a village in the time of the monks, who had an abbey there. Many of the cottages are strange old places; others, again, are built of the abbey stones, mixed up with the shale from the neighboring quarries; and you may see many a quaint bit of carving worked into the walls, or forming the lintels of the doors. There is a row of houses, built still more recently, where one Mr Peel came to live there for the sake of the water-power, and gave the place a fillip into something like life; though a different kind of life, as I take it, from the grand, slow ways folks had when the monks were about.

Now it was — six o'clock, ring the bell, throng to the factory; sharp home at twelve; and even at night, when work was done, we hardly knew how to walk slowly, we had been so bustled all day long. I can't recollect the time when I did not go to the factory. My father used to drag me there when I was quite a little fellow, in order to wind reels for him. I never remember my mother. I should have been a better man than I have been, if I had only had a notion of the sound of her voice, or the look on her face.

My father and I lodged in the house of a man who also worked in the factory. We were sadly thronged in Sawley, so many people came from different parts of the country to earn a livelihood at the new work; and it was some time before the row of cottages I have spoken of could be built. While they were building, my father was turned out of his lodgings for drinking and being disorderly, and he and I slept in the brick-kiln; that is to say, when we did sleep o' nights; but, often and often, we went poaching; and many a hare and pheasant have I rolled up in clay, and roasted in the embers of the kiln. Then, as followed to reason, I was drowsy next day over my work; but father had no mercy on me for sleeping, for all he knew the cause of it, but kicked me where I lay, a heavy lump on the factory floor, and cursed and swore at me till I got up for very fear, and to my winding again. But, when his back was turned, I paid him off with heavier curses than he had given me, and longed to be a man, that I might be revenged on him. The words I then spoke I would not now dare to repeat; and worse than hating words, a hating heart went with them. I forget the time when I did not know how to hate. When I first came to read, and learnt about Ishmael, I thought I must be of his doomed race, for my hand was against every man, and every man's against me. But I was seventeen or more before I cared for my book enough to learn to read.

After the row of works was finished, father took one, and set up for himself, in letting lodgings. I can't say much for the furnishing; but there was plenty of straw, and we kept up good fires; and there is a set of people who value warmth above everything. The worst lot about the place lodged with us. We used to have a supper in the middle of the night; there was game enough, or if there was not game, there was poultry to be had for the stealing. By day, we all made a show of working in the factory. By night, we feasted and drank.

Now this web of my life was black enough, and coarse enough; but, by-and-by, a little golden, filmy thread began to be woven in; the dawn of God's mercy was at hand.

One blowy October morning, as I sauntered lazily along to the mill, I came to the little wooden bridge over a brook that falls into the Bribble. On the plank there stood a child, balancing the pitcher on her head, with which she had been to fetch water. She was so light on her feet that, had it not been for the weight of the pitcher, I almost believe the wind would have taken her up, and wafted her away as it carries off a blow-ball in seed-time; her blue cotton dress was blown before her, as if she were spreading her wings for a flight; she turned her face round, as if to ask me for something, but when she saw who it was, she hesitated, for I had a bad name in the village, and I doubt not she had been warned against me. But her heart was too innocent to be distrustful; so she said to me, timidly, -

"Please, John Middleton, will you carry me this heavy jug just over the bridge?"

10

It was the very first time I had ever been spoken to gently. I was ordered here and there by my father and his rough companions; I was abused, and cursed by them if I failed in doing what they wished; if I succeeded, there came no expression of thanks or gratitude. I was informed of facts necessary for me to know. But the gentle words of request or entreaty were aforetime unknown to me, and now their tones fell on my ear soft and sweet as a distant peal of bells. I wished that I knew how to speak properly in reply; but though we were of the same standing as regarded worldly circumstances, there was some mighty difference between us, which made me unable to speak in her language of soft words and modest entreaty. There was nothing for me but to take up the pitcher in a kind of gruff, shy silence, and carry it over the bridge, as she had asked me. When I gave it her back again, she thanked me and tripped away, leaving me, wordless, gazing after her like an awkward lout as I was. I knew well enough who she was. She was grandchild to Eleanor Hadfield, an aged woman, who was reputed as a witch by my father and his set, for no other reason, that I can make out, than her scorn, dignity, and fearlessness of rancor. It was true we often met her in the grey dawn of the morning, when we returned from poaching, and my father used to curse her, under his breath, for a witch, such as were burnt long ago on Pendle Hill top; but I had heard that Eleanor was a skilful sick nurse, and ever ready to give her services to those who were ill; and I believe that she had been sitting up through the night (the night that we had been spending under the wild heavens, in deeds as wild), with those who were appointed to die. Nelly was her orphan granddaughter; her little hand-maiden; her treasure; her one ewe lamb. Many and many a day have I watched by the brook-side, hoping that some happy gust of wind, coming with opportune bluster down the hollow of the dale, might make me necessary once more to her. I longed to hear her speak to me again. I said the words she had used to myself, trying to catch her tone; but the chance never came again. I do not know that she ever knew how I watched for her there. I found out that she went to school, and nothing would serve me but that I must go too. My father scoffed at me; I did not care. I knew nought of what reading was, nor that it was likely that I should be laughed at; I, a great hulking lad of seventeen or upwards, for going to learn my A, B, C, in the midst of a crowd of little ones. I stood just this way in my mind. Nelly was at school; it was the best place for seeing her, and hearing her voice again. Therefore I would go too. My father talked, and swore, and threatened, but I stood to it. He said I should leave school, weary of it in a month. I swore a deeper oath than I like to remember, that I would stay a year, and come out a reader and a writer. My father hated the notion of folks learning to read, and said it took all the spirit out of them; besides, he thought he had a right to every penny of my wages, and though, when he was in good humor, he might have given me many a jug of ale, he grudged my twopence a week for schooling. However, to school I went. It was a different place to what I had thought it before I went inside. The girls sat on one side, and the boys on the other; so I was not near Nelly. She, too, was in the first class; I was put with the little toddling things that could hardly run alone. The master sat in the middle, and kept pretty strict watch over us. But I could see Nelly, and hear her read her chapter; and even when it was one with a long list of hard names, such as the master was very fond of giving her, to show how well she could hit them off without spelling, I thought I had never heard a prettier music. Now and then she read other things. I did not know what they were, true or false; but I listened because she read; and, by-and-by, I began to wonder. I remember the first word I ever spoke to her was to ask her (as we were coming out of school) who was the Father of whom she had been reading, for when she said the words 'Our Father,' her voice dropped into a soft, holy kind of low sound, which struck me more than any loud reading, it seemed so loving and tender. When I asked her this, she looked at me with her great blue wondering eyes, at first shocked; and then, as it were, melted down into pity and sorrow, she said in the same way, below her breath, in which she read the words, "Our Father," -

"Don't you know? It is God."

"God?"

"Yes; the God that grandmother tells me about."

"Tell me what she says, will you?" So we sat down on the hedge-bank, she a little above me, while I looked up into her face, and she told me all the holy texts her grandmother had taught her, as explaining all that could be explained of the Almighty. I listened in silence, for indeed I was overwhelmed with astonishment. Her knowledge was principally rote-knowledge; she was too young for much more; but we, in Lancashire, speak a rough kind of Bible language, and the texts seemed very clear to me. I rose up, dazed and overpowered. I was going away in silence, when I bethought me of my manners, and turned hack, and said, 'Thank you,' for the first time I ever remember saying it in my life. That was a great day for me, in more ways than one.

I was always one who could keep very steady to an object when once I had set it before me. My object was to know Nelly. I was conscious of nothing more. But it made me regardless of all other things. The master might scold, the little ones might laugh; I bore it all without giving it a second thought. I kept to my year, and came out a reader and writer; more, however, to stand well in Nelly's good opinion, than because of my oath. About this time, my father committed some bad, cruel deed, and had to fly the country. I was glad he went; for I had never loved or cared for him, and wanted to shake myself clear of his set. But it was no easy matter. Honest folk stood aloof; only bad men held out their arms to me with a welcome. Even Nelly seemed to have a mixture of fear now with her kind ways towards me. I was the son of John Middleton, who, if he were caught, would be hung at Lancaster Castle. I thought she looked at me sometimes with a sort of sorrowful horror. Others were not forbearing enough to keep their expression of feeling confined to looks. The son of the overlooker at the mill never ceased twitting me with my father's crime; he now brought up his poaching against him, though I knew very well how many a good supper he himself had made on game which had been given him to make him and his father wink at late hours in the morning. And how were such as my father to come honestly by game?

This lad, Dick Jackson, was the bane of my life. He was a year or two older than I was, and had much power over the men who worked at the mill, as he could report to his father what he chose. I could not always hold my peace when he "threaped" me with my father's sins, but gave it him back sometimes in a storm of passion. It did me no good; only threw me farther from the company of better men, who looked aghast and shocked at the oaths I poured out - blasphemous words learnt in my childhood, which I could not forget now that I would fain have purified myself of them; while all the time Dick Jackson stood by, with a mocking smile of intelligence; and when I had ended, breathless and weary with spent passion, he would run to those whose respect I longed to earn, and ask if I were not a worthy son of my father, and likely to tread in his steps. But this smiling indifference of his to my miserable vehemence was not all, though it was the worst part of his conduct, for it made the rankling hatred grow up in my heart, and overshadow it like the great gourd-tree of the prophet Jonah. But his was a merciful shade, keeping out the burning sun; mine blighted what it fell upon.

What Dick Jackson did besides, was this. His father was a skilful overlooker, and a good man. Mr Peel valued him so much, that he was kept on, although his health was failing; and when he was unable, through illness, to come to the mill, he deputed his son to watch over, and report the men. It was too much power for one so young — I speak it calmly now. Whatever Dick Jackson became, he had strong temptations when he was young, which will be allowed for hereafter. But at the time of which I am telling, my hate raged like a fire. I believed that he was the one sole obstacle to my being received as fit to mix with good and honest men. I was sick of crime and disorder, and would fain have come over to a different kind of life, and have been industrious, sober, honest, and right-spoken (I had no idea of higher virtue then), and at every turn Dick Jackson met me with his sneers. I have walked the night through, in the old abbey field, planning how I could outwit him, and win men's respect in spite of him. The first time I ever prayed, was underneath the silent stars, kneeling by the old abbey walls, throwing up my arms, and asking God for the power of revenge upon him.

I had heard that if I prayed earnestly, God would give me what I asked for, and I looked upon it as a kind of chance for the fulfilment of my wishes. If earnestness would have won the boon for me, never were wicked words so earnestly spoken. And oh, later on, my prayer was heard, and my wish granted! All this time I saw little of Nelly. Her grandmother was failing, and she had much to do indoors. Besides, I believed I had read her looks aright, when I took them to speak of aversion; and I planned to hide myself from her sight, as it were, until I could stand upright before men, with fearless eyes, dreading no face of accusation. It was possible to acquire a good character; I would do it — I did it: but no one brought up among respectable untempted people can tell the unspeakable hardness of the task. In the evenings I would not go forth among the village throng; for the acquaintances that claimed me were my father's old associates, who would have been glad enough to enlist a strong young man like me in their projects; and the men who would have shunned me and kept aloof, were the steady and orderly. So I stayed indoors, and practised myself in reading. You will say, I should have found it easier to earn a good character away from Sawley, at some place where neither I nor my father was known. So I should; but it would not have been the same thing to my mind. Besides, representing all good men, all goodness to me, in Sawley Nelly lived. In her sight I would work out my life, and fight my way upwards to men's respect. Two years passed on. Every. day I strove fiercely; every day my struggles were made fruitless by the son of the overlooker; and I seemed but where I was — but where I must ever be esteemed by all who knew me - but as the son of the criminal - wild, reckless, ripe for crime myself Where was the use of my reading and writing? These acquirements were disregarded and scouted by those among whom I was thrust back to take my portion. I could have read any chapter in the Bible now; and Nelly seemed as though she would never know it. I was driven in upon my books; and few enough of them I had. The pedlars brought them round in their packs, and I bought what I could. I had the *Seven Champions*, and the *Pilgrim's Progress*, and both seemed to me equally wonderful, and equally founded on fact. I got Byron's *Narrative*, and Milton's *Paradise Lost*; but I lacked the knowledge which would give a clue to all. Still they afforded me pleasure, because they took me out of myself, and made me forget my miserable position, and made me unconscious (for the time at least) of my one great passion of hatred against Dick Jackson.

When Nelly was about seventeen her grandmother died. I stood aloof in the churchyard, behind the great yew-tree, and watched the funeral. It was the first religious service that ever I heard; and, to my shame, as I thought, it affected me to tears. The words seemed so peaceful and holy that I longed to go to church, but I durst not, because I had never been. The parish church was at Bolton, far enough away to serve as an excuse for all who did not care to go. I heard Nelly's sobs filling up every pause in the clergyman's voice; and every sob of hers went to my heart. She passed me on her way out of the churchyard; she was so near I might have touched her; but her head was hanging down, and I durst not speak to her. Then the question arose, what was to become of her? She must earn her living! Was it to be as a farm-servant, or by working at the mill? I knew enough of both kinds of life to make me tremble for her. My wages were such as to enable me to marry, if I chose; and I never thought of woman, for my wife, but Nelly. Still, I would not have married her now, if I could; for, as yet, I had not risen up to the character which I determined it was fit that Nelly's husband should have. When I was rich in good report, I would come forwards, and take my chance, but until then I would hold my peace. I had faith in the power of my long-continued dogged breasting of opinion. Sooner or later it must, it should, yield, and I be received among the ranks of good men. But, meanwhile, what was to become of Nelly? I reckoned up my wages; I went to inquire what the board of a girl would be who should help her in her household work, and live with her as a daughter, at the house of one of the most decent women of the place; she looked at me suspiciously. I kept down my temper, and told her I would never come near the place; that I would keep away from that end of the village, and that the girl for whom I made the inquiry should never know but what the parish paid for her keep. It would not do; she suspected me; but I know I had power over myself to have kept my word; and besides, I would not for worlds have had Nelly put under any obligation to me, which should speck the purity of her love, or dim it by a mixture of gratitude, — the love that I craved to earn, not for my money, not for my kindness, but for myself. I heard that Nelly had met with a place in Bolland; and I could see no reason why I might not speak to her once before she left our neighborhood. I meant it to be a quiet friendly telling her of my sympathy in her sorrow. I felt I could command myself. So, on the Sunday before she was to leave Sawley, I waited near the wood-path, by which I knew that she would return from afternoon church. The birds made such a melodious warble, such a busy sound among the leaves, that I did not hear approaching footsteps till they were close at hand; and then there were sounds of two persons' voices. The wood was near that part of Sawley where Nelly was staying with friends; the path through it led to their house, and theirs only, so I knew it must be she, for I had watched her setting out to church alone.

But who was the other?

The blood went to my heart and head, as if I were shot, when I saw that it was Dick Jackson. Was this the end of it all? In the steps of sin which my father had trod, I would rush to my death and my doom. Even where I stood I longed for a weapon to slay him. How dared he come near my Nelly? She too— I thought her faithless, and forgot how little I had ever been to her in outward action; how few words, and those how uncouth, I had ever spoken to her; and I hated her for a traitress. These feelings passed through me before

I could see, my eyes and head were so dizzy and blind. When I looked I saw Dick Jackson holding her hand, and speaking quick and low and thick, as a man speaks in great vehemence. She seemed white and dismayed; but all at once, at some word of his (and what it was she never would tell me), she looked as though she defied a fiend, and wrenched herself out of his grasp. He caught hold of her again, and began once more the thick whisper that I loathed. I could bear it no longer, nor did I see why I should. I stepped out from behind the tree where I had been lying. When she saw me, she lost her look of one strung up to desperation and came and clung to me; and I felt like a giant in strength and might. I held her with one arm, but I did not take my eyes off him; I felt as if they blazed down into his soul, and scorched him up. He never spoke, but tried to look as though he defied me. At last, his eyes fell before mine, I dared not speak; for the old horrid oaths thronged up to my mouth; and I dreaded giving them way, and terrifying my poor, trembling Nelly.

At last, he made to go past me: I drew her out of the pathway. By instinct she wrapped her garments round her, as if to avoid his accidental touch; and he was stung by this, I suppose — I believe — to the mad, miserable revenge he took. As my back was turned to him, in an endeavour to speak some words to Nelly that might soothe her into calmness, she, who was looking after him, like one fascinated with terror, saw him take a sharp, shaley stone, and aim it at me. Poor darling! She clung round me as a shield, making her sweet body into a defence for mine. It hit her, and she spoke no word, kept back her cry of pain, but fell at my feet in a swoon. He — the coward! — ran off as soon as he saw what he had done. I was with Nelly alone in the green gloom of the wood. The quivering and leaf-tinted light made her look as if she were dead. I carried her, not knowing if I bore a corpse or not, to her friend's house. I did not stay to explain, but ran madly for the doctor.

Well! I cannot bear to recur to that time again. Five weeks I lived in the agony of suspense; from which my only relief was in laying savage plans for revenge. If I hated him before, what think ye I did now? It seemed as if earth could not hold us twain, but that one of us must go down to Gehenna. I could have killed him; and would have done it without a scruple, but that seemed too poor and bold a revenge. At length — oh! the weary waiting — oh! the sickening of my heart - Nelly grew better; as well as she was ever to grow. The bright color had left her cheek; the mouth quivered with repressed pain, the eyes were dim with tears that agony had forced into them; and I loved her a thousand times better and more than when she was bright and blooming! What was best of all, I began to perceive that she cared for me. I know her grandmother's friends warned her against me, and told her I came of a bad stock; but she had passed the point where remonstrance from bystanders can take effect — she loved me as I was, a strange mixture of bad and good—all unworthy of her. We spoke together now, as those do whose lives are bound up in each other. I told her I would marry her as soon as she had recovered her health. Her friends shook their heads; but they saw she would be unfit for farm-service or heavy work, and they perhaps thought, as many a one does, that a bad husband was better than none at all. Anyhow, we were married; and I learnt to bless God for my happiness, so far beyond my deserts. I kept her like a lady. I was a skilful workman, and earned good wages; and every want she had I tried to gratify. Her wishes were few and simple enough, poor Nelly! If they had been ever so fanciful, I should have had my reward in the new feeling of the holiness of home. She could lead me as a little child, with the charm of her gentle voice, and her ever-kind words. She would plead for all when I was frill of anger and passion; only Dick Jackson's name passed never between our lips during all that time. In the evening she lay back in her beehive chair, and read to me. I think I see her now, pale and weak, with her sweet, young face, lighted by her holy, earnest eyes, telling me of the Saviour's life and death, till they were filled with tears. I longed to have been there, to have avenged him on the wicked Jews. I liked Peter the best of all the disciples. But I got the Bible myself, and read the mighty act of God's vengeance, in the Old Testament, with a kind of triumphant faith that, sooner or later, He would take my cause in hand, and revenge me on mine enemy.

In a year or so, Nelly had a baby — a little girl—with eyes that looked with a grave openness right into yours. Nelly recovered but slowly. It was just before winter, the cotton-crop had failed, and master had to turn off many hands. I thought I was sure of being kept on, for I had earned a steady character, and did my work well; but once again it was permitted that Dick Jackson should do me wrong. He induced his father to dismiss me among the first in my branch of the business; and there was I, just before winter set in, with a wife and new-born child, and a small enough store of money to keep body and soul together, till I could get to work again. All my savings had gone by Christmas Eve, and we sat in the house, foodless for the morrow's festival. Nelly looked pinched and worn; the baby cried for a larger supply of milk than its poor, starving mother could give it. My right hand had not forgot its cunning, and I went out once more to my poaching. I knew where the gang met; and I knew what a welcome back I should have, — a far warmer and more hearty welcome than good men had given me when I tried to enter their ranks. On the road to the meeting-place I fell in with an old man, — one who had been a companion to my father in his early days.

"What, lad!" said he, "art thou turning back to the old trade? It's the better business, now that cotton has failed."

"Ay," said I, "cotton is starving us outright. A man may bear a deal himself, but he'll do aught bad and sinful to save his wife and child."

"Nay, lad," said he, "poaching is not sinful; it goes against man's laws, but not against God's."

I was too weak to argue or talk much. I had not tasted food for two days. But I murmured, "At any rate, I trusted to have been clear of it for the rest of my days. It led my father wrong at first. I have tried and I have striven. Now I give all up. Right or wrong shall be the same to me. Some are foredoomed; and so am I." And as I spoke, some notion of the futurity that would separate Nelly, the pure and holy, from me, the reckless and desperate one, came over me with an irrepressible burst of anguish. Just then the bells of Bolton-in-Bolland struck up a glad peal, which came over the woods, in the solemn midnight air, like the sons of the morning shouting for joy — they seemed so clear and jubilant. It was Christmas Day: and I felt like an outcast from the gladness and the salvation. Old Jonah spoke out: —

"Yon's the Christmas bells. I say, Johnny, my lad, I've no notion of taking such a spiritless chap as thou into the thick of it, with thy rights and thy wrongs. We don't trouble ourselves with such fine lawyer's stuff, and we bring down the 'varmint' all the better. Now, I'll not have thee in our gang, for thou art not up to the fun, and thou'd hang fire when the time came to be doing. But I've a shrewd guess that plaguy wife and child of thine are at the bottom of thy half-and-half joining. Now, I was thy father's friend afore he took to them helter-skelter ways, and I've five shillings and a neck of mutton at thy service. I'll not list a fasting man; but if thou'lt come to us with a full stomach, and say, 'I like your life, my lads, and I'll make one of you with pleasure, the first shiny night,' why, we'll give you a welcome and a half; but, to-night, make no more ado. but turn back with me for the mutton and the money."

I was not proud: nay, I was most thankful. I took the meat, and boiled some broth for my poor Nelly. She was in a sleep, or a faint, I know not which; but I roused her, and held her up in bed, and fed her with a teaspoon, and the light came back to her eyes, and the faint, moonlight smile to her lips; and when she had ended, she said her innocent grace, and fell asleep, with her baby on her breast. I sat over the fire, and listened to the bells, as they swept past my cottage on the gusts of the wind. I longed and yearned for the second coming of Christ, of which Nelly had told me. The world seemed cruel, and hard, and strong — too strong for me; and I prayed to cling to the hem of His garment, and be borne over the rough places when I fainted, and bled, and found no man to pity or help me, but poor old Jonah, the publican and sinner. All this time my own woes and my own self were uppermost in my mind, as they are in the minds of most who have been hardly used. As I thought of my wrongs, and my sufferings, my heart burned against Dick Jackson; and as the bells rose and fell, so my hopes waxed and waned, that in those mysterious days, of which they were both the remembrance and the prophecy, he would be purged from off the earth. I took Nelly's Bible, and turned, not to the gracious story of the Saviour's birth, but to the records of the former days, when the Jews took such wild revenge upon all their opponents. I was a Jew, — a leader among the people. Dick Jackson was as Pharaoh, as the King Agag, who walked delicately, thinking the bitterness of death was past, — in short, he was the conquered enemy, over whom I gloated, with my Bible in my hand — that Bible which contained our Saviour's words on the Cross. As yet, those words seemed faint and meaningless to me, like a tract of country seen in the starlight haze; while the histories of the Old Testament were grand and distinct in the blood-red color of sunset. By-and-by that night passed into day, and little piping voices came round, carol-singing. They wakened Nelly. I went to her as soon as I heard her stirring.

"Nelly," said I, 'there's money and food in the house; I will be off to Padiham seeking work, while thou hast something to go upon.

"Not to-day," said she; "stay to-day with me. If thou wouldst only go to church with me this once" — for you see I had never been inside a church but when we were married, and she was often praying me to go; and now she looked at me, with a sigh just creeping forth from her lips, as she expected a refusal. But I did not refuse. I had been kept away from church before because I dared not go; and now I was desperate, and dared do anything. If I did look like a heathen in the face of all men, why, I was a heathen in my heart; for I was falling back into all my evil ways. I had resolved if my search of work at Padiham should fail, I would follow my father's footsteps, and take with my own right hand and by my strength of arm what it was denied me to obtain honestly. I had resolved to leave Sawley, where a curse seemed to hang over me; so, what did it matter if I went to church, all unbeknowing what strange ceremonies were there performed? I walked thither as a sinful man — sinful in my heart. Nelly hung on my arm, but even she could not get me to speak. I went in; she found my places, and pointed to the words, and looked up into my eyes with hers, so frill of faith and joy. But I saw nothing but Richard Jackson — I heard nothing but his loud nasal voice, making response, and desecrating all the holy words. He was in broadcloth of the best — I in my fustian jacket. He was prosperous and glad — I was starving and desperate. Nelly grew pale, as she saw the expression in my eyes; and she prayed ever, and ever more fervently as the thought of me tempted by the Devil even at that very moment came more fully before her.

By-and-by she forgot even me, and laid her soul bare before God, in a long, silent, weeping prayer, before we left the church. Nearly all had gone; and I stood by her, unwilling to disturb her, unable to join her. At last she rose up, heavenly calm. She took my arm, and we went home through the woods, where all the birds seemed tame and familiar. Nelly said she thought all living creatures knew it was Christmas Day, and rejoiced, and were loving together. I believed it was the frost that had tamed them; and I felt the hatred that was in me, and knew that whatever else was loving, I was full of malice and uncharitableness, nor did I wish to be otherwise. That afternoon I bade Nelly and our child farewell, and tramped to Padiham. I got work — how I hardly know; for stronger and stronger came the force of the temptation to lead a wild, free life of sin; legions seemed whispering evil thoughts to me, and only my gentle, pleading Nelly to pull me back from the great gulf. However, as I said before, I got work, and set off homewards to move my wife and child to that neighborhood. I hated Sawley, and yet I was fiercely indignant to leave it, with my purposes unaccomplished. I was still an outcast from the more respectable, who stood afar off from such as I; and mine enemy lived and flourished in their regard. Padiham, however, was not so far away for me to despair — to relinquish my fixed determination. It was on the eastern side of the great Pendle Hill, ten miles away — maybe. Hate will overleap a greater obstacle. I took a cottage on the Fell, high up on the side of the hill. We saw a long black moorland slope before us, and then the grey stone houses of Padiham, over which a black cloud hung, different from the blue wood or turf smoke about Sawley. The wild winds came down and whistled round our house many a day when all was still below. But I was happy then. I rose in men's esteem. I had work in plenty. Our child lived and throve. But I forgot not our country proverb — "Keep a stone in thy pocket for seven years: turn it, and keep it seven years more; but have it ever ready to cast at thine enemy when the time comes."

One day a fellow-workman asked me to go to a hill-side preaching. Now, I never cared to go to church; but there was something newer and freer in the notion of praying to God right under His great dome; and the open air had had a charm to me ever since my wild boyhood. Besides, they said, these ranters had strange ways with them, and I thought it would be fun to see their way of setting about it; and this ranter of all others had made himself a name in our parts. Accordingly we went; it was a fine summer's evening, after work was done. When we got to the place we saw such a crowd as I never saw before — men, women, and children; all ages were gathered together, and sat on the hill-side. They were care-worn, diseased, sorrowful, criminal; all that was told on their faces, which were hard and strongly marked. In the midst, standing in a cart, was the preacher. When I first saw him, I said to my companion, "Lord! What a little man to make all this pother! I could trio him up with one of my fingers," and then I sat down, and looked about me a bit. All eyes were fixed on the preacher; and I turned mine upon him too. He began to speak; it was in no fine-drawn language, but in words such as we heard every day of our lives, and about things we did every day of our lives. He did not call our shortcomings pride or worldliness, or pleasure-seeking, which would have given us no clear notion of what he meant, but he just told us outright what we did, and then he gave it a name, and said

22

that it was accursed, and that we were lost if we went on so doing.

By this time the tears and sweat were running down his face; he was wrestling for our souls. We wondered how he knew our innermost lives as he did, for each one of us saw his sin set before him in plain-spoken words. Then he cried out to us to repent; and spoke first to us, and then to God, in a way that would have shocked many — but it did not shock me. I liked strong things; and I liked the bare, hill truth: and I felt brought nearer to God in that hour — the summer darkness creeping over us, and one after one the stars coming out above us, like the eyes of the angels watching us — than I had ever done in my life before. When he had brought us to our tears and sighs, he stopped his loud voice of upbraiding, and there was a hush, only broken by sobs and quivering moans, in which I heard through the gloom the voices of strong men in anguish and supplication, as well as the shriller tones of women. Suddenly he was heard again; by this time we could not see him; but his voice was now tender as the voice of an angel, and he told us of Christ, and implored us to come to Him. I never heard such passionate entreaty. He spoke as if he saw Satan hovering near us in the dark, dense night, and as if our only safety lay in a very present coming to the Cross; I believe he did see Satan; we know he haunts the desolate old hills, awaiting his time, and now or never it was with many a soul. At length there was a sudden silence; and by the cries of those nearest to the preacher, we heard that he had fainted. We had all crowded round him, as if he were our safety and our guide; and he was overcome by the heat and the fatigue, for we were the fifth set of people whom he had addressed that day. I left the crowd who were leading him down, and took a lonely path myself.

Here was the earnestness I needed. To this weak and weary fainting man, religion was a life and a passion. I look back now, and wonder at my blindness as to what was the root of all my Nelly's patience and longsuffering; for I thought, now I had found out what religion was, and that hitherto it had been all an unknown thing to me.

Henceforward, my life was changed. I was zealous and fanatical. Beyond the set to whom I had affiliated myself, I had no sympathy. I would have persecuted all who differed from me, if I had only had the power. I became an ascetic in all bodily enjoyments. And, strange and inexplicable mystery, I had some thoughts that by every act of self-denial I was attaining to my unholy end, and that, when I had fasted and prayed long enough, God would place my vengeance in my hands. I have knelt by Nelly's bedside, and vowed to live a self-denying life, as regarded all outward things, if so that God would grant my prayer. I left it in His hands. I felt sure He would trace out the token and the word; and Nelly would listen to my passionate words, and lie awake sorrowful and heart-sore through the night; and I would get up and make her tea, and rearrange her pillows, with a strange and willful blindness that my bitter words and blasphemous prayers had cost her miserable, sleepless nights. My Nelly was suffering yet from that blow. How or where the stone had hurt her, I never understood; but in consequence of that one moment's action, her limbs became numb and dead, and, by slow degrees, she took to her bed, from whence she was never carried alive. There she lay, propped up by pillows, her meek face ever bright, and smiling forth a greeting; her white, pale hands ever busy with some kind of work; and our little Grace was as the power of motion to her. Fierce as I was away from her, I never could speak to her but in my gentlest tones. She seemed to me as if she had never wrestled for salvation as I had; and when away from her, I resolved many a time and oft, that I would rouse her up to her state of danger when I returned home that evening - even if strong reproach were required I would rouse her up to her soul's need. But I came in and heard her voice singing softly some holy word of patience, some psalm which, maybe, had comforted the martyrs, and when I saw her face like the face of an angel, full of patience and happy faith, I put off my awakening speeches til another time.

One night, long ago, when I was yet young and strong, although my years were past forty, I sat alone in my houseplace. Nelly was always in bed, as I have told you, and Grace lay in a cot by her side. I believed them to be both asleep; though how they could sleep I could not conceive, so wild and terrible was the night. The wind came sweeping down from the hill-top in great beats, like the pulses of heaven; and, during the pauses, while I listened for the coming roar, I felt the earth shiver beneath me. The rain beat against windows and doors, and sobbed for entrance. I thought the Prince of the Air was abroad; and I heard, or fancied I heard, shrieks come on the blast, like the cries of sinful souls given over to his power.

The sounds came nearer and nearer. I got up and saw to the fastenings of the door, for though I cared not for mortal man, I did care for what I believed was surrounding the house, in evil might and power. But the door shook as though it, too, were in deadly terror, and I thought the fastenings would give way. I stood facing the entrance, lashing my heart up to defy the spiritual enemy that I looked to see, every instant, in bodily presence; and the door did burst open; and before me stood — what was it? Man or demon? A grey-haired man, with poor, worn clothes all wringing wet, and he himself battered and piteous to look upon, from the storm he had passed through.

"Let me in!" he said. "Give me shelter. I am poor, or I would reward you. And I am friendless, too," he said, looking up in my face, like one seeking what he cannot find. In that look, strangely changed, I knew that God had heard me; for it was the old cowardly look of my life's enemy. Had he been a stranger, I might not have welcomed him; but as he was mine enemy, I gave him welcome in a lordly dish. I sat opposite to him. "Whence do you come?" said I. "It is a strange night to be out on the fells."

He looked up at me sharp; but in general he held his head down like a beast or hound.

"You won't betray me. I'll not trouble you long. As soon as the storm abates, I'll go.'

"Friend!" said I, "what have I to betray?" And I trembled lest he should keep himself out of my power and not tell me. "You come for shelter, and I give you of my best. Why do you suspect me?"

"Because," said he, in his abject bitterness, "all the world is against me. I never met with goodness or kindness; and now I am hunted like a wild beast. I'll tell you — I'm a convict returned before my time. I was a Sawley man" (as if I, of all men, did nor know it!), "and I went back, like a fool, to the old place. They've hunted me out where I would fain have lived rightly and quietly, and they'll send me back to that hell upon earth, if they catch me. I did nor know it would be such a night. Only let me rest and get warm once more, and I'll go away. Good, kind man, have pity upon me!" I smiled all his doubts away; I promised him a bed on the floor, and I thought of Jael and Sisera. My heart leaped up like a war-horse at the sound of the trumpet, and said, "Ha, ha, the Lord hath heard my prayer and supplication; I shall have vengeance at last!"

He did not dream who I was. He was changed; so that I, who had learned his features with all the diligence of hatred, did not, at first, recognize him; and he thought not of me, only of his own woe and affright. He looked into the fire with the dreamy gaze of one whose strength of character, if he had any, is beaten out of him, and cannot return at any emergency whatsoever. He sighed and pitied himself, yet could not decide on what to do. I went softly about my business, which was to make him up a bed on the floor, and, when he was lulled to sleep and security, to make the best of my way to Padiham, and summon the constable, into whose hands I would give him up, to be taken back to his "hell upon earth." I went into Nelly's room. She was awake and anxious. I saw she had been listening to the voices.

"Who is there?" said she. "John, tell me; it sounded like a voice I knew. For God's sake, speak!"

I smiled a quiet smile. "It is a poor man, who has lost his way. Go to sleep, my dear — I shall make him up on the floor. I may not come for some time. Go to sleep;" and I kissed her. I thought she was soothed, but not fully satisfied. However, I hastened away before there was any further time for questioning. I made up the bed, and Richard Jackson, tired out, lay down and fell asleep. My contempt for him almost equalled my hate. If I were avoiding return to a place which I thought to be a hell upon earth, think you I would have taken a quiet sleep under any man's roof till, somehow or another, I was secure. Now comes this man, and, with incontinence of tongue, blabs out the very thing he most should conceal, and then lies down to a good, quiet, snoring sleep. I looked again. His face was old, and worn, and miserable. So should mine enemy look. And yet it was sad to gaze upon him, poor, hunted creature!

I would gaze no more, lest I grew weak and pitiful. Thus I took my hat, and softly opened the door. The wind blew in, but did not disturb him, he was so utterly weary. I was out in the open air of night. The storm was ceasing, and, instead of the black sky of doom that I had seen when I last looked forth, the moon was come out, wan and pale, as if wearied with the fight in the heavens, and her white light fell ghostly and calm on many a well-known object. Now and then, a dark, torn cloud was blown across her home in the sky; but they grew fewer and fewer, and at last she shone out steady and clear. I could see Padiham down before me. I heard the noise of the watercourses down the hill-side. My mind was full of one thought, and strained upon that one thought, and yet my senses were most acute and observant. When I came to the brook, it was swollen to a rapid, tossing river; and the little bridge, with its handrail, was utterly swept away. It was like the bridge at Sawrey, where I had first seen Newly; and I remembered that day even then in the midst of my vexation at having to go round. I turned away from the brook, and there stood a little figure facing me. No spirit from the dead could have affrighted me as it did; for I saw it was Grace, whom I had left in bed by her mother's side.

She came to me, and took my hand. Her bare feet glittered white in the moonshine, and sprinkled the light upwards, as they plashed through the pool.

"Father," said she, "mother bade me say this." Then pausing to gather breath and memory, she repeated these words, like a lesson of which she feared to forget a syllable: —

"Mother says, 'There is a God in heaven; and in His house are many mansions. If you hope to meet her there, you will come back and speak to her; if you are to be separate for ever and ever, you will go on, and may God have mercy on her and on you!' Father, I have said it right — every word." I was silent. At last, I said, —

"What made mother say this? How came she to send you out?"

"I was asleep, father, and I heard her cry. I wakened up, and I think you had but just left the house, and that she was calling for you. Then she prayed, with the tears rolling down her cheeks, and kept saying — 'Oh, that I could walk! - Oh, that for one hour I could run and walk!' So I said, 'Mother, I can run and walk. Where must I go?' And she clutched at my arm, and bade God bless me, and told me not to fear, for that He would compass me about, and taught me my message: and now, father, dear father, you will meet mother in heaven, won't you, and not be separate for ever and ever?" She clung to my knees, and pleaded once more in her mother's words. I took her up in my arms, and turned homewards.

"Is yon man there, on the kitchen floor?" asked I.

"Yes!" she answered. At any rate, my vengeance was not out of my power yet.

When we got home I passed him, dead asleep.

In our room, to which my child guided me, was Nelly. She sat up in bed, a most unusual attitude for her, and one of which I thought she had been incapable of attaining to without help. She had her hands clasped, and her face rapt, as if in prayer; and when she saw me, she lay back with a sweet ineffable smile. She could not speak at first; but when I came near, she took my hand and kissed it, and then she called Grace to her, and made her take off her cloak and her wet things, and dressed in her short scanty nightgown, she slipped in to her mother's warm side; and all this time my Nelly never told me why she summoned me: it seemed enough that she should hold my hand, and feel that I was there. I believed she had read my heart; and yet I durst not speak to ask her. At last, she looked up. "My husband," said she, "God has saved you and me from a great sorrow this night." I would not understand, and I felt her look die away into disappointment.

"That poor wanderer in the house-place is Richard Jackson, is it not?"

I made no answer. Her face grew white and wan. "Oh," said she, "this is hard to bear. Speak what is in your mind, I beg of you. I will not thwart you harshly; dearest John, only speak to me."

"Why need I speak? You seem to know all."

"I do know that his is a voice I can never forget; and I do know the awful prayers you have prayed; and I know how I have lain awake, to pray that your words might never be heard; and I am a powerless cripple. I put my cause in God's hands. You shall not do the man any harm. What you have it in your thoughts to do, I cannot tell. But I know that you cannot do it. My eyes are dim with a strange mist; but some voice tells me that you will forgive even Richard Jackson. Dear husband — dearest John, it is so dark, I cannot see you: but speak once to me."

I moved the candle; but when I saw her face, I saw what was drawing the mist over those loving eyes — how strange and woeful that she could die! Her little girl lying by her side looked in my face, and then at her; and the wild knowledge of death shot through her young heart, and she screamed aloud.

Nelly opened her eyes once more. They fell upon the gaunt, sorrow-worn man who was the cause of all. He roused him from his sleep, at that child's piercing cry, and stood at the doorway, looking in. He knew Nelly, and understood where the storm had driven him to shelter. He came towards her —

"Oh, woman — dying woman — you have haunted me in the loneliness of the Bush far away — you have been in my dreams for ever — the hunting of men has not been so terrible as the hunting of your spirit, — that stone — that stone!" He fell down by her bedside in an agony; above which her saint-like face looked on us all, for the last time, glorious with the coming light of heaven. She spoke once again: —

"It was a moment of passion; I never bore you malice for it. I forgive you; and so does John, I trust."

Could I keep my purpose there? It faded into nothing. But, above my choking tears, I strove to speak clear and distinct, for her dying ear to hear, and her sinking heart to be gladdened.

"I forgive you, Richard; I will befriend you in your trouble."

She could not see; but, instead of the dim shadow of death stealing over her face, a quiet light came over it, which we knew was the look of a soul at rest.

That night I listened to his tale for her sake; and I learned that it is better to be sinned against than to sin. In the storm of the night mine enemy came to me; in the calm of the grey morning I led him forth, and bade him "God speed." And a woe had come upon me, but the burning burden of a sinful, angry heart was taken off. I am old now, and my daughter is married. I try to go about preaching and teaching in my rough, rude way; and what I teach is, how Christ lived and died, and what was Nelly's faith of love.

The Cost of Kindness
Jerome K. Jerome

"Kindness," argued little Mrs. Pennycoop, "costs nothing."

"And, speaking generally, my dear, is valued precisely at cost price," retorted Mr. Pennycoop, who, as an auctioneer of twenty years experience, had enjoyed much opportunity of testing the attitude of the public towards sentiment.

"I don't care what you say, George," persisted his wife; "he may be a disagreeable, cantankerous old brute—I don't say he isn't. All the same, the man is going away, and we may never see him again."

"If I thought there was any fear of our doing so," observed Mr. Pennycoop, "I'd turn my back on the Church of England tomorrow and become a Methodist."

"Don't talk like that, George," his wife admonished him, reprovingly; "the Lord might be listening to you."

"If the Lord had to listen to old Cracklethorpe He'd sympathize with me," was the opinion of Mr. Pennycoop.

"The Lord sends us our trials, and they are meant for our good," explained his wife. "They are meant to teach us patience."

"You are not churchwarden," retorted her husband; "you can get away from him. You hear him when he is in the pulpit, where, to a certain extent, he is bound to keep his temper."

"You forget the rummage sale, George," Mrs. Pennycoop reminded him; "to say nothing of the church decorations."

"The rummage sale," Mr. Pennycoop pointed out to her, "occurs only once a year, and at that time your own temper, I have noticed—"

"I always try to remember I am a Christian," interrupted little Mrs. Pennycoop. "I do not pretend to be a saint, but whatever I say I am always sorry for it afterwards—you know I am, George."

"It's what I am saying," explained her husband. "A vicar who has contrived in three years to make every member of his congregation hate the very sight of a church—well, there's something wrong about it somewhere."

Mrs. Pennycoop, gentlest of little women, laid her plump and still pretty hands upon her husband's shoulders. "Don't think, dear, I haven't sympathized with you. You have borne it nobly. I have marvelled sometimes that you have been able to control yourself as you have done, most times; the things that he has said to you."

Mr. Pennycoop had slid unconsciously into an attitude suggestive of petrified virtue, lately discovered.

"One's own poor self," observed Mr. Pennycoop, in accents of proud humility—"insults that are merely personal one can put up with. Though even there," added the senior churchwarden, with momentary descent towards the plane of human nature, "nobody cares to have it hinted publicly across the vestry table that one has chosen to collect from the left side for the express purpose of artfully passing over one's own family."

"The children have always had their three-penny-bits ready waiting in their hands," explained Mrs. Pennycoop, indignantly.

"It's the sort of thing he says merely for the sake of making a disturbance," continued the senior churchwarden. "It's the things he does I draw the line at."

"The things he has done, you mean, dear," laughed the little woman, with the accent on the "has." "It is all over now, and we are going to be rid of him. I expect, dear, if we only knew, we should find it was his liver. You know, George, I remarked to you the first day that he came how pasty he looked and what a singularly unpleasant mouth he had. People can't help these things, you know, dear. One should look upon them in the light of afflictions and be sorry for them."

"I could forgive him doing what he does if he didn't seem to enjoy it," said the senior churchwarden. "But, as you say, dear, he is going, and all I hope and pray is that we never see his like again."

"And you'll come with me to call upon him, George," urged kind little Mrs. Pennycoop. "After all, he has been our vicar for three years, and he must be feeling it, poor man—whatever he may pretend—going away like this, knowing that everybody is glad to see the back of him.".

"Well, I sha'n't say anything I don't really feel," stipulated Mr. Pennycoop.

"That will be all right, dear," laughed his wife, "so long as you don't say what you do feel. And we'll both of us keep our temper," further suggested the little woman, "whatever happens. Remember, it will be for the last time."

Little Mrs. Pennycoop's intention was kind and Christianlike. The Rev. Augustus Cracklethorpe would be quitting Wychwood-on-the-Heath the following Monday, never to set foot—so the Rev. Augustus Cracklethorpe himself and every single member of his congregation hoped sincerely—in the neighbourhood again. Hitherto no pains had been taken on either side to disguise the mutual joy with which the parting was looked forward to. The Rev. Augustus Cracklethorpe, M.A., might possibly have been of service to his Church in, say, some East-end parish of unsavoury reputation, some mission station far advanced amid the hordes of heathendom. There his inborn instinct of antagonism to everybody and everything surrounding him, his unconquerable disregard for other people's views and feelings, his inspired conviction that everybody but himself was bound to be always wrong about everything, combined with determination to act and speak fearlessly in such belief, might have found their uses. In picturesque little Wychwood-on-the-Heath, among the Kentish hills, retreat beloved of the retired tradesman, the spinster of moderate means, the reformed Bohemian developing latent instincts towards respectability, these qualities made only for scandal and disunion.

For the past two years the Rev. Cracklethorpe's parishioners, assisted by such other of the inhabitants of Wychwood-on-the-Heath as had happened to come into personal contact with the reverend gentleman, had sought to impress upon him, by hints and innuendoes difficult to misunderstand, their cordial and daily-increasing dislike of him, both as a parson and a man. Matters had come to a head by the determination officially announced to him that, failing other alternatives, a deputation of his leading parishioners would wait upon his bishop. This it was that had brought it home to the Rev. Augustus Cracklethorpe that, as the spiritual guide and comforter of Wychwood-on-the Heath, he had proved a failure. The Rev. Augustus had sought and secured the care of other souls. The following Sunday morning he had arranged to preach his farewell sermon, and the occasion promised to be a success from every point of view. Churchgoers who had not visited St. Jude's for months had promised themselves the luxury of feeling they were listening to the Rev. Augustus Cracklethorpe for the last time. The Rev. Augustus Cracklethorpe had prepared a sermon that for plain speaking and directness was likely to leave an impression. The parishioners of St. Jude's, Wychwood-on-the-Heath, had their failings, as we all have. The Rev. Augustus flattered himself that he had not missed out a single one, and was looking forward with pleasurable anticipation to the sensation that his remarks, from his "firstly" to his "sixthly and lastly," were likely to create.

What marred the entire business was the impulsiveness of little Mrs. Pennycoop. The Rev. Augustus Cracklethorpe, informed in his study on the Wednesday afternoon that Mr. and Mrs. Pennycoop had called, entered the drawing-room a quarter of an hour later, cold and severe; and, without offering to shake hands, requested to be informed as shortly as possible for what purpose he had been disturbed. Mrs. Pennycoop had had her speech ready to her tongue. It was just what it should have been, and no more.

It referred casually, without insisting on the point, to the duty incumbent upon all of us to remember on occasion we were Christians; that our privilege it was to forgive and forget; that, generally speaking, there are faults on both sides; that partings should never take place in anger; in short, that little Mrs. Pennycoop and George, her husband, as he was waiting to say for himself, were sorry for everything and anything they may have said or done in the past to hurt the feelings of the Rev. Augustus Cracklethorpe, and would like to shake hands with him and wish him every happiness for the future. The chilling attitude of the Rev. Augustus scattered that carefully-rehearsed speech to the winds. It left Mrs. Pennycoop nothing but to retire in choking silence, or to fling herself upon the inspiration of the moment and make up something new. She choose the latter alternative.

At first the words came halting. Her husband, man-like, had deserted her in her hour of utmost need and was fumbling with the door-knob. The steely stare with which the Rev. Cracklethorpe regarded her, instead of chilling her, acted upon her as a spur. It put her on her mettle. He should listen to her. She would make him understand her kindly feeling towards him if she had to take him by the shoulders and shake it into him. At the end of five minutes the Rev. Augustus Cracklethorpe, without knowing it, was looking pleased. At the end of another five Mrs. Pennycoop stopped, not for want of words, but for want of breath. The Rev. Augustus Cracklethorpe replied in a voice that, to his own surprise, was trembling with emotion. Mrs. Pennycoop had made his task harder for him. He had thought to leave Wychwood-on-the-Heath without a regret. The knowledge he now possessed, that at all events one member of his congregation understood him, as Mrs. Pennycoop had proved to him she understood him, sympathized with him—the knowledge that at least one heart, and that heart Mrs. Pennycoop's, had warmed to him, would transform what he had looked forward to as a blessed relief into a lasting grief.

Mr. Pennycoop, carried away by his wife's eloquence, added a few halting words of his own. It appeared from Mr. Pennycoop's remarks that he had always regarded the Rev. Augustus Cracklethorpe as the vicar of his dreams, but misunderstandings in some unaccountable way will arise. The Rev. Augustus Cracklethorpe, it appeared, had always secretly respected Mr. Pennycoop. If at any time his spoken words might have conveyed the contrary impression, that must have arisen from the poverty of our language, which does not lend itself to subtle meanings.

Then following the suggestion of tea, Miss Cracklethorpe, sister to the Rev. Augustus—a lady whose likeness to her brother in all respects was startling, the only difference between them being that while he was clean-shaven she wore a slight moustache— was called down to grace the board. The visit was ended by Mrs. Pennycoop's remembrance that it was Wilhelmina's night for a hot bath.

"I said more than I intended to," admitted Mrs. Pennycoop to George, her husband, on the way home; "but he irritated me."

Rumor of the Pennycoops' visit flew through the parish. Other ladies felt it their duty to show to Mrs. Pennycoop that she was not the only Christian in Wychwood-on-the-Heath. Mrs. Pennycoop, it was feared, might be getting a swelled head over this matter. The Rev. Augustus, with pardonable pride, repeated some of the things that Mrs. Pennycoop had said to him. Mrs. Pennycoop was not to imagine herself the only person in Wychwood-on-the-Heath capable of generosity that cost nothing. Other ladies could say graceful nothings—could say them even better. Husbands dressed in their best clothes and carefully rehearsed were brought in to grace the almost endless procession of disconsolate parishioners hammering at the door of St. Jude's parsonage. Between Thursday morning and Saturday night the Rev. Augustus, much to his own astonishment, had been forced to the conclusion that five-sixths of his parishioners had loved him from the first without hitherto having had opportunity of expressing their real feelings.

The eventful Sunday arrived. The Rev. Augustus Cracklethorpe had been kept so busy listening to regrets at his departure, assurances of an esteem hitherto disguised from him, explanations of seeming discourtesies that had been intended as tokens of affectionate regard, that no time had been left to him to think of other matters. Not till he entered the vestry at five minutes to eleven did recollection of his farewell sermon come to him. It haunted him throughout the service. To deliver it after the revelations of the last three days would be impossible. It was the sermon that Moses might have preached to Pharaoh the Sunday prior to the exodus. To crush with it this congregation of broken-hearted adorers sorrowing for his departure would be inhuman. The Rev. Augustus tried to think of passages that might be selected, altered. There were none. From beginning to end it contained not a single sentence capable of being made to sound pleasant by any ingenuity whatsoever.

The Rev. Augustus Cracklethorpe climbed slowly up the pulpit steps without an idea in his head of what he was going to say. The sunlight fell upon the upturned faces of a crowd that filled every corner of the church. So happy, so buoyant a congregation the eyes of the Rev. Augustus Cracklethorpe had never till that day looked down upon. The feeling came to him that he did not want to leave them. That they did not wish him to go, could he doubt? Only by regarding them as a collection of the most shameless hypocrites ever gathered together under one roof. The Rev. Augustus Cracklethorpe dismissed the passing suspicion as a suggestion of the Evil One, folded the neatly-written manuscript that lay before him on the desk, and put it aside. He had no need of a farewell sermon. The arrangements made could easily be altered. The Rev. Augustus Cracklethorpe spoke from his pulpit for the first time an impromptu.

The Rev. Augustus Cracklethorpe wished to acknowledge himself in the wrong. Foolishly founding his judgment upon the evidence of a few men, whose names there would be no need to mention, members of the congregation who, he hoped, would one day be sorry for the misunderstandings they had caused, brethren whom it was his duty to forgive, he had assumed the parishioners of St. Jude's, Wychwood-on-the-Heath, to have taken a personal dislike to him. He wished to publicly apologize for the injustice he had unwittingly done to their heads and to their hearts. He now had it from their own lips that a libel had been put upon them. So far from their wishing his departure, it was self-evident that his going would inflict upon them a great sorrow. With the knowledge he now possessed of the respect—one might almost say the veneration—with which the majority of that congregation regarded him—knowledge, he admitted, acquired somewhat late— it was clear to him he could still be of help to them in their spiritual need. To leave a flock so devoted would stamp him as an unworthy shepherd. The ceaseless stream of regrets at his departure that had been poured into his ear during the last four days he had decided at the last moment to pay heed to. He would remain with them—on one condition.

There quivered across the sea of humanity below him a movement that might have suggested to a more observant watcher the convulsive clutchings of some drowning man at some chance straw. But the Rev. Augustus Cracklethorpe was thinking of himself.

The parish was large and he was no longer a young man. Let them provide him with a conscientious and energetic curate. He had such a one in his mind's eye, a near relation of his own, who, for a small stipend that was hardly worth mentioning, would, he knew it for a fact, accept the post. The pulpit was not the place in which to discuss these matters, but in the vestry afterwards he would be pleased to meet such members of the congregation as might choose to stay.

The question agitating the majority of the congregation during the singing of the hymn was the time it would take them to get outside the church. There still remained a faint hope that the Rev. Augustus Cracklethorpe, not obtaining his curate, might consider it due to his own dignity to shake from his feet the dust of a parish generous in sentiment, but obstinately close-fisted when it came to putting its hands into its pockets.

But for the parishioners of St. Jude's that Sunday was a day of misfortune. Before there could be any thought of moving, the Rev. Augustus raised his surpliced arm and begged leave to acquaint them with the contents of a short note that had just been handed up to him. It would send them all home, he felt sure, with joy and thankfulness in their hearts. An example of Christian benevolence was among them that did honour to the Church.

Here a retired wholesale clothier from the East-end of London—a short, tubby gentleman who had recently taken the Manor House—was observed to turn scarlet.

A gentleman hitherto unknown to them had signalled his advent among them by an act of munificence that should prove a shining example to all rich men. Mr. Horatio Copper—the reverend gentleman found some difficulty, apparently, in deciphering the name.

"Cooper-Smith, sir, with an hyphen," came in a thin whisper, the voice of the still scarlet-faced clothier.

Mr. Horatio Cooper-Smith, taking—the Rev. Augustus felt confident—a not unworthy means of grappling to himself thus early the hearts of his fellow-townsmen, had expressed his desire to pay for the expense of a curate entirely out of his own pocket. Under these circumstances, there would be no further talk of a farewell between the Rev. Augustus Cracklethorpe and his parishioners. It would be the hope of the Rev. Augustus Cracklethorpe to live and die the pastor of St. Jude's.

A more solemn-looking, sober congregation than the congregation that emerged that Sunday morning from St. Jude's in Wychwood-on-the-Heath had never, perhaps, passed out of a church door.

"He'll have more time upon his hands," said Mr. Biles, retired wholesale ironmonger and junior churchwarden, to Mrs. Biles, turning the corner of Acacia Avenue—"he'll have more time to make himself a curse and a stumbling-block."

"And if this 'near relation' of his is anything like him—"

"Which you may depend upon it is the case, or he'd never have thought of him," was the opinion of Mr. Biles.

"I shall give that Mrs. Pennycoop," said Mrs. Biles, "a piece of my mind when I meet her."

But of what use was that?

God Sees The Truth, But Waits
Leo Tolstoy

In the town of Vladimir lived a young merchant named Ivan Dmitrich Aksionov. He had two shops and a house of his own.

Aksionov was a handsome, fair-haired, curly-headed fellow, full of fun, and very fond of singing. When quite a young man he had been given to drink, and was riotous when he had had too much; but after he married he gave up drinking, except now and then.

One summer Aksionov was going to the Nizhny Fair, and as he bade good-bye to his family, his wife said to him, "Ivan Dmitrich, do not start to-day; I have had a bad dream about you."

Aksionov laughed, and said, "You are afraid that when I get to the fair I shall go on a spree."

His wife replied: "I do not know what I am afraid of; all I know is that I had a bad dream. I dreamt you returned from the town, and when you took off your cap I saw that your hair was quite grey."

Aksionov laughed. "That's a lucky sign," said he. "See if I don't sell out all my goods, and bring you some presents from the fair."

So he said good-bye to his family, and drove away.

When he had travelled half-way, he met a merchant whom he knew, and they put up at the same inn for the night. They had some tea together, and then went to bed in adjoining rooms.

It was not Aksionov's habit to sleep late, and, wishing to travel while it was still cool, he aroused his driver before dawn, and told him to put in the horses.

Then he made his way across to the landlord of the inn (who lived in a cottage at the back), paid his bill, and continued his journey.

When he had gone about twenty-five miles, he stopped for the horses to be fed. Aksionov rested awhile in the passage of the inn, then he stepped out into the porch, and, ordering a samovar to be heated, got out his guitar and began to play.

Suddenly a troika drove up with tinkling bells and an official alighted, followed by two soldiers. He came to Aksionov and began to question him, asking him who he was and whence he came. Aksionov answered him fully, and said, "Won't you have some tea with me?" But the official went on cross-questioning him and asking him. "Where did you spend last night? Were you alone, or with a fellow-merchant? Did you see the other merchant this morning? Why did you leave the inn before dawn?"

Aksionov wondered why he was asked all these questions, but he described all that had happened, and then added, "Why do you cross-question me as if I were a thief or a robber? I am travelling on business of my own, and there is no need to question me."

Then the official, calling the soldiers, said, "I am the police-officer of this district, and I question you because the merchant with whom you spent last night has been found with his throat cut. We must search your things."

They entered the house. The soldiers and the police-officer unstrapped Aksionov's luggage and searched it. Suddenly the officer drew a knife out of a bag, crying, "Whose knife is this?"

Aksionov looked, and seeing a blood-stained knife taken from his bag, he was frightened.

"How is it there is blood on this knife?"

Aksionov tried to answer, but could hardly utter a word, and only stammered: "I—don't know—not mine." Then the police-officer said: "This morning the merchant was found in bed with his throat cut. You are the only person who could have done it. The house was locked from inside, and no one else was there. Here is this blood-stained knife in your bag and your face and manner betray you! Tell me how you killed him, and how much money you stole?"

Aksionov swore he had not done it; that he had not seen the merchant after they had had tea together; that he had no money except eight thousand rubles of his own, and that the knife was not his. But his voice was broken, his face pale, and he trembled with fear as though he were guilty.

The police-officer ordered the soldiers to bind Aksionov and to put him in the cart. As they tied his feet together and flung him into the cart, Aksionov crossed himself and wept. His money and goods were taken from him, and he was sent to the nearest town and imprisoned there. Enquiries as to his character were made in Vladimir. The merchants and other inhabitants of that town said that in former days he used to drink and waste his time, but that he was a good man. Then the trial came on: he was charged with murdering a merchant from Ryazan, and robbing him of twenty thousand rubles.

His wife was in despair, and did not know what to believe. Her children were all quite small; one was a baby at her breast. Taking them all with her, she went to the town where her husband was in jail. At first she was not allowed to see him; but after much begging, she obtained permission from the officials, and was taken to him. When she saw her husband in prison-dress and in chains, shut up with thieves and criminals, she fell down, and did not come to her senses for a long time. Then she drew her children to her, and sat down near him. She told him of things at home, and asked about what had happened to him. He told her all, and she asked, "What can we do now?"

"We must petition the Czar not to let an innocent man perish."

His wife told him that she had sent a petition to the Czar, but it had not been accepted.

Aksionov did not reply, but only looked downcast.

Then his wife said, "It was not for nothing I dreamt your hair had turned grey. You remember? You should not have started that day." And passing her fingers through his hair, she said: "Vanya dearest, tell your wife the truth; was it not you who did it?"

"So you, too, suspect me!" said Aksionov, and, hiding his face in his hands, he began to weep. Then a soldier came to say that the wife and children must go away; and Aksionov said good-bye to his family for the last time.

When they were gone, Aksionov recalled what had been said, and when he remembered that his wife also had suspected him, he said to himself, "It seems that only God can know the truth; it is to Him alone we must appeal, and from Him alone expect mercy."

And Aksionov wrote no more petitions; gave up all hope, and only prayed to God.

Aksionov was condemned to be flogged and sent to the mines. So he was flogged with a knot, and when the wounds made by the knot were healed, he was driven to Siberia with other convicts.

For twenty-six years Aksionov lived as a convict in Siberia. His hair turned white as snow, and his beard grew long, thin, and grey. All his mirth went; he stooped; he walked slowly, spoke little, and never laughed, but he often prayed.

In prison Aksionov learnt to make boots, and earned a little money, with which he bought *The Lives of the Saints*. He read this book when there was light enough in the prison; and on Sundays in the prison-church he read the lessons and sang in the choir; for his voice was still good.

The prison authorities liked Aksionov for his meekness, and his fellow-prisoners respected him: they called him "Grandfather," and "The Saint." When they wanted to petition the prison authorities about anything, they always made Aksionov their spokesman, and when there were quarrels among the prisoners they came to him to put things right, and to judge the matter.

No news reached Aksionov from his home, and he did not even know if his wife and children were still alive.

One day a fresh gang of convicts came to the prison. In the evening the old prisoners collected round the new ones and asked them what towns or villages they came from, and what they were sentenced for. Among the rest Aksionov sat down near the newcomers, and listened with downcast air to what was said.

One of the new convicts, a tall, strong man of sixty, with a closely-cropped grey beard, was telling the others what he had been arrested for.

"Well, friends," he said, "I only took a horse that was tied to a sledge, and I was arrested and accused of stealing. I said I had only taken it to get home quicker, and had then let it go; besides, the driver was a personal friend of mine. So I said, 'It's all right.' 'No,' said they, 'you stole it.' But how or where I stole it they could not say. I once really did something wrong, and ought by rights to have come here long ago, but that time I was not found out. Now I have been sent here for nothing at all... Eh, but it's lies I'm telling you; I've been to Siberia before, but I did not stay long."

"Where are you from?" asked some one.

"From Vladimir. My family are of that town. My name is Makar, and they also call me Semyonich."

Aksionov raised his head and said: "Tell me, Semyonich, do you know anything of the merchants Aksionov of Vladimir? Are they still alive?"

"Know them? Of course I do. The Aksionovs are rich, though their father is in Siberia: a sinner like ourselves, it seems! As for you, Gran'dad, how did you come here?"

Aksionov did not like to speak of his misfortune. He only sighed, and said, "For my sins I have been in prison these twenty-six years."

"What sins?" asked Makar Semyonich.

But Aksionov only said, "Well, well—I must have deserved it!" He would have said no more, but his companions told the newcomers how Aksionov came to be in Siberia; how some one had killed a merchant, and had put the knife among Aksionov's things, and Aksionov had been unjustly condemned.

When Makar Semyonich heard this, he looked at Aksionov, slapped his own knee, and exclaimed, "Well, this is wonderful! Really wonderful! But how old you've grown, Gran'dad!"

The others asked him why he was so surprised, and where he had seen Aksionov before; but Makar Semyonich did not reply. He only said: "It's wonderful that we should meet here, lads!"

These words made Aksionov wonder whether this man knew who had killed the merchant; so he said, "Perhaps, Semyonich, you have heard of that affair, or maybe you've seen me before?"

"How could I help hearing? The world's full of rumours. But it's a long time ago, and I've forgotten what I heard."

"Perhaps you heard who killed the merchant?" asked Aksionov.

Makar Semyonich laughed, and replied: "It must have been him in whose bag the knife was found! If some one else hid the knife there, 'He's not a thief till he's caught,' as the saying is. How could any one put a knife into your bag while it was under your head? It would surely have woke you up."

When Aksionov heard these words, he felt sure this was the man who had killed the merchant. He rose and went away. All that night Aksionov lay awake. He felt terribly unhappy, and all sorts of images rose in his mind. There was the image of his wife as she was when he parted from her to go to the fair. He saw her as if she were present; her face and her eyes rose before him; he heard her speak and laugh. Then he saw his children, quite little, as they were at that time: one with a little cloak on, another at his mother's breast. And then he remembered himself as he used to be—young and merry. He remembered how he sat playing the guitar in the porch of the inn where he was arrested, and how free from care he had been. He saw, in his mind, the place where he was flogged, the executioner, and the people standing around; the chains, the convicts, all the twenty-six years of his prison life, and his premature old age. The thought of it all made him so wretched that he was ready to kill himself.

"And it's all that villain's doing!" thought Aksionov. And his anger was so great against Makar Semyonich that he longed for vengeance, even if he himself should perish for it. He kept repeating prayers all night, but could get no peace. During the day he did not go near Makar Semyonich, nor even look at him.

A fortnight passed in this way. Aksionov could not sleep at night, and was so miserable that he did not know what to do.

One night as he was walking about the prison he noticed some earth that came rolling out from under one of the shelves on which the prisoners slept. He stopped to see what it was. Suddenly Makar Semyonich crept out from under the shelf, and looked up at Aksionov with frightened face. Aksionov tried to pass without looking at him, but Makar seized his hand and told him that he had dug a hole under the wall, getting rid of the earth by putting it into his high-boots, and emptying it out every day on the road when the prisoners were driven to their work.

"Just you keep quiet, old man, and you shall get out too. If you blab, they'll flog the life out of me, but I will kill you first."

Aksionov trembled with anger as he looked at his enemy. He drew his hand away, saying, "I have no wish to escape, and you have no need to kill me; you killed me long ago! As to telling of you—I may do so or not, as God shall direct."

Next day, when the convicts were led out to work, the convoy soldiers noticed that one or other of the prisoners emptied some earth out of his boots. The prison was searched and the tunnel found. The Governor came and questioned all the prisoners to find out who had dug the hole. They all denied any knowledge of it. Those who knew would not betray Makar Semyonich, knowing he would be flogged almost to death. At last the Governor turned to Aksionov whom he knew to be a just man, and said:

"You are a truthful old man; tell me, before God, who dug the hole?"

Makar Semyonich stood as if he were quite unconcerned, looking at the Governor and not so much as glancing at Aksionov.

Aksionov's lips and hands trembled, and for a long time he could not utter a word. He thought, "Why should I screen him who ruined my life? Let him pay for what I have suffered. But if I tell, they will probably flog the life out of him, and maybe I suspect him wrongly. And, after all, what good would it be to me?"

"Well, old man," repeated the Governor, "tell me the truth: who has been digging under the wall?"

Aksionov glanced at Makar Semyonich, and said, "I cannot say, your honour. It is not God's will that I should tell! Do what you like with me; I am in your hands."

However much the Governor! tried, Aksionov would say no more, and so the matter had to be left.

That night, when Aksionov was lying on his bed and just beginning to doze, some one came quietly and sat down on his bed. He peered through the darkness and recognised Makar.

"What more do you want of me?" asked Aksionov. "Why have you come here?"

Makar Semyonich was silent. So Aksionov sat up and said, "What do you want? Go away, or I will call the guard!"

Makar Semyonich bent close over Aksionov, and whispered, "Ivan Dmitrich, forgive me!"

"What for?" asked Aksionov.

"It was I who killed the merchant and hid the knife among your things. I meant to kill you too, but I heard a noise outside, so I hid the knife in your bag and escaped out of the window."

Aksionov was silent, and did not know what to say. Makar Semyonich slid off the bed-shelf and knelt upon the ground. "Ivan Dmitrich," said he, "forgive me! For the love of God, forgive me! I will confess that it was I who killed the merchant, and you will be released and can go to your home."

"It is easy for you to talk," said Aksionov, "but I have suffered for you these twenty-six years. Where could I go to now?... My wife is dead, and my children have forgotten me. I have nowhere to go..."

Makar Semyonich did not rise, but beat his head on the floor. "Ivan Dmitrich, forgive me!" he cried. "When they flogged me with the knot it was not so hard to bear as it is to see you now ... yet you had pity on me, and did not tell. For Christ's sake forgive me, wretch that I am!" And he began to sob.

When Aksionov heard him sobbing he, too, began to weep. "God will forgive you!" said he. "Maybe I am a hundred times worse than you." And at these words his heart grew light, and the longing for home left him. He no longer had any desire to leave the prison, but only hoped for his last hour to come.

In spite of what Aksionov had said, Makar Semyonich confessed, his guilt. But when the order for his release came, Aksionov was already dead.

Jean Francois
Maurice Baring

Jean Francois was a vagabond by nature, a ballad-monger by profession. Like many poets in many times, he found that the business of writing verse was more amusing than lucrative; and he was constrained to supplement the earnings of his pen and his guitar by other and more profitable work. He had run away from what had been his home at the age of seven (he was a foundling, and his adopted father was a shoe-maker), without having learnt a trade. When the necessity arose he decided to supplement the art of ballad-mongering by that of stealing. He was skilful in both arts: he wrote verse, sang ballads, picked pockets (in the city), and stole horses (in the country) with equal facility and success. Some of his verse has reached posterity, for instance the *"Ballads du Paradis Peint,"* which he wrote on white vellum, and illustrated himself with illuminations in red, blue and gold, for the Dauphin. It ends thus in the English version of a Balliol scholar:—

> *Prince, do not let your nose, your Royal nose,*
> *Your large Imperial nose get out of joint;*
> *Forbear to criticise my perfect prose—*
> *Painting on vellum is my weakest point.*

Again, the ballad of which the "Envoi" runs:—

> *Prince, when you light your pipe with radium spills,*
> *Especially invented for the King—*
> *Remember this, the worst of human ills:*
> *Life without matches is a dismal thing,*

is, in reality, only a feeble adaptation of his *"Priez pour feu le vrai tresor de vie."*

But although Jean Francois was not unknown during his

lifetime, and although, as his verse testifies, he knew his name would live among those of the enduring poets after his death, his life was one of rough hardship, brief pleasures, long anxieties, and constant uncertainty. Sometimes for a few days at a time he would live in riotous luxury, but these rare epochs would immediately be succeeded by periods of want bordering on starvation. Besides which he was nearly always in peril of his life; the shadow of the gallows darkened his merriment, and the thought of the wheel made bitter his joy. Yet in spite of this hazardous and harassing life, in spite of the sharp and sudden transitions in his career, in spite of the menace of doom, the hint of the wheel and the gallows, his fund of joy remained undiminished, and this we see in his verse, which reflects with equal vividness his alternate moods of infinite enjoyment and unmitigated despair. For instance, the only two triolets which have survived from his *"Trente deux Triolets joyeux and tristes"* are an example of his twofold temperament. They run thus in the literal and exact translations of them made by an eminent official: —

> *I wish I was dead,*
> *And lay deep in the grave.*
> *I've a pain in my head,*
> *I wish I was dead.*
> *In a coffin of lead —*
> *With the Wise and the Brave —*
> *I wish I was dead,*
> *And lay deep in the grave.*

This passionate utterance immediately preceded, in the original text, the following verses in which his buoyant spirits rise once more to the surface: —

> *Thank God I'm alive*
> *In the light of the Sun!*
> *It's a quarter to five;*
> *Thank God I'm alive!*
> *Now the hum of the hive*
> *Of the world has begun,*
> *Thank God I'm alive*
> *In the light of the Sun!*

A more plaintive, in fact a positively wistful note, which is almost incongruous amongst the definite and sharply defined moods of Jean Francois, is struck in the sonnet of which only the

48

first line has reached us: "I wish I had a hundred thousand pounds." ("*Voulentiers serais pauvre avec dix mille escus.*") But in nearly all his verse, whether joyous as in the "*Chant de vin et vie,*" or gloomy as in the "*Ballade des Treize Pendus,*" there is a curious recurrent aspiration towards a warm fire, a sure and plentiful supper, a clean bed, and a long, long sleep. Whether Jean Francois moped or made merry, and in spite of the fact that he enjoyed his roving career and would not have exchanged it for the throne of an Emperor or the money-bags of Croesus, there is no doubt that he experienced the burden of an immense fatigue. He was never quite warm enough; always a little hungry; and never got as much sleep as he desired. A place where he could sleep his fill represented the highest joys of Heaven to him; and he looked forward to Death as a traveller looks forward to a warm inn where (its terrible threshold once passed), a man can sleep the clock round. Witness the sonnet which ends (the translation is mine): —

> *For thou has never turned*
> *A stranger from thy gates or hast denied,*
> *O hospitable Death, a place to rest.*

And it is of his death and not of his life or works which I wish to tell, for it was singular. He died on Christmas Eve, 1432. The winter that year in the north of France was, as is well known, terrible for its severe cold. The rich stayed at home, the poor died, and the unfortunate third estate of gipsies, ballad-mongers, tinkers, tumblers, and thieves had no chance of displaying their dexterity. In fact, they starved. Ever since the 1st of December Jean Francois had been unable to make a silver penny either by his song or his sleight of hand. Christmas was drawing near, and he was starving; and this was especially bitter to him, as it was his custom (for he was not only a lover of good cheer, but a good Catholic and a strict observer of fasts and feasts) to keep the great day of Christendom fittingly. This year he had nothing to keep it with. Luck seemed to be against him; for three days before Christmas he met in a dark side street of the town the rich and stingy Sieur de Ranquet. He picked the pocket of that nobleman, but owing to the extreme cold his fingers faltered, and he was discovered. He ran like a hare and managed easily enough to outstrip the miser, and to conceal himself in a den where he was well known. But unfortunately the matter did not end there. The Sieur de Ranquet was influential at Court; he was implacable as well as avaricious, and his disposition positively forbade him to forgive any one who had nearly picked his pocket. Besides which he knew that Jean had often stolen his horses. He made a formal complaint at high quarters, and a warrant was issued against Jean, offering a large sum in silver coin to the man who should bring him, alive or dead, to justice.

Now the police were keenly anxious to make an end of Jean. They knew he was guilty of a hundred thefts, but such was his skill that they had never been able to convict him; he had often been put in prison, but he had always been released for want of evidence. This time no mistake was possible. So Jean, aware of the danger, fled from the city and sought a gipsy encampment in a neighboring forest, where he had friends. These gipsy friends of his were robbers, outlaws, murderers and horse-stealers all of them, and hardened criminals; they called themselves gipsies, but it was merely a courtesy title.

On Christmas Eve—it was snowing hard—Jean was walking through the forest towards the town, ready for a desperate venture, for in the camp they were starving, and he was sick almost to death of his hunted, miserable life. As he plunged through the snow he heard a moan, and he saw a child sitting at the roots of a tall tree crying. He asked what was the matter. The child—it was a little boy about five years old—said that it had run away from home because its nurse had beaten it, and had lost its way.

"Where do you live?" asked Jean.

"My father is the Sieur de Ranquet," said the child.

At that moment Jean heard the shouts of his companions in the distance.

"I want to go home," said the little boy quietly. "You must take me home," and he put his hand into Jean's hand and looked up at him and smiled.

Jean thought for a moment. The boy was richly dressed; he had a large ruby cross hanging from a golden collar worth many hundred gold pieces. Jean knew well what would happen if his gipsy companions came across the child. They would kill it instantly.

"All right," said Jean, "climb on my back."

The little boy climbed on to his back, and Jean trudged through the snow. In an hour's time they reached the Sieur de Ranquet's castle; the place was alive with bustling men and flaring torches, for the Sieur's heir had been missed.

The Sieur looked at Jean and recognized him immediately.

Jean was a public character, and especially well known to the Sieur de Ranquet. A few words were whispered. The child was sent to bed, and the archers civilly lead Jean to his dungeon. Jean was tired and sleepy. He fell asleep at once on the straw. They told him he would have to get up early the next morning, in time for a long, cold journey. The gallows, they added, would be ready.

But in the night Jean dreamed a dream: he saw a child in glittering clothes and with a shining face who came into the dungeon and broke the bars.

The child said: "I am little St. Nicholas, the children's friend, and I think you are tired, so I'm going to take you to a quiet place."

Jean followed the child, who led him by the hand till they came to a nice inn, very high up on the top of huge mountains. There was a blazing log fire in the room, a clean warm bed, and the windows opened on a range of snowy mountains, bright as diamonds. And the stars twinkled in the sky like the candles of a Christmas tree.

"You can go to bed here," said St. Nicholas, "nobody will disturb you, and when you do wake you will be quite happy and rested. Good-night, Jean." And he went away.

* * * * *

The next day in the dawn, when the archers came to fetch Jean, they found he was fast asleep. They thought it was almost a pity to wake him, because he looked so happy and contented in his sleep; but when they tried they found it was impossible.

The Star-Child
Oscar Wilde

Once upon a time two poor Woodcutters were making their way home through a great pine-forest. It was winter, and a night of bitter cold. The snow lay thick upon the ground, and upon the branches of the trees: the frost kept snapping the little twigs on either side of them, as they passed: and when they came to the Mountain-Torrent she was hanging motionless in air, for the Ice-King had kissed her.

So cold was it that even the animals and the birds did not know what to make of it.

"Ugh!" snarled the Wolf as he limped through the brushwood with his tail between his legs, "this is perfectly monstrous weather. Why doesn't the Government look to it?"

"Weet! weet! weet! twittered the green Linnets, "the old Earth is dead, and they have laid her out in her white shroud."

"The Earth is going to be married, and this is her bridal dress," whispered the Turtle-doves to each other. Their little pink feet were quite frost-bitten, but they felt that it was their duty to take a romantic view of the situation.

"Nonsense!" growled the Wolf. "I tell you that it is all the fault of the Government, and if you don't believe me I shall eat you." The Wolf had a thoroughly practical mind, and was never at a loss for a good argument.

"Well, for my own part, said the Woodpecker, who was a born philosopher, "I don't care an atomic theory for explanations. If a thing is so, it is so, and at present it is terribly cold."

Terribly cold it certainly was. The little Squirrels, who lived inside the tall fir-tree, kept rubbing each other's noses to keep themselves warm, and the Rabbits curled themselves up in their holes, and did not venture even to look out of doors. The only people who seemed to enjoy it were the great horned Owls. Their feathers were quite stiff with rime, but they did not mind, and they rolled their large yellow eyes, and called out to each other across the forest, "Tu-whit! Tu-whoo! Tu-whit! Tu-whoo! what delightful weather we are having!"

On and on went the two Woodcutters, blowing lustily upon their fingers, and stamping with their huge iron-shod boots upon the caked snow. Once they sank into a deep drift, and came out as white as millers are, when the stones are grinding; and once they slipped on the hard smooth ice where the marsh-water was frozen, and their faggots fell out of their bundles, and they had to pick them up and bind them together again; and once they thought that they had lost their way, and a great terror seized on them, for they knew that the Snow is cruel to those who sleep in her arms. But they put their trust in the good Saint Martin, who watches over all travellers, and retraced their steps, and went warily, and at last they reached the outskirts of the forest, and saw, far down in the valley beneath them, the lights of the village in which they dwelt.

So overjoyed were they at their deliverance that they laughed aloud, and the Earth seemed to them like a flower of silver, and the Moon like a flower of gold.

Yet, after that they had laughed they became sad, for they remembered their poverty, and one of them said to the other, "Why did we make merry, seeing that life is for the rich, and not for such as we are? Better that we had died of cold in the forest, or that some wild beast had fallen upon us and slain us."

"Truly," answered his companion, much is given to some, and little is given to others. Injustice has parcelled out the world, nor is there equal division of aught save of sorrow."

But as they were bewailing their misery to each other this strange thing happened. There fell from heaven a very bright and beautiful star. It slipped down the side of the sky, passing by the other stars in its course, and, as they watched it wondering, it seemed to them to sink behind a clump of willow-trees that stood hard by a little sheep-fold no more than a stone's throw away.

"Why! there is a crock of gold for whoever finds it," they cried, and they set to and ran, so eager were they for the gold.

And one of them ran faster than his mate, and outstripped

him, and forced his way through the willows, and came out on the other side, and lo! there was indeed a thing of gold lying on the white snow. So he hastened towards it, and stooping down placed his hands upon it, and it was a cloak of golden tissue, curiously wrought with stars, and wrapped in many folds. And he cried out to his comrade that he had found the treasure that had fallen from the sky, and when his comrade had come up, they sat them down in the snow, and loosened the folds of the cloak that they might divide the pieces of gold. But, alas! no gold was in it, nor silver, nor, indeed, treasure of any kind, but only a little child who was asleep.

And one of them said to the other: "This is a bitter ending to our hope, nor have we any good fortune, for what doth a child profit to a man? Let us leave it here, and go our way, seeing that we are poor men, and have children of our own whose bread we may not give to another."

But his companion answered him: "Nay, but it were an evil thing to leave the child to perish here in the snow, and though I am as poor as thou art, and have many mouths to feed, and but little in the pot, yet will I bring it home with me, and my wife shall have care of it."

So very tenderly he took up the child, and wrapped the cloak around it to shield it from the harsh cold, and made his way down the hill to the village, his comrade marvelling much at his foolishness and softness of heart.

And when they came to the village, his comrade said to him, "Thou hast the child, therefore give me the cloak, for it is meet that we should share."

But he answered him: "Nay, for the cloak is neither mine nor thine, but the child's only," and he bade him Godspeed, and went to his own house and knocked.

And when his wife opened the door and saw that her husband had returned safe to her, she put her arms round his neck and kissed him, and took from his back the bundle of faggots, and brushed the snow off his boots, and bade him come in.

But he said to her, "I have found something in the forest, and I have brought it to thee to have care of it," and he stirred not from the threshold.

"What is it?" she cried. "Show it to me, for the house is bare, and we have need of many things." And he drew the cloak back, and showed her the sleeping child.

"Alack, goodman!" she murmured, "have we not children enough of our own, that thou must needs bring a changeling to sit by the hearth? And who knows if it will not bring us bad fortune? And how shall we tend it?" And she was wroth against him.

"Nay, but it is a Star-Child," he answered; and he told her the strange manner of the finding of it.

But she would not be appeased, but mocked at him, and spoke angrily, and cried: "Our children lack bread, and shall we feed the child of another? Who is there who careth for us? And who giveth us food?"

"Nay, but God careth for the sparrows even, and feedeth them," he answered.

"Do not the sparrows die of hunger in the winter?" she asked. And is it not winter now?" And the man answered nothing, but stirred not from the threshold.

And a bitter wind from the forest came in through the open door, and made her tremble, and she shivered, and said to him: "Wilt thou not close the door? There cometh a bitter wind into the house, and I am cold."

"Into a house where a heart is hard cometh there not always a bitter wind?" he asked. And the woman answered him nothing, but crept closer to the fire.

And after a time she turned round and looked at him, and her eyes were full of tears. And he came in swiftly, and placed the child in her arms, and she kissed it, and laid it in a little bed where the youngest of their own children was lying. And on the morrow the Woodcutter took the curious cloak of gold and placed it in a great chest, and a chain of amber that was round the child's neck his wife took and set it in the chest also.

So the Star-Child was brought up with the children of the Woodcutter, and sat at the same board with them, and was their playmate. And every year he became more beautiful to look at, so that all those who dwelt in the village were filled with wonder, for, while they were swarthy and black-haired, he was white and delicate as sawn ivory, and his curls were like the rings of the daffodil. His lips, also, were like the petals of a red flower, and his eyes were like violets by a river of pure water, and his body like the narcissus of a field where the mower comes not.

Yet did his beauty work him evil. For he grew proud, and cruel, and selfish. The children of the Woodcutter, and the other children of the village, he despised, saying that they were of mean parentage, while he was noble, being sprung from a Star, and he made himself master over them, and called them his servants. No pity had he for the poor, or for those who were blind or maimed or in any way afflicted, but would cast stones at them and drive them forth on to the highway, and bid them beg their bread elsewhere, so that none save the outlaws came twice to that village to ask for alms. Indeed, he was as one enamoured of beauty, and would mock at the weakly and ill-favoured, and make jest of them; and himself he loved, and in summer, when the winds were still, he would lie by the well in the priest's orchard and look down at the marvel of his own face, and laugh for the pleasure he had in his fairness.

Often did the Woodcutter and his wife chide him, and say: "We did not deal with thee as thou dealest with those who are left desolate, and have none to succor them. Wherefore art thou so cruel to all who need pity?"

Often did the old priest send for him, and seek to teach him the love of living things, saying to him: "The fly is thy brother. Do it no harm. The wild birds that roam through the forest have their freedom. Snare them not for thy pleasure. God made the blind-worm and the mole, and each has its place. Who art thou to bring pain into God's world? Even the cattle of the field praise Him."

But the Star-Child heeded not their words, but would frown and flout, and go back to his companions, and lead them. And his companions followed him, for he was fair, and fleet of foot, and could dance, and pipe, and make music. And wherever the Star-Child led them they followed, and whatever the Star-Child bade them do, that did they. And when he pierced with a sharp reed the dim eyes of the mole, they laughed, and when he cast stones at the leper they laughed also. And in all things he ruled them, and they became hard of heart, even as he was.

Now there passed one day through the village a poor beggar-woman. Her garments were torn and ragged, and her feet were bleeding from the rough road on which she had travelled, and she was in very evil plight. And being weary she sat her down under a chestnut-tree to rest.

But when the Star-Child saw her, he said to his companions, "See! There sitteth a foul beggar-woman under that fair and green-leaved tree. Come, let us drive her hence, for she is ugly and ill-favoured."

So he came near and threw stones at her, and mocked her, and she looked at him with terror in her eyes, nor did she move her gaze from him. And when the Woodcutter, who was cleaving logs in a haggard hard by, saw what the Star-Child was doing, he ran up and rebuked him, and said to him: "Surely thou art hard of heart and knowest not mercy, for what evil has this poor woman done to thee that thou should'st treat her in this wise?"

And the Star-Child grew red with anger, and stamped his foot upon the ground, and said, "Who art thou to question me what I do? I am no son of thine to do thy bidding."

"Thou speakest truly," answered the Woodcutter, "yet did I show thee pity when I found thee in the forest."

And when the woman heard these words she gave a loud cry, and fell into a swoon. And the Woodcutter carried her to his own house, and his wife had care of her, and when she rose up from the swoon into which she had fallen, they set meat and drink before her, and bade her have comfort.

But she would neither eat nor drink, but said to the Woodcutter, "Didst thou not say that the child was found in the forest? And was it not ten years from this day?"

And the Woodcutter answered, "Yea, it was in the forest that I found him, and it is ten years from this day."

"And what signs didst thou find with him?" she cried. "Bore he not upon his neck a chain of amber? Was not round him a cloak of gold tissue broidered with stars?"

"Truly," answered the Woodcutter, "it was even as thou sayest." And he took the cloak and the amber chain from the chest where they lay, and showed them to her.

And when she saw them she wept for joy, and said, "He is my little son whom I lost in the forest. I pray thee send for him quickly, for in search of him have I wandered over the whole world."

So the Woodcutter and his wife went out and called to the Star-Child, and said to him, "Go into the house, and there shalt thou find thy mother, who is waiting for thee."

So he ran in, filled with wonder and great gladness. But when he saw her who was waiting there, he laughed scornfully and said, "Why, where is my mother? For I see none here but this vile beggar-woman."

And the woman answered him, "I am thy mother."

"Thou art mad to say so," cried the Star-Child angrily. "I am no son of thine, for thou art a beggar, and ugly, and in rags. Therefore get thee hence, and let me see thy foul face no more."

"Nay, but thou art indeed my little son, whom I bare in the forest," she cried, and she fell on her knees, and held out her arms to him. "The robbers stole thee from me, and left thee to die," she murmured, "but I recognized thee when I saw thee, and the signs also have I recognized, the cloak of golden tissue and the amber-chain. Therefore I pray thee come with me, for over the whole world have I wandered in search of thee. Come with me, my son, for I have need of thy love."

But the Star-Child stirred not from his place, but shut the doors of his heart against her, nor was there any sound heard save the sound of the woman weeping for pain.

And at last he spoke to her, and his voice was hard and bitter. "If in very truth thou art my mother," he said, "it had been better hadst thou stayed away, and not come here to bring me to shame, seeing that I thought I was the child of some Star and not a beggar's child, as thou tellest me that I am. Therefore get thee hence, and let me see thee no more."

"Alas! my son," she cried, "wilt thou not kiss me before I go? For I have suffered much to find thee."

"Nay," said the Star-Child, "but thou art too foul to look at and rather would I kiss the adder or the toad than thee."

So the woman rose up, and went away into the forest weeping bitterly, and when the Star-Child saw that she had gone, he was glad, and ran back to his playmates that he might play with them.

But when they beheld him coming, they mocked him and said, "Why, thou art as foul as the toad, and as loathsome as the adder. Get thee hence, for we will not suffer thee to play with us," and they drove him out of the garden.

And the Star-Child frowned and said to himself, "What is this that they say to me? I will go to the well of water and look into it, and it shall tell me of my beauty."

So he went to the well of water and looked into it, and lo! his face was as the face of a toad, and his body was scaled like an adder. And he flung himself down on the grass and wept, and said to himself, "Surely this has come upon me by reason of my sin. For I have denied my mother, and driven her away, and been proud, and cruel to her. Wherefore I will go and seek her through the whole world, nor will I rest till I have found her."

And there came to him the little daughter of the Woodcutter, and she put her hand upon his shoulder and said, "What doth it matter if thou hast lost thy comeliness? Stay with us, and I will not mock at thee."

And he said to her, "Nay, but I have been cruel to my mother, and as a punishment has this evil been sent to me. Wherefore I must go hence, and wander through the world till I find her, and she give me her forgiveness."

So he ran away into the forest and called out to his mother to come to him, but there was no answer. All day long he called to her, and when the sun set he lay down to sleep on a bed of leaves, and the birds and the animals fled from him, as they remembered his cruelty, and he was alone save for the toad that watched him, and the slow adder that crawled past.

And in the morning he rose up, and plucked some bitter berries from the trees and ate them, and took his way through the great wood, weeping sorely. And of everything that he met he made enquiry if perchance they had seen his mother.

He said to the Mole, "Thou canst go beneath the earth. Tell me, is my mother there?"

And the Mole answered, "Thou hast blinded mine eyes. How should I know?"

He said to the Linnet, "Thou canst fly over the tops of the tall trees, and canst see the whole world. Tell me, canst thou see my mother?"

And the Linnet answered, "Thou hast clipt my wings for thy pleasure. How should I fly?"

And to the little Squirrel who lived in the fir-tree, and was lonely, he said, "Where is my mother?"

And the Squirrel answered, "Thou hast slain mine. Dost thou seek to slay thine also?"

And the Star-Child wept and bowed his head, and prayed forgiveness of God's things, and went on through the forest, seeking for the beggar-woman. And on the third day he came to the other side of the forest and went down into the plain.

And when he passed through the villages the children mocked him, and threw stones at him, and the carlots would not suffer him even to sleep in the byres lest he might bring mildew on the stored corn, so foul was he to look at, and their hired men drove him away, and there was none who had pity on him. Nor could he hear anywhere of the beggar-woman who was his mother, though for the space of three years he wandered over the world, and often seemed to see her on the road in front of him, and would call to her, and run after her till the sharp flints made his feet to bleed. But overtake her he could not, and those who dwelt by the way did ever deny that they had seen her, or any like to her, and they made sport of his sorrow.

For the space of three years he wandered over the world, and in the world there was neither love nor loving-kindness nor charity for him, but it was even such a world as he had made for himself in the days of his great pride.

And one evening he came to the gate of a strong-walled city that stood by a river, and, weary and footsore though he was, he made to enter in. But the soldiers who stood on guard dropped their halberts across the entrance, and said roughly to him, "What is thy business in the city?"

"I am seeking for my mother," he answered, "and I pray ye to suffer me to pass, for it may be that she is in this city."

But they mocked at him, and one of them wagged a black beard, and set down his shield and cried, "Of a truth, thy mother will not be merry when she sees thee, for thou art more ill-favoured than the toad of the marsh, or the adder that crawls in the fen. Get thee gone. Get thee gone. Thy mother dwells not in this city."

And another, who held a yellow banner in his hand, said to him, "Who is thy mother, and wherefore art thou seeking for her?"

And he answered, "My mother is a beggar even as I am, and I have treated her evilly, and I pray ye to suffer me to pass that she may give me her forgiveness, if it be that she tarrieth in this city." But they would not, and pricked him with their spears.

And, as he turned away weeping, one whose armor was inlaid with gilt flowers, and on whose helmet couched a lion that had wings, came up and made enquiry of the soldiers who it was who had sought entrance. And they said to him, "It is a beggar and the child of a beggar, and we have driven him away."

"Nay," he cried, laughing, "but we will sell the foul thing for a slave, and his price shall be the price of a bowl of sweet wine."

And an old and evil-visaged man who was passing by called out, and said, "I will buy him for that price," and, when he had paid the price, he took the Star-Child by the hand and led him into the city.

And after that they had gone through many streets they came to a little door that was set in a wall that was covered with a pomegranate tree. And the old man touched the door with a ring of graved jasper and it opened, and they went down five steps of brass into a garden filled with black poppies and green jars of burnt clay. And the old man took then from his turban a scarf of figured silk, and bound with it the eyes of the Star-Child, and drove him in front of him. And when the scarf was taken off his eyes, the Star-Child found himself in a dungeon, that was lit by a lantern of horn.

And the old man set before him some moldy bread on a trencher and said, "Eat," and some brackish water in a cup and said, "Drink," and when he had eaten and drunk, the old man went out, locking the door behind him and fastening it with an iron chain.

And on the morrow the old man, who was indeed the subtlest of the magicians of Libya and had learned his art from one who dwelt in the tombs of the Nile, came in to him and frowned at him, and said, "In a wood that is nigh to the gate of this city of Giaours there are three pieces of gold. One is of white gold, and another is of yellow gold, and the gold of the third one is red. Today thou shalt bring me the piece of white gold, and if thou bringest it not back, I will beat thee with a hundred stripes. Get thee away quickly, and at sunset I will be waiting for thee at the door of the garden. See that thou bringest the white gold, or it shall go ill with thee, for thou art my slave, and I have bought thee for the price of a bowl of sweet wine." And he bound the eyes of the Star-Child with the scarf of figured silk, and led him through the house, and through the garden of poppies, and up the five steps of brass. And having opened the little door with his ring he set him in the street.

And the Star-Child went out of the gate of the city, and came to the wood of which the Magician had spoken to him.

Now this wood was very fair to look at from without, and seemed full of singing birds and of sweet-scented flowers, and the Star-Child entered it gladly. Yet did its beauty profit him little, for wherever he went harsh briars and thorns shot up from the ground and encompassed him, and evil nettles stung him, and the thistle pierced him with her daggers, so that he was in sore distress. Nor could he anywhere find the piece of white gold of which the Magician had spoken, though he sought for it from morn to noon, and from noon to sunset. And at sunset he set his face towards home, weeping bitterly, for he knew what fate was in store for him.

But when he had reached the outskirts of the wood, he heard from a thicket a cry as of someone in pain. And forgetting his own sorrow he ran back to the place, and saw there a little Hare caught in a trap that some hunter had set for it.

And the Star-Child had pity on it, and released it, and said to it, "I am myself but a slave, yet may I give thee thy freedom."

And the Hare answered him, and said: "Surely thou hast given me freedom, and what shall I give thee in return?"

And the Star-Child said to it, "I am seeking for a piece of white gold, nor can I anywhere find it, and if I bring it not to my master he will beat me."

"Come thou with me," said the Hare, "and I will lead thee to it, for I know where it is hidden, and for what purpose."

So the Star-Child went with the Hare, and lo! in the cleft of a great oak-tree he saw the piece of white gold that he was seeking. And he was filled with joy, and seized it, and said to the Hare, "The service that I did to thee thou hast rendered back again many times over and the kindness that I showed thee thou hast repaid a hundredfold."

"Nay," answered the Hare, "but as thou dealt with me, so I did deal with thee," and it ran away swiftly, and the Star-Child went towards the city.

Now at the gate of the city there was seated one who was a leper. Over his face hung a cowl of grey linen, and through the eyelets his eyes gleamed like red coals. And when he saw the Star-Child coming, he struck upon a wooden bowl, and clattered his bell, and called out to him, and said, "Give me a piece of money, or I must die of hunger. For they have thrust me out of the city, and there is no one who has pity on me."

"Alas! cried the Star-Child, "I have but one piece of money in my wallet, and if I bring it not to my master he will beat me for I am his slave."

But the leper entreated him, and prayed of him, till the Star-Child had pity, and gave him the piece of white gold.

And when he came to the Magician's house, the Magician opened to him, and brought him in, and said to him, "Hast thou the piece of white gold?" And the Star-Child answered, "I have it not." So the Magician fell upon him, and beat him, and set before him an empty trencher, and said "Eat," and an empty cup, and said, "Drink," and flung him again into the dungeon.

And on the morrow the Magician came to him, and said, "If today thou bringest me not the piece of yellow gold, I will surely keep thee as my slave, and give thee three hundred stripes."

So the Star-Child went to the wood, and all day long he searched for the piece of yellow gold, but nowhere could he find it. And at sunset he sat him down and began to weep, and as he was weeping there came to him the little Hare that he had rescued from the trap.

And the Hare said to him, "Why art thou weeping? And what dost thou seek in the wood?"

And the Star-Child answered, "I am seeking for a piece of yellow gold that is hidden here, and if I find it not, my master will beat me, and keep me as a slave."

"Follow me," cried the Hare, and it ran through the wood till it came to a pool of water. And at the bottom of the pool the piece of yellow gold was lying.

"How shall I thank thee?" said the Star-Child, "for lo! this is the second time that you have succored me."

"Nay, but thou hadst pity on me first," said the Hare, and it ran away swiftly.

And the Star-Child took the piece of yellow gold, and put it in his wallet, and hurried to the city. But the leper saw him coming, and ran to meet him and knelt down and cried, "Give me a piece of money or I shall die of hunger."

And the Star-Child said to him, "I have in my wallet but one piece of yellow gold, and if I bring it not to my master he will beat me and keep me as his slave."

But the leper entreated him sore, so that the Star-Child had pity on him, and gave him the piece of yellow gold.

And when he came to the Magician's house, the Magician opened to him, and brought him in, and said to him, "Hast thou the piece of yellow gold?" And the Star-Child said to him, "I have it not." So the Magician fell upon him, and beat him, and loaded him with chains, and cast him again into the dungeon.

And on the morrow the Magician came to him, and said, "If today thou bringest me the piece of red gold I will set thee free, but if thou bringest it not I will surely slay thee."

So the Star-Child went to the wood, and all day long he searched for the piece of red gold, but nowhere could he find it. And at evening he sat him down, and wept, and as he was weeping there came to him the little Hare.

And the Hare said to him, "The piece of red gold that thou seekest is in the cavern that is behind thee. Therefore weep no more but be glad."

"How shall I reward thee," cried the Star-Child, "for lo! this is the third time thou hast succored me."

"Nay, but thou hadst pity on me first," said the Hare, and it ran away swiftly.

And the Star-Child entered the cavern, and in its farthest corner he found the piece of red gold. So he put it in his wallet, and hurried to the city. And the leper seeing him coming, stood in the centre of the road, and cried out, and said to him, "Give me the piece of red money, or I must die," and the Star-Child had pity on him again, and gave him the piece of red gold, saying, "Thy need is greater than mine." Yet was his heart heavy, for he knew what evil fate awaited him.

But lo! as he passed through the gate of the city, the guards bowed down and made obeisance to him, saying, "How beautiful is our lord!" and a crowd of citizens followed him, and cried out, 'Surely there is none so beautiful in the whole world!" so that the Star-Child wept, and said to himself, "They are mocking me, and making light of my misery." And so large was the concourse of the people, that he lost the threads of his way, and found himself at last in a great square, in which there was a palace of a King.

And the gate of the palace opened, and the priests and the high officers of the city ran forth to meet him, and they abased themselves before him, and said, "Thou art our lord for whom we have been waiting, and the son of our King."

And the Star-Child answered them and said, "I am no king's son, but the child of a poor beggar-woman. And how say ye that I am beautiful, for I know that I am evil to look at?"

Then he, whose armor was inlaid with gilt flowers, and on whose helmet couched a lion that had wings, held up a shield, and cried, "How saith my lord that he is not beautiful?"

And the Star-Child looked, and lo! his face was even as it had been, and his comeliness had come back to him, and he saw that in his eyes which he had not seen there before.

And the priests and the high officers knelt down and said to him, "It was prophesied of old that on this day should come he who was to rule over us. Therefore, let our lord take this crown and this sceptre, and be in his justice and mercy our King over us."

But he said to them, "I am not worthy, for I have denied the mother who bore me, nor may I rest till I have found her, and known her forgiveness. Therefore, let me go, for I must wander again over the world, and may not tarry here, though ye bring me the crown and the sceptre." And as he spake he turned his face from them towards the street that led to the gate of the city, and lo! amongst the crowd that pressed round the soldiers, he saw the beggar-woman who was his mother, and at her side stood the leper, who had sat by the road.

And a cry of joy broke from his lips, and he ran over, and kneeling down he kissed the wounds on his mother's feet, and wet them with his tears. He bowed his head in the dust, and sobbing, as one whose heart might break, he said to her: "Mother, I denied thee in the hour of my pride. Accept me in the hour of my humility. Mother, I gave thee hatred. Do thou give me love. Mother, I rejected thee. Receive thy child now." But the beggar-woman answered him not a word.

And he reached out his hands, and clasped the white feet of the leper, and said to him: "Thrice did I give thee of my mercy. Bid my mother speak to me once." But the leper answered him not a word.

And he sobbed again, and said: "Mother, my suffering is greater than I can bear. Give me thy forgiveness, and let me go back to the forest." And the beggar-woman put her hand on his head, and said to him, "Rise," and the leper put his hand on his head, and said to him "Rise," also.

And he rose up from his feet, and looked at them, and lo! they were a King and a Queen.

And the Queen said to him, "This is thy father whom thou hast succored."

And the King said, "This is thy mother, whose feet thou hast washed with thy tears."

And they fell on his neck and kissed him, and brought him into the palace, and clothed him in fair raiment, and set the crown upon his head, and the sceptre in his hand, and over the city that stood by the river he ruled, and was its lord. Much justice and mercy did he show to all, and the evil Magician he banished, and to the Woodcutter and his wife he sent many rich gifts, and to their children he gave high honor. Nor would he suffer any to be cruel to bird or beast, but taught love and loving-kindness and charity, and to the poor he gave bread, and to the naked he gave raiment, and there was peace and plenty in the land.

Yet ruled he not long, so great had been his suffering, and so bitter the fire of his testing, for after the space of three years he died. And he who came after him ruled evilly.

For Conscience' Sake

Thomas Hardy

CHAPTER I

Whether the utilitarian or the intuitive theory of the moral sense be upheld, it is beyond question that there are a few subtle-souled persons with whom the absolute gratuitousness of an act of reparation is an inducement to perform it; while exhortation as to its necessity would breed excuses for leaving it undone. The case of Mr. Millborne and Mrs. Frankland particularly illustrated this, and perhaps something more.

There were few figures better known to the local crossing-sweeper than Mr. Millborne's, in his daily comings and goings along a familiar and quiet London street, where he lived inside the door marked eleven, though not as householder. In age he was fifty at least, and his habits were as regular as those of a person can be who has no occupation but the study of how to keep himself employed. He turned almost always to the right on getting to the end of his street, then he went onward down Bond Street to his club, whence he returned by precisely the same course about six o'clock, on foot; or, if he went to dine, later on in a cab. He was known to be a man of some means, though apparently not wealthy. Being a bachelor he seemed to prefer his present mode of living as a lodger in Mrs. Towney's best rooms, with the use of furniture which he had bought ten times over in rent during his tenancy, to having a house of his own.

None among his acquaintance tried to know him well, for his manner and moods did not excite curiosity or deep friendship. He was not a man who seemed to have anything on his mind, anything to conceal, anything to impart. From his casual remarks it was generally understood that he was country-born, a native of some place in Wessex; that he had come to London as a young man in a banking-house, and had risen to a post of responsibility; when, by the death of his father, who had been fortunate in his investments, the son succeeded to an income which led him to retire from a business life somewhat early.

One evening, when he had been unwell for several days, Doctor Bindon came in, after dinner, from the adjoining medical quarter, and smoked with him over the fire. The patient's ailment was not such as to require much thought, and they talked together on indifferent subjects.

"I am a lonely man, Bindon—a lonely man," Millborne took occasion to say, shaking his head gloomily. "You don't know such loneliness as mine . . . And the older I get the more I am dissatisfied with myself. And to-day I have been, through an accident, more than usually haunted by what, above all other events of my life, causes that dissatisfaction—the recollection of an unfulfilled promise made twenty years ago. In ordinary affairs I have always been considered a man of my word and perhaps it is on that account that a particular vow I once made, and did not keep, comes back to me with a magnitude out of all proportion (I daresay) to its real gravity, especially at this time of day. You know the discomfort caused at night by the half-sleeping sense that a door or window has been left unfastened, or in the day by the remembrance of unanswered letters. So does that promise haunt me from time to time, and has done to-day particularly."

There was a pause, and they smoked on. Millborne's eyes, though fixed on the fire, were really regarding attentively a town in the West of England.

"Yes," he continued, "I have never quite forgotten it, though during the busy years of my life it was shelved and buried under the pressure of my pursuits. And, as I say, to-day in particular, an incident in the law- report of a somewhat similar kind has brought it back again vividly. However, what it was I can tell you in a few words, though no doubt you, as a man of the world, will smile at the thinness of my skin when you hear it . . . I came up to town at one-and-twenty, from Toneborough, in Outer Wessex, where I was born, and where, before I left, I had won the heart of a young woman of my own age. I promised her marriage, took advantage of my promise, and—am a bachelor."

"The old story."

The other nodded.

"I left the place, and thought at the time I had done a very clever thing in getting so easily out of an entanglement. But I have lived long enough for that promise to return to bother me—to be honest, not altogether as a pricking of the conscience, but as a dissatisfaction with myself as a specimen of the heap of flesh called humanity. If I were to ask you to lend me fifty pounds, which I would repay you next midsummer, and I did not repay you, I should consider myself a shabby sort of fellow, especially if you wanted the money badly. Yet I promised that girl just as distinctly; and then coolly broke my word, as if doing so were rather smart conduct than a mean action, for which the poor victim herself, encumbered with a child, and not I, had really to pay the penalty, in spite of certain pecuniary aid that was given. There, that's the retrospective trouble that I am always unearthing; and you may hardly believe that though so many years have elapsed, and it is all gone by and done with, and she must be getting on for an old woman now, as I am for an old man, it really often destroys my sense of self-respect still."

"O, I can understand it. All depends upon the temperament. Thousands of men would have forgotten all about it; so would you, perhaps, if you had married and had a family. Did she ever marry?"

"I don't think so. O no—she never did. She left Toneborough, and later on appeared under another name at Exonbury, in the next county, where she was not known. It is very seldom that I go down into that part of the country, but in passing through Exonbury, on one occasion, I learnt that she was quite a settled resident there, as a teacher of music, or something of the kind. That much I casually heard when I was there two or three years ago. But I have never set eyes on her since our original acquaintance, and should not know her if I met her."

"Did the child live?" asked the doctor.

"For several years, certainly," replied his friend. "I cannot say if she is living now. It was a little girl. She might be married by this time as far as years go."

"And the mother—was she a decent, worthy young woman?"

"O yes; a sensible, quiet girl, neither attractive nor unattractive to the ordinary observer; simply commonplace. Her position at the time of our acquaintance was not so good as mine. My father was a solicitor, as I think I have told you. She was a young girl in a music-shop; and it was represented to me that it would be beneath my position to marry her. Hence the result."

"Well, all I can say is that after twenty years it is probably too late to think of mending such a matter. It has doubtless by this time mended itself. You had better dismiss it from your mind as an evil past your control. Of course, if mother and daughter are alive, or either, you might settle something upon them, if you were inclined, and had it to spare."

"Well, I haven't much to spare; and I have relations in narrow circumstances—perhaps narrower than theirs. But that is not the point. Were I ever so rich I feel I could not rectify the past by money. I did not promise to enrich her. On the contrary, I told her it would probably be dire poverty for both of us. But I did promise to make her my wife."

"Then find her and do it," said the doctor jocularly as he rose to leave.

"Ah, Bindon. That, of course, is the obvious jest. But I haven't the slightest desire for marriage; I am quite content to live as I have lived. I am a bachelor by nature, and instinct, and habit, and everything. Besides, though I respect her still (for she was not an atom to blame), I haven't any shadow of love for her. In my mind she exists as one of those women you think well of, but find uninteresting. It would be purely with the idea of putting wrong right that I should hunt her up, and propose to do it off-hand."

"You don't think of it seriously?" said his surprised friend.

"I sometimes think that I would, if it were practicable; simply, as I say, to recover my sense of being a man of honor."

"I wish you luck in the enterprise," said Doctor Bindon. "You'll soon be out of that chair, and then you can put your impulse to the test. But—after twenty years of silence—I should say, don't!"

CHAPTER II

The doctor's advice remained counterpoised, in Millborne's mind, by the aforesaid mood of seriousness and sense of principle, approximating often to religious sentiment, which had been evolving itself in his breast for months, and even years.

The feeling, however, had no immediate effect upon Mr. Millborne's actions. He soon got over his trifling illness, and was vexed with himself for having, in a moment of impulse, confided such a case of conscience to anybody.

But the force which had prompted it, though latent, remained with him and ultimately grew stronger. The upshot was that about four months after the date of his illness and disclosure, Millborne found himself on a mild spring morning at Paddington Station, in a train that was starting for the west. His many intermittent thoughts on his broken promise from time to time, in those hours when loneliness brought him face to face with his own personality, had at last resulted in this course.

The decisive stimulus had been given when, a day or two earlier, on looking into a Post-Office Directory, he learnt that the woman he had not met for twenty years was still living on at Exonbury under the name she had assumed when, a year or two after her disappearance from her native town and his, she had returned from abroad as a young widow with a child, and taken up her residence at the former city. Her condition was apparently but little changed, and her daughter seemed to be with her, their names standing in the Directory as "Mrs. Leonora Frankland and Miss Frankland, Teachers of Music and Dancing."

Mr. Millborne reached Exonbury in the afternoon, and his first business, before even taking his luggage into the town, was to find the house occupied by the teachers. Standing in a central and open place it was not difficult to discover, a well-burnished brass doorplate bearing their names prominently. He hesitated to enter without further knowledge, and ultimately took lodgings over a toyshop opposite, securing a sitting-room which faced a similar drawing or sitting-room at the Franklands', where the dancing lessons were given. Installed here he was enabled to make indirectly, and without suspicion, inquiries and observations on the character of the ladies over the way, which he did with much deliberateness.

He learnt that the widow, Mrs. Frankland, with her one daughter, Frances, was of cheerful and excellent repute, energetic and painstaking with her pupils, of whom she had a good many, and in whose tuition her daughter assisted her. She was quite a recognized townswoman, and though the dancing branch of her profession was perhaps a trifle worldly, she was really a serious-minded lady who, being obliged to live by what she knew how to teach, balanced matters by lending a hand at charitable bazaars, assisting at sacred concerts, and giving musical recitations in aid of funds for bewildering happy savages, and other such enthusiasms of this enlightened country. Her daughter was one of the foremost of the bevy of young women who decorated the churches at Easter and Christmas, was organist in one of those edifices, and had subscribed to the testimonial of a silver broth-basin that was presented to the Reverend Mr. Walker as a token of gratitude for his faithful and arduous intonations of six months as sub-precentor in the Cathedral. Altogether mother and daughter appeared to be a typical and innocent pair among the genteel citizens of Exonbury.

As a natural and simple way of advertising their profession they allowed the windows of the music-room to be a little open, so that you had the pleasure of hearing all along the street at any hour between sunrise and sunset fragmentary gems of classical music as interpreted by the young people of twelve or fourteen who took lessons there. But it was said that Mrs. Frankland made most of her income by letting out pianos on hire, and by selling them as agent for the makers.

The report pleased Millborne; it was highly creditable, and far better than he had hoped. He was curious to get a view of the two women who led such blameless lives.

He had not long to wait to gain a glimpse of Leonora. It was when she was standing on her own doorstep, opening her parasol, on the morning after his arrival. She was thin, though not gaunt; and a good, well-wearing, thoughtful face had taken the place of the one which had temporarily attracted him in the days of his nonage. She wore black, and it became her in her character of widow. The daughter next appeared; she was a smoothed and rounded copy of her mother, with the same decision in her mien that Leonora had, and a bounding gait in which he traced a faint resemblance to his own at her age.

For the first time he absolutely made up his mind to call on them. But his antecedent step was to send Leonora a note the next morning, stating his proposal to visit her, and suggesting the evening as the time, because she seemed to be so greatly occupied in her professional capacity during the day. He purposely worded his note in such a form as not to require an answer from her which would be possibly awkward to write.

No answer came. Naturally he should not have been surprised at this; and yet he felt a little checked, even though she had only refrained from volunteering a reply that was not demanded.

At eight, the hour fixed by himself, he crossed over and was passively admitted by the servant. Mrs. Frankland, as she called herself, received him in the large music-and-dancing room on the first-floor front, and not in any private little parlour as he had expected. This cast a distressingly business-like colour over their first meeting after so many years of severance. The woman he had wronged stood before him, well-dressed, even to his metropolitan eyes, and her manner as she came up to him was dignified even to hardness. She certainly was not glad to see him. But what could he expect after a neglect of twenty years!

"How do you do, Mr. Millborne?" she said cheerfully, as to any chance caller. "I am obliged to receive you here because my daughter has a friend downstairs."

"Your daughter—and mine."

"Ah—yes, yes," she replied hastily, as if the addition had escaped her memory. "But perhaps the less said about that the better, in fairness to me. You will consider me a widow, please."

"Certainly, Leonora . . . " He could not get on, her manner was so cold and indifferent. The expected scene of sad reproach, subdued to delicacy by the run of years, was absent altogether. He was obliged to come to the point without preamble.

"You are quite free, Leonora—I mean as to marriage? There is nobody who has your promise, or—"

"O yes; quite free, Mr. Millborne," she said, somewhat surprised.

"Then I will tell you why I have come. Twenty years ago I promised to make you my wife; and I am here to fulfil that promise. Heaven forgive my tardiness!"

Her surprise was increased, but she was not agitated. She seemed to become gloomy, disapproving. "I could not entertain such an idea at this time of life," she said after a moment or two. "It would complicate matters too greatly. I have a very fair income, and require no help of any sort. I have no wish to marry . . . What could have induced you to come on such an errand now? It seems quite extraordinary, if I may say so!"

"It must—I daresay it does," Millborne replied vaguely; "and I must tell you that impulse—I mean in the sense of passion—has little to do with it. I wish to marry you, Leonora; I much desire to marry you. But it is an affair of conscience, a case of fulfilment. I promised you, and it was dishonorable of me to go away. I want to remove that sense of dishonor before I die. No doubt we might get to love each other as warmly as we did in old times?"

She dubiously shook her head. "I appreciate your motives, Mr. Millborne; but you must consider my position; and you will see that, short of the personal wish to marry, which I don't feel, there is no reason why I should change my state, even though by so doing I should ease your conscience. My position in this town is a respected one; I have built it up by my own hard labours, and, in short, I don't wish to alter it. My daughter, too, is just on the verge of an engagement to be married, to a young man who will make her an excellent husband. It will be in every way a desirable match for her. He is downstairs now."

"Does she know—anything about me?"

"O no, no; God forbid! Her father is dead and buried to her. So that, you see, things are going on smoothly, and I don't want to disturb their progress."

He nodded. "Very well," he said, and rose to go. At the door, however, he came back again.

"Still, Leonora," he urged, "I have come on purpose; and I don't see what disturbance would be caused. You would simply marry an old friend. Won't you reconsider? It is no more than right that we should be united, remembering the girl."

She shook her head, and patted with her foot nervously.

"Well, I won't detain you," he added. "I shall not be leaving Exonbury yet. You will allow me to see you again?"

"Yes; I don't mind," she said reluctantly.

The obstacles he had encountered, though they did not reanimate his dead passion for Leonora, did certainly make it appear indispensable to his peace of mind to overcome her coldness. He called frequently. The first meeting with the daughter was a trying ordeal, though he did not feel drawn towards her as he had expected to be; she did not excite his sympathies. Her mother confided to Frances the errand of "her old friend," which was viewed by the daughter with strong disfavor. His desire being thus uncongenial to both, for a long time Millborne made not the least impression upon Mrs. Frankland. His attentions pestered her rather than pleased her. He was surprised at her firmness, and it was only when he hinted at moral reasons for their union that she was ever shaken. "Strictly speaking," he would say, "we ought, as honest persons, to marry; and that's the truth of it, Leonora."

"I have looked at it in that light," she said quickly. "It struck me at the very first. But I don't see the force of the argument. I totally deny that after this interval of time I am bound to marry you for honor's sake. I would have married you, as you know well enough, at the proper time. But what is the use of remedies now?"

They were standing at the window. A scantly-whiskered young man, in clerical attire, called at the door below. Leonora flushed with interest.

"Who is he?" said Mr. Millborne.

"My Frances's lover. I am so sorry—she is not at home! Ah! they have told him where she is, and he has gone to find her . . . I hope that suit will prosper, at any rate!"

"Why shouldn't it?"

"Well, he cannot marry yet; and Frances sees but little of him now he has left Exonbury. He was formerly doing duty here, but now he is curate of St. John's, Ivell, fifty miles up the line. There is a tacit agreement between them, but—there have been friends of his who object, because of our vocation. However, he sees the absurdity of such an objection as that, and is not influenced by it."

"Your marriage with me would help the match, instead of hindering it, as you have said."

"Do you think it would?"

"It certainly would, by taking you out of this business altogether."

By chance he had found the way to move her somewhat, and he followed it up. This view was imparted to Mrs. Frankland's daughter, and it led her to soften her opposition. Millborne, who had given up his lodging in Exonbury, journeyed to and fro regularly, till at last he overcame her negations, and she expressed a reluctant assent.

They were married at the nearest church; and the goodwill—whatever that was—of the music-and-dancing connection was sold to a successor only too ready to jump into the place, the Millbornes having decided to live in London.

CHAPTER III

Millborne was a householder in his old district, though not in his old street, and Mrs. Millborne and their daughter had turned themselves into Londoners. Frances was well reconciled to the removal by her lover's satisfaction at the change. It suited him better to travel from Ivell a hundred miles to see her in London, where he frequently had other engagements, than fifty in the opposite direction where nothing but herself required his presence. So here they were, furnished up to the attics, in one of the small but popular streets of the West district, in a house whose front, till lately of the complexion of a chimney-sweep, had been scraped to show to the surprised wayfarer the bright yellow and red brick that had lain lurking beneath the soot of fifty years.

The social lift that the two women had derived from the alliance was considerable; but when the exhilaration which accompanies a first residence in London, the sensation of standing on a pivot of the world, had passed, their lives promised to be somewhat duller than when, at despised Exonbury, they had enjoyed a nodding acquaintance with three- fourths of the town. Mr. Millborne did not criticise his wife; he could not. Whatever defects of hardness and acidity his original treatment and the lapse of years might have developed in her, his sense of a realized idea, of a re-established self-satisfaction, was always thrown into the scale on her side, and out-weighed all objections.

It was about a month after their settlement in town that the household decided to spend a week at a watering-place in the Isle of Wight, and while there the Reverend Percival Cope (the young curate aforesaid) came to see them, Frances in particular. No formal engagement of the young pair had been announced as yet, but it was clear that their mutual understanding could not end in anything but marriage without grievous disappointment to one of the parties at least. Not that Frances was sentimental. She was rather of the imperious sort, indeed; and, to say all, the young girl had not fulfilled her father's expectations of her. But he hoped and worked for her welfare as sincerely as any father could do.

Mr. Cope was introduced to the new head of the family, and stayed with them in the Island two or three days. On the last day of his visit they decided to venture on a two hours' sail in one of the small yachts which lay there for hire. The trip had not progressed far before all, except the curate, found that sailing in a breeze did not quite agree with them; but as he seemed to enjoy the experience, the other three bore their condition as well as they could without grimace or complaint, till the young man, observing their discomfort, gave immediate directions to tack about. On the way back to port they sat silent, facing each other.

Nausea in such circumstances, like midnight watching, fatigue, trouble, fright, has this marked effect upon the countenance, that it often brings out strongly the divergences of the individual from the norm of his race, accentuating superficial peculiarities to radical distinctions. Unexpected physiognomies will uncover themselves at these times in well- known faces; the aspect becomes invested with the spectral presence of entombed and forgotten ancestors; and family lineaments of special or exclusive cast, which in ordinary moments are masked by a stereotyped expression and mien, start up with crude insistence to the view.

Frances, sitting beside her mother's husband, with Mr. Cope opposite, was naturally enough much regarded by the curate during the tedious sail home; at first with sympathetic smiles. Then, as the middle-aged father and his child grew each gray-faced, as the pretty blush of Frances disintegrated into spotty stains, and the soft rotundities of her features diverged from their familiar and reposeful beauty into elemental lines, Cope was gradually struck with the resemblance between a pair in their discomfort who in their ease presented nothing to the eye in common. Mr. Millborne and Frances in their indisposition were strangely, startlingly alike.

The inexplicable fact absorbed Cope's attention quite. He forgot to smile at Frances, to hold her hand; and when they touched the shore he remained sitting for some moments like a man in a trance.

As they went homeward, and recovered their complexions and contours, the similarities one by one disappeared, and Frances and Mr. Millborne were again masked by the commonplace differences of sex and age. It was as if, during the voyage, a mysterious veil had been lifted, temporarily revealing a strange pantomime of the past.

During the evening he said to her casually: "Is your step-father a cousin of your mother, dear Frances?"

"Oh, no," said she. "There is no relationship. He was only an old friend of hers. Why did you suppose such a thing?"

He did not explain, and the next morning started to resume his duties at Ivell.

Cope was an honest young fellow, and shrewd withal. At home in his quiet rooms in St. Peter's Street, Ivell, he pondered long and unpleasantly on the revelations of the cruise. The tale it told was distinct enough, and for the first time his position was an uncomfortable one. He had met the Franklands at Exonbury as parishioners, had been attracted by Frances, and had floated thus far into an engagement which was indefinite only because of his inability to marry just yet. The Franklands' past had apparently contained mysteries, and it did not coincide with his judgment to marry into a family whose mystery was of the sort suggested. So he sat and sighed, between his reluctance to lose Frances and his natural dislike of forming a connection with people whose antecedents would not bear the strictest investigation.

A passionate lover of the old-fashioned sort might possibly never have halted to weigh these doubts; but though he was in the church Cope's affections were fastidious—distinctly tempered with the alloys of the century's decadence. He delayed writing to Frances for some while, simply because he could not tune himself up to enthusiasm when worried by suspicions of such a kind.

Meanwhile the Millbornes had returned to London, and Frances was growing anxious. In talking to her mother of Cope she had innocently alluded to his curious inquiry if her mother and her step-father were connected by any tie of cousinship. Mrs. Millborne made her repeat the words. Frances did so, and watched with inquisitive eyes their effect upon her elder.

"What is there so startling in his inquiry then?" she asked. "Can it have anything to do with his not writing to me?"

Her mother flinched, but did not inform her, and Frances also was now drawn within the atmosphere of suspicion. That night when standing by chance outside the chamber of her parents she heard for the first time their voices engaged in a sharp altercation.

The apple of discord had, indeed, been dropped into the house of the Millbornes. The scene within the chamber-door was Mrs. Millborne standing before her dressing-table, looking across to her husband in the dressing-room adjoining, where he was sitting down, his eyes fixed on the floor.

"Why did you come and disturb my life a second time?" she harshly asked. "Why did you pester me with your conscience, till I was driven to accept you to get rid of your importunity? Frances and I were doing well: the one desire of my life was that she should marry that good young man. And now the match is broken off by your cruel interference! Why did you show yourself in my world again, and raise this scandal upon my hard-won respectability—won by such weary years of labour as none will ever know!" She bent her face upon the table and wept passionately.

There was no reply from Mr. Millborne. Frances lay awake nearly all that night, and when at breakfast-time the next morning still no letter appeared from Mr. Cope, she entreated her mother to go to Ivell and see if the young man were ill.

Mrs. Millborne went, returning the same day. Frances, anxious and haggard, met her at the station.

Was all well? Her mother could not say it was; though he was not ill.

One thing she had found out, that it was a mistake to hunt up a man when his inclinations were to hold aloof. Returning with her mother in the cab Frances insisted upon knowing what the mystery was which plainly had alienated her lover. The precise words which had been spoken at the interview with him that day at Ivell Mrs. Millborne could not be induced to repeat; but thus far she admitted, that the estrangement was fundamentally owing to Mr. Millborne having sought her out and married her.

"And why did he seek you out—and why were you obliged to marry him?" asked the distressed girl. Then the evidences pieced themselves together in her acute mind, and, her colour gradually rising, she asked her mother if what they pointed to was indeed the fact. Her mother admitted that it was.

A flush of mortification succeeded to the flush of shame upon the young woman's face. How could a scrupulously correct clergyman and lover like Mr. Cope ask her to be his wife after this discovery of her irregular birth? She covered her eyes with her hands in a silent despair.

In the presence of Mr. Millborne they at first suppressed their anguish. But by and by their feelings got the better of them, and when he was asleep in his chair after dinner Mrs. Millborne's irritation broke out. The embittered Frances joined her in reproaching the man who had come as the spectre to their intended feast of Hymen, and turned its promise to ghastly failure.

"Why were you so weak, mother, as to admit such an enemy to your house—one so obviously your evil genius—much less accept him as a husband, after so long? If you had only told me all, I could have advised you better! But I suppose I have no right to reproach him, bitter as I feel, and even though he has blighted my life for ever!"

"Frances, I did hold out; I saw it was a mistake to have any more to say to a man who had been such an unmitigated curse to me! But he would not listen; he kept on about his conscience and mine, till I was bewildered, and said Yes! . . . Bringing us away from a quiet town where we were known and respected—what an ill-considered thing it was! O the content of those days! We had society there, people in our own position, who did not expect more of us than we expected of them. Here, where there is so much, there is nothing! He said London society was so bright and brilliant that it would be like a new world. It may be to those who are in it; but what is that to us two lonely women; we only see it flashing past! . . . O the fool, the fool that I was!"

Now Millborne was not so soundly asleep as to prevent his hearing these animadversions that were almost execrations, and many more of the same sort. As there was no peace for him at home, he went again to his club, where, since his reunion with Leonora, he had seldom if ever been seen. But the shadow of the troubles in his household interfered with his comfort here also; he could not, as formerly, settle down into his favorite chair with the evening paper, reposeful in the celibate's sense that where he was his world's centre had its fixture. His world was now an ellipse, with a dual centrality, of which his own was not the major.

The young curate of Ivell still held aloof, tantalizing Frances by his elusiveness. Plainly he was waiting upon events. Millborne bore the reproaches of his wife and daughter almost in silence; but by degrees he grew meditative, as if revolving a new idea. The bitter cry about blighting their existence at length became so impassioned that one day Millborne calmly proposed to return again to the country; not necessarily to Exonbury, but, if they were willing, to a little old manor-house which he had found was to be let, standing a mile from Mr. Cope's town of Ivell.

They were surprised, and, despite their view of him as the bringer of ill, were disposed to accede. "Though I suppose," said Mrs. Millborne to him, "it will end in Mr. Cope's asking you flatly about the past, and your being compelled to tell him; which may dash all my hopes for Frances. She gets more and more like you every day, particularly when she is in a bad temper. People will see you together, and notice it; and I don't know what may come of it!"

"I don't think they will see us together," he said; but he entered into no argument when she insisted otherwise. The removal was eventually resolved on; the town-house was disposed of; and again came the invasion by furniture-men and vans, till all the movables and servants were whisked away. He sent his wife and daughter to an hotel while this was going on, taking two or three journeys himself to Ivell to superintend the refixing, and the improvement of the grounds. When all was done he returned to them in town.

The house was ready for their reception, he told them, and there only remained the journey. He accompanied them and their personal luggage to the station only, having, he said, to remain in town a short time on business with his lawyer. They went, dubious and discontented—for the much-loved Cope had made no sign.

"If we were going down to live here alone," said Mrs Millborne to her daughter in the train; "and there was no intrusive tell-tale presence! . . . But let it be!"

The house was a lovely little place in a grove of elms, and they liked it much. The first person to call upon them as new residents was Mr. Cope. He was delighted to find that they had come so near, and (though he did not say this) meant to live in such excellent style. He had not, however, resumed the manner of a lover.

"Your father spoils all!" murmured Mrs. Millborne.

But three days later she received a letter from her husband, which caused her no small degree of astonishment. It was written from Boulogne.

It began with a long explanation of settlements of his property, in which he had been engaged since their departure. The chief feature in the business was that Mrs. Millborne found herself the absolute owner of a comfortable sum in personal estate, and Frances of a life-interest in a larger sum, the principal to be afterwards divided amongst her children if she had any. The remainder of his letter ran as hereunder:—

"I have learnt that there are some derelictions of duty which cannot be blotted out by tardy accomplishment. Our evil actions do not remain isolated in the past, waiting only to be reversed: like locomotive plants they spread and re-root, till to destroy the original stem has no material effect in killing them. I made a mistake in searching you out; I admit it; whatever the remedy may be in such cases it is not marriage, and the best thing for you and me is that you do not see me more. You had better not seek me, for you will not be likely to find me: you are well provided for, and we may do ourselves more harm than good by meeting again.

"F. M."

Millborne, in short, disappeared from that day forward. But a searching inquiry would have revealed that, soon after the

Millbornes went to Ivell, an Englishman, who did not give the name of Millborne, took up his residence in Brussels; a man who might have been recognized by Mrs. Millborne if she had met him. One afternoon in the ensuing summer, when this gentleman was looking over the English papers, he saw the announcement of Miss Frances Frankland's marriage. She had become the Reverend Mrs. Cope.

"Thank God!" said the gentleman.

But his momentary satisfaction was far from being happiness. As he formerly had been weighted with a bad conscience, so now was he burdened with the heavy thought which oppressed Antigone, that by honourable observance of a rite he had obtained for himself the reward of dishonorable laxity. Occasionally he had to be helped to his lodgings by his servant from the *Cercle* he frequented, through having imbibed a little too much liquor to be able to take care of himself. But he was harmless, and even when he had been drinking said little.

The Woman Who Tried to be Good
Edna Ferber

Before she tried to be a good woman she had been a very bad woman—so bad that she could trail her wonderful apparel up and down Main Street, from the Elm Tree Bakery to the railroad tracks, without once having a man doff his hat to her or a woman bow. You passed her on the street with a surreptitious glance, though she was well worth looking at— in her furs and laces and plumes. She had the only full-length mink coat in our town, and Ganz's shoe store sent to Chicago for her shoes. Hers were the miraculously small feet you frequently see in stout women.

Usually she walked alone; but on rare occasions, especially round Christmastime, she might have been seen accompanied by some silent, dull-eyed, stupid-looking girl, who would follow her dumbly in and out of stores, stopping now and then to admire a cheap comb or a chain set with flashy imitation stones—or, queerly enough, a doll with yellow hair and blue eyes and very pink cheeks. But, alone or in company, her appearance in the stores of our town was the signal for a sudden jump in the cost of living. The storekeepers mulcted her; and she knew it and paid in silence, for she was of the class that has no redress. She owned the House with the Closed Shutters, near the freight depot—did Blanche Devine.

In a larger town than ours she would have passed unnoticed. She did not look like a bad woman. Of course she used too much make-up, and as she passed you caught the oversweet breath of a certain heavy scent. Then, too, her diamond eardrops would have made any woman's features look hard; but her plump face, in spite of its heaviness, wore an expression of good-humored intelligence, and her eyeglasses gave her somehow a look of respectability. We do not associate vice with eyeglasses. So in a large city she would have passed for a well-dressed, prosperous, comfortable wife and mother who was in danger of losing her figure from an overabundance of good living; but with us she was a town character, like Old Man Givins, the drunkard, or the weak-minded Binns girl. When she passed the drug-store corner there would be a sniggering among the vacant-eyed loafers idling there, and they would leer at each other and jest in undertones.

So, knowing Blanche Devine as we did, there was something resembling a riot in one of our most respectable neighborhoods when it was learned that she had given up her interest in the house near the freight depot and was going to settle down in the white cottage on the corner and be good. All the husbands in the block, urged on by righteously indignant wives, dropped in on Alderman Mooney after supper to see if the thing could not be stopped. The fourth of the protesting husbands to arrive was the Very Young Husband who lived next door to the corner cottage that Blanche Devine had bought. The Very Young Husband had a Very Young Wife, and they were the joint owners of Snooky. Snooky was three-going- on-four, and looked something like an angel—only healthier and with grimier hands. The whole neighborhood borrowed her and tried to spoil her; but Snooky would not spoil.

Alderman Mooney was down in the cellar, fooling with the furnace.

He was in his furnace overalls; a short black pipe in his mouth. Three protesting husbands had just left. As the Very Young Husband, following Mrs. Mooney's directions, descended the cellar stairs, Alderman Mooney looked up from his tinkering. He peered through a haze of pipe smoke.

"Hello!" he called, and waved the haze away with his open palm.

"Come on down! Been tinkering with this blamed furnace since supper. She don't draw like she ought. 'Long toward spring a furnace always gets balky. How many tons you used this winter?"

"Oh-five," said the Very Young Husband shortly. Alderman Mooney considered it thoughtfully. The Young Husband leaned up against the side of the water tank, his hands in his pockets. "Say, Mooney, is that right about Blanche Devine's having bought the house on the corner?"

"You're the fourth man that's been in to ask me that this evening. I'm expecting the rest of the block before bedtime. She bought it all right."

The Young Husband flushed and kicked at a piece of coal with the toe of his boot.

"Well, it's a darned shame!" he began hotly. "Jen was ready to cry at supper. This'll be a fine neighborhood for Snooky to grow up in! What's a woman like that want to come into a respectable street for, anyway? I own my home and pay my taxes—"

Alderman Mooney looked up.

"So does she," he interrupted. "She's going to improve the place—paint it, and put in a cellar and a furnace, and build a porch, and lay a cement walk all round."

The Young Husband took his hands out of his pockets in order to emphasize his remarks with gestures.

"What's that got to do with it? I don't care if she puts in diamonds for windows and sets out Italian gardens and a terrace with peacocks on it. You're the alderman of this ward, aren't you? Well, it was up to you to keep her out of this block! You could have fixed it with an injunction or somethng. I'm going to get up a petition—that's what I'm going——"

Alderman Mooney closed the furnace door with a bang that drowned the rest of the threat. He turned the draft in a pipe overhead and brushed his sooty palms briskly together like one who would put an end to a profitless conversation.

"She's bought the house," he said mildly, "and paid for it. And it's hers. She's got a right to live in this neighborhood as long as she acts respectable."

The Very Young Husband laughed.

"She won't last! They never do."

Alderman Mooney had taken his pipe out of his mouth and was rubbing his thumb over the smooth bowl, looking down at it with unseeing eyes. On his face was a queer look—the look of one who is embarrassed because he is about to say something honest.

"Look here! I want to tell you something: I happened to be up in the mayor's office the day Blanche signed for the place. She had to go through a lot of red tape before she got it—had quite a time of it, she did! And say, kid, that woman ain't so—bad."

The Very Young Husband exclaimed impatiently:

"Oh, don't give me any of that, Mooney! Blanche Devine's a

town character. Even the kids know what she is. If she's got religion or something, and wants to quit and be decent, why doesn't she go to another town— Chicago or someplace—where nobody knows her?"

That motion of Alderman Mooney's thumb against the smooth pipe bowl stopped. He looked up slowly.

"That's what I said—the mayor too. But Blanche Devine said she wanted to try it here. She said this was home to her. Funny—ain't it? Said she wouldn't be fooling anybody here. They know her. And if she moved away, she said, it'd leak out some way sooner or later. It does, she said. Always! Seems she wants to live like—well, like other women. She put it like this: she says she hasn't got religion, or any of that. She says she's no different than she was when she was twenty. She says that for the last ten years the ambition of her life has been to be able to go into a grocery store and ask the price of, say, celery; and, if the clerk charged her ten when it ought to be seven, to be able to sass him with a regular piece of her mind— and then sail out and trade somewhere else until he saw that she didn't have to stand anything from storekeepers, any more than any other woman that did her own marketing. She's a smart woman, Blanche is! God knows I ain't taking her part—exactly; but she talked a little, and the mayor and me got a little of her history."

A sneer appeared on the face of the Very Young Husband. He had been known before he met Jen as a rather industrious sower of wild oats. He knew a thing or two, did the Very Young Husband, in spite of his youth! He always fussed when Jen wore even a V-necked summer gown on the street.

"Oh, she wasn't playing for sympathy," went on Alderman Mooney in answer to the sneer. "She said she'd always paid her way and always expected to. Seems her husband left her without a cent when she was eighteen—with a baby. She worked for four dollars a week in a cheap eating house. The two of 'em couldn't live on that. Then the baby——"

"Good night!" said the Very Young Husband. "I suppose Mrs. Mooney's going to call?"

"Minnie! It was her scolding all through supper that drove me down to monkey with the furnace. She's wild—Minnie is." He peeled off his overalls and hung them on a nail. The Young Husband started to ascend the cellar stairs. Alderman Mooney laid a detaining finger on his sleeve. "Don't say anything in front of

Minnie! She's boiling! Minnie and the kids are going to visit her folks out West this summer; so I wouldn't so much as dare to say `Good morning!' to the Devine woman. Anyway, a person wouldn't talk to her, I suppose. But I kind of thought I'd tell you about her.

"Thanks!" said the Very Young Husband dryly.

In the early spring, before Blanche Devine moved in, there came stone- masons, who began to build something. It was a great stone fireplace that rose in massive incongruity at the side of the little white cottage. Blanche Devine was trying to make a home for herself.

Blanche Devine used to come and watch them now and then as the work progressed. She had a way of walking round and round the house, looking up at it and poking at plaster and paint with her umbrella or finger tip. One day she brought with her a man with a spade. He spaded up a neat square of ground at the side of the cottage and a long ridge near the fence that separated her yard from that of the Very Young Couple next door. The ridge spelled sweet peas and nasturtiums to our small-town eyes.

On the day that Blanche Devine moved in there was wild agitation among the white-ruffed bedroom curtains of the neighborhood. Later on certain odors, as of burning dinners, pervaded the atmosphere. Blanche Devine, flushed and excited, her hair slightly askew, her diamond eardrops flashing, directed the moving, wrapped in her great fur coat; but on the third morning we gasped when she appeared out-of-doors, carrying a little household ladder, a pail of steaming water, and sundry voluminous white cloths. She reared the little ladder against the side of the house, mounted it cautiously, and began to wash windows with housewifely thoroughness. Her stout figure was swathed in a gray sweater and on her head was a battered felt hat—the sort of window-washing costume that has been worn by women from time immemorial. We noticed that she used plenty of hot water and clean rags, and that she rubbed the glass until it sparkled, leaning perilously sideways on the ladder to detect elusive streaks. Our keenest housekeeping eye could find no fault with the way Blanche Devine washed windows.

By May, Blanche Devine had left off her diamond eardrops—perhaps it was their absence that gave her face a new expression. When she went downtown we noticed that her hats were more like the hats the other women in our town wore; but she still affected extravagant footgear, as is right and proper for a stout woman who has cause to be vain of her feet. We noticed that her trips downtown were rare that spring and summer. She used to come home laden with little bundles; and before supper she would change her street clothes for a neat, washable housedress, as is our thrifty custom. Through her bright windows we could see her moving briskly about from kitchen to sitting room; and from the smells that floated out from her kitchen door, she seemed to be preparing for her solitary supper the same homely viands that were frying or stewing or baking in our kitchens. Sometimes you could detect the delectable scent of browning, hot tea biscuit. It takes a determined woman to make tea biscuit for no one but herself.

Blanche Devine joined the church. On the first Sunday morning she came to the service there was a little flurry among the ushers at the vestibule door. They seated her well in the rear. The second Sunday morning a dreadful thing happened. The woman next to whom they seated her turned, regarded her stonily for a moment, then rose agitatedly and moved to a pew across the aisle.

Blanche Devine's face went a dull red beneath her white powder. She never came again—though we saw the minister visit her once or twice. She always accompanied him to the door pleasantly, holding it well open until he was down the little flight of steps and on the sidewalk. The minister's wife did not call.

She rose early, like the rest of us; and as summer came on we used to see her moving about in her little garden patch in the dewy, golden morning. She wore absurd pale-blue negligees that made her stout figure loom immense against the greenery of garden and apple tree. The neighborhood women viewed these negligees with Puritan disapproval as they smoothed down their own prim, starched gingham skirts. They said it was disgusting — and perhaps it was; but the habit of years is not easily overcome. Blanche Devine—snipping her sweet peas, peering anxiously at the Virginia creeper that clung with such fragile fingers to the trellis, watering the flower baskets that hung from her porch—was blissfully unconscious of the disapproving eyes. I wish one of us had just stopped to call good morning to her over the fence, and to say in our neighborly, small-town way: "My, ain't this a scorcher! So early too! It'll be fierce by noon!"

But we did not.

I think perhaps the evenings must have been the loneliest for her. The summer evenings in our little town are filled with intimate, human, neighborly sounds. After the heat of the day it is pleasant to relax in the cool comfort of the front porch, with the life of the town eddying about us. We sew and read out there until it grows dusk. We call across lots to our next- door neighbor. The men water the lawns and the flower boxes and get together in little, quiet groups to discuss the new street paving. I have even known Mrs. Hines to bring her cherries out there when she had canning to do, and pit them there on the front porch partially shielded by her porch vine, but not so effectually that she was deprived of the sights and sounds about her. The kettle in her lap and the dishpan full of great ripe cherries on the porch floor by her chair, she would pit and chat and peer out through the vines, the red juice staining her plump bare arms.

I have wondered since what Blanche Devine thought of us those lonesome evenings—those evenings filled with friendly sights and sounds. It must have been difficult for her, who had dwelt behind closed shutters so long, to seat herself on the new front porch for all the world to stare at; but she did sit there—resolutely—watching us in silence.

She seized hungrily upon the stray crumbs of conversation that fell to her. The milkman and the iceman and the butcher boy used to hold daily conversation with her. They—sociable gentlemen— would stand on her door- step, one grimy hand resting against the white of her doorpost, exchanging the time of day with Blanche in the doorway—a tea towel in one hand, perhaps, and a plate in the other. Her little house was a miracle of cleanliness. It was no uncommon sight to see her down on her knees on the kitchen floor, wielding her brush and rag like the rest of us. In canning and preserving time there floated out from her kitchen the pungent scent of pickled crab apples; the mouth-watering smell that meant sweet pickles; or the cloying, divinely sticky odor that meant raspberry jam. Snooky, from her side of the fence, often used to peer through the pickets, gazing in the direction of the enticing smells next door.

Early one September morning there floated out from Blanche Devine's kitchen that fragrant, sweet scent of fresh-baked cookies— cookies with butter in them, and spice, and with nuts on top. Just by the smell of them your mind's eye pictured them coming from the oven-crisp brown circlets, crumbly, delectable. Snooky, in her scarlet sweater and cap, sniffed them from afar and straightway deserted her sand pile to take her stand at the fence. She peered through the restraining bars, standing on tiptoe. Blanche Devine, glancing up from her board and rolling pin, saw the eager golden head. And Snooky, with guile in her heart, raised one fat, dimpled hand above the fence and waved it friendlily. Blanche Devine waved back. Thus encouraged, Snooky's two hands wigwagged frantically above the pickets. Blanche Devine hesitated a moment, her floury hand on her hip. Then she went to the pantry shelf and took out a clean white saucer. She selected from the brown jar on the table three of the brownest, crumbliest, most perfect cookies, with a walnut meat perched atop of each, placed them temptingly on the saucer and, descending the steps, came swiftly across the grass to the triumphant Snooky. Blanche Devine held out the saucer, her lips smiling, her eyes tender. Snooky reached up with one plump white arm.

"Snooky!" shrilled a high voice. "Snooky!" A voice of horror and of wrath. "Come here to me this minute! And don't you dare to touch those!" Snooky hesitated rebelliously, one pink finger in her pouting mouth.

"Snooky! Do you hear me?"

And the Very Young Wife began to descend the steps of her back porch. Snooky, regretful eyes on the toothsome dainties, turned away aggrieved. The Very Young Wife, her lips set, her eyes flashing, advanced and seized the shrieking Snooky by one arm and dragged her away toward home and safety.

Blanche Devine stood there at the fence, holding the saucer in her hand. The saucer tipped slowly, and the three cookies slipped off and fell to the grass. Blanche Devine stood staring at them a moment. Then she turned quickly, went into the house, and shut the door.

It was about this time we noticed that Blanche Devine was away much of the time. The little white cottage would be empty for weeks. We knew she was out of town because the expressman would come for her trunk. We used to lift our eyebrows significantly. The newspapers and handbills would accumulate in a dusty little heap on the porch; but when she returned there was always a grand cleaning, with the windows open, and Blanche—her head bound turbanwise in a towel—appearing at a window every few minutes to shake out a dustcloth. She seemed to put an enormous amount of energy into those cleanings—as if they were a sort of safety valve.

As winter came on she used to sit up before her grate fire long, long after we were asleep in our beds. When she neglected to pull down the shades we could see the flames of her cosy fire dancing gnomelike on the wall. There came a night of sleet and snow, and wind and rattling hail—one of those blustering, wild nights that are followed by morning-paper reports of trains stalled in drifts, mail delayed, telephone and telegraph wires down. It must have been midnight or past when there came a hammering at Blanche Devine's door—a persistent, clamorous rapping. Blanche Devine, sitting before her dying fire half asleep, started and cringed when she heard it, then jumped to her feet, her hand at her breast—her eyes darting this way and that, as though seeking escape.

She had heard a rapping like that before. It had meant bluecoats swarming up the stairway, and frightened cries and pleadings, and wild confusion. So she started forward now, quivering. And then she remembered, being wholly awake now—she remembered, and threw up her head and smiled a little bitterly and walked toward the door. The hammering continued, louder than ever. Blanche Devine flicked on the porch light and opened the door. The half-clad figure of the Very Young Wife next door staggered into the room. She seized Blanche Devine's arm with both her frenzied hands and shook her, the wind and snow beating in upon both of them.

"The baby!" she screamed in a high, hysterical voice. "The baby! The baby——!"

Blanche Devine shut the door and shook the Young Wife smartly by the shoulders.

"Stop screaming," she said quietly. "Is she sick?"

The Young Wife told her, her teeth chattering:

"Come quick! She's dying! Will's out of town. I tried to get the doctor. The telephone wouldn't—— I saw your light! For God's sake——"

Blanche Devine grasped the Young Wife's arm, opened the door, and together they sped across the little space that separated the two houses. Blanche Devine was a big woman, but she took the stairs like a girl and found the right bedroom by some miraculous woman instinct. A dreadful choking, rattling sound was coming from Snooky's bed.

"Croup," said Blanche Devine, and began her fight.

It was a good fight. She marshaled her inadequate forces, made up of the half-fainting Young Wife and the terrified and awkward hired girl.

"Get the hot water on—lots of it!" Blanche Devine pinned up her sleeves. "Hot cloths! Tear up a sheet—or anything! Got an oilstove? I want a tea- kettle boiling in the room. She's got to have the steam. If that don't do it we'll raise an umbrella over her and throw a sheet over, and hold the kettle under till the steam gets to her that way. Got any ipecac?"

The Young Wife obeyed orders, white-faced and shaking. Once Blanche Devine glanced up at her sharply.

"Don't you dare faint!" she commanded.

And the fight went on. Gradually the breathing that had been so frightful became softer, easier. Blanche Devine did not relax. It was not until the little figure breathed gently in sleep that Blanche Devine sat back, satisfied. Then she tucked a cover at the side of the bed, took a last satisfied look at the face on the pillow, and turned to look at the wan, disheveled Young Wife.

"She's all right now. We can get the doctor when morning comes— though I don't know's you'll need him."

The Young Wife came round to Blanche Devine's side of the bed and stood looking up at her.

"My baby died," said Blanche Devine simply. The Young Wife gave a little inarticulate cry, put her two hands on Blanche Devine's broad shoulders, and laid her tired head on her breast.

"I guess I'd better be going," said Blanche Devine.

The Young Wife raised her head. Her eyes were round with fright.

"Going! Oh, please stay! I'm so afraid. Suppose she should take sick again! That awful—breathing——"

"I'll stay if you want me to."

"Oh, please! I'll make up your bed and you can rest——"

"I'm not sleepy. I'm not much of a hand to sleep anyway. I'll sit up here in the hall, where there's a light. You get to bed. I'll watch and see that everything's all right. Have you got something I can read out here—something kind of lively—with a love story in it?"

So the night went by. Snooky slept in her white bed. The Very Young Wife half dozed in her bed, so near the little one. In the hall, her stout figure looming grotesque in wall shadows, sat Blanche Devine, pretending to read. Now and then she rose and tiptoed into the bedroom with miraculous quiet, and stooped over the little bed and listened and looked—and tiptoed away again, satisfied.

The Young Husband came home from his business trip next

day with tales of snowdrifts and stalled engines. Blanche Devine breathed a sigh of relief when she saw him from her kitchen window. She watched the house now with a sort of proprietary eye. She wondered about Snooky; but she knew better than to ask. So she waited. The Young Wife next door had told her husband all about that awful night—had told him with tears and sobs. The Very Young Husband had been very, very angry with her— angry, he said, and astonished! Snooky could not have been so sick! Look at her now! As well as ever. And to have called such a woman! Well, he did not want to be harsh; but she must understand that she must never speak to the woman again. Never!

So the next day the Very Young Wife happened to go by with the Young Husband. Blanche Devine spied them from her sitting-room window, and she made the excuse of looking in her mailbox in order to go to the door. She stood in the doorway and the Very Young Wife went by on the arm of her husband. She went by— rather white-faced—without a look or a word or a sign!

And then this happened! There came into Blanche Devine's face a look that made slits of her eyes, and drew her mouth down into an ugly, narrow line, and that made the muscles of her jaw tense and hard. It was the ugliest look you can imagine. Then she smiled—if having one's lips curl away from one's teeth can be called smiling.

Two days later there was great news of the white cottage on the corner. The curtains were down; the furniture was packed; the rugs were rolled. The wagons came and backed up to the house and took those things that had made a home for Blanche Devine. And when we heard that she had bought back her interest in the House with the Closed Shutters, near the freight depot, we sniffed.

"I knew she wouldn't last!" we said.

"They never do!" said we.

Cain's Atonement
Algernon Blackwood

So many thousands today have deliberately put Self aside, and are ready to yield their lives for an ideal, that it is not surprising a few of them should have registered experiences of a novel order. For to step aside from Self is to enter a larger world, to be open to new impressions. If Powers of Good exist in the universe at all, they can hardly be inactive at the present time. . . .

The case of two men, who may be called Jones and Smith, occurs to the mind in this connection. Whether a veil actually was lifted for a moment, or whether the tension of long and terrible months resulted in an exaltation of emotion, the experience claims significance. Smith, to whom the experience came, holds the firm belief that it was real. Jones, though it involved him too, remained unaware.

It is a somewhat personal story, their peculiar relationship dating from early youth: a kind of unwilling antipathy was born between them, yet an antipathy that had no touch of hate or even of dislike. It was rather in the nature of an instinctive rivalry. Some tie operated that flung them ever into the same arena with strange persistence, and ever as opponents. An inevitable fate delighted to throw them together in a sense that made them rivals; small as well as large affairs betrayed this malicious tendency of the gods. It showed itself in earliest days, at school, at Cambridge, in travel, even in house-parties and the lighter social intercourse. Though distant cousins, their families were not intimate, and there was no obvious reason why their paths should fall so persistently together. Yet their paths did so, crossing and recrossing in the way described.

Sooner or later, in all his undertakings, Smith would note the shadow of Jones darkening the ground in front of him; and later, when called to the Bar in his chosen profession, he found most frequently that the learned counsel in opposition to him was the owner of this shadow, Jones. In another matter, too, they became rivals, for the same girl, oddly enough, attracted both, and though she accepted neither offer of marriage (during Smith's lifetime!), the attitude between them was that of unwilling rivals. For they were friends as well.

Jones, it appears, was hardly aware that any rivalry existed; he did not think of Smith as an opponent, and as an adversary, never. He did notice, however, the constantly recurring meetings, for more than once he commented on them with good-humoured amusement. Smith, on the other hand, was conscious of a depth and strength in the tie that certainly intrigued him; being of a thoughtful, introspective nature, he was keenly sensible of the strange competition in their lives, and sought in various ways for its explanation, though without success. The desire to find out was very strong in him. And this was natural enough, owing to the singular fact that in all their battles he was the one to lose. Invariably Jones got the best of every conflict. Smith always paid; sometimes he paid with interest.

Occasionally, too, he seemed forced to injure himself while contributing to his cousin's success. It was very curious. He reflected much upon it; he wondered what the origin of their tie and rivalry might be, but especially why it was that he invariably lost, and why he was so often obliged to help his rival to the point even of his own detriment. Tempted to bitterness sometimes, he did not yield to it, however; the relationship remained frank and pleasant; if anything, it deepened.

He remembered once, for instance, giving his cousin a chance introduction which yet led, a little later, to the third party offering certain evidence which lost him an important case—Jones, of course, winning it. The third party, too, angry at being dragged into the case, turned hostile to him, thwarting various subsequent projects. In no other way could Jones have procured this particular evidence; he did not know of its existence even. That chance introduction did it all. There was nothing the least dishonorable on the part of Jones—it was just the chance of the dice. The dice were always loaded against Smith and there were other instances of similar kind.

About this time, moreover, a singular feeling that had lain vaguely in his mind for some years past, took more definite form. It suddenly assumed the character of a conviction, that yet had no evidence to support it. A voice, long whispering in the depths of him, became much louder, grew into a statement that he accepted without further ado: "I'm paying off a debt," he phrased it, "an old, old debt is being discharged. I owe him this—my help and so forth." He accepted it, that is, as just; and this certainty of justice kept sweet his heart and mind, shutting the door on bitterness or envy. The thought, however, though it recurred persistently with each encounter, brought no explanation.

When the war broke out both offered their services; as members of the O.T.C., they got commissions quickly; but it was a chance remark of Smith's that made his friend join the very regiment he himself was in. They trained together, were in the same retreats and the same advances together. Their friendship deepened. Under the stress of circumstances the tie did not dissolve, but strengthened. It was indubitably real, therefore. Then, oddly enough, they were both wounded in the same engagement.

And it was here the remarkable fate that jointly haunted them betrayed itself more clearly than in any previous incident of their long relationship. Smith was wounded in the act of protecting his cousin. How it happened is confusing to a layman, but each apparently was leading a bombing-party, and the two parties came together. They found themselves shoulder to shoulder, both brimmed with that pluck which is complete indifference to Self; they exchanged a word of excited greeting; and the same second one of those rare opportunities of advantage presented itself which only the highest courage could make use of. Neither, certainly, was thinking of personal reward; it was merely that each saw the chance by which instant heroism might gain a surprise advantage for their side. The risk was heavy, but there was a chance; and success would mean a decisive result, to say nothing of high distinction for the man who obtained it if he survived. Smith, being a few yards ahead of his cousin, had the moment in his grasp. He was in the act of dashing forward when something made him pause. A bomb in mid-air, flung from the opposing trench, was falling; it seemed immediately above him; he saw that it would just miss himself, but land full upon his cousin whose head was turned the other way. By stretching out his hand, Smith knew he could field it like a cricket ball. There was an interval of a second and a half, he judged. He hesitated perhaps a quarter of a second then he acted. He caught it. It was the obvious thing to do. He flung it back into the opposing trench.

The rapidity of thought is hard to realize. In that second and a half Smith was aware of many things: He saved his cousin's life unquestionably; unquestionably also Jones seized the opportunity that otherwise was his cousin's. But it was neither of these reflections that filled Smith's mind. The dominant impression was another. It flashed into actual words inside his excited brain: "I must risk it. I owe it to him and more besides!"

He was, further, aware of another impulse than the obvious one. In the first fraction of a second it was overwhelmingly established. And it was this: that the entire episode was familiar to him. A subtle familiarity was present. All this had happened before. He had already somewhere, somehow seen death descending upon his cousin from the air. Yet with a difference. The "difference" escaped him; the familiarity was vivid. That he missed the deadly detonators in making the catch, or that the fuse delayed, he called good luck. He only remembers that he flung the gruesome weapon back whence it had come, and that its explosion in the opposite trench materially helped his cousin to find glory in the place of death. The slight delay, however, resulted in his receiving a bullet through the chest a bullet he would not otherwise have received, presumably.

It was some days later, gravely wounded, that he discovered his cousin in another bed across the darkened floor. They exchanged remarks. Jones was already "decorated," it seemed, having snatched success from his cousin's hands, while little aware whose help had made it easier. . . . And once again there stole across the inmost mind of Smith that strange, insistent whisper: "I owed it to him . . . but, by God, I owe more than that . . . I mean to pay it too . . .!"

There was not a trace of bitterness or envy now; only this profound conviction, of obscurest origin, that it was right and absolutely just full, honest repayment of a debt incurred. Some ancient balance of account was being settled; there was no "chance"; injustice and caprice played no role at all. . . . And a deeper understanding of life's ironies crept into him; for if everything was just, there was no room for whimpering.

And the voice persisted above the sound of busy footsteps in the ward : "I owe it ... I'll pay it gladly . . . !"

Through the pain and weakness the whisper died away. He was exhausted. There were periods of unconsciousness, but there were periods of half -consciousness as well; then flashes of another kind of consciousness altogether, when, bathed in high, soft light, he was aware of things he could not quite account for. He saw. It was absolutely real. Only, the critical faculty was gone. He did not question what he saw, as he stared across at his cousin's bed. He knew. Perhaps the beaten, worn-out body let something through at last. The nerves, over-strained to numbness, lay very still. The physical system, battered and depleted, made no cry. The clamor of the flesh was hushed. He was aware, however, of an undeniable exaltation of the spirit in him, as he lay and gazed towards his cousin's bed. . . .

Across the night of time, it seemed to him, the picture stole before his inner eye with a certainty that left no room for doubt. It was not the cells of memory in his brain of To-day that gave up their dead, it was the eternal Self in him that remembered and understood the soul. . . .

With that satisfaction which is born of full comprehension, he watched the light glow and spread about the little bed. Thick matting deadened the footsteps of nurses, orderlies, doctors. New cases were brought in, "old" cases were carried out; he ignored them; he saw only the light above his cousin's bed grow stronger. He lay still and stared. It came neither from the ceiling nor the floor; it unfolded like a cloud of shining smoke. And the little lamp, the sheets, the figure framed between them all these slid cleverly away and vanished utterly. He stood in another place that had lain behind all these appearances a landscape with wooded hills, a foaming river, the sun just sinking below the forest, and dusk creeping from a gorge along the lonely banks. In the warm air there was a perfume of great flowers and heavy-scented trees; there were fire-flies, and the taste of spray from the tumbling river was on his lips. Across the water a large bird, flapped its heavy wings, as it moved down-stream to find another fishing place. For he and his companion had disturbed it as they broke out of the thick foliage and reached the river-bank. The companion, moreover, was his brother; they ever hunted together; there was a passionate link between them born of blood and of affection they were twins. . . .

It all was as clear as though of Yesterday. In his heart was the lust of the hunt; in his blood was the lust of woman; and thick behind these lurked the jealousy and fierce desire of a primitive day. But, though clear as of Yesterday, he knew that it was of long, long ago. . . . And his brother came up close beside him, resting his bloody spear with a clattering sound against the boulders on the shore. He saw the gleaming of the metal in the sunset, he saw the shining glitter of the spray upon the boulders, he saw his brother's eyes look straight into his own. And in them shone a light that was neither the reflection of the sunset, nor the excitement of the hunt just over.

"It escaped us," said his brother. "Yet I know my first spear struck."

"It followed the fawn that crossed," was the reply. "Besides, we came down wind, thus giving it warning. Our flocks, at any rate, are safer ."

The other laughed significantly.

"It is not the safety of our flocks that troubles me just now, brother," he interrupted eagerly, while the light burned more deeply in his eyes. "It is, rather, that she waits for me by the fire across the river, and that I would get to her. With your help added to my love," he went on in a trusting voice, "the gods have shown me the favour of true happiness!" He pointed with his spear to a camp-fire on the farther bank, turning his head as he strode to plunge into the stream and swim across.

For an instant, then, the other felt his natural love turn into bitter hate. His own fierce passion, unconfessed, concealed, burst into instant flame. That the girl should become his brother's wife sent the blood surging through his veins in fury. He felt his life and all that he desired go down in ashes. . . . He watched his brother stride towards the water, the deer-skin cast across one naked shoulder when another object caught his practised eye. In mid-air it passed suddenly, like a shining gleam; it seemed to hang a second; then it swept swiftly forward past his head and downward. It had leaped with a blazing fury from the overhanging-bank behind; he saw the blood still streaming from its wounded flank. It must land—he saw it with a secret, awful pleasure—full upon the striding figure, whose head was turned away!

The swiftness of that leap, however, was not so swift but that he could easily have used his spear. Indeed, he gripped it strongly.

His skill, his strength, his aim—he knew them well enough. But hate and love, fastening upon his heart, held all his muscles still. He hesitated. He was no murderer, yet he paused. He heard the roar, the ugly thud, the crash, the cry for help too late . . . and when, an instant afterwards, his steel plunged into the great beast's heart, the human heart and life he might have saved lay still for ever. . . . He heard the water rushing past, an icy wind came down the gorge against his naked back, he saw the fire shine upon the farther bank . . . and the figure of a girl in skins was wading across, seeking out the shallow places in the dusk, and calling wildly as she came. . . . Then darkness hid the entire landscape, yet a darkness that was deeper, bluer than the velvet of the night alone. . . .

And he shrieked aloud in his remorseful anguish: "May the gods forgive me, for I did not mean it! Oh, that I might undo . . . that I might repay. . . .!"

That his cries disturbed the weary occupants in more than one bed is certain, but he remembers chiefly that a nurse was quickly by his side, and that something she gave him soothed his violent pain and helped him into deeper sleep again. There was, he noticed, anyhow, no longer the soft, clear, blazing light about his cousin's bed. He saw only the faint glitter of the oil-lamps down the length of the great room. . . .

And some weeks later he went back to fight. The picture, however, never left his memory. It stayed with him as an actual reality that was neither delusion nor hallucination. He believed that he understood at last the meaning of the tie that had fettered him and puzzled him so long. The memory of those far-off days— of shepherding beneath the stars of long ago—remained vividly beside him. He kept his secret, however. In many a talk with his cousin beneath the nearer stars of Flanders no word of it ever passed his lips.

The friendship between them, meanwhile, experienced a curious deepening, though unacknowledged in any spoken words. Smith, at any rate, on his side, put into it an affection that was a brave man's love. He watched over his cousin. In the fighting especially, when possible, he sought to protect and shield him, regardless of his own personal safety. He delighted secretly in the honours his cousin had already won. He himself was not yet even mentioned in dispatches, and no public distinction of any kind had come his way.

His V.C.* eventually—well, he was no longer occupying his body when it was bestowed. He had already "left." . . . He was now conscious, possibly, of other experiences besides that one of ancient, primitive days when he and his brother were shepherding beneath other stars. But the reckless heroism which saved his cousin under fire may later enshrine another memory which, at some far future time, shall reawaken as a "hallucination" from a Past that today is called the Present. . . . The notion, at any rate, flashed across his mind before he "left."

---

* Victoria Cross

The Fiend
F. Scott Fitzgerald

On June 3, 1895, on a country road near Stillwater, Minnesota, Mrs. Crenshaw Engels and her seven year old son, Mark, were waylaid and murdered by a fiend, under circumstances so atrocious that, fortunately, it is not necessary to set them down here.

Crenshaw Engels, the husband and father, was a photographer in Stillwater. He was a great reader and considered "a little unsafe," for he had spoken his mind frankly about the railroad-agrarian struggles of the time—but no one denied that he was a devoted family man, and the catastrophe visited upon him hung over the little town for many weeks. There was a move to lynch the perpetrator of the horror, for Minnesota did not permit the capital punishment it deserved, but the instigators were foiled by the big stone penitentiary close at hand.

The cloud hung over Engel's home so that folks went there only in moods of penitence, of fear or guilt, hoping that they would be visited in turn should their lives ever chance to trek under a black sky. The photography studio suffered also: the routine of being posed, the necessary silences and pauses in the process, permitted the clients too much time to regard the prematurely aged face of Crenshaw Engels, and high school students, newly married couples, mothers of new babies, were always glad to escape from the place into the open air. So Crenshaw's business fell off and he went through a time of hardship—finally liquidating the lease, the apparatus and the good will, and wearing out the money obtained. He sold his house for a little more than its two mortgages, went to board and took a position clerking in Radamacher's Department Store.

In the sight of his neighbors he had become a man ruined by adversity, a man manqué, a man emptied. But in the last opinion they were wrong—he was empty of all save one thing. His memory was long as a Jew's, and though his heart was in the grave he was sane as when his wife and son had started on their last walk that summer morning. At the first trial he lost control and got at the Fiend, seizing him by the necktie—and then had been dragged off with the Fiend's tie in such a knot that the man was nearly garotted.

At the second trial Crenshaw cried aloud once. Afterwards he went to all the members of the state legislature in the county and handed them a bill he had written himself for the introduction of capital punishment in the state—the bill to be retroactive on criminals condemned to life imprisonment. The bill fell through; it was on the day Crenshaw heard this that he got inside the penitentiary by a ruse and was only apprehended in time to be prevented from shooting the Fiend in his cell.

Crenshaw was given a suspended sentence and for some months it was assumed that the agony was fading gradually from his mind. In fact when he presented himself to the warden in another rôle a year after the crime, the official was sympathetic to his statement that he had had a change of heart and felt he could only emerge from the valley of shadow by forgiveness, that he wanted to help the Fiend, show him the True Path by means of good books and appeals to his buried better nature. So, after being carefully searched, Crenshaw was permitted to sit for half an hour in the corridor outside the Fiend's cell.

But had the warden suspected the truth he would not have permitted the visit—for, far from forgiving, Crenshaw's plan was to wreak upon the Fiend a mental revenge to replace the physical one of which he was subjected.

When he faced the Fiend, Crenshaw felt his scalp tingle. From behind the bars a roly-poly man, who somehow made his convict's uniform resemble a business suit, a man with thick brown-rimmed glasses and the trim air of an insurance salesman, looked at him uncertainly. Feeling faint Crenshaw sat down in the chair that had been brought for him.

"The air around you stinks!" he cried suddenly. "This whole corridor, this whole prison."

"I suppose it does," admitted the Fiend, "I noticed it too."

"You'll have time to notice it," Crenshaw muttered. "All your life you'll pace up and down stinking in that little cell, with everything getting blacker and blacker. And after that there'll be hell waiting for you. For all eternity you'll be shut in a little space, but in hell it'll be so small that you can't stand up or stretch out."

"Will it now?" asked the Fiend concerned.

"It will!" said Crenshaw. "You'll be alone with your own vile thoughts in that little space, forever and ever and ever. You'll itch with corruption so that you can never sleep, and you'll always be thirsty, with water just out of reach."

"Will I now?" repeated the Fiend, even more concerned. "I remember once—"

"All the time you'll be full of horror," Crenshaw interrupted. "You'll be like a person just about to go crazy but can't go crazy. All the time you'll be thinking that it's forever and ever."

"That's bad," said the Fiend, shaking his head gloomily. "That's real bad."

"Now listen here to me," went on Crenshaw. "I've brought you some books you're going to read. It's arranged that you get no books or papers except what I bring you."

As a beginning Crenshaw had brought half a dozen books which his vagarious curiosity had collected over as many years. They comprised a German doctor's thousand case histories of sexual abnormality—cases with no cures, no hopes, no prognoses, cases listed cold; a series of sermons by a New England Divine of the Great Revival which pictured the tortures of the damned in hell; a collection of horror stories; and a volume of erotic pieces from each of which the last two pages, containing the consummations, had been torn out; a volume of detective stories mutilated in the same manner. A tome of the Newgate calendar completed the batch. These Crenshaw handed through the bars—the Fiend took them and put them on his iron cot.

This was the first of Crenshaw's long series of fortnightly visits. Always he brought with him something somber and menacing to say, something dark and terrible to read—save that once when the Fiend had had nothing to read for a long time he brought him four inspiringly titled books—that proved to have nothing but blank paper inside. Another time, pretending to concede a point, he promised to bring newspapers—he brought ten copies of the yellowed journal that had reported the crime and the arrest. Sometimes he obtained medical books that showed in color the red and blue and green ravages of leprosy and skin disease, the mounds of shattered cells, the verminous tissue and brown corrupted blood.

And there was no sewer of the publishing world from which he did not obtain records of all that was gross and vile in man.

Crenshaw could not keep this up indefinitely both because of the expense and because of the exhaustibility of such books. When five years had passed he leaned toward another form of torture. He built up false hopes in the Fiend with protests of his own change of heart and manoeuvres for a pardon, and then dashed the hopes to pieces. Or else he pretended to have a pistol with him, or an inflammatory substance that would make the cell a raging Inferno and consume the Fiend in two minutes—once he threw a dummy bottle into the cell and listened in delight to the screams as the Fiend ran back and forth waiting for the explosion. At other times he would pretend grimly that the legislature had passed a new law which provided that the Fiend would be executed in a few hours.

A decade passed. Crenshaw was gray at forty—he was white at fifty when the alternating routine of his fortnightly visits to the graves of his loved ones and to the penitentiary had become the only part of his life—the long days at Radamacher's were only a weary dream. Sometimes he went and sat outside the Fiend's cell, with no word said during the half hour he was allowed to be there. The Fiend too had grown white in twenty years. He was very respectable-looking with his horn-rimmed glasses and his white hair. He seemed to have a great respect for Crenshaw and even when the latter, in a renewal of diminishing vitality, promised him one day that on his very next visit he was going to bring a revolver and end the matter, he nodded gravely as if in agreement, said, "I suppose so. Yes, I suppose you're perfectly right," and did not mention the matter to the guards. On the occasion of the next visit he was waiting with his hands on the bars of the cell looking at Crenshaw both hopefully and desperately. At certain tensions and strains death takes on, indeed, the quality of a great adventure as any soldier can testify.

Years passed. Crenshaw was promoted to floor manager at Radamacher's—there were new generations now that did not know of his tragedy and regarded him as an austere nonentity. He came into a little legacy and bought new stones for the graves of his wife and son. He knew he would soon be retired and while a third decade lapsed through the white winters, the short sweet smoky summers, it became more and more plain to him that the time had come to put an end to the Fiend; to avoid any mischance by which the other would survive him.

The moment he fixed upon came at the exact end of thirty years. Crenshaw had long owned the pistol with which it would be accomplished; he had fingered the shells lovingly and calculated the lodgement of each in the Fiend's body, so that death would be sure but lingering—he studied the tales of abdominal wounds in the war news and delighted in the agony that made victims pray to be killed.

After that, what happened to him did not matter.

When the day came he had no trouble in smuggling the pistol into the penitentiary. But to his surprise he found the Fiend scrunched up upon his iron cot, instead of waiting for him avidly by the bars.

"I'm sick," the Fiend said. "My stomach's been burning me up all morning. They gave me a physic but now it's worse and nobody comes."

Crenshaw fancied momentarily that this was a premonition in the man's bowels of a bullet that would shortly ride ragged through that spot.

"Come up to the bars," he said mildly.

"I can't move."

"Yes, you can."

"I'm doubled up. All doubled up."

"Come doubled up then."

With an effort the Fiend moved himself, only to fall on his side on the cement floor. He groaned and then lay quiet for a minute, after which, still bent in two, he began to drag himself a foot at a time toward the bars.

Suddenly Crenshaw set off at a run toward the end of the corridor.

"I want the prison doctor," he demanded of the guard, "That man's sick—sick, I tell you."

"The doctor has—"

"Get him—get him now!"

The guard hesitated, but Crenshaw had become a tolerated, even privileged person around the prison, and in a moment the guard took down his phone and called the infirmary.

All that afternoon Crenshaw waited in the bare area inside the gates, walking up and down with his hands behind his back. From time to time he went to the front entrance and demanded of the guard:

"Any news?"

"Nothing yet. They'll call me when there's anything."

Late in the afternoon the Warden appeared at the door, looked about and spotted Crenshaw. The latter, all alert, hastened over.

"He's dead," the Warden said. "His appendix burst. They did everything they could."

"Dead," Crenshaw repeated.

"I'm sorry to bring you this news. I know how—"

"It's all right," said Crenshaw, and licking his lips. "So he's dead."

The Warden lit a cigarette.

"While you're here, Mr. Engels, I wonder if you can let me have that pass that was issued to you—I can turn it in to the office. That is—I suppose you won't need it any more."

Crenshaw took the blue card from his wallet and handed it over. The Warden shook hands with him.

"One thing more," Crenshaw demanded as the Warden turned away. "Which is the—the window of the infirmary?"

"It's on the interior court, you can't see it from here."

"Oh."

When the Warden had gone Crenshaw still stood there a long time, the tears running out down his face. He could not collect his thoughts and he began by trying to remember what day it was; Saturday, the day, every other week, on which he came to see the Fiend.

He would not see the Fiend two weeks from now.

In a misery of solitude and despair he muttered aloud: "So he is dead. He has left me." And then with a long sigh of mingled grief and fear, "So I have lost him—my only friend—now I am alone."

He was still saying that to himself as he passed through the outer gate, and as his coat caught in the great swing of the outer door the guard opened up to release it, he heard a reiteration of the words:

"I'm alone. At last—at last I am alone."

Once more he called on the Fiend, after many weeks.

"But he's dead," the Warden told him kindly.

"Oh, yes," Crenshaw said. "I guess I must have forgotten."

And he set off back home, his boots sinking deep into the white diamond surface of the flats.

FAMILY

The Parable of the Lost Son
Luke 15: 11-32

Jesus continued: "There was a man who had two sons. The younger one said to his father, 'Father, give me my share of the estate.' So he divided his property between them.

Not long after that, the younger son got together all he had, set off for a distant country and there squandered his wealth in wild living. After he had spent everything, there was a severe famine in that whole country, and he began to be in need. So he went and hired himself out to a citizen of that country, who sent him to his fields to feed pigs. He longed to fill his stomach with the pods that the pigs were eating, but no one gave him anything.

"When he came to his senses, he said, 'How many of my father's hired men have food to spare, and here I am starving to death! I will set out and go back to my father and say to him: Father, I have sinned against heaven and against you. I am no longer worthy to be called your son; make me like one of your hired men.' So he got up and went to his father.

"But while he was still a long way off, his father saw him and was filled with compassion for him; he ran to his son, threw his arms around him and kissed him.

"The son said to him, 'Father, I have sinned against heaven and against you. I am no longer worthy to be called your son.'

"But the father said to his servants, 'Quick! Bring the best robe and put it on him. Put a ring on his finger and sandals on his feet. Bring the fattened calf and kill it. Let's have a feast and celebrate. For this son of mine was dead and is alive again; he was lost and is found.' So they began to celebrate.

"Meanwhile, the older son was in the field. When he came

near the house, he heard music and dancing. So he called one of the servants and asked him what was going on. 'Your brother has come,' he replied, 'and your father has killed the fattened calf because he has him back safe and sound.'

"The older brother became angry and refused to go in. So his father went out and pleaded with him. But he answered his father, 'Look! All these years I've been slaving for you and never disobeyed your orders. Yet you never gave me even a young goat so I could celebrate with my friends. But when this son of yours who has squandered your property with prostitutes comes home, you kill the fattened calf for him!'

"'My son,' the father said, 'you are always with me, and everything I have is yours. But we had to celebrate and be glad, because this brother of yours was dead and is alive again; he was lost and is found.'"

The Mirror Of Matsuyama, A Story Of Old Japan

Yei Theodora Ozaki

L ong years ago in old Japan there lived in the Province of Echigo, a very remote part of Japan even in these days, a man and his wife. When this story begins they had been married for some years and were blessed with one little daughter. She was the joy and pride of both their lives, and in her they stored an endless source of happiness for their old age.

What golden letter days in their memory were these that had marked her growing up from babyhood; the visit to the temple when she was just thirty days old, her proud mother carrying her, robed in ceremonial kimono, to be put under the patronage of the family's household god; then her first dolls festival, when her parents gave her a set of dolls and their miniature belongings, to be added to as year succeeded year; and perhaps the most important occasion of all, on her third birthday, when her first OBI (broad brocade sash) of scarlet and gold was tied round her small waist, a sign that she had crossed the threshold of girlhood and left infancy behind. Now that she was seven years of age, and had learned to talk and to wait upon her parents in those several little ways so dear to the hearts of fond parents, their cup of happiness seemed full. There could not be found in the whole of the Island Empire a happier little family.

One day there was much excitement in the home, for the father had been suddenly summoned to the capital on business. In these days of railways and jinrickshas and other rapid modes of traveling, it is difficult to realize what such a journey as that from Matsuyama to Kyoto meant. The roads were rough and bad, and ordinary people had to walk every step of the way, whether the distance were one hundred or several hundred miles. Indeed, in those days it was as great an undertaking to go up to the capital as it is for a Japanese to make a voyage to Europe now.

So the wife was very anxious while she helped her husband get ready for the long journey, knowing what an arduous task lay before him. Vainly she wished that she could accompany him, but the distance was too great for the mother and child to go, and besides that, it was the wife's duty to take care of the home.

All was ready at last, and the husband stood in the porch with his little family round him.

"Do not be anxious, I will come back soon," said the man. "While I am away take care of everything, and especially of our little daughter."

"Yes, we shall be all right—but you—you must take care of yourself and delay not a day in coming back to us," said the wife, while the tears fell like rain from her eyes.

The little girl was the only one to smile, for she was ignorant of the sorrow of parting, and did not know that going to the capital was at all different from walking to the next village, which her father did very often. She ran to his side, and caught hold of his long sleeve to keep him a moment.

"Father, I will be very good while I am waiting for you to come back, so please bring me a present."

As the father turned to take a last look at his weeping wife and smiling, eager child, he felt as if some one were pulling him back by the hair, so hard was it for him to leave them behind, for they had never been separated before. But he knew that he must go, for the call was imperative. With a great effort he ceased to think, and resolutely turning away he went quickly down the little garden and out through the gate. His wife, catching up the child in her arms, ran as far as the gate, and watched him as he went down the road between the pines till he was lost in the haze of the distance and all she could see was his quaint peaked hat, and at last that vanished too.

"Now father has gone, you and I must take care of everything till he comes back," said the mother, as she made her way back to the house.

"Yes, I will be very good," said the child, nodding her head, "and when father comes home please tell him how good I have been, and then perhaps he will give me a present."

"Father is sure to bring you something that you want very much. I know, for I asked him to bring you a doll. You must think of father every day, and pray for a safe journey till he comes back."

"O, yes, when he comes home again how happy I shall be," said the child, clapping her hands, and her face growing bright with joy at the glad thought. It seemed to the mother as she looked at the child's face that her love for her grew deeper and deeper.

Then she set to work to make the winter clothes for the three of them. She set up her simple wooden spinning-wheel and spun the thread before she began to weave the stuffs. In the intervals of her work she directed the little girl's games and taught her to read the old stories of her country. Thus did the wife find consolation in work during the lonely days of her husband's absence. While the time was thus slipping quickly by in the quiet home, the husband finished his business and returned.

It would have been difficult for any one who did not know the man well to recognize him. He had traveled day after day, exposed to all weathers, for about a month altogether, and was sunburnt to bronze, but his fond wife and child knew him at a glance, and flew to meet him from either side, each catching hold of one of his sleeves in their eager greeting. Both the man and his wife rejoiced to find each other well. It seemed a very long time to all until—the mother and child helping—his straw sandals were untied, his large umbrella hat taken off, and he was again in their midst in the old familiar sitting-room that had been so empty while he was away.

As soon as they had sat down on the white mats, the father opened a bamboo basket that he had brought in with him, and took out a beautiful doll and a lacquer box full of cakes.

"Here," he said to the little girl, "is a present for you. It is a prize for taking care of mother and the house so well while I was away."

"Thank you," said the child, as she bowed her head to the ground, and then put out her hand just like a little maple leaf with its eager wide-spread fingers to take the doll and the box, both of which, coming from the capital, were prettier than anything she had ever seen. No words can tell how delighted the little girl was— her face seemed as if it would melt with joy, and she had no eyes and no thought for anything else.

Again the husband dived into the basket, and brought out this time a square wooden box, carefully tied up with red and white string, and handing it to his wife, said:

"And this is for you."

The wife took the box, and opening it carefully took out a metal disk with a handle attached. One side was bright and shining like a crystal, and the other was covered with raised figures of pine-trees and storks, which had been carved out of its smooth surface in lifelike reality. Never had she seen such a thing in her life, for she had been born and bred in the rural province of Echigo. She gazed into the shining disk, and looking up with surprise and wonder pictured on her face, she said:

"I see somebody looking at me in this round thing! What is it that you have given me?"

The husband laughed and said:

"Why, it is your own face that you see. What I have brought you is called a mirror, and whoever looks into its clear surface can see their own form reflected there. Although there are none to be found in this out of the way place, yet they have been in use in the capital from the most ancient times. There the mirror is considered a very necessary requisite for a woman to possess. There is an old proverb that 'As the sword is the soul of a samurai, so is the mirror the soul of a woman,' and according to popular tradition, a woman's mirror is an index to her own heart—if she keeps it bright and clear, so is her heart pure and good. It is also one of the treasures that form the insignia of the Emperor. So you must lay great store by your mirror, and use it carefully."

The wife listened to all her husband told her, and was pleased at learning so much that was new to her. She was still more pleased at the precious gift—his token of remembrance while he had been away.

"If the mirror represents my soul, I shall certainly treasure it as a valuable possession, and never will I use it carelessly." Saying so, she lifted it as high as her forehead, in grateful acknowledgment of the gift, and then shut it up in its box and put it away.

The wife saw that her husband was very tired, and set about serving the evening meal and making everything as comfortable as she could for him. It seemed to the little family as if they had not known what true happiness was before, so glad were they to be together again, and this evening the father had much to tell of his journey and of all he had seen at the great capital.

Time passed away in the peaceful home, and the parents saw

their fondest hopes realized as their daughter grew from childhood into a beautiful girl of sixteen. As a gem of priceless value is held in its proud owner's hand, so had they reared her with unceasing love and care: and now their pains were more than doubly rewarded. What a comfort she was to her mother as she went about the house taking her part in the housekeeping, and how proud her father was of her, for she daily reminded him of her mother when he had first married her.

But, alas! in this world nothing lasts forever. Even the moon is not always perfect in shape, but loses its roundness with time, and flowers bloom and then fade. So at last the happiness of this family was broken up by a great sorrow. The good and gentle wife and mother was one day taken ill.

In the first days of her illness the father and daughter thought that it was only a cold, and were not particularly anxious. But the days went by and still the mother did not get better; she only grew worse, and the doctor was puzzled, for in spite of all he did the poor woman grew weaker day by day. The father and daughter were stricken with grief, and day or night the girl never left her mother's side. But in spite of all their efforts the woman's life was not to be saved.

One day as the girl sat near her mother's bed, trying to hide with a cheery smile the gnawing trouble at her heart, the mother roused herself and taking her daughter's hand, gazed earnestly and lovingly into her eyes. Her breath was labored and she spoke with difficulty:

"My daughter. I am sure that nothing can save me now. When I am dead, promise me to take care of your dear father and to try to be a good and dutiful woman."

"Oh, mother," said the girl as the tears rushed to her eyes, "you must not say such things. All you have to do is to make haste and get well—that will bring the greatest happiness to father and myself."

"Yes, I know, and it is a comfort to me in my last days to know how greatly you long for me to get better, but it is not to be. Do not look so sorrowful, for it was so ordained in my previous state of existence that I should die in this life just at this time; knowing this, I am quite resigned to my fate. And now I have something to give you whereby to remember me when I am gone."

Putting her hand out, she took from the side of the pillow a square wooden box tied up with a silken cord and tassels. Undoing this very carefully, she took out of the box the mirror that her husband had given her years ago.

"When you were still a little child your father went up to the capital and brought me back as a present this treasure; it is called a mirror. This I give you before I die. If, after I have ceased to be in this life, you are lonely and long to see me sometimes, then take out this mirror and in the clear and shining surface you will always see me—so will you be able to meet with me often and tell me all your heart; and though I shall not be able to speak, I shall understand and sympathize with you, whatever may happen to you in the future." With these words the dying woman handed the mirror to her daughter.

The mind of the good mother seemed to be now at rest, and sinking back without another word her spirit passed quietly away that day.

The bereaved father and daughter were wild with grief, and they abandoned themselves to their bitter sorrow. They felt it to be impossible to take leave of the loved woman who till now had filled their whole lives and to commit her body to the earth. But this frantic burst of grief passed, and then they took possession of their own hearts again, crushed though they were in resignation. In spite of this the daughter's life seemed to her desolate. Her love for her dead mother did not grow less with time, and so keen was her remembrance, that everything in daily life, even the falling of the rain and the blowing of the wind, reminded her of her mother's death and of all that they had loved and shared together. One day when her father was out, and she was fulfilling her household duties alone, her loneliness and sorrow seemed more than she could bear. She threw herself down in her mother's room and wept as if her heart would break. Poor child, she longed just for one glimpse of the loved face, one sound of the voice calling her pet name, or for one moment's forgetfulness of the aching void in her heart. Suddenly she sat up. Her mother's last words had rung through her memory hitherto dulled by grief.

"Oh! my mother told me when she gave me the mirror as a parting gift, that whenever I looked into it I should be able to meet her—to see her. I had nearly forgotten her last words—how stupid I am; I will get the mirror now and see if it can possibly be true!"

She dried her eyes quickly, and going to the cupboard took

out the box that contained the mirror, her heart beating with expectation as she lifted the mirror out and gazed into its smooth face. Behold, her mother's words were true! In the round mirror before her she saw her mother's face; but, oh, the joyful surprise! It was not her mother thin and wasted by illness, but the young and beautiful woman as she remembered her far back in the days of her own earliest childhood. It seemed to the girl that the face in the mirror must soon speak, almost that she heard the voice of her mother telling her again to grow up a good woman and a dutiful daughter, so earnestly did the eyes in the mirror look back into her own.

"It is certainly my mother's soul that I see. She knows how miserable I am without her and she has come to comfort me. Whenever I long to see her she will meet me here; how grateful I ought to be!"

And from this time the weight of sorrow was greatly lightened for her young heart. Every morning, to gather strength for the day's duties before her, and every evening, for consolation before she lay down to rest, did the young girl take out the mirror and gaze at the reflection which in the simplicity of her innocent heart she believed to be her mother's soul. Daily she grew in the likeness of her dead mother's character, and was gentle and kind to all, and a dutiful daughter to her father.

A year spent in mourning had thus passed away in the little household, when, by the advice of his relations, the man married again, and the daughter now found herself under the authority of a step-mother. It was a trying position; but her days spent in the recollection of her own beloved mother, and of trying to be what that mother would wish her to be, had made the young girl docile and patient, and she now determined to be filial and dutiful to her father's wife, in all respects. Everything went on apparently smoothly in the family for some time under the new regime; there were no winds or waves of discord to ruffle the surface of every-day life, and the father was content.

But it is a woman's danger to be petty and mean, and step-mothers are proverbial all the world over, and this one's heart was not as her first smiles were. As the days and weeks grew into months, the step-mother began to treat the motherless girl unkindly and to try and come between the father and child.

Sometimes she went to her husband and complained of her

step-daughter's behavior, but the father knowing that this was to be expected, took no notice of her ill-natured complaints. Instead of lessening his affection for his daughter, as the woman desired, her grumblings only made him think of her the more. The woman soon saw that he began to show more concern for his lonely child than before. This did not please her at all, and she began to turn over in her mind how she could, by some means or other, drive her step-child out of the house. So crooked did the woman's heart become.

She watched the girl carefully, and one day peeping into her room in the early morning, she thought she discovered a grave enough sin of which to accuse the child to her father. The woman herself was a little frightened too at what she had seen.

So she went at once to her husband, and wiping away some false tears she said in a sad voice:

"Please give me permission to leave you today."

The man was completely taken by surprise at the suddenness of her request, and wondered whatever was the matter.

"Do you find it so disagreeable," he asked, "in my house, that you can stay no longer?"

"No! no! It has nothing to do with you—even in my dreams I have never thought that I wished to leave your side; but if I go on living here I am in danger of losing my life, so I think it best for all concerned that you should allow me to go home!"

And the woman began to weep afresh. Her husband, distressed to see her so unhappy, and thinking that he could not have heard aright, said:

"Tell me what you mean! How is your life in danger here?"

"I will tell you since you ask me. Your daughter dislikes me as her step-mother. For some time past she has shut herself up in her room morning and evening, and looking in as I pass by, I am convinced that she has made an image of me and is trying to kill me by magic art, cursing me daily. It is not safe for me to stay here, such being the case; indeed, indeed, I must go away, we cannot live under the same roof any more."

The husband listened to the dreadful tale, but he could not believe his gentle daughter guilty of such an evil act. He knew that by popular superstition people believed that one person could cause the gradual death of another by making an image of the hated one and cursing it daily; but where had his young daughter learned such knowledge?—the thing was impossible. Yet he remembered having noticed that his daughter stayed much in her room of late and kept herself away from every one, even when visitors came to the house. Putting this fact together with his wife's alarm, he thought that there might be something to account for the strange story.

His heart was torn between doubting his wife and trusting his child, and he knew not what to do. He decided to go at once to his daughter and try to find out the truth. Comforting his wife and assuring her that her fears were groundless, he glided quietly to his daughter's room.

The girl had for a long time past been very unhappy. She had tried by amiability and obedience to show her goodwill and to mollify the new wife, and to break down that wall of prejudice and misunderstanding that she knew generally stood between step-parents and their step-children. But she soon found that her efforts were in vain. The step-mother never trusted her, and seemed to misinterpret all her actions, and the poor child knew very well that she often carried unkind and untrue tales to her father. She could not help comparing her present unhappy condition with the time when her own mother was alive only a little more than a year ago — so great a change in this short time! Morning and evening she wept over the remembrance. Whenever she could she went to her room, and sliding the screens to, took out the mirror and gazed, as she thought, at her mother's face. It was the only comfort that she had in these wretched days.

Her father found her occupied in this way. Pushing aside the fusama, he saw her bending over something or other very intently. Looking over her shoulder, to see who was entering her room, the girl was surprised to see her father, for he generally sent for her when he wished to speak to her. She was also confused at being found looking at the mirror, for she had never told any one of her mother's last promise, but had kept it as the sacred secret of her heart. So before turning to her father she slipped the mirror into her long sleeve. Her father noting her confusion, and her act of hiding something, said in a severe manner:

"Daughter, what are you doing here? And what is that that you have hidden in your sleeve?"

The girl was frightened by her father's severity. Never had he spoken to her in such a tone. Her confusion changed to apprehension, her color from scarlet to white. She sat dumb and shamefaced, unable to reply.

Appearances were certainly against her; the young girl looked guilty, and the father thinking that perhaps after all what his wife had told him was true, spoke angrily:

"Then, is it really true that you are daily cursing your step-mother and praying for her death? Have you forgotten what I told you, that although she is your step-mother you must be obedient and loyal to her? What evil spirit has taken possession of your heart that you should be so wicked? You have certainly changed, my daughter! What has made you so disobedient and unfaithful?"

And the father's eyes filled with sudden tears to think that he should have to upbraid his daughter in this way.

She on her part did not know what he meant, for she had never heard of the superstition that by praying over an image it is possible to cause the death of a hated person. But she saw that she must speak and clear herself somehow. She loved her father dearly, and could not bear the idea of his anger. She put out her hand on his knee deprecatingly:

"Father! father! do not say such dreadful things to me. I am still your obedient child. Indeed, I am. However stupid I may be, I should never be able to curse any one who belonged to you, much less pray for the death of one you love. Surely some one has been telling you lies, and you are dazed, and you know not what you say—or some evil spirit has taken possession of YOUR heart. As for me I do not know—no, not so much as a dew-drop, of the evil thing of which you accuse me."

But the father remembered that she had hidden something away when he first entered the room, and even this earnest protest did not satisfy him. He wished to clear up his doubts once for all.

"Then why are you always alone in your room these days? And tell me what is that that you have hidden in your sleeve—show it to me at once."

Then the daughter, though shy of confessing how she had cherished her mother's memory, saw that she must tell her father all in order to clear herself. So she slipped the mirror out from her long sleeve and laid it before him.

"This," she said, "is what you saw me looking at just now."

"Why," he said in great surprise, "this is the mirror that I brought as a gift to your mother when I went up to the capital many years ago! And so you have kept it all this time? Now, why do you spend so much of your time before this mirror?"

Then she told him of her mother's last words, and of how she had promised to meet her child whenever she looked into the glass. But still the father could not understand the simplicity of his daughter's character in not knowing that what she saw reflected in the mirror was in reality her own face, and not that of her mother.

"What do you mean?" he asked. "I do not understand how you can meet the soul of your lost mother by looking in this mirror?"

"It is indeed true," said the girl: "and if you don't believe what I say, look for yourself," and she placed the mirror before her. There, looking back from the smooth metal disk, was her own sweet face. She pointed to the reflection seriously:

"Do you doubt me still?" she asked earnestly, looking up into his face.

With an exclamation of sudden understanding the father smote his two hands together.

"How stupid I am! At last I understand. Your face is as like your mother's as the two sides of a melon—thus you have looked at the reflection of your face ail this time, thinking that you were brought face to face with your lost mother! You are truly a faithful child. It seems at first a stupid thing to have done, but it is not really so, It shows how deep has been your filial piety, and how innocent your heart. Living in constant remembrance of your lost mother has helped you to grow like her in character. How clever it was of her to tell you to do this. I admire and respect you, my daughter, and I am ashamed to think that for one instant I believed your suspicious step-mother's story and suspected you of evil, and came with the intention of scolding you severely, while all this time you have been so true and good. Before you I have no countenance left, and I beg you to forgive me."

And here the father wept. He thought of how lonely the poor girl must have been, and of all that she must have suffered under her step-mother's treatment. His daughter steadfastly keeping her faith and simplicity in the midst of such adverse circumstances—bearing all her troubles with so much patience and amiability—made him compare her to the lotus which rears its blossom of dazzling beauty out of the slime and mud of the moats and ponds, fitting emblem of a heart which keeps itself unsullied while passing through the world.

The step-mother, anxious to know what would happen, had

all this while been standing outside the room. She had grown interested, and had gradually pushed the sliding screen back till she could see all that went on. At this moment she suddenly entered the room, and dropping to the mats, she bowed her head over her outspread hands before her step-daughter.

"I am ashamed! I am ashamed!" she exclaimed in broken tones. "I did not know what a filial child you were. Through no fault of yours, but with a step-mother's jealous heart, I have disliked you all the time. Hating you so much myself, it was but natural that I should think you reciprocated the feeling, and thus when I saw you retire so often to your room I followed you, and when I saw you gaze daily into the mirror for long intervals, I concluded that you had found out how I disliked you, and that you were out of revenge trying to take my life by magic art. As long as I live I shall never forget the wrong I have done you in so misjudging you, and in causing your father to suspect you. From this day I throw away my old and wicked heart, and in its place I put a new one, clean and full of repentance. I shall think of you as a child that I have borne myself. I shall love and cherish you with all my heart, and thus try to make up for all the unhappiness I have caused you. Therefore, please throw into the water all that has gone before, and give me, I beg of you, some of the filial love that you have hitherto given to your own lost mother."

Thus did the unkind step-mother humble herself and ask forgiveness of the girl she had so wronged.

Such was the sweetness of the girl's disposition that she willingly forgave her step-mother, and never bore a moment's resentment or malice towards her afterwards. The father saw by his wife's face that she was truly sorry for the past, and was greatly relieved to see the terrible misunderstanding wiped out of remembrance by both the wrong-doer and the wronged.

From this time on, the three lived together as happily as fish in water. No such trouble ever darkened the home again, and the young girl gradually forgot that year of unhappiness in the tender love and care that her step-mother now bestowed on her. Her patience and goodness were rewarded at last.

The Christmas Peace
Thomas Nelson Page

I

They had lived within a mile of each other for fifty-odd years, old Judge Hampden and old Colonel Drayton; that is, all their lives, for they had been born on adjoining plantations within a month of each other. But though they had thus lived and were accounted generally good men and good neighbors, to each other they had never been neighbors any more than the Levite was neighbor to him who went down to Jericho.

Kindly to everyone·else and ready to do their part by all other men, the Draytons and the Hampdens, whenever they met each other, always passed by on the other side.

It was an old story—the feud between the families—and, perhaps, no one now knew just how the trouble started. They had certainly been on opposite sides ever since they established themselves in early Colonial days on opposite hills in the old county from which the two mansions looked at each other across the stream like hostile forts. The earliest records of the county were those of a dispute between one Colonel Drayton and one Captain Hampden, growing out of some claim to land; but in which the chief bitterness appeared to have been injected by Captain Hampden's having claimed precedence over Colonel Drayton on the ground that his title of "Captain" was superior to Colonel Drayton's title, because he had held a real commission and had fought for it, whereas the Colonel's title was simply honorary and "Ye sayd Collonel had never smelled enough powder to kill a tom-cat."

However this might be and there was nothing in the records to show how this contention was adjudicated—in the time of Major Wilmer Drayton and Judge Oliver Hampden, the breach between the two families had been transmitted from father to son for several generations and showed no signs of abatement. Other neighborhood families intermarried, but not the Drayton-Hall and the Hampden-Hill families, and in time it came to be an accepted tradition that a Drayton and a Hampden would not mingle any more than would fire and water.

The Hampdens were dark and stout, hot-blooded, fierce, and impetuous. They were apparently vigorous; but many of them died young. The Draytons, on the other hand, were slender and fair, and usually lived to a round old age; a fact of which they were wont to boast in contrast with the briefer span of the Hampdens.

"Their tempers burn them out," the Major used to say of the Hampdens.

Moreover, the Draytons were generally cool-headed, deliberate, and self-contained. Thus, the Draytons had mainly prospered throughout the years.

Even the winding creek which ran down through the strip of meadow was a fruitful cause of dissension and litigation between the families. "It is as ungovernable as a Hampden's temper, sir," once said Major Drayton, On the mere pretext of a thunder-storm, it would burst forth from its banks, tear the fences to pieces and even change its course, cutting a new channel, now to one side and now to the other through the soft and loamy soil. A lawsuit arose over the matter, in which the costs alone amounted to far more than the value of the whole land involved; but no one doubted that old Major Drayton spoke the truth when he declared that his father would rather have lost his entire estate with all its rolling hills and extensive forests than the acre or two which was finally awarded to Judge Hampden.

As neither owner would join the other even in keeping up a partition fence, there were two fences run within three feet of each other along the entire boundary line between the two places. With these double fences, there could hardly be peace between the two families; for neither owner ever saw the two lines running side by side without at once being reminded of his neighbor's obstinacy and—of his own.

Thus, in my time the quarrel between the Drayton-Hall people and the Hampden-Hill folks was a factor in every neighborhood problem or proposition from a "church dressing" or a "sewing society meeting" to a political campaign. It had to be considered in every invitation and in every discussion.

It is not meant that there was no intercourse between the two families. Major Drayton and Judge Hampden regularly paid each other a visit every year—and oftener when there was serious illness in one house or the other—but even on such occasions their differences were liable to crop out. One of them held an opinion that when one gentleman was spending the night in another gentleman's house, it was the part of the host to indicate when bedtime had arrived; whilst the other maintained with equal firmness the doctrine that no gentleman could inform his guest that he was fatigued: that this duty devolved upon the guest himself. This difference of opinion worked comfortably enough on both sides until an occasion when Judge Hampden, who held the former view, was spending the night at Colonel Drayton's. When bedtime arrived, the rest of the household retired quietly, leaving the two gentlemen conversing, and when the servants appeared in the morning to open the blinds and light the fires, the two gentlemen were still found seated opposite each other conversing together quite as if it were the ordinary thing to sit up and talk all night long.

On another occasion, it is said that Major Drayton, hearing of his neighbor's serious illness, rode over to make inquiry about him, and owing to a slip of the tongue, asked in a voice of deepest sympathy, "Any hopes of the old gentleman dying!"

II

Yet, they had once been friends.

Before Wilmer Drayton and Oliver Hampden were old enough to understand that by all the laws of heredity and custom they should be enemies, they had learned to like each other. When they were only a few years old, the little creek winding between the two plantations afforded in its strip of meadow a delightful neutral territory where the two boys could enjoy themselves together, safe from the interference of their grave seniors; wading, sailing mimic fleets upon its uncertain currents, fishing together, or bathing in the deepest pools it offered in its winding course.

It looked, indeed, for a time as if in the fellowship of these two lads the long-standing feud of the Hampdens and Draytons might be ended, at last. They went to school together at the academy, where their only contests were a generous rivalry. At college they were known as Damon and Pythias, and though a natural rivalry, which might in any event have existed between them, developed over the highest prize of the institution—the debater's medal—the generosity of youth saved them. It was even said that young Drayton, who for some time had apparently been certain of winning, had generously retired in order to defeat a third candidate and throw the prize to Oliver Hampden.

They came home and both went to the Bar, but with different results. Young Drayton was learned and unpractical. Oliver Hampden was clever, able, and successful, and soon had a thriving practice; while his neighbor's learning was hardly known outside the circle of the Bar.

Disappointed in his ambition, Drayton shortly retired from the Bar and lived the life of a country gentleman, while his former friend rapidly rose to be the head of the Bar.

The old friendship might have disappeared in any event, but a new cause arose which was certain to end it.

Lucy Fielding was, perhaps, the prettiest girl in all that region. Oliver Hampden had always been in love with her. However, Fortune, ever capricious, favored Wilmer Drayton, who entered the lists when it looked as if Miss Lucy were almost certain to marry her old lover. It appeared that Mr. Drayton's indifference had counted for more than the other's devotion. He carried off the prize with a dash.

If Oliver Hampden, however, was severely stricken by his disappointment, he masked it well; for he married not long afterward, and though some said it was from pique, there was no more happily married pair in all the county.

A year later a new Oliver came to keep up the name and tenets of the Hampdens. Oliver Hampden, now the head of the Bar, would not have envied any man on earth had not his wife died a few years later and left him alone with his boy in his big house.

Lucy Drayton was born two years after young Oliver Hampden.

The mammies of the two children, as the mammies of their parents had done before them, used to walk them over on the edge of the shaded meadow which divided the places, and thus young Oliver Hampden, a lusty boy of five, came to know little Lucy Drayton fully three years before his father ever laid eyes on her.

Mr. Hampden was riding around his fences one summer afternoon, and was making his way along the double division line with a cloud on his brow as the double rows recalled the wide breach with his neighbor and former friend, and many memories came trooping at the recollection. Passing through a small grove which had been allowed to grow up to shut off a part of his view of the Drayton place, as he came out into the meadow his eye fell on a scene which made him forget the present with all its wrongs. On the green turf before him where butter-cups speckled the ground with golden blossoms, was a little group of four persons busily engaged and wholly oblivious of the differences which divided the masters of the two estates. The two mammies were seated side by side on a bank, sewing and talking busily—their large aprons and caps making a splotch of white against the green willows beyond— and in front of them at a little distance a brown-haired boy of five and a yellow-ringleted girl of three were at play on the turf, rolling over and over, shouting and laughing in their glee.

As the father rested his eyes on the group, the frown which had for a second lowered on his brow passed away and he pulled in his horse so as not to disturb them. He was about to turn back and leave them in their happiness when his black-eyed boy caught sight of him and ran toward him, shouting for a ride and calling over his shoulder for "Luthy" to "come on too." As there was no escape, Mr. Hampden went forward and, ignoring the confusion of the mammies at being caught together, took the boy up before him and gave him a ride up and down the meadow. Then nothing else would do for Master Oliver but he "must take Luthy up, too."

"Perhaps 'Luthy' may be afraid of the horse!" suggested Mr. Hampden with a smile.

But far from it. Led by the little boy who had run to fetch her, she came to Mr. Hampden as readily as his own son had done, and, though she gave him one of those quick searching glances with which childhood reads character, having made sure that he was friendly, she was no more afraid of his horse than the boy was.

Oliver tried to lift her, and as he tugged at her, the father sat and watched with a smile, then leant down and picked her up while the two mammies gasped with mingled astonishment and fear.

"I tell you, she's pretty heavy," said the little boy.

"Indeed, she is," said the father, gaily.

Mr. Hampden would have taken his son home with him, but the latter declined the invitation. He wished to "stay with Luthy." So, Mr. Hampden, having first set the nurses' minds at ease by complimenting the little girl in warm terms to her mammy, rode home alone with his face set in deep reflection.

The breach between the Hampdens and the Draytons was nearer being closed that evening than it had been in three generations, for as Oliver Hampden rode up the bridle path across his fields, he heard behind him the merry laughter of the two children in the quiet meadow below, and old memories of his childhood and college life softened his heart. He forgot the double-line fences and determined to go on the morrow to Drayton Hall and make up the quarrel. He would offer the first overture and a full declaration of regret, and this, he was quite sure, would make it up. Once he actually turned his horse around to go straight across the fields as he used to do in his boyhood, but there below him were the double-line fences stretching brown and clear. No horse could get over them, and around the road it was a good five miles, so he turned back again and rode home and the chance was lost.

On his arrival he found a summons in a suit which had been instituted that day by Wilmer Drayton for damages to his land by reason of his turning the water of the creek upon him.

Mr. Hampden did not forbid old Lydia to take his boy down there again, but he went to the meadow no more himself, and when he and Wilmer Drayton met next, which was not for some time, they barely spoke.

III

Young Oliver Hampden grew up clear eyed, strong, and good to look at, and became shy where girls were concerned, and most of all appeared to be shy with Lucy Drayton. He went to college and as he got his broad shoulders and manly stride he got over his shyness with most girls, but not with Lucy Drayton. With her, he appeared to have become yet more reserved. She had inherited her mother's eyes and beauty, with the fairness of a lily; a slim, willowy figure; a straight back and a small head set on her shoulders in a way that showed both blood and pride. Moreover, she had character enough, as her friends knew: those gray eyes that smiled could grow haughty with disdain or flash with indignation, and she had taught many an uppish young man to feel her keen irony.

"She gets only her intellect from the Draytons; her beauty and her sweetness come from her mother," said a lady of the neighborhood to Judge Hampden, thinking to please him.

"She gets both her brains and beauty from her mother and only her name from her father," snapped the Judge, who had often seen her at church, and never without recalling Lucy Fielding as he knew her.

That she and young Oliver Hampden fought goes without saying. But no one knew why she was cruelly bitter to a young man who once spoke slightingly of Oliver, or why Oliver, who rarely saw her except at church, took up a quarrel of hers so furiously.

*****

The outbreak of the war, or rather the conditions preceding that outbreak, finally fixed forever the gulf between the two families. Judge Hampden was an ardent follower of Calhoun and "stumped" the State in behalf of Secession, whereas Major Drayton, as the cloud that had been gathering so long rolled nearer, emerged from his seclusion and became one of the sternest opponents of a step which he declared was not merely revolution, but actual rebellion. So earnest was he, that believing that slavery was the ultimate bone of contention, he emancipated his slaves on a system which he thought would secure their welfare. Nothing could have more deeply stirred Judge Hampden's wrath. He declared that such a measure at such a crisis was a blow at every Southern man. He denounced Major Drayton as "worse than Garrison, Phillips, and Greeley all put together."

They at last met in debate at the Court House. Major Drayton exasperated the Judge by his coolness, until the latter lost his temper and the crowd laughed.

"I do not get as hot as you do," said the Major, blandly. He looked as cool as a cucumber, but his voice betrayed him.

"Oh, yes, you do," snorted the Judge. "A mule gets as hot as a horse, but he does not sweat."

This saved him.

There came near being a duel. Everyone expected it. Only the interposition of friends prevented their meeting on the field. Only this and one other thing.

Though no one in the neighborhood knew it until long afterward—and then only in a conjectural way by piecing together fragments of rumors that floated about—young Oliver Hampden really prevented the duel. He told his father that he loved Lucy Drayton. There was a fierce outbreak on the Judge's part.

"Marry that girl!—the daughter of Wilmer Drayton! I will

disinherit you if you but so much as — — "

"Stop!" The younger man faced him and held up his hand with an imperious gesture. "Stop! Do not say a word against her or I may never forget it."

The father paused with his sentence unfinished, for his son stood before him suddenly revealed in a strength for which the Judge had never given him credit, and he recognized in his level eyes, tense features, and the sudden set of the square jaw, the Hampden firmness at its best or worst.

"I have nothing to say against her," said the Judge, with a sudden rush of recollection of Lucy Fielding. "I have no doubt she is in one way all you think her; but she is Wilmer Drayton 's daughter. You will never win her."

"I will win her," said the young man.

That night Judge Hampden thought deeply over the matter, and before daylight he had despatched a note to Major Drayton making an apology for the words he had used.

Both Judge Hampden and his son went into the army immediately on the outbreak of hostilities. Major Drayton, who to the last opposed Secession bitterly, did not volunteer until after the State had seceded; but then he, also, went in, and later was desperately wounded.

A few nights before they went off to the war, Judge Hampden and his son rode over together to Major Drayton's to offer the olive-branch of peace in shape of young Oliver and all that he possessed.

Judge Hampden did not go all the way, for he had sworn never to put foot again in Major Drayton's house so long as he lived, and, moreover, he felt that his son would be the better ambassador alone. Accordingly, he waited in the darkness at the front gate while his son presented himself and laid at Lucy Drayton's feet what the Judge truly believed was more than had ever been offered to any other woman. He, however, sent the most conciliatory messages to Major Drayton.

"Tell him," he said, "that I will take down my fence and he shall run the line to suit himself." He could not have gone further.

The time that passed appeared unending to the Judge waiting in the darkness; but in truth it was not long, for the interview was brief. It was with Major Drayton and not with his daughter.

Major Drayton declined, both on his daughter's part and on his own, the honor which had been proposed.

At this moment the door opened and Lucy herself appeared. She was a vision of loveliness. Her face was white, but her eyes were steady. If she knew what had occurred, she gave no sign of it in words. She walked straight to her father's side and took his hand.

"Lucy," he said, "Mr. Hampden has done us the honor to ask your hand and I have declined it."

"Yes, papa." Her eyelids fluttered and her bosom heaved, but she did not move, and Lucy was too much a Drayton to unsay what her father had said, or to undo what he had done.

Oliver Hampden's eyes did not leave her face. For him the Major had disappeared, and he saw only the girl who stood before him with a face as white as the dress she wore.

"Lucy, I love you. Will you ever care for me? I am going — going away to-morrow, and I shall not see you any more; but I would like to know if there is any hope." The young man's voice was strangely calm.

The girl held out her hand to him.

"I will never marry anyone else."

"I will wait for you all my life," said the young man.

Bending low, he kissed her hand in the palm, and with a bow to her father, strode from the room.

The Judge, waiting at the gate in the darkness, heard the far-off, monotonous galloping of Oliver's horse on the hard plantation road. He rode forward to meet him.

"Well!"

It was only a word.

"They declined."

The father scarcely knew his son's voice, it was so wretched.

"What! Who declined? Did you see—"

"Both!"

Out in the darkness Judge Hampden broke forth into such a torrent of rage that his son was afraid for his life and had to devote all his attention to soothing him. He threatened to ride straight to Drayton's house and horsewhip him on the spot. This, however, the young man prevented, and the two rode home together in a silence which was unbroken until they had dismounted at their own gate and given their horses to the waiting servants. As they entered the house, Judge Hampden spoke.

"I hope you are satisfied," he said, sternly. "I make but one request of you—that from this time forth, you will never mention the name of Drayton to me again as long as you live."

"I suppose I should hate her," said the son, bitterly, "but I do not. I love her and I believe she cares for me."

His father turned in the door-way and faced him.

"Cares for you! Not so much as she cares for the smallest negro on that place. If you ever marry her, I will disinherit you."

"Disinherit me!" burst from the young man. "Do you think I care for this place? What has it ever brought to us but unhappiness? I have seen your life embittered by a feud with your nearest neighbor, and now it wrecks my happiness and robs me of what I would give all the rest of the world for."

Judge Hampden looked at him curiously. He started to say, "Before I would let her enter this house, I would burn it with my own hands"; but as he met his son's steadfast gaze there was that in it which made him pause. The Hampden look was in his eyes. The father knew that another word might sever them forever.

*****

If ever a man tried to court death, young Oliver Hampden did. But Death, that struck many a happier man, passed him by, and he secured instead only a reputation for reckless courage and was promoted on the field.

His father rose to the command of a brigade, and Oliver himself became a captain.

At last the bullet Oliver had sought found him; but it spared his life and only incapacitated him for service.

There were no trained nurses during the war, and Lucy Drayton, like so many girls, when the war grew fiercer, went into the hospitals, and by devotion supplied their place.

Believing that life was ended for her, she had devoted herself wholly to the cause, and self-repression had given to her face the gentleness and consecration of a nun.

It was said that once as she bent over a wounded common soldier, he returned to consciousness, and after gazing up at her a moment, asked vaguely, "Who are you, Miss?"

"I am one of the sisters whom our Father has sent to nurse you and help you to get well. But you must not talk."

The wounded man closed his eyes and then opened them with a faint smile.

"All right; just one word. Will you please ask your pa if I may be his son-in-law?"

Into the hospital was brought one day a soldier so broken and bandaged that no one but Lucy Drayton might have recognized Oliver Hampden.

For a long time his life was despaired of; but he survived.

When consciousness returned to him, the first sound he heard was a voice which had often haunted him in his dreams, but which he had never expected to hear again.

"Who is that!" he asked, feebly.

"It is I, Oliver—it is Lucy."

The wounded man moved slightly and the girl bending over him caught the words, whispered brokenly to himself:

"I am dreaming."

But he was not dreaming.

Lucy Drayton's devotion probably brought him back from death and saved his life.

In the hell of that hospital one man at least found the balm for his wounds. When he knew how broken he was he offered Lucy her release. Her reply was in the words of the English girl to the wounded Napier, "If there is enough of you left to hold your soul, I will marry you."

As soon as he was sufficiently convalescent, they were married.

Lucy insisted that General Hampden should be informed, but the young man knew his father's bitterness, and refused. He relied on securing his consent later, and Lucy, fearing for her patient's life, and having secured her own father's consent, yielded.

It was a mistake.

Oliver Hampden misjudged the depth of his father's feeling, and General Hampden was mortally offended by his having married without informing him.

Oliver adored his father and he sent him a present in token of his desire for forgiveness; but the General had been struck deeply. The present was returned. He wrote: "I want obedience; not sacrifice."

Confident of his wife's ability to overcome any obstacle, the young man bided his time. His wounds, however, and his breach with his father affected his health so much that he went with his wife to the far South, where Major Drayton, now a colonel, had a remnant of what had once been a fine property. Here, for a time, amid the live-oaks and magnolias he appeared to improve. But his father's obdurate refusal to forgive his disobedience preyed on his health, and just after the war closed, he died a few months before his son was born.

In his last days he dwelt much on his father. He made excuses for him, over which his wife simply tightened her lips, while her gray eyes burned with deep resentment.

"He was brought up that way. He cannot help it. He never had anyone to gainsay him. Do not be hard on him. And if he ever sues for pardon, be merciful to him for my sake."

His end came too suddenly for his wife to notify his father in advance, even if she would have done so; for he had been fading gradually and at the last the flame had flared up a little.

Lucy Hampden was too upright a woman not to do what she believed her duty, however contrary to her feelings it might be. So, although it was a bitter thing to her, she wrote to inform General Hampden of his son's death.

It happened by one of the malign chances of fortune that this letter never reached its destination, General Hampden did not learn of Oliver's death until some weeks later, when he heard of it by accident. It was a terrible blow to him, for time was softening the asperity of his temper, and he had just made up his mind to make friends with his son. He attributed the failure to inform him of Oliver's illness and death to the malignity of his wife.

Thus it happened that when her son was born, Lucy Hampden made no announcement of his birth to the General, and he remained in ignorance of it.

IV

The war closed, and about the only thing that appeared to remain unchanged was the relation between General Hampden and Colonel Drayton. Everything else underwent a change, for war eats up a land.

General Hampden, soured and embittered by his domestic troubles, but stern in his resolve and vigorous in his intellect, was driven by his loneliness to adapt himself to the new conditions. He applied his unabated energies to building up a new fortune. His decision, his force, and his ability soon placed him at the head of one of the earliest new enterprises in the State—a broken-down railway—which he re-organized and brought to a full measure of success.

Colonel Drayton, on the other hand, broken in body and in fortunes, found it impossible to adapt himself to the new conditions.

He possessed none of the practical qualities of General Hampden. With a mind richly stored with the wisdom of others, he had the temperament of a dreamer and poet and was unable to apply it to any practical end. As shy and reserved as his neighbor was bold and aggressive, he lived in his books and had never been what is known as a successful man. Even before the war he had not been able to hold his own. The exactions of hospitality and of what he deemed his obligations to others had consumed a considerable part of the handsome estate he had inherited, and his plantation was mortgaged. What had been thus begun, the war had completed.

When his plantation was sold, his old neighbor and enemy bought it, and the Colonel had the mortification of knowing that Drayton Hall was at last in the hands of a Hampden. What he did not know was that General Hampden, true to his vow, never put his foot on the plantation except to ride down the road and see that all his orders for its proper cultivation were carried out.

Colonel Drayton tried teaching school, but it appeared that everyone else was teaching at that time, and after attempting it for a year or two, he gave it up and confined himself to writing philosophical treatises for the press, which were as much out of date as the Latin and Greek names which he signed to them. As these contributions were usually returned, he finally devoted himself to writing agricultural essays for an agricultural paper, in which he met with more success than he had done when he was applying his principles himself.

"If farms were made of paper he'd beat Cincinnatus," said the General.

Lucy Hampden, thrown on her own resources, in the town in the South in which her husband had died, had for some time been supporting herself and her child by teaching. She had long urged her father to come to them, but he had always declined, maintaining that a man was himself only in the country, and in town was merely a unit. When, however, the plantation was sold and his daughter wrote for him, he went to her, and the first time that the little boy was put in his arms, both he and she knew that he would never go away again. That evening as they sat together in the fading light on the veranda of the little house which Lucy had taken, amid the clambering roses and jasmine, the old fellow said, "I used to think that I ought to have been killed in battle at the head of my men when I was shot, but perhaps, I may have been saved to bring up this young man."

His daughter's smile, as she leant over and kissed him, showed very clearly what she thought of it, and before a week was out, the Colonel felt that he was not only still of use, but was, perhaps, the most necessary, and, with one exception, the most important member of the family.

Nevertheless, there were hard times before them. The Colonel was too old-fashioned; too slow for the new movement of life, and just enough behind the times to be always expecting to succeed and always failing.

But where the father failed the daughter succeeded. She soon came to be known as one of the efficient women of the community, as her father, who was now spoken of as "the old Colonel," came to be recognized as one of the picturesque figures of that period. He was always thought of in connection with the boy. The two were hardly ever apart, and they were soon known throughout the town—the tall, thin old gentleman who looked out on the world with his mild blue eyes and kindly face, and the chubby, red-cheeked, black-eyed boy, whose tongue was always prattling, and who looked out with his bright eyes on all the curious things which, common-place to the world, are so wonderful to a boy.

The friendship between an old man and a little child is always touching; they grew nearer together day by day, and the old Colonel and little Oliver soon appeared to understand each other, and to be as dependent on each other as if they had both been of the same age. The child, somewhat reserved with others, was bold enough with his grandfather. They held long discussions together over things that interested the boy; went sight-seeing in company to where the water ran over an old mill-wheel, or where a hen and her chickens lived in a neighbor's yard, or a litter of puppies gamboled under an outhouse, or a bird had her nest and little ones in a jasmine in an old garden, and Colonel Drayton told the boy wonderful stories of the world which was as unknown to him as the present world was to the Colonel.

So matters went, until the Christmas when the boy was seven years old.

V

Meantime, General Hampden was facing a new foe. His health had suddenly given way, and he was in danger of becoming blind. His doctor had given him his orders—orders which possibly he might not have taken had not the spectre of a lonely old man in total darkness begun to haunt him. He had been "working too hard," the doctor told him.

"Working hard! Of course, I have been working hard!" snapped the General, fiercely, with his black eyes glowering. "What else have I to do but work? I shall always work hard."

The doctor knew something of the General's trouble. He had been a surgeon in the hospital where young Oliver Hampden had been when Lucy Drayton found him.

"You must stop," he said, quietly. "You will not last long unless you do."

"How long!" demanded the General, quite calmly.

"Oh! I cannot say that. Perhaps, a year—perhaps, less. You have burned your candle too fast." He glanced at the other's unmoved face. "You need change. You ought to go South this winter."

"I should only change my skies and not my thoughts," said the General, his memory swinging back to the past.

The doctor gazed at him curiously. "What is the use of putting out your eyes and working yourself to death when you have everything that money can give?"

"I have nothing! I work to forget that," snarled the General, fiercely.

The doctor remained silent.

The General thought over the doctor's advice and finally followed it, though not for the reason the physician supposed.

Something led him to select the place where his son had gone and where his body lay amid the magnolias. If he was going to die, he would carry out a plan which he had formed in the lonely hours when he lay awake between the strokes of the clock. He would go and see that his son's grave was cared for, and if he could, would bring him back home at last. Doubtless, "that woman's" consent could be bought. She had possibly married again. He hoped she had.

VI

Christmas is always the saddest of seasons to a lonely man, and General Hampden, when he landed in that old Southern town on the afternoon of Christmas Eve, would not have been lonelier in a desert. The signs of Christmas preparation and the sounds of Christmas cheer but made him lonelier. For years, flying from the Furies, he had immersed himself in work and so, in part, had forgotten his troubles; but the removal of this prop let him fall flat to the earth.

As soon as the old fellow had gotten settled in his room at the hotel he paid a visit to his son's grave, piloted to the cemetery by a friendly and garrulous old Negro hackman, who talked much about Christmas and "the holidays."

"Yes, suh, dat he had known Cap'n Ham'n. He used to drive him out long as he could drive out. He had been at his funeral. He knew Mrs. Ham'n, too. She sutney is a fine lady," he wound up in sincere eulogy.

The General gave a grunt.

He was nearer to his son than he had ever been since the day he last saw him in all the pride and beauty of a gallant young soldier.

The grave, at least, was not neglected. It was marked by a modest cross, on which was the Hampden coat-of-arms and the motto, "*Loyal*," and it was banked in fresh evergreens, and some flowers had been placed on it only that afternoon. It set the General to thinking.

When he returned to his hotel, he found the loneliness unbearable. His visit to his son's grave had opened the old wound and awakened all his memories. He knew now that he had ruined his life. The sooner the doctor's forecast came true, the better. He had no care to live longer. He would return to work and die in harness.

He sent his servant to the office and arranged for his car to be put on the first train next morning.

Then, to escape from his thoughts, he strolled out in the street where the shopping crowds streamed along, old and young, poor and well-to-do, their arms full of bundles, their faces eager, and their eyes alight.

General Hampden seemed to himself to be walking among ghosts.

As he stalked on, bitter and lonely, he was suddenly run into by a very little boy, in whose small arms was so big a bundle that he could scarcely see over it. The shock of the collision knocked the little fellow down, sitting flat on the pavement, still clutching his bundle. But his face after the first shadow of surprise lit up again.

"I beg your pardon, sir—that was my fault," he said, with so quaint an imitation of an old person that the General could not help smiling. With a cheery laugh, he tried to rise to his feet, but the bundle was too heavy, and he would not let it go.

The General bent over him and, with an apology, set him on his feet.

"I beg *your* pardon, sir. That was *my* fault. That is a pretty big bundle you have."

"Yes, sir; and I tell you, it is pretty heavy, too," the manikin said, proudly. "It's a Christmas gift." He started on, and the General turned with him.

"A Christmas gift! It must be a fine one. Who gave it to you?" demanded the General, with a smile at the little fellow's confidence.

"It is a fine one! Didn't anybody give it to me. We're giving it to somebody."

"Oh! You are? To whom?"

"I'll tell you; but you must promise not to tell."

"I promise I will not tell a soul. I cross my heart."

He made a sign as he remembered he used to do in his boyhood.

The boy looked up at him doubtfully with a shade of disapproval.

"My grandfather says that you must not cross your heart—'t a gentleman's word is enough," he said, quaintly.

"Oh, he does? Well, I give my word."

"Well—" He glanced around to see that no one was listening, and sidling a little nearer, lowered his voice: "It's a great-coat for grandfather!"

"A great-coat! That's famous!" exclaimed the General.

"Yes, isn't it? You see—he's mighty old and he's got a bad cough—he caught it in the army, and I have to take care of him. Don't you think that's right?"

"Of course, I do," said the General, envying one grandfather.

"That's what I tell him. So mamma and I have bought this for him."

"He must be a proud grandfather," said the General, with envy biting deeper at his heart.

"I have another grandfather; but I don't like *him*," continued the little fellow.

"I am sorry for that," said the General, sincerely. "Why is that?"

"He was mean to my father, and he is mean to my mother." His voice conveyed a sudden bitterness.

"Oh!"

"Mamma says I must like him; but I do not. I just can't. You would not like a man who was mean to your mother, would you!"

143

"I would not," declared the General, truthfully.

"And I am not going to like him," asserted the boy, with firmness.

The General suddenly pitied one grandfather.

They had come to a well-lighted corner, and as the boy lifted his face, the light fell on it. Something about the bright, sturdy countenance with its frank, dark eyes and brown hair suddenly sent the General back thirty years to a strip of meadow on which two children were playing: one a dark-eyed boy as sturdy as this one. It was like an arrow in his heart. "With a gasp he came back to the present. His thoughts pursued him even here.

"What is your name?" he asked as he was feeling in his pocket for a coin.

"Oliver Drayton Hampden, sir."

The words were perfectly clear.

The General's heart stopped beating and then gave a bound. The skies suddenly opened for him and then shut up again.

His exclamation brought the child to a stop and he glanced up at him in vague wonder. The General stooped and gazed at him searchingly, almost fiercely. The next second he had pounced upon him and lifted him in his arms while the bundle fell to the pavement.

"My boy! I am your grandfather," he cried, kissing him violently. "I am your grandfather Hampden."

The child was lost in amazement for a moment, and then, putting his hands against the General's face, he pushed him slowly away.

"Put me down, please," he said, with that gravity which in a child means so much.

General Hampden set him down on the pavement. The boy looked at him searchingly for a second, and then turned in silence and lifted his bundle. The General's face wore a puzzled look— he had solved many problems, but he had never had one more difficult than this. His heart yearned toward the child, and he knew that on his own wisdom at that moment might depend his future happiness. On his next words might hang for him life or death. The expression on the boy's face, and the very set of his little back as he sturdily tugged at his burden, recalled his father, and with it the General recognized the obstinacy which he knew lurked in the Hampden blood, which had once been his pride.

"Oliver," he said, gravely, leaning down over the boy and

putting his hand on him gently, "there has been a great mistake. I am going home with you to your mother and tell her so. I want to see her and your grandfather, and I think I can explain everything."

The child turned and gazed at him seriously, and then his face relaxed. He recognized his deep sincerity.

"All right." He turned and walked down the street, bending under his burden. The General offered to carry it for him, but he declined.

"I can carry it," was the only answer he made except once when, as the General rather insisted, he said firmly, "I want to carry it myself," and tottered on.

A silence fell on them for a moment. A young man passing them spoke to the child cheerily.

"Hullo, Oliver! A Christmas present? — That's a great boy," he said, in sheer friendliness to the General, and passed on. The boy was evidently well known.

Oliver nodded; then feeling that some civility was due on his part to his companion, he said briefly, "That's a friend of mine."

"Evidently."

The General, even in his perplexity, smiled at the quaint way the child imitated the manners of older men.

Just then they came to a little gate and the boy's manner changed.

"If you will wait, I will run around and put my bundle down. I am afraid my grandfather might see it." He lowered his voice for the first time since the General had introduced himself. Then he disappeared around the house.

Oliver, having slipped in at the back door and carefully reconnoitred the premises, tripped up stairs with his bundle to his mother's room. He was so excited over his present that he failed to observe her confusion at his sudden entrance, or her hasty hiding away of something on which she was working. Colonel Drayton was not the only member of that household that Christmas who was to receive a great-coat.

When Oliver had untied his bundle, nothing would serve but he must put on the coat to show his mother how his grandfather would look in it. As even with the sleeves rolled up and with his arms held out to keep it from falling off him, the tails dragged for some distance on the floor and only the top of his head was visible above the collar, the resemblance was possibly not wholly exact. But it appeared to satisfy the boy. He was showing how his grandfather walked, when he suddenly recalled his new acquaintance.

"I met my other grandfather, on the street, mamma, and he came home with me." He spoke quite naturally.

"Met your other grandfather!" Mrs. Hampden looked mystified.

"He says he is my grandfather, and he looks like papa. I reckon he 's my other grandfather. He ran against me in the street and knocked me down, and then came home with me."

"Came home with you!" repeated Mrs. Hampden, still in a maze, and with a vague trouble dawning in her face.

"Yes 'm."

Oliver went over the meeting again.

His mother's face meantime showed the tumult of emotion that was sweeping over her. Why had General Hampden come? What had he come for? To try and take her boy from her?

At the thought her face and form took on something of the lioness that guards her whelp. Then as the little boy repeated what his grandfather had said of his reason for coming home with him, her face softened again. She heard a voice saying, "If he ever sues for pardon, be merciful to him for my sake." She remembered what day it was: the Eve of the day of Peace and Good-will toward all men. He must have come for Peace, and Peace it should be. She would not bring up her boy under the shadow of that feud which had blighted both sides of his race so long.

"Oliver," she said, "you must go down and let him in. Say I will come down."

"I will not like him," said the child, his eyes on her face.

"Oh, yes, you must; he is your grandfather."

"You do not love him, and I will not." The sturdy little figure and the serious face with the chin already firm for such a child, the dark, grave eyes and the determined speech, were so like his father that the widow gave half a cry.

"You must, my son, and I will try. Your father would wish it."

The little boy pondered for a second.

"Very well, mamma; but he must be good to you."

As the little fellow left the room, the widow threw herself on her knees.

VII

As General Hampden stood and waited in the dusk, he felt that his whole life and future depended on the issue of the next few moments. He determined to take matters in his own hand. Every moment might tell against him and might decide his fate. So, without waiting longer, he rang the bell. A minute later he heard steps within, and the door was opened by one who he knew must be Colonel Drayton, though had he met him elsewhere he should not have recognized the white hair and the thin, bent form as that of his old friend and enemy. Colonel Drayton had evidently not seen his grandson yet, for he spoke as to a stranger.

"Will you not walk in, sir!" he said cordially. "I was expecting my little grandson who went out a short while ago." He peered up the street. "Did you wish to see my daughter? You will find us in a little confusion—Christinas time is always a busy season with us on account of our young man: my grandson." He lingered with pride over the words.

The General stepped into the light.

"Wilmer Drayton! Don't you know me? I am Oliver Hampden, and I have come to apologize to you for all I have done which has offended you, and to ask you to be friends with me." He held out his hand.

The old Colonel stepped back, and under the shock of surprise paused for a moment.

"Oliver Hampden!" The next moment he stepped forward and took his hand.

"Come in, Oliver," he said, gently, and putting his other arm around the General's shoulder, he handed him into the little cosy, fire-lighted room as though nothing had happened since he had done the same the last time fifty years before.

At this moment the door opened and the little boy entered with mingled mysteriousness and importance. Seeing the two gentlemen standing together, he paused with a mystified look in his wide-open eyes, trying to comprehend the situation.

"Oliver, come here," said the Colonel, quietly. "This is your other grandfather."

The boy came forward, and, wheeling, stood close beside the Colonel, facing General Hampden, like a soldier dressing by his file-closer.

"*You* are my grandfather," he said, glancing up at the Colonel.

The Colonel's eyes glowed with a soft light.

"Yes, my boy; and so is he. We are friends again, and you must love him—just as you do me."

"I will not love him as much," was the sturdy answer.

It was the General who spoke next.

"That is right, my boy. All I ask is that you will love me some." He was pleading with this young commissioner.

"I will, if you are good to my mother." His eyes were fastened on him without a tremor, and the General's deep-set eyes began to glow with hope.

"That's a bargain," he said holding out his hand. The boy took it gravely.

Just then the door opened and Lucy Hampden entered. Her face was calm and her form was straight. Her eyes, deep and burning, showed that she was prepared either for peace or war. It was well for the General that he had chosen peace. Better otherwise had he charged once more the deadliest battle line he had ever faced. For a moment the General saw only Lucy Fielding.

With a woman's instinct the young widow comprehended at the first glance what had taken place, and although her face was white, her eyes softened as she advanced. The General had turned and faced her. He could not utter a word, but the boy sprang towards her and, wheeling, stood by her side.

Taking his hand, she led him forward.

"Oliver," she said, gently, "this is your father's father." Then to the General, in a dead silence—"Father, this is your son's son."

The General clasped them both in his arms.

"Forgive me. Forgive me. I have prayed for *his* forgiveness, for I can never forgive myself."

"He forgave you," said the widow, simply.

VIII

No young king was ever put to bed with more ceremony or more devotion than was that little boy that night. Two old gentlemen were his grooms of the bedchamber and saw him to bed together.

The talk was all of Christmas, and the General envied the ease with which the other grandfather carried on the conversation. But when the boy, having kissed his grandfather, said of his own accord, "Now, I must kiss my *other* grandfather," he envied no man on earth.

The next morning when Oliver Hampden, before the first peep of light, waked in his little bed, which stood at the foot of his grandfather's bed in the tiny room which they occupied together, and standing up, peeped over the footboard to catch his grandfather's "Christmas gift," he was surprised to find that the bed was empty and undisturbed. Then having tiptoed in and caught his mother, he stole down the stairs and softly opened the sitting-room door where he heard the murmur of voices. The fire was burning dim, and on either side sat the two old gentlemen in their easy chairs, talking amicably and earnestly as they had been talking when he kissed them "good-night." Neither one had made the suggestion that it was bedtime; but when at the first break of day the rosy boy in his night-clothes burst in upon them with his shout of "Christmas gift," and his ringing laughter, they both knew that the long feud was at last ended, and peace was established forever.

The Silent Sisters
Israel Zangwill

They had quarrelled in girlhood, and mutually declared their intention never to speak to each other again, wetting and drying their forefingers to the accompaniment of an ancient childish incantation, and while they lived on the paternal farm they kept their foolish oath with the stubbornness of a slow country stock, despite the alternate coaxing and chastisement of their parents, notwithstanding the perpetual everyday contact of their lives, through every vicissitude of season and weather, of sowing and reaping, of sun and shade, of joy and sorrow.

Death and misfortune did not reconcile them, and when their father died and the old farm was sold up, they travelled to London in the same silence, by the same train, in search of similar situations. Service separated them for years, though there was only a stone's throw between them. They often stared at each other in the streets.

Honor, the elder, married a local artisan, and two and a half years later, Mercy, the younger, married a fellow-workman of Honor's husband. The two husbands were friends, and often visited each other's houses, which were on opposite sides of the same sordid street, and the wives made them welcome. Neither Honor nor Mercy suffered an allusion to their breach; it was understood that their silence must be received in silence. Each of the children had a quiverful of children who played and quarrelled together in the streets and in one another's houses, but not even the street affrays and mutual grievances of the children could provoke the mothers to words. They stood at their doors in impotent fury, almost bursting with the torture of keeping their mouths shut against the effervescence of angry speech. When either lost a child the other watched the funeral from her window, dumb as the mutes.

The years rolled on, and still the river of silence flowed between their lives. Their good looks faded, the burden of life and child-bearing was heavy upon them. Grey hairs streaked their brown tresses, then brown hairs streaked their grey tresses. The puckers of age replaced the dimples of youth. The years rolled on, and Death grew busy among the families. Honor's husband died, and Mercy lost a son, who died a week after his wife. Cholera took several of the younger children. But the sisters themselves lived on, bent and shrivelled by toil and sorrow, even more than by the slow frost of the years.

Then one day Mercy took to her death-bed. An internal disease, too long neglected, would carry her off within a week. So the doctor told Jim, Mercy's husband.

Through him, the news travelled to Honor's eldest son, who still lived with her. By the evening it reached Honor.

She went upstairs abruptly when her son told her, leaving him wondering at her stony aspect. When she came down she was bonneted and shawled. He was filled with joyous amaze to see her hobble across the street and for the first time in her life pass over her sister Mercy's threshold.

As Honor entered the sick-room, with pursed lips, a light leapt into the wasted, wrinkled countenance of the dying creature. She raised herself slightly in bed, her lips parted, then shut tightly, and her face darkened.

Honor turned angrily to Mercy's husband, who hung about impotently. "Why did you let her run down so low?" she said.

"I didn't know," the old man stammered, taken aback by her presence even more than by her question. "She was always a woman to say nothin'."

Honor put him impatiently aside and examined the medicine bottle on the bedside table.

"Isn't it time she took her dose?"

"I dessay."

Honor snorted wrathfully. "What's the use of a man?" she inquired, as she carefully measured out the fluid and put it to her sister's lips, which opened to receive it, and then closed tightly again.

"How is your wife feeling now?" Honor asked after a pause.

"How are you, now, Mercy?" asked the old man awkwardly.

The old woman shook her head. "I'm a-goin' fast, Jim," she grumbled weakly, and a tear of self-pity trickled down her parchment cheek.

"What rubbidge she do talk!" cried Honor, sharply. "Why d'ye stand there like a tailor's dummy? Why don't you tell her to cheer up?"

"Cheer up, Mercy," quavered the old man, hoarsely.

But Mercy groaned instead, and turned fretfully on her other side, with her face to the wall.

"I'm too old, I'm too old," she moaned, "this is the end o' me."

"Did you ever hear the like?" Honor asked Jim, angrily, as she smoothed his wife's pillow. "She was always conceited about her age, settin' herself up as the equals of her elders, and here am I, her elder sister, as carried her in my arms when I was five and she was two, still hale and strong, and with no mind for underground for many a day. Nigh three times her age I was once, mind you, and now she has the imperence to talk of dyin' before me."

She took off her bonnet and shawl. "Send one o' the kids to tell my boy I'm stayin' here," she said, "and then just you get 'em all to bed—there's too much noise about the house."

The children, who were orphaned grandchildren of the dying woman, were sent to bed, and then Jim himself was packed off to refresh himself for the next day's labours, for the poor old fellow still doddered about the workshop.

The silence of the sick-room spread over the whole house. About ten o'clock the doctor came again and instructed Honor how to alleviate the patient's last hours. All night long she sat watching her dying sister, hand and eye alert to anticipate every wish. No word broke the awful stillness.

The first thing in the morning, Mercy's married daughter, the only child of hers living in London, arrived to nurse her mother. But Honor indignantly refused to be dispossessed.

"A nice daughter you are," she said, "to leave your mother lay a day and a night without a sight o' your ugly face."

"I had to look after the good man, and the little 'uns," the daughter pleaded.

"Then what do you mean by desertin' them now?" the irate old woman retorted. "First you deserts your mother, and then your husband and children. You must go back to them as needs your care. I carried your mother in my arms before you was born, and if she wants anybody else now to look after her, let her just tell me so, and I'll be off in a brace o' shakes."

She looked defiantly at the yellow, dried-up creature in the bed. Mercy's withered lips twitched, but no sound came from them. Jim, strung up by the situation, took the word. "You can't do no good up here, the doctor says. You might look after the kids downstairs a bit, when you can spare an hour, and I've got to go to the shop. I'll send you a telegraph if there's a change," he whispered to the daughter, and she, not wholly discontented to return to her living interests, kissed her mother, lingered a little, and then stole quietly away.

All that day the old women remained together in solemn silence, broken only by the doctor's visit. He reported that Mercy might last a couple of days more. In the evening Jim replaced his sister-in-law, who slept perforce. At midnight she reappeared and sent him to bed. The sufferer tossed about restlessly. At half-past two she awoke, and Honor fed her with some broth, as she would have fed a baby. Mercy, indeed, looked scarcely bigger than an infant, and Honor only had the advantage of her by being puffed out with clothes. A church clock in the distance struck three. Then the silence fell deeper. The watcher drowsed, the lamp flickered, tossing her shadow about the walls as if she, too, were turning feverishly from side to side. A strange ticking made itself heard in the wainscoting. Mercy sat up with a scream of terror. "Jim!" she shrieked, "Jim!"

Honor started up, opened her mouth to cry "Hush!" then checked herself, suddenly frozen.

"Jim," cried the dying woman, "listen! Is that the death spider?"

Honor listened, her blood curdling. Then she went towards the door and opened it. "Jim," she said, in low tones, speaking towards the landing, "tell her it's nothing, it's only a mouse. She was always a nervous little thing." And she closed the door softly, and pressing her trembling sister tenderly back on the pillow, tucked her up snugly in the blanket.

Next morning, when Jim was really present, the patient begged pathetically to have a grandchild with her in the room, day and night. "Don't leave me alone again," she quavered, "don't leave me alone with not a soul to talk to." Honor winced, but said nothing.

The youngest child, who did not have to go to school, was brought—a pretty little boy with brown curls, which the sun, streaming through the panes, turned to gold. The morning passed slowly. About noon Mercy took the child's hand, and smoothed his curls.

"My sister Honor had golden curls like that," she whispered.

"They were in the family, Bobby," Honor answered. "Your granny had them, too, when she was a girl."

There was a long pause. Mercy's eyes were half-glazed. But her vision was inward now.

"The mignonette will be growin' in the gardens, Bobby," she murmured.

"Yes, Bobby, and the heart's-ease," said Honor, softly. "We lived in the country, you know, Bobby."

"There is flowers in the country," Bobby declared gravely.

"Yes, and trees," said Honor. "I wonder if your granny remembers when we were larruped for stealin' apples."

"Ay, that I do, Bobby, he, he," croaked the dying creature, with a burst of enthusiasm. "We was a pair o' tomboys. The farmer he ran after us cryin' 'Ye! ye!' but we wouldn't take no gar. He, he, he!"

Honor wept at the laughter. The native idiom, unheard for half a century, made her face shine under the tears. "Don't let your granny excite herself, Bobby. Let me give her her drink." She moved the boy aside, and Mercy's lips automatically opened to the draught.

"Tom was wi' us, Bobby," she gurgled, still vibrating with amusement, "and he tumbled over on the heather. He, he!"

"Tom is dead this forty year, Bobby," whispered Honor.

Mercy's head fell back, and an expression of supreme exhaustion came over the face. Half an hour passed. Bobby was called down to dinner. The doctor had been sent for. The silent sisters were alone. Suddenly Mercy sat up with a jerk.

"It be growin' dark, Tom," she said hoarsely, "'haint it time to call the cattle home from the ma'shes?"

"She's talkin' rubbidge again," said Honor, chokingly. "Tell her she's in London, Bobby."

A wave of intelligence traversed the sallow face. Still sitting up, Mercy bent towards the side of the bed. "Ah, is Honor still there? Kiss me—Bobby." Her hands groped blindly. Honor bent down and the old women's withered lips met.

And in that kiss Mercy passed away into the greater Silence.

The Hatred of the Queen: A Story of Burma
L. Adams Beck

Most wonderful is the Irawadi, the mighty river of Burma. In all the world elsewhere is no such river, bearing the melted snows from its mysterious sources in the high places of the mountains. The dawn rises upon its league-wide flood; the moon walks upon it with silver feet. It is the pulsing heart of the land, living still though so many rules and rulers have risen and fallen beside it, their pomps and glories drifting like flotsam down the river to the eternal ocean that is the end of all — and the beginning. Dead civilizations strew its banks, dreaming in the torrid sunshine of glories that were of blood-stained gold, jewels wept from woeful crowns, nightmare dreams of murder and terror; dreaming also of heavenly beauty, for the Lord Buddha looks down in moonlight peace upon the land that leaped to kiss His footprints, that has laid its heart in the hand of the Blessed One, and shares therefore in His bliss and content. The Land of the Lord Buddha, where the myriad pagodas lift their golden flames of worship everywhere, and no idlest wind can pass but it ruffles the bells below the *htees* until they send forth their silver ripple of music to swell the hymn of praise!

There is a little bay on the bank of the flooding river — a silent, deserted place of sand-dunes and small hills. When a ship is in sight, some poor folk come and spread out the red lacquer that helps their scanty subsistence, and the people from the passing ship land and barter and in a few minutes are gone on their busy way and silence settles down once more. They neither know nor care that, near by, a mighty city spread its splendor for miles along the river bank, that the king known as Lord of the Golden Palace, The Golden Foot, Lord of the White Elephant, held his state there with

157

balls of magnificence, obsequious women, fawning courtiers and all the riot and color of an Eastern tyranny. How should they care? Now there are ruins — ruins, and the cobras slip in and out through the deserted holy places. They breed their writhing young in the sleeping-chambers of queens, the tigers mew in the moonlight, and the giant spider, more terrible than the cobra, strikes with its black poison-claw and, paralyzing the life of the victim, sucks its brain with slow, lascivious pleasure.

Are these foul creatures more dreadful than some of the men, the women, who dwelt in these palaces — the more evil because of the human brain that plotted and foresaw? That is known only to the mysterious Law that in silence watches and decrees.

But this is a story of the dead days of Pagan, by the Irawadi, and it will be shown that, as the Lotus of the Lord Buddha grows up a white splendor from the black mud of the depths, so also may the soul of a woman.

In the days of the Lord of the White Elephant, the King Pagan Men, was a boy named Mindon, son of second Queen and the King. So, at least, it was said in the Golden Palace, but those who knew the secrets of such matters whispered that, when the King had taken her by the hand she came to him no maid, and that the boy was the son of an Indian trader. Furthermore it was said that she herself was woman of the Rajputs, knowledgeable in spells, incantations and elemental spirits such as the Beloos that terribly haunt waste places, and all Powers that move in the dark, and that thus she had won the King. Certainly she had been captured by the King's war-boats off the coast from a trading-ship bound for Ceylon, and it was her story that, because of her beauty, she was sent thither to serve as concubine to the King, Tissa of Ceylon. Being captured, she was brought to the Lord of the Golden Palace. The tongue she spoke was strange to all the fighting men, but it was wondrous to see how swiftly she learnt theirs and spoke it with a sweet ripple such as is in the throat of a bird.

She was beautiful exceedingly, with a color of pale gold upon her and lengths of silk-spun hair, and eyes like those of a jungle-deer, and water might run beneath the arch of her foot without wetting it, and her breasts were like the cloudy pillows where the sun couches at setting. Now, at Pagan, the name they called her was Dwaymenau, but her true name, known only to herself, was Sundari, and she knew not the Law of the Blessed Buddha but was a heathen accursed. In the strong hollow of her hand she held the heart of the King, so that on the birth of her son she had risen from a mere concubine to be the second Queen and a power to whom all bowed. The First Queen, Maya, languished in her palace, her pale beauty wasting daily, deserted and lonely, for she had been the light of the King's eyes until the coming of the Indian woman, and she loved her lord with a great love and was a noble woman brought up in honour and all things becoming a queen. But sigh as she would, the King came never. All night he lay in the arms of Dwaymenau, all day he sat beside her, whether at the great water pageants or at the festival when the dancing-girls swayed and postured before him in her gilded chambers. Even when be went forth to hunt the tiger, she went with him as far as a woman may go, and then stood back only because he would not risk his jewel, her life. So all that was evil in the man she fostered and all that was good she cherished not at all, fearing lest he should return to the Queen. At her will he had consulted the Hlwot Daw, the Council of the Woon-gyees or Ministers, concerning a divorce of the Queen, but this they told him could not be since she had kept all the laws of Manu, being faithful, noble and beautiful and having borne him a son.

For, before the Indian woman had come to the King, the Queen had borne a son, Ananda, and he was pale and slender and the King despised him because of the wiles of Dwaymenau, saying he was fit only to sit among the women, having the soul of a slave, and he laughed bitterly as the pale child crouched in the corner to see him pass. If his eyes had been clear, he would have known that here was no slave, but a heart as much greater than his own as the spirit is stronger than the body. But this he did not know and he strode past with Dwaymenau's boy on his shoulder, laughing with cruel glee.

And this boy, Mindon, was beautiful and strong as his mother, pale olive of face, with the dark and crafty eyes of the cunning Indian traders, with black hair and a body straight, strong and long in the leg for his years — apt at the beginnings of bow, sword and spear — full of promise, if the promise was only words and looks.

And so matters rested in the palace until Ananda had ten years and Mindon nine.

It was the warm and sunny winter and the days were pleasant, and on a certain day the Queen, Maya, went with her ladies to worship the Blessed One at the Thapinyu Temple, looking down upon the swiftly flowing river. The temple was exceedingly rich and magnificent, so gilded with pure gold-leaf that it appeared of solid gold. And about the upper part were golden bells beneath the jewelled *htee*, which wafted very sweetly in the wind and gave forth a crystal-clear music. The ladies bore in their hands more gold-leaf, that they might acquire merit by offering this for the service of the Master of the Law, and indeed this temple was the offering of the Queen herself, who, because she bore the name of the Mother of the Lord, excelled in good works and was the Moon of this lower world in charity and piety.

Though wan with grief and anxiety, this Queen was beautiful. Her eyes, like mournful lakes of darkness, were lovely in the pale ivory of her face. Her lips were nobly cut and calm, and by the favour of the Guardian Nats, she was shaped with grace and health, a worthy mother of kings. Also she wore her jewels like a mighty princess, a magnificence to which all the people shikoed as she passed, folding their hands and touching the forehead while they bowed down, kneeling.

Before the colossal image of the Holy One she made her offering and, attended by her women, she sat in meditation, drawing consolation from the Tranquillity above her and the silence of the shrine. This ended, the Queen rose and did obeisance to the Lord and, retiring, paced back beneath the White Canopy and entered the courtyard where the palace stood — a palace of noble teakwood, brown and golden and carved like lace into strange fantasies of spires and pinnacles and branches where Nats and Tree Spirits and Beloos and swaying river maidens mingled and met amid fruits and leaves and flowers in a wild and joyous confusion. The faces, the blowing garments, whirled into points with the swiftness of the dance, were touched with gold, and so glad was the building that it seemed as if a very light wind might whirl it to the sky, and even the sad Queen stopped to rejoice in its beauty as it blossomed in the sunlight.

And even as she paused, her little son Ananda rushed to meet her, pale and panting, and flung himself into her arms with dry sobs like those of an overrun man. She soothed him until he could speak, and then the grief made way in a rain of tears.

"Mindon has killed my deer. He bared his knife, slit his throat and cast him in the ditch and there he lies."

"There will he not lie long!" shouted Mindon, breaking from the palace to the group where all were silent now. "For the worms will eat him and the dogs pick clean his bones, and he will show his horns at his lords no more. If you loved him, White-liver, you should have taught him better manners to his betters.

With a stifled shriek Ananda caught the slender knife from his girdle and flew at Mindon like a cat of the woods. Such things were done daily by young and old, and this was a long sorrow come to a head between the boys.

Suddenly, lifting the hangings of the palace gateway, before them stood the mother of Mindon, the Lady Dwaymenau, pale as wool, having heard the shout of her boy, so that the two Queens faced each other, each holding the shoulders of her son, and the ladies watched, mute as fishes, for it was years since these two had met.

"What have you done to my son?" breathed Maya the Queen, dry in the throat and all but speechless with passion. For indeed his face, for a child, was ghastly.

"Look at his knife! What would he do to my son?" Dwaymenau was stiff with hate and spoke as to a slave.

"He has killed my deer and mocks me because I loved him, He is the devil in this place. Look at the devils in his eyes. Look quick before he smiles, my mother."

And indeed, young as the boy was, an evil thing sat in either eye and glittered upon them. Dwaymenau passed her hand across his brow, and he smiled and they were gone.

"The beast ran at me and would have flung me with his horns," he said, looking up brightly at his mother. "He had the madness upon him. I struck once and he was dead. My father would have done the same.

"That would he not!" said Queen Maya bitterly. "Your father would have crept up, fawning on the deer, and offered him the fruits he loved, stroking him the while. And in trust the beast would have eaten, and the poison in the fruit would have slain him. For the people of your father meet neither man nor beast in fair fight. With a kiss they stab!"

Horror kept the women staring and silent. No one had dreamed that the scandal had reached the Queen. Never had she spoken or looked her knowledge but endured all in patience. Now it sprang out like a sword among them, and they feared for Maya, whom all loved.

Mindon did not understand. It was beyond him, but he saw

he was scorned. Dwaymenau, her face rigid as a mask, looked pitilessly at the shaking Queen, and each word dropped from her mouth, hard and cold as the falling of diamonds. She refused the insult.

"If it is thus you speak of our lord and my love, what wonder he forsakes you? Mother of a craven milk runs in your veins and his for blood. Take your slinking brat away and weep together! My son and I go forth to meet the King as he comes from hunting, and to welcome him kingly!" She caught her boy to her with a magnificent gesture; he flung his little arm about her, and laughing loudly they went off together.

The tension relaxed a little when they were out of sight. The women knew that, since Dwaymenau had refused to take the Queen's meaning, she would certainly not carry her complaint to the King. They guessed at her reason for this forbearance, but, be that as it might, it was certain that no other person would dare to tell him and risk the fate that waits the messenger of evil.

The eldest lady led away the Queen, now almost tottering in the reaction of fear and pain. Oh, that she had controlled her speech! Not for her own sake — for she had lost all and the beggar can lose no more — but for the boy's sake, the unloved child that stood between the stranger and her hopes. For him she had made a terrible enemy. Weeping, the boy followed her.

"Take comfort, little son," she said, drawing him to her tenderly. "The deer can suffer no more. For the tigers, he does not fear them. He runs in green woods now where there is none to hunt. He is up and away. The Blessed One was once a deer as gentle as yours."

But still the child wept, and the Queen broke down utterly. "Oh, if life be a dream, let us wake, let us wake!" she sobbed. "For evil things walk in it that cannot live in the light. Or let us dream deeper and forget. Go, little son, yet stay — for who can tell what waits us when the King comes. Let us meet him here."

For she believed that Dwaymenau would certainly carry the tale of her speech to the King, and, if so, what hope but death together?

That night, after the feasting, when the girls were dancing the dance of the fairies and spirits, in gold dresses, winged on the legs and shoulders, and high, gold-spired and pinnacled caps, the King missed the little Prince, Ananda, and asked why he was absent.

No one answered, the women looking upon each other, until

Dwaymenau, sitting beside him, glimmering with rough pearls and rubies, spoke smoothly: "Lord, worshipped and beloved, the two boys quarreled this day, and Ananda's deer attacked our Mindon. He had a madness upon him and thrust with his horns. But, Mindon, your true son, flew in upon him and in a great fight he slit the beast's throat with the knife you gave him. Did he not well?"

"Well," said the King briefly. "But is there no hurt? Have you searched? For he is mine."

There was arrogance in the last sentence and her proud soul rebelled, but smoothly as ever she spoke: "I have searched and there is not the littlest scratch. But Ananda is weeping because the deer is dead, and his mother is angry. What should I do?"

"Nothing. Ananda is worthless and worthless let him be! And for that pale shadow that was once a woman, let her be forgotten. And now, drink, my Queen!"

And Dwaymenau drank but the drink was bitter to her, for a ghost had risen upon her that day. She had never dreamed that such a scandal had been spoken, and it stunned her very soul with fear, that the Queen should know her vileness and the cheat she had put upon the King. As pure maid he had received her, and she knew, none better, what the doom would be if his trust were broken and he knew the child not his. She herself had seen this thing done to a concubine who had a little offended. She was thrust living in a sack and this hung between two earthen jars pierced with small holes, and thus she was set afloat on the terrible river. And not till the slow filling and sinking of the jars was the agony over and the cries for mercy stilled. No, the Queen's speech was safe with her, but was it safe with the Queen? For her silence, Dwaymenau must take measures.

Then she put it all aside and laughed and jested with the King and did indeed for a time forget, for she loved him for his black-browed beauty and his courage and royalty and the childlike trust and the man's passion that mingled in him for her. Daily and nightly such prayers as she made to strange gods were that she might bear a son, true son of his.

Next day, in the noonday stillness when all slept, she led her young son by the hand to her secret chamber, and, holding him upon her knees in that rich and golden place, she lifted his face to hers and stared into his eyes. And so unwavering was her gaze, so mighty the hard, unblinking stare that his own was held against

163

it, and he stared back as the earth stares breathless at the moon. Gradually the terror faded out of his eyes; they glazed as if in a trance; his head fell stupidly against her bosom; his spirit stood on the borderland of being and waited.

Seeing this, she took his palm and, molding it like wax, into the cup of it she dropped clear fluid from a small vessel of pottery with the fylfot upon its side and the disks of the god Shiva. And strange it was to see that lore of India in the palace where the Blessed Law reigned in peace. Then, fixing her eyes with power upon Mindon, she bade him, a pure child, see for her in its clearness.

"Only virgin-pure can see!" she muttered, staring into his eyes. "See! See!"

The eyes of Mindon were closing. He half opened them and looked dully at his palm. His face was pinched and yellow.

"A woman — a child, on a long couch. Dead! I see!"

"See her face. Is her head crowned with the Queen's jewels? See!"

"Jewels. I cannot see her face. It is hidden."

"Why is it hidden?"

"A robe across her face. Oh, let me go!"

"And the child? See!"

"Let me go. Stop — my head — my head! I cannot see. The child is hidden. Her arm holds it. A woman stoops above them."

"A woman? Who? Is it like me? Speak! See!"

"A woman. It is like you, mother — it is like you. I fear very greatly. A knife — a knife! Blood! I cannot see — I cannot speak! I — I sleep."

His face was ghastly white now, his body cold and collapsed. Terrified, she caught him to her breast and relaxed the power of her will upon him. For that moment, she was only the passionate mother and quaked to think she might have hurt him. An hour passed and he slept heavily in her arms, and in agony she watched to see the color steal back into the olive cheek and white lips. In the second hour he waked and stretched himself indolently, yawning like a cat. Her tears dropped like rain upon him as she clasped him violently to her.

He writhed himself free, petulant and spoilt. "Let me be. I hate kisses and women's tricks. I want to go forth and play. I have had a devil's dream.

"What did you see in your dream, prince of my heart?" She

caught frantically at the last chance.

"A deer — a tiger. I have forgotten. Let me go." He ran off and she sat alone with her doubts and fears. Yet triumph colored them too. She saw a dead woman, a dead child, and herself bending above them. She hid the vessel in her bosom and went out among her women.

Weeks passed, and never a word that she dreaded from Maya the Queen. The women of Dwaymenau, questioning the Queen's women, heard that she seemed to have heavy sorrow upon her. Her eyes were like dying lamps and she faded as they. The King never entered her palace. Drowned in Dwaymenau's wiles and beauty, her slave, her thrall, he forgot all else but his fighting, his hunting and his long war-boats, and whether the Queen lived or died, he cared nothing. Better indeed she should die and her place be emptied for the beloved, without offence to her powerful kindred.

And now he was to sail upon a raid against the Shan Tsaubwa, who had denied him tribute of gold and jewels and slaves. Glorious were the boats prepared for war, of brown teak and gilded until they shone like gold. Seventy men rowed them, sword and lance beside each. Warriors crowded them, flags and banners fluttered about them; the shining water reflected the pomp like a mirror and the air rang with song. Dwaymenau stood beside the water with her women, bidding the King farewell, and so he saw her, radiant in the dawn, with her boy beside her, and waved his hand to the last.

The ships were gone and the days languished a little at Pagan. They missed the laughter and royalty of the King, and few men, and those old and weak, were left in the city. The pulse of life beat slower.

And Dwaymenau took rule in the Golden Palace. Queen Maya sat like one in a dream and questioned nothing, and Dwaymenau ruled with wisdom but none loved her. To all she was the interloper, the witch-woman, the out-land upstart. Only the fear of the King guarded her and her boy, but that was strong. The boys played together sometimes, Mindon tyrannizing and cruel, Ananda fearing and complying, broken in spirit.

Maya the Queen walked daily in the long and empty Golden Hall of Audience, where none came now that the King was gone, pacing up and down, gazing wearily at the carved screens and all their woodland beauty of gods that did not hear, of happy spirits that had no pity. Like a spirit herself she passed between the red pillars, appearing and reappearing with steps that made no sound, consumed with hate of the evil woman that had stolen her joy. Like a slow fire it burned in her soul, and the face of the Blessed One was hidden from her, and she had forgotten His peace. In that atmosphere of hate her life dwindled. Her son's dwindled also, and there was talk among the women of some potion that Dwaymenau had been seen to drop into his noontide drink as she went swiftly by. That might he the gossip of malice, but he pined. His eyes were large like a young bird's; his hands like little claws. They thought the departing year would take him with it. What harm? Very certainly the King would shed no tear.

It was a sweet and silent afternoon and she wandered in the great and lonely hall, sickened with the hate in her soul and her fear for her boy. Suddenly she heard flying footsteps — a boy's, running in mad haste in the outer hall, and, following them, bare feet, soft, thudding.

She stopped dead and every pulse cried — Danger! No time to think or breathe when Mindon burst into sight, wild with terror and following close beside him a man — a madman, a short bright dah in his grasp, his jaws grinding foam, his wild eyes starting — one passion to murder. So sometimes from the Nats comes pitiless fury, and men run mad and kill and none knows why.

Maya the Queen stiffened to meet the danger. Joy swept through her soul; her weariness was gone. A fierce smile showed her teeth — a smile of hate, as she stood there and drew her dagger for defense. For defense — the man would rend the boy and turn on her and she would not die. She would live to triumph that the mongrel was dead, and her son, the Prince again and his father's joy — for his heart would turn to the child most surely. Justice was rushing on its victim. She would see it and live content, the long years of agony wiped out in blood, as was fitting. She would not flee; she would see it and rejoice. And as she stood in gladness — these broken thoughts rushing through her like flashes of lightning — Mindon saw her by the pillar and, screaming in anguish for the first time, fled to her for refuge.

She raised her knife to meet the staring eyes, the chalk white face, and drive him back on the murderer. If the man failed, she would not! And even as she did this a strange thing befell. Something stronger than hate swept her away like a leaf on the river; something primeval that lives in the lonely pangs of childbirth, that hides in the womb and breasts of the mother. It was stronger than she. It was not the hated Mindon — she saw him no more. Suddenly it was the eternal Child, lifting dying, appealing eyes to the Woman, as he clung to her knees. She did not think this — she felt it, and it dominated her utterly. The Woman answered. As if it had been her own flesh and blood, she swept the panting body behind her and faced the man with uplifted dagger and knew her victory assured, whether in life or death. On came the horrible rush, the flaming eyes, and, if it was chance that set the dagger against his throat, it was cool strength that drove it home and never wavered until the blood welling from the throat quenched the flame in the wild eyes, and she stood triumphing like a war-goddess, with the man at her feet. Then, strong and flushed, Maya the Queen gathered the half-dead boy in her arms, and, both drenched with blood, they moved slowly down the hall and outside met the hurrying crowd, with Dwaymenau, whom the scream had brought to find her son.

"You have killed him! She has killed him!" Scarcely could the Rajput woman speak. She was kneeling beside him — he hideous with blood. "She hated him always. She has murdered him. Seize her!"

"Woman, what matter your hates and mine?" the Queen said slowly. "The boy is stark with fear. Carry him in and send for old Meh Shway Gon. Woman, be silent!"

When a Queen commands, men and women obey, and a Queen commanded then. A huddled group lifted the child and carried him away, Dwaymenau with them, still uttering wild threats, and the Queen was left alone.

She could not realize what she had done and left undone. She could not understand it. She had hated, sickened with loathing, as it seemed for ages, and now, in a moment it had blown away like a whirlwind that is gone. Hate was washed out of her soul and had left it cool and white as the Lotus of the Blessed One. What power had Dwaymenau to hurt her when that other Power walked beside her? She seemed to float above her in high air and look down upon her with compassion. Strength, virtue flowed in her veins; weakness, fear were fantasies. She could not understand, but knew that here was perfect enlightenment. About her echoed the words of the Blessed One: "Never in this world doth hatred cease by hatred, but only by love. This is an old rule."

"Whereas I was blind, now I see," said Maya the Queen slowly to her own heart. She had grasped the hems of the Mighty.

Words cannot speak the still passion of strength and joy that possessed her. Her step was light. As she walked, her soul sang within her, for thus it is with those that have received the Law. About them is the Peace.

In the dawn she was told that the Queen, Dwaymenau, would speak with her, and without a tremor she who had shaken like a leaf at that name commanded that she should enter. It was Dwaymenau that trembled as she came into that unknown place.

With cloudy brows and eyes that would reveal no secret, she stood before the high seat where the Queen sat pale and majestic.

"Is it well with the boy?" the Queen asked earnestly.

"Well," said Dwaymenau, fingering the silver bosses of her girdle.

"Then — is there more to say?" The tone was that of the great lady who courteously ends an audience. "There is more. The men brought in the body and in its throat your dagger was sticking. And my son has told me that your body was a shield to him. You offered your life for his. I did not think to thank you — but I thank you." She ended abruptly and still her eyes had never met the Queen's.

"I accept your thanks. Yet a mother could do no less."

The tone was one of dismissal but still Dwaymenau lingered.

"The dagger," she said and drew it from her bosom. On the clear, pointed blade the blood had curdled and dried. "I never thought to ask a gift of you, but this dagger is a memorial of my son's danger. May I keep it?"

"As you will. Here is the sheath." From her girdle she drew it —rough silver, encrusted with rubies from the mountains.

The hand rejected it.

"Jewels I cannot take, but bare steel is a fitting gift between us two."

"As you will."

The Queen spoke compassionately, and Dwaymenau, still with veiled eyes, was gone without fare well. The empty sheath lay on the seat — a symbol of the sharp-edged hate that had passed out of her life. She touched the sheath to her lips and, smiling, laid it away.

And the days went by and Dwaymenau came no more before her, and her days were fulfilled with peace. And now again the Queen ruled in the palace wisely and like a Queen, and this Dwaymenau did not dispute, but what her thoughts were no man could tell.

Then came the end.

One night the city awakened to a wild alarm. A terrible fleet of war-boats came sweeping along the river thick as locusts — the war fleet of the Lord of Prome. Battle shouts broke tile peace of the night to horror; axes battered on the outer doors; the roofs of the outer buildings were all aflame. It was no wonderful incident, but a common one enough of those turbulent days — reprisal by a powerful ruler with raids and hates to avenge on the Lord of the Golden Palace. It was indeed a right to be gainsaid only by the strong arm, and the strong arm was absent; as for the men of Pagan, if the guard failed and the women's courage sank, they would return to blackened walls, empty chambers and desolation.

At Pagan the guard was small, indeed, for the King's greed of plunder had taken almost every able man with him. Still, those who were left did what they could, and the women, alert and brave, with but few exceptions, gathered the children and handed such weapons as they could muster to the men, and themselves, taking knives and daggers, helped to defend the inner rooms.

In the farthest, the Queen, having given her commands and encouraged all with brave words, like a wise, prudent princess, sat with her son beside her. Her duty was now to him. Loved or unloved, he was still the heir, the root of the House tree. If all failed, she must make ransom and terms for him, and, if they died, it must be together. He, with sparkling eyes, gray in the danger, stood by her. Thus Dwaymenau found them.

She entered quietly and without any display of emotion and stood before the high seat.

"Great Queen" — she used that title for the first time — "the leader is Meng Kyinyo of Prome. There is no mercy. The end is near. Our men fall fast, the women are fleeing. I have come to say this thing: Save the Prince."

"And how?" asked the Queen, still seated. "I have no power."

"I have sent to Maung Tin, abbot of the Golden Monastery, and he has said this thing. In the Kyoung across the river he can hide one child among the novices. Cut his hair swiftly and put upon him this yellow robe. The time is measured in minutes."

Then the Queen perceived, standing by the pillar, a monk of a stern, dark presence, the creature of Dwaymenau. For an instant she pondered. Was the woman selling the child to death? Dwaymenau spoke no word. Her face was a mask. A minute that seemed an hour drifted by, and the yelling and shrieks for mercy drew nearer.

"There will be pursuit," said the Queen. "They will slay him on the river. Better here with me."

"There will be no pursuit." Dwaymenau fixed her strange eyes on the Queen for the first time.

What moved in those eyes? The Queen could not tell. But despairing, she rose and went to the silent monk, leading the Prince by the hand. Swiftly he stripped the child of the silk pasoh of royalty, swiftly he cut the long black tresses knotted on the little head, and upon the slender golden body he set the yellow robe worn by the Lord Himself on earth, and in the small hand he placed the begging-bowl of the Lord. And now, remote and holy, in the dress that is of all most sacred, the Prince, standing by the monk, turned to his mother and looked with grave eyes upon her, as the child Buddha looked upon his Mother — also a Queen. But Dwaymenau stood by silent and lent no help as the Queen folded the Prince in her arms and laid his hand in the hand of the monk and saw them pass away among the pillars, she standing still and white.

She turned to her rival. "If you have meant truly, I thank you."

"I have meant truly."

She turned to go, but the Queen caught her by the hand.

"Why have you done this?" she asked, looking into the strange eyes of the strange woman.

Something like tears gathered in them for a moment, but she brushed them away as she said hurriedly:

"I was grateful. You saved my son. Is it not enough?"

"No, not enough!" cried the Queen. "There is more. Tell me, for death is upon us."

"His footsteps are near," said the Indian. "I will speak. I love my lord. In death I will not cheat him. What you have known is true. My child is no child of his. I will not go down to death with a lie upon my lips. Come and see."

Dwaymenau was no more. Sundari, the Indian woman, awful and calm, led the Queen down the long hall and into her own chamber, where Mindon, the child, slept a drugged sleep. The Queen felt that she had never known her; she herself seemed diminished in stature as she followed the stately figure, with its still, dark face. Into this room the enemy were breaking, shouldering their way at the door — a rabble of terrible faces. Their fury was partly checked when only a sleeping child and two women confronted them, but their leader, a grim and evil-looking man, strode from the huddle.

"Where is the son of the King?" be shouted. "Speak, women! Whose is this boy?"

Sundari laid her hand upon her son's shoulder. Not a muscle of her face flickered.

"This is his son."

"His true son — the son of Maya the Queen?"

"His true son, the son of Maya the Queen."

"Not the younger — the mongrel?"

"The younger — the mongrel died last week of a fever."

Every moment of delay was precious. Her eyes saw only a monk and a boy fleeing across the wide river.

"Which is Maya the Queen?"

"This," said Sundari. "She cannot speak. It is her son — the Prince."

Maya had veiled her face with her hands. Her brain swam, but she understood the noble lie. This woman could love. Their lord would not be left childless. Thought beat like pulses in her — raced along her veins. She held her breath and was dumb.

His doubt was assuaged and the lust of vengeance was on him — a madness seized the man. But even his own wild men shrank back a moment, for to slay a sleeping child in cold blood is no man's work.

"You swear it is the Prince. But why? Why do you not lie to save him if you are the King's woman?"

"Because his mother has trampled me to the earth. I am the Indian woman — the mother of the younger, who is dead and safe. She jeered at me — she mocked me. It is time I should see her suffer. Suffer now as I have suffered, Maya the Queen!"

This was reasonable — this was like the women he had known. His doubt was gone — he laughed aloud.

"Then feed full of vengeance!" he cried, and drove his knife through the child's heart.

For a moment Sundari wavered where she stood, but she held herself and was rigid as the dead.

"Tha-du! Well done!" she said with an awful smile. "The tree is broken, the roots cut. And now for us women — our fate, O master?"

"Wait here," he answered. "Let not a hair of their heads be touched. Both are fair. The two for me. For the rest draw lots when all is done."

The uproar surged away. The two stood by the dead boy. So swift had been his death that he lay as though he still slept — the black lashes pressed upon his cheek.

With the heredity of their different races upon them, neither wept. But silently the Queen opened her arms; wide as a woman that entreats she opened them to the Indian Queen, and speechlessly the two clung together. For a while neither spoke.

"My sister!" said Maya the Queen. And again, "O great of heart!"

She laid her cheek against Sundari's, and a wave of solemn joy seemed to break in her soul and flood it with life and light.

"Had I known sooner!" she said. "For now the night draws on."

"What is time?" answered the Rajput woman. "We stand before the Lords of Life and Death. The life you gave was yours, and I am unworthy to kiss the feet of the Queen. Our lord will return and his son is saved. The House can be rebuilt. My son and I were waifs washed up from the sea. Another wave washes us back to nothingness. Tell him my story and he will loathe me."

"My lips are shut," said the Queen. "Should I betray my sister's honor? When he speaks of the noble women of old, your name will be among them. What matters which of us he loves and remembers? Your soul and mine have seen the same thing, and we are one. But I — what have I to do with life? The ship and the bed of the conqueror await us. Should we await them, my sister?"

The bright tears glittered in the eyes of Sundari at the tender name and the love in the face of the Queen. At last she accepted it.

"My sister, no," she said, and drew from her bosom the dagger of Maya, with the man's blood rusted upon it. "Here is the way. I have kept this dagger in token of my debt. Nightly have I kissed it, swearing that, when the time came, I would repay my debt to the great Queen. Shall I go first or follow, my sister?"

Her voice lingered on the word. It was precious to her. It was like clear water, laying away the stain of the shameful years.

"Your arm is strong," answered the Queen. "I go first. Because the King's son is safe, I bless you. For your love of the King, I love you. And here, standing on the verge of life, I testify that the words of the Blessed One are truth — that love is All; that hatred is Nothing."

She bared the breast that this woman had made desolate — that, with the love of this woman, was desolate ho longer, and, stooping, laid her hand on the brow of Mindon. Once more they embraced, and then, strong and true, and with the Rajput passion behind the blow, the stroke fell and Sundari had given her sister the crowning mercy of deliverance. She laid the body beside her own son, composing the stately limbs, the quiet eyelids, the black lengths of hair into majesty. So, she thought, in the great temple of the Rajput race, the Mother Goddess shed silence and awe upon her worshippers. The two lay like mother and son — one slight hand of the Queen she laid across the little body as if to guard it.

Her work done, she turned to the entrance and watched the dawn coming glorious over the river. The men shouted and quarreled in the distance, but she heeded them no more than the chattering of apes. Her heart was away over the distance to the King, but with no passion now: so might a mother have thought of her son. He was sleeping, forgetful of even her in his dreams. What matter? She was glad at heart. The Queen was dearer to her than the King — so strange is life; so healing is death. She remembered without surprise that she had asked no forgiveness of the Queen for all the cruel wrongs, for the deadly intent - had made no confession. Again what matter? What is forgiveness when love is all?

She turned from the dawn-light to the light in the face of the Queen. It was well. Led by such a hand, she could present herself without fear before the Lords of Life and Death — she and the child. She smiled. Life is good, but death, which is more life, is better. The son of the King was safe, but her own son safer.

When the conqueror reentered the chamber, he found the dead Queen guarding the dead child, and across her feet, as not worthy to lie beside her, was the body of the Indian woman, most beautiful in death.

A Problem
Anton Chekhov

The strictest measures were taken that the Uskovs' family secret might not leak out and become generally known. Half of the servants were sent off to the theatre or the circus; the other half were sitting in the kitchen and not allowed to leave it. Orders were given that no one was to be admitted. The wife of the Colonel, her sister, and the governess, though they had been initiated into the secret, kept up a pretence of knowing nothing; they sat in the dining-room and did not show themselves in the drawing-room or the hall.

Sasha Uskov, the young man of twenty-five who was the cause of all the commotion, had arrived some time before, and by the advice of kind-hearted Ivan Markovitch, his uncle, who was taking his part, he sat meekly in the hall by the door leading to the study, and prepared himself to make an open, candid explanation. The other side of the door, in the study, a family council was being held. The subject under discussion was an exceedingly disagreeable and delicate one. Sasha Uskov had cashed at one of the banks a false promissory note, and it had become due for payment three days before, and now his two paternal uncles and Ivan Markovitch, the brother of his dead mother, were deciding the question whether they should pay the money and save the family honour, or wash their hands of it and leave the case to go for trial.

To outsiders who have no personal interest in the matter such questions seem simple; for those who are so unfortunate as to have to decide them in earnest they are extremely difficult. The uncles had been talking for a long time, but the problem seemed no nearer decision.

"My friends!" said the uncle who was a colonel, and there was a note of exhaustion and bitterness in his voice. "Who says that family honour is a mere convention? I don't say that at all. I am only warning you against a false view; I am pointing out the possibility of an unpardonable mistake. How can you fail to see it? I am not speaking Chinese; I am speaking Russian!"

"My dear fellow, we do understand," Ivan Markovitch protested mildly.

"How can you understand if you say that I don't believe in family honour? I repeat once more: fa-mil-y ho-nour fal-sely un-der-stood is a prejudice! Falsely understood! That's what I say: whatever may be the motives for screening a scoundrel, whoever he may be, and helping him to escape punishment, it is contrary to law and unworthy of a gentleman. It's not saving the family honour; it's civic cowardice! Take the army, for instance. . . . The honour of the army is more precious to us than any other honour, yet we don't screen our guilty members, but condemn them. And does the honour of the army suffer in consequence? Quite the opposite!"

The other paternal uncle, an official in the Treasury, a taciturn, dull-witted, and rheumatic man, sat silent, or spoke only of the fact that the Uskovs' name would get into the newspapers if the case went for trial. His opinion was that the case ought to be hushed up from the first and not become public property; but, apart from publicity in the newspapers, he advanced no other argument in support of this opinion.

The maternal uncle, kind-hearted Ivan Markovitch, spoke smoothly, softly, and with a tremor in his voice. He began with saying that youth has its rights and its peculiar temptations. Which of us has not been young, and who has not been led astray? To say nothing of ordinary mortals, even great men have not escaped errors and mistakes in their youth. Take, for instance, the biography of great writers. Did not every one of them gamble, drink, and draw down upon himself the anger of right-thinking people in his young days? If Sasha's error bordered upon crime, they must remember that Sasha had received practically no education; he had been expelled from the high school in the fifth class; he had lost his parents in early childhood, and so had been left at the tenderest age without guidance and good, benevolent influences. He was nervous, excitable, had no firm ground under his feet, and, above all, he had been unlucky. Even if he were guilty, anyway he deserved indulgence and the sympathy of all compassionate souls. He ought, of course, to be punished, but he was punished as it was by his conscience and the agonies he was enduring now while awaiting the sentence of his relations. The comparison with the army made by the Colonel was delightful, and did credit to his lofty intelligence; his appeal to their feeling of public duty spoke for the chivalry of his soul, but they must not forget that in each individual the citizen is closely linked with the Christian. . . .

"Shall we be false to civic duty," Ivan Markovitch exclaimed passionately, "if instead of punishing an erring boy we hold out to him a helping hand?"

Ivan Markovitch talked further of family honour. He had not the honour to belong to the Uskov family himself, but he knew their distinguished family went back to the thirteenth century; he did not forget for a minute, either, that his precious, beloved sister had been the wife of one of the representatives of that name. In short, the family was dear to him for many reasons, and he refused to admit the idea that, for the sake of a paltry fifteen hundred roubles, a blot should be cast on the escutcheon that was beyond all price. If all the motives he had brought forward were not sufficiently convincing, he, Ivan Markovitch, in conclusion, begged his listeners to ask themselves what was meant by crime? Crime is an immoral act founded upon ill-will. But is the will of man free? Philosophy has not yet given a positive answer to that question. Different views were held by the learned. The latest school of Lombroso, for instance, denies the freedom of the will, and considers every crime as the product of the purely anatomical peculiarities of the individual.

"Ivan Markovitch," said the Colonel, in a voice of entreaty, "we are talking seriously about an important matter, and you bring in Lombroso, you clever fellow. Think a little, what are you saying all this for? Can you imagine that all your thunderings and rhetoric will furnish an answer to the question?"

Sasha Uskov sat at the door and listened. He felt neither terror, shame, nor depression, but only weariness and inward emptiness. It seemed to him that it made absolutely no difference to him whether they forgave him or not; he had come here to hear his sentence and to explain himself simply because kind-hearted Ivan Markovitch had begged him to do so. He was not afraid of the future. It made no difference to him where he was: here in the hall, in prison, or in Siberia.

"If Siberia, then let it be Siberia, damn it all!"

He was sick of life and found it insufferably hard. He was inextricably involved in debt; he had not a farthing in his pocket; his family had become detestable to him; he would have to part from his friends and his women sooner or later, as they had begun to be too contemptuous of his sponging on them. The future looked black.

Sasha was indifferent, and was only disturbed by one circumstance; the other side of the door they were calling him a scoundrel and a criminal. Every minute he was on the point of jumping up, bursting into the study and shouting in answer to the detestable metallic voice of the Colonel:

"You are lying!"

"Criminal" is a dreadful word — that is what murderers, thieves, robbers are; in fact, wicked and morally hopeless people. And Sasha was very far from being all that. . . . It was true he owed a great deal and did not pay his debts. But debt is not a crime, and it is unusual for a man not to be in debt. The Colonel and Ivan Markovitch were both in debt. . . .

"What have I done wrong besides?" Sasha wondered.

He had discounted a forged note. But all the young men he knew did the same. Handrikov and Von Burst always forged IOU's from their parents or friends when their allowances were not paid at the regular time, and then when they got their money from home they redeemed them before they became due. Sasha had done the same, but had not redeemed the IOU because he had not got the money which Handrikov had promised to lend him. He was not to blame; it was the fault of circumstances. It was true that the use of another person's signature was considered reprehensible; but, still, it was not a crime but a generally accepted dodge, an ugly formality which injured no one and was quite harmless, for in forging the Colonel's signature Sasha had had no intention of causing anybody damage or loss.

"No, it doesn't mean that I am a criminal . . ." thought Sasha. "And it's not in my character to bring myself to commit a crime. I am soft, emotional. . . . When I have the money I help the poor. . . ."

Sasha was musing after this fashion while they went on talking the other side of the door.

"But, my friends, this is endless," the Colonel declared, getting excited. "Suppose we were to forgive him and pay the money. You know he would not give up leading a dissipated life, squandering money, making debts, going to our tailors and ordering suits in our names! Can you guarantee that this will be his last prank? As far as I am concerned, I have no faith whatever in his reforming!"

The official of the Treasury muttered something in reply; after him Ivan Markovitch began talking blandly and suavely again. The Colonel moved his chair impatiently and drowned the other's words with his detestable metallic voice. At last the door opened and Ivan Markovitch came out of the study; there were patches of red on his lean shaven face.

"Come along," he said, taking Sasha by the hand. "Come and speak frankly from your heart. Without pride, my dear boy, humbly and from your heart."

Sasha went into the study. The official of the Treasury was sitting down; the Colonel was standing before the table with one hand in his pocket and one knee on a chair. It was smoky and stifling in the study. Sasha did not look at the official or the Colonel; he felt suddenly ashamed and uncomfortable. He looked uneasily at Ivan Markovitch and muttered:

"I'll pay it . . . I'll give it back. . . ."

"What did you expect when you discounted the IOU?" he heard a metallic voice.

"I . . . Handrikov promised to lend me the money before now."

Sasha could say no more. He went out of the study and sat down again on the chair near the door.

He would have been glad to go away altogether at once, but he was choking with hatred and he awfully wanted to remain, to tear the Colonel to pieces, to say something rude to him. He sat trying to think of something violent and effective to say to his hated uncle, and at that moment a woman's figure, shrouded in the twilight, appeared at the drawing-room door. It was the Colonel's wife. She beckoned Sasha to her, and, wringing her hands, said, weeping:

"Alexandre, I know you don't like me, but . . . listen to me; listen, I beg you. . . . But, my dear, how can this have happened? Why, it's awful, awful! For goodness' sake, beg them, defend yourself, entreat them."

Sasha looked at her quivering shoulders, at the big tears that were rolling down her cheeks, heard behind his back the hollow, nervous voices of worried and exhausted people, and shrugged his shoulders. He had not in the least expected that his aristocratic relations would raise such a tempest over a paltry fifteen hundred roubles! He could not understand her tears nor the quiver of their voices.

An hour later he heard that the Colonel was getting the best of it; the uncles were finally inclining to let the case go for trial.

"The matter's settled," said the Colonel, sighing. "Enough."

After this decision all the uncles, even the emphatic Colonel, became noticeably depressed. A silence followed.

"Merciful Heavens!" sighed Ivan Markovitch. "My poor sister!"

And he began saying in a subdued voice that most likely his sister, Sasha's mother, was present unseen in the study at that moment. He felt in his soul how the unhappy, saintly woman was weeping, grieving, and begging for her boy. For the sake of her peace beyond the grave, they ought to spare Sasha.

The sound of a muffled sob was heard. Ivan Markovitch was weeping and muttering something which it was impossible to catch through the door. The Colonel got up and paced from corner to corner. The long conversation began over again.

But then the clock in the drawing-room struck two. The family council was over. To avoid seeing the person who had moved him to such wrath, the Colonel went from the study, not into the hall, but into the vestibule. . . . Ivan Markovitch came out into the hall. . . . He was agitated and rubbing his hands joyfully. His tear-stained eyes looked good-humoured and his mouth was twisted into a smile.

"Capital," he said to Sasha. "Thank God! You can go home, my dear, and sleep tranquilly. We have decided to pay the sum, but on condition that you repent and come with me tomorrow into the country and set to work."

A minute later Ivan Markovitch and Sasha in their great-coats and caps were going down the stairs. The uncle was muttering something edifying. Sasha did not listen, but felt as though some uneasy weight were gradually slipping off his shoulders. They had forgiven him; he was free! A gust of joy sprang up within him and sent a sweet chill to his heart. He longed to breathe, to move swiftly, to live! Glancing at the street lamps and the black sky, he remembered that Von Burst was celebrating his name-day that evening at the "Bear," and again a rush of joy flooded his soul. . . .

"I am going!" he decided.

But then he remembered he had not a farthing, that the

companions he was going to would despise him at once for his empty pockets. He must get hold of some money, come what may!

"Uncle, lend me a hundred roubles," he said to Ivan Markovitch.

His uncle, surprised, looked into his face and backed against a lamp-post.

"Give it to me," said Sasha, shifting impatiently from one foot to the other and beginning to pant. "Uncle, I entreat you, give me a hundred roubles."

His face worked; he trembled, and seemed on the point of attacking his uncle. . . .

"Won't you?" he kept asking, seeing that his uncle was still amazed and did not understand. "Listen. If you don't, I'll give myself up tomorrow! I won't let you pay the IOU! I'll present another false note tomorrow!"

Petrified, muttering something incoherent in his horror, Ivan Markovitch took a hundred-rouble note out of his pocket-book and gave it to Sasha. The young man took it and walked rapidly away from him. . . .

Taking a sledge, Sasha grew calmer, and felt a rush of joy within him again. The "rights of youth" of which kind-hearted Ivan Markovitch had spoken at the family council woke up and asserted themselves. Sasha pictured the drinking-party before him, and, among the bottles, the women, and his friends, the thought flashed through his mind:

"Now I see that I am a criminal; yes, I am a criminal."

The Requium
Anton Chekhov

In the village church of Verhny Zaprudy mass was just over. The people had begun moving and were trooping out of church. The only one who did not move was Andrey Andreyitch, a shopkeeper and old inhabitant of Verhny Zaprudy. He stood waiting, with his elbows on the railing of the right choir. His fat and shaven face, covered with indentations left by pimples, expressed on this occasion two contradictory feelings: resignation in the face of inevitable destiny, and stupid, unbounded disdain for the smocks and striped kerchiefs passing by him. As it was Sunday, he was dressed like a dandy. He wore a long cloth overcoat with yellow bone buttons, blue trousers not thrust into his boots, and sturdy goloshes — the huge clumsy goloshes only seen on the feet of practical and prudent persons of firm religious convictions.

His torpid eyes, sunk in fat, were fixed upon the ikon stand. He saw the long familiar figures of the saints, the verger Matvey puffing out his cheeks and blowing out the candles, the darkened candle stands, the threadbare carpet, the sacristan Lopuhov running impulsively from the altar and carrying the holy bread to the churchwarden. . . . All these things he had seen for years, and seen over and over again like the five fingers of his hand. . . . There was only one thing, however, that was somewhat strange and unusual. Father Grigory, still in his vestments, was standing at the north door, twitching his thick eyebrows angrily.

"Who is it he is winking at? God bless him!" thought the shopkeeper. "And he is beckoning with his finger! And he stamped his foot! What next! What's the matter, Holy Queen and Mother! Whom does he mean it for?"

Andrey Andreyitch looked round and saw the church completely deserted. There were some ten people standing at the door, but they had their backs to the altar.

"Do come when you are called! Why do you stand like a graven image?" he heard Father Grigory's angry voice. "I am calling you."

The shopkeeper looked at Father Grigory's red and wrathful face, and only then realized that the twitching eyebrows and beckoning finger might refer to him. He started, left the railing, and hesitatingly walked towards the altar, tramping with his heavy goloshes.

"Andrey Andreyitch, was it you asked for prayers for the rest of Mariya's soul?" asked the priest, his eyes angrily transfixing the shopkeeper's fat, perspiring face.

"Yes, Father."

"Then it was you wrote this? You?" And Father Grigory angrily thrust before his eyes the little note.

And on this little note, handed in by Andrey Andreyitch before mass, was written in big, as it were staggering, letters:

"For the rest of the soul of the servant of God, the harlot Mariya."

"Yes, certainly I wrote it, ..." answered the shopkeeper.

"How dared you write it?" whispered the priest, and in his husky whisper there was a note of wrath and alarm.

The shopkeeper looked at him in blank amazement; he was perplexed, and he, too, was alarmed. Father Grigory had never in his life spoken in such a tone to a leading resident of Verhny Zaprudy. Both were silent for a minute, staring into each other's face. The shopkeeper's amazement was so great that his fat face spread in all directions like spilt dough.

"How dared you?" repeated the priest.

"Wha . . . what?" asked Andrey Andreyitch in bewilderment.

"You don't understand?" whispered Father Grigory, stepping back in astonishment and clasping his hands. "What have you got on your shoulders, a head or some other object? You send a note up to the altar, and write a word in it which it would be unseemly even to utter in the street! Why are you rolling your eyes? Surely you know the meaning of the word?"

"Are you referring to the word harlot?" muttered the shopkeeper, flushing crimson and blinking. "But you know, the Lord in His mercy . . . forgave this very thing, . . . forgave a harlot.

. . . He has prepared a place for her, and indeed from the life of the holy saint, Mariya of Egypt, one may see in what sense the word is used — excuse me . . ."

The shopkeeper wanted to bring forward some other argument in his justification, but took fright and wiped his lips with his sleeve

"So that's what you make of it!" cried Father Grigory, clasping his hands. "But you see God has forgiven her — do you understand? He has forgiven, but you judge her, you slander her, call her by an unseemly name, and whom! Your own deceased daughter! Not only in Holy Scripture, but even in worldly literature you won't read of such a sin! I tell you again, Andrey, you mustn't be over-subtle! No, no, you mustn't be over-subtle, brother! If God has given you an inquiring mind, and if you cannot direct it, better not go into things. . . . Don't go into things, and hold your peace!"

"But you know, she, . . . excuse my mentioning it, was an actress!" articulated Andrey Andreyitch, overwhelmed.

"An actress! But whatever she was, you ought to forget it all now she is dead, instead of writing it on the note."

"Just so, . . ." the shopkeeper assented.

"You ought to do penance," boomed the deacon from the depths of the altar, looking contemptuously at Andrey Andreyitch's embarrassed face, "that would teach you to leave off being so clever! Your daughter was a well-known actress. There were even notices of her death in the newspapers. . . . Philosopher!"

"To be sure, . . . certainly," muttered the shopkeeper, "the word is not a seemly one; but I did not say it to judge her, Father Grigory, I only meant to speak spiritually, . . . that it might be clearer to you for whom you were praying. They write in the memorial notes the various callings, such as the infant John, the drowned woman Pelagea, the warrior Yegor, the murdered Pavel, and so on. . . . I meant to do the same."

"It was foolish, Andrey! God will forgive you, but beware another time. Above all, don't be subtle, but think like other people. Make ten bows and go your way."

"I obey," said the shopkeeper, relieved that the lecture was over, and allowing his face to resume its expression of importance and dignity. "Ten bows? Very good, I understand. But now, Father, allow me to ask you a favor. . . . Seeing that I am, anyway, her father, . . . you know yourself, whatever she was, she was still my daughter, so I was, . . . excuse me, meaning to ask you to sing the requiem today. And allow me to ask you, Father Deacon!"

"Well, that's good," said Father Grigory, taking off his vestments. "That I commend. I can approve of that! Well, go your way. We will come out immediately."

Andrey Andreyitch walked with dignity from the altar, and with a solemn, requiem-like expression on his red face took his stand in the middle of the church. The verger Matvey set before him a little table with the memorial food upon it, and a little later the requiem service began.

There was perfect stillness in the church. Nothing could be heard but the metallic click of the censer and slow singing. . . . Near Andrey Andreyitch stood the verger Matvey, the midwife Makaryevna, and her one-armed son Mitka. There was no one else. The sacristan sang badly in an unpleasant, hollow bass, but the tune and the words were so mournful that the shopkeeper little by little lost the expression of dignity and was plunged in sadness. He thought of his Mashutka, . . . he remembered she had been born when he was still a lackey in the service of the owner of Verhny Zaprudy. In his busy life as a lackey he had not noticed how his girl had grown up. That long period during which she was being shaped into a graceful creature, with a little flaxen head and dreamy eyes as big as kopeck-pieces passed unnoticed by him. She had been brought up like all the children of favorite lackeys, in ease and comfort in the company of the young ladies. The gentry, to fill up their idle time, had taught her to read, to write, to dance; he had had no hand in her bringing up. Only from time to time casually meeting her at the gate or on the landing of the stairs, he would remember that she was his daughter, and would, so far as he had leisure for it, begin teaching her the prayers and the scripture. Oh, even then he had the reputation of an authority on the church rules and the holy scriptures! Forbidding and stolid as her father's face was, yet the girl listened readily. She repeated the prayers after him yawning, but on the other hand, when he, hesitating and trying to express himself elaborately, began telling her stories, she was all attention. Esau's pottage, the punishment of Sodom, and the troubles of the boy Joseph made her turn pale and open her blue eyes wide.

Afterwards when he gave up being a lackey, and with the money he had saved opened a shop in the village, Mashutka had gone away to Moscow with his master's family. . . .

Three years before her death she had come to see her father.

He had scarcely recognized her. She was a graceful young woman with the manners of a young lady, and dressed like one. She talked cleverly, as though from a book, smoked, and slept till midday. When Andrey Andreyitch asked her what she was doing, she had announced, looking him boldly straight in the face: "I am an actress." Such frankness struck the former flunkey as the acme of cynicism. Mashutka had begun boasting of her successes and her stage life; but seeing that her father only turned crimson and threw up his hands, she ceased. And they spent a fortnight together without speaking or looking at one another till the day she went away. Before she went away she asked her father to come for a walk on the bank of the river. Painful as it was for him to walk in the light of day, in the sight of all honest people, with a daughter who was an actress, he yielded to her request.

"What a lovely place you live in!" she said enthusiastically. "What ravines and marshes! Good heavens, how lovely my native place is!"

And she had burst into tears.

"The place is simply taking up room, ..." Andrey Andreyvitch had thought, looking blankly at the ravines, not understanding his daughter's enthusiasm. "There is no more profit from them than milk from a billy-goat."

And she had cried and cried, drawing her breath greedily with her whole chest, as though she felt she had not a long time left to breathe.

Andrey Andreyitch shook his head like a horse that has been bitten, and to stifle painful memories began rapidly crossing himself. . . .

"Be mindful, O Lord," he muttered, "of Thy departed servant, the harlot Mariya, and forgive her sins, voluntary or involuntary. . . ."

The unseemly word dropped from his lips again, but he did not notice it: what is firmly imbedded in the consciousness cannot be driven out by Father Grigory's exhortations or even knocked out by a nail. Makaryevna sighed and whispered something, drawing in a deep breath, while one-armed Mitka was brooding over something. . . .

"Where there is no sickness, nor grief, nor sighing," droned the sacristan, covering his right cheek with his hand.

Bluish smoke coiled up from the censer and bathed in the broad, slanting patch of sunshine which cut across the gloomy, lifeless emptiness of the church. And it seemed as though the soul of the dead woman were soaring into the sunlight together with the smoke. The coils of smoke like a child's curls eddied round and round, floating upwards to the window and, as it were, holding aloof from the woes and tribulations of which that poor soul was full.

A Sister's Confession
Guy de Maupassant

Marguerite de Therelles was dying. Although she was only fifty-six years old she looked at least seventy-five. She gasped for breath, her face whiter than the sheets, and had spasms of violent shivering, with her face convulsed and her eyes haggard as though she saw a frightful vision.

Her elder sister, Suzanne, six years older than herself, was sobbing on her knees beside the bed. A small table close to the dying woman's couch bore, on a white cloth, two lighted candles, for the priest was expected at any moment to administer extreme unction and the last communion.

The apartment wore that melancholy aspect common to death chambers; a look of despairing farewell. Medicine bottles littered the furniture; linen lay in the corners into which it had been kicked or swept. The very chairs looked, in their disarray, as if they were terrified and had run in all directions. Death—terrible Death—was in the room, hidden, awaiting his prey.

This history of the two sisters was an affecting one. It was spoken of far and wide; it had drawn tears from many eyes.

Suzanne, the elder, had once been passionately loved by a young man, whose affection she returned. They were engaged to be married, and the wedding day was at hand, when Henry de Sampierre suddenly died.

The young girl's despair was terrible, and she took an oath never to marry. She faithfully kept her vow and adopted widow's weeds for the remainder of her life.

But one morning her sister, her little sister Marguerite, then only twelve years old, threw herself into Suzanne's arms, sobbing:

"Sister, I don't want you to be unhappy. I don't want you to mourn all your life. I'll never leave you—never, never, never! I shall never marry, either. I'll stay with you always—always!"

Suzanne kissed her, touched by the child's devotion, though not putting any faith in her promise.

But the little one kept her word, and, despite her parents' remonstrances, despite her elder sister's prayers, never married. She was remarkably pretty and refused many offers. She never left her sister.

They spent their whole life together, without a single day's separation. They went everywhere together and were inseparable. But Marguerite was pensive, melancholy, sadder than her sister, as if her sublime sacrifice had undermined her spirits. She grew older more quickly; her hair was white at thirty; and she was often ill, apparently stricken with some unknown, wasting malady.

And now she would be the first to die.

She had not spoken for twenty-four hours, except to whisper at daybreak:

"Send at once for the priest."

And she had since remained lying on her back, convulsed with agony, her lips moving as if unable to utter the dreadful words that rose in her heart, her face expressive of a terror distressing to witness.

Suzanne, distracted with grief, her brow pressed against the bed, wept bitterly, repeating over and over again the words:

"Margot, my poor Margot, my little one!"

She had always called her "my little one," while Marguerite's name for the elder was invariably "sister."

A footstep sounded on the stairs. The door opened. An acolyte appeared, followed by the aged priest in his surplice. As soon as she saw him the dying woman sat up suddenly in bed, opened her lips, stammered a few words and began to scratch the bed-clothes, as if she would have made hole in them.

Father Simon approached, took her hand, kissed her on the forehead and said in a gentle voice:

"May God pardon your sins, my daughter. Be of good courage. Now is the moment to confess them—speak!"

Then Marguerite, shuddering from head to foot, so that the very bed shook with her nervous movements, gasped:

"Sit down, sister, and listen."

The priest stooped toward the prostrate Suzanne, raised her to her feet, placed her in a chair, and, taking a hand of each of the sisters, pronounced:

"Lord God! Send them strength! Shed Thy mercy upon them."

And Marguerite began to speak. The words issued from her lips one by one—hoarse, jerky, tremulous.

"Pardon, pardon, sister! pardon me! Oh, if only you knew how I have dreaded this moment all my life!"

Suzanne faltered through her tears:

"But what have I to pardon, little one? You have given me everything, sacrificed all to me. You are an angel."

But Marguerite interrupted her:

"Be silent, be silent! Let me speak! Don't stop me! It is terrible. Let me tell all, to the very end, without interruption. Listen. You remember—you remember—Henry—"

Suzanne trembled and looked at her sister. The younger one went on:

"In order to understand you must hear everything. I was twelve years old—only twelve—you remember, don't you? And I was spoilt; I did just as I pleased. You remember how everybody spoilt me? Listen. The first time he came he had on his riding boots; he dismounted, saying that he had a message for father. You remember, don't you? Don't speak. Listen. When I saw him I was struck with admiration. I thought him so handsome, and I stayed in a corner of the drawing-room all the time he was talking. Children are strange—and terrible. Yes, indeed, I dreamt of him.

"He came again—many times. I looked at him with all my eyes, all my heart. I was large for my age and much more precocious than—any one suspected. He came often. I thought only of him. I often whispered to myself:

"'Henry-Henry de Sampierre!'

"Then I was told that he was going to marry you. That was a blow! Oh, sister, a terrible blow—terrible! I wept all through three sleepless nights.

He came every afternoon after lunch. You remember, don't you? Don't answer. Listen. You used to make cakes that he was very fond of—with flour, butter and milk. Oh, I know how to make them. I could make them still, if necessary. He would swallow them at one mouthful and wash them down with a glass of wine, saying: 'Delicious!' Do you remember the way he said it?

"I was jealous—jealous! Your wedding day was drawing near. It was only a fortnight distant. I was distracted. I said to myself: 'He shall not marry Suzanne—no, he shall not! He shall marry me when I am old enough! I shall never love any one half so much.' But one evening, ten days before the wedding, you went for a stroll with him in the moonlight before the house—and yonder—under the pine tree, the big pine tree—he kissed you—kissed you—and held you in his arms so long—so long! You remember, don't you? It was probably the first time. You were so pale when you carne back to the drawing-room!

"I saw you. I was there in the shrubbery. I was mad with rage! I would have killed you both if I could!

"I said to myself: 'He shall never marry Suzanne—never! He shall marry no one! I could not bear it.' And all at once I began to hate him intensely.

"Then do you know what I did? Listen. I had seen the gardener prepare pellets for killing stray dogs. He would crush a bottle into small pieces with a stone and put the ground glass into a ball of meat.

"I stole a small medicine bottle from mother's room. I ground it fine with a hammer and hid the glass in my pocket. It was a glistening powder. The next day, when you had made your little cakes; I opened them with a knife and inserted the glass. He ate three. I ate one myself. I threw the six others into the pond. The two swans died three days later. You remember? Oh, don't speak! Listen, listen. I, I alone did not die. But I have always been ill. Listen—he died—you know—listen—that was not the worst. It was afterward, later—always—the most terrible— listen.

"My life, all my life—such torture! I said to myself: 'I will never leave my sister. And on my deathbed I will tell her all.' And now I have told. And I have always thought of this moment—the moment when all would be told. Now it has come. It is terrible— oh!—sister—

"I have always thought, morning and evening, day and night: 'I shall have to tell her some day!' I waited. The horror of it! It is done. Say nothing. Now I am afraid—I am afraid! Oh! Supposing I should see him again, by and by, when I am dead! See him again! Only to think of it! I dare not—yet I must. I am going to die. I want you to forgive me. I insist on it. I cannot meet him without your forgiveness. Oh, tell her to forgive me, Father! Tell her. I implore you! I cannot die without it."

She was silent and lay back, gasping for breath, still plucking at the sheets with her fingers.

Suzanne had hidden her face in her hands and did not move. She was thinking of him whom she had loved so long. What a life of happiness they might have had together! She saw him again in the dim and distant past-that past forever lost. Beloved dead! how the thought of them rends the heart! Oh! that kiss, his only kiss! She had retained the memory of it in her soul. And, after that, nothing, nothing more throughout her whole existence!

The priest rose suddenly and in a firm, compelling voice said:

"Mademoiselle Suzanne, your sister is dying!"

Then Suzanne, raising her tear-stained face, put her arms round her sister, and kissing her fervently, exclaimed:

"I forgive you, I forgive you, little one!"

The Reckoning
Edith Wharton

I

"The marriage law of the new dispensation will be: THOU SHALT NOT BE UNFAITHFUL — TO THYSELF."

A discreet murmur of approval filled the studio, and through the haze of cigarette smoke Mrs. Clement Westall, as her husband descended from his improvised platform, saw him merged in a congratulatory group of ladies. Westall's informal talks on "The New Ethics" had drawn about him an eager following of the mentally unemployed — those who, as he had once phrased it, liked to have their brain-food cut up for them. The talks had begun by accident. Westall's ideas were known to be "advanced," but hitherto their advance had not been in the direction of publicity. He had been, in his wife's opinion, almost pusillanimously careful not to let his personal views endanger his professional standing. Of late, however, he had shown a puzzling tendency to dogmatize, to throw down the gauntlet, to flaunt his private code in the face of society; and the relation of the sexes being a topic always sure of an audience, a few admiring friends had persuaded him to give his after-dinner opinions a larger circulation by summing them up in a series of talks at the Van Sideren studio.

The Herbert Van Siderens were a couple who subsisted, socially, on the fact that they had a studio. Van Sideren's pictures were chiefly valuable as accessories to the *mise en scene* which differentiated his wife's "afternoons" from the blighting functions held in long New York drawing-rooms, and permitted her to offer their friends whiskey-and-soda instead of tea. Mrs. Van Sideren, for her part, was skilled in making the most of the kind of atmosphere which a lay-figure and an easel create; and if at times she found the illusion hard to maintain, and lost courage to the extent of almost wishing that Herbert could paint, she promptly overcame such moments of weakness by calling in some fresh talent, some extraneous re-enforcement of the "artistic" impression. It was in quest of such aid that she had seized on Westall, coaxing him, somewhat to his wife's surprise, into a flattered participation in her fraud. It was vaguely felt, in the Van Sideren circle, that all the audacities were artistic, and that a teacher who pronounced marriage immoral was somehow as distinguished as a painter who depicted purple grass and a green sky. The Van Sideren set were tired of the conventional color-scheme in art and conduct.

Julia Westall had long had her own views on the immorality of marriage; she might indeed have claimed her husband as a disciple. In the early days of their union she had secretly resented his disinclination to proclaim himself a follower of the new creed; had been inclined to tax him with moral cowardice, with a failure to live up to the convictions for which their marriage was supposed to stand. That was in the first burst of propagandism, when, womanlike, she wanted to turn her disobedience into a law. Now she felt differently. She could hardly account for the change, yet being a woman who never allowed her impulses to remain unaccounted for, she tried to do so by saying that she did not care to have the articles of her faith misinterpreted by the vulgar. In this connection, she was beginning to think that almost every one was vulgar; certainly there were few to whom she would have cared to intrust the defence of so esoteric a doctrine. And it was precisely at this point that Westall, discarding his unspoken principles, had chosen to descend from the heights of privacy, and stand hawking his convictions at the street-corner!

It was Una Van Sideren who, on this occasion, unconsciously focussed upon herself Mrs. Westall's wandering resentment. In the first place, the girl had no business to be there. It was "horrid" — Mrs. Westall found herself slipping back into the old feminine vocabulary -simply "horrid" to think of a young girl's being allowed to listen to such talk. The fact that Una smoked cigarettes and sipped an occasional cocktail did not in the least tarnish a certain radiant innocency which made her appear the victim, rather than the accomplice, of her parents' vulgarities. Julia Westall felt in a hot helpless way that something ought to be done — that some one ought to speak to the girl's mother. And just then Una glided up.

"Oh, Mrs. Westall, how beautiful it was!" Una fixed her with large limpid eyes. "You believe it all, I suppose?" she asked with seraphic gravity.

"All — what, my dear child?"

The girl shone on her. "About the higher life — the freer expansion of the individual — the law of fidelity to one's self," she glibly recited.

Mrs. Westall, to her own wonder, blushed a deep and burning blush.

"My dear Una," she said, "you don't in the least understand what it's all about!"

Miss Van Sideren stared, with a slowly answering blush. "Don't you, then?" she murmured.

Mrs. Westall laughed. "Not always — or altogether! But I should like some tea, please."

Una led her to the corner where innocent beverages were dispensed. As Julia received her cup she scrutinized the girl more carefully. It was not such a girlish face, after all-definite lines were forming under the rosy haze of youth. She reflected that Una must be six-and-twenty, and wondered why she had not married. A nice stock of ideas she would have as her dower! If they were to be a part of the modern girl's trousseau —

Mrs. Westall caught herself up with a start. It was as though some one else had been speaking — a stranger who had borrowed her own voice: she felt herself the dupe of some fantastic mental ventriloquism. Concluding suddenly that the room was stifling and Una's tea too sweet, she set down her cup, and looked about for Westall: to meet his eyes had long been her refuge from every uncertainty. She met them now, but only, as she felt, in transit; they included her parenthetically in a larger flight. She followed the flight, and it carried her to a corner to which Una had withdrawn — one of the palmy nooks to which Mrs. Van Sideren attributed the success of her Saturdays. Westall, a moment later, had overtaken his look, and found a place at the girl's side. She bent forward, speaking eagerly; he leaned back, listening, with the depreciatory smile which acted as a filter to flattery, enabling him to swallow the strongest doses without apparent grossness of appetite. Julia winced at her own definition of the smile.

On the way home, in the deserted winter dusk, Westall

surprised his wife by a sudden boyish pressure of her arm. "Did I open their eyes a bit? Did I tell them what you wanted me to?" he asked gaily.

Almost unconsciously, she let her arm slip from his. "What I wanted — ?"

"Why, haven't you — all this time?" She caught the honest wonder of his tone. "I somehow fancied you'd rather blamed me for not talking more openly — before — You've made me feel, at times, that I was sacrificing principles to expediency."

She paused a moment over her reply; then she asked quietly: "What made you decide not to — any longer?"

She felt again the vibration of a faint surprise. "Why — the wish to please you!" he answered, almost too simply.

"I wish you would not go on, then," she said abruptly.

He stopped in his quick walk, and she felt his stare through the darkness.

"Not go on — ?"

"Call a hansom, please. I'm tired," broke from her with a sudden rush of physical weariness.

Instantly his solicitude enveloped her. The room had been infernally hot — and then that confounded cigarette smoke — he had noticed once or twice that she looked pale — she mustn't come to another Saturday. She felt herself yielding, as she always did, to the warm influence of his concern for her, the feminine in her leaning on the man in him with a conscious intensity of abandonment. He put her in the hansom, and her hand stole into his in the darkness. A tear or two rose, and she let them fall. It was so delicious to cry over imaginary troubles!

That evening, after dinner, he surprised her by reverting to the subject of his talk. He combined a man's dislike of uncomfortable questions with an almost feminine skill in eluding them; and she knew that if he returned to the subject he must have some special reason for doing so.

"You seem not to have cared for what I said this afternoon. Did I put the case badly?"

"No — you put it very well."

"Then what did you mean by saying that you would rather not have me go on with it?"

She glanced at him nervously, her ignorance of his intention deepening her sense of helplessness.

"I don't think I care to hear such things discussed in public."

"I don't understand you," he exclaimed. Again the feeling that his surprise was genuine gave an air of obliquity to her own attitude. She was not sure that she understood herself.

"Won't you explain?" he said with a tinge of impatience. Her eyes wandered about the familiar drawing-room which had been the scene of so many of their evening confidences. The shaded lamps, the quiet-colored walls hung with mezzotints, the pale spring flowers scattered here and there in Venice glasses and bowls of old Sevres, recalled, she hardly knew why, the apartment in which the evenings of her first marriage had been passed — a wilderness of rosewood and upholstery, with a picture of a Roman peasant above the mantel-piece, and a Greek slave in "statuary marble" between the folding-doors of the back drawing-room. It was a room with which she had never been able to establish any closer relation than that between a traveller and a railway station; and now, as she looked about at the surroundings which stood for her deepest affinities — the room for which she had left that other room — she was startled by the same sense of strangeness and unfamiliarity. The prints, the flowers, the subdued tones of the old porcelains, seemed to typify a superficial refinement that had no relation to the deeper significances of life.

Suddenly she heard her husband repeating his question.

"I don't know that I can explain," she faltered.

He drew his arm-chair forward so that he faced her across the hearth. The light of a reading-lamp fell on his finely drawn face, which had a kind of surface-sensitiveness akin to the surface-refinement of its setting.

"Is it that you no longer believe in our ideas?" he asked.

"In our ideas — ?"

"The ideas I am trying to teach. The ideas you and I are supposed to stand for." He paused a moment. "The ideas on which our marriage was founded."

The blood rushed to her face. He had his reasons, then — she was sure now that he had his reasons! In the ten years of their marriage, how often had either of them stopped to consider the ideas on which it was founded? How often does a man dig about the basement of his house to examine its foundation? The foundation is there, of course — the house rests on it — but one lives abovestairs and not in the cellar. It was she, indeed, who in the beginning had insisted on reviewing the situation now and then, on recapitulating the reasons which justified her course, on proclaiming, from time to time, her adherence to the religion of personal independence; but she had long ceased to feel the need of any such ideal standards, and had accepted her marriage as frankly and naturally as though it had been based on the primitive needs of the heart, and needed no special sanction to explain or justify it.

"Of course I still believe in our ideas!" she exclaimed.

"Then I repeat that I don't understand. It was a part of your theory that the greatest possible publicity should be given to our view of marriage. Have you changed your mind in that respect?"

She hesitated. "It depends on circumstances — on the public one is addressing. The set of people that the Van Siderens get about them don't care for the truth or falseness of a doctrine. They are attracted simply by its novelty."

"And yet it was in just such a set of people that you and I met, and learned the truth from each other."

"That was different."

"In what way?"

"I was not a young girl, to begin with. It is perfectly unfitting that young girls should be present at — at such times-should hear such things discussed —"

"I thought you considered it one of the deepest social wrongs that such things never are discussed before young girls; but that is beside the point, for I don't remember seeing any young girl in my audience to-day —"

"Except Una Van Sideren!"

He turned slightly and pushed back the lamp at his elbow.

"Oh, Miss Van Sideren — naturally —"

"Why naturally?"

"The daughter of the house — would you have had her sent out with her governess?"

"If I had a daughter I should not allow such things to go on in my house!"

Westall, stroking his mustache, leaned back with a faint smile. "I fancy Miss Van Sideren is quite capable of taking care of herself."

"No girl knows how to take care of herself — till it's too late."

"And yet you would deliberately deny her the surest means of self-defense?"

"What do you call the surest means of self-defence?"

"Some preliminary knowledge of human nature in its relation to the marriage tie."

She made an impatient gesture. "How should you like to marry that kind of a girl?"

"Immensely — if she were my kind of girl in other respects."

She took up the argument at another point.

"You are quite mistaken if you think such talk does not affect young girls. Una was in a state of the most absurd exaltation —" She broke off, wondering why she had spoken.

Westall reopened a magazine which he had laid aside at the beginning of their discussion. "What you tell me is immensely flattering to my oratorical talent — but I fear you overrate its effect. I can assure you that Miss Van Sideren doesn't have to have her thinking done for her. She's quite capable of doing it herself."

"You seem very familiar with her mental processes!" flashed unguardedly from his wife.

He looked up quietly from the pages he was cutting.

"I should like to be," he answered. "She interests me."

II

If there be a distinction in being misunderstood, it was one denied to Julia Westall when she left her first husband. Every one was ready to excuse and even to defend her. The world she adorned agreed that John Arment was "impossible," and hostesses gave a sigh of relief at the thought that it would no longer be necessary to ask him to dine.

There had been no scandal connected with the divorce: neither side had accused the other of the offence euphemistically described as "statutory." The Arments had indeed been obliged to transfer their allegiance to a State which recognized desertion as a cause for divorce, and construed the term so liberally that the seeds of desertion were shown to exist in every union. Even Mrs. Arment's second marriage did not make traditional morality stir in its sleep. It was known that she had not met her second husband till after she had parted from the first, and she had, moreover, replaced a rich man by a poor one. Though Clement Westall was acknowledged to be a rising lawyer, it was generally felt that his fortunes would not rise as rapidly as his reputation. The Westalls would probably always have to live quietly and go out to dinner in cabs. Could there be better evidence of Mrs. Arment's complete disinterestedness?

If the reasoning by which her friends justified her course was somewhat cruder and less complex than her own elucidation of the matter, both explanations led to the same conclusion: John Arment was impossible. The only difference was that, to his wife, his impossibility was something deeper than a social disqualification. She had once said, in ironical defence of her marriage, that it had at least preserved her from the necessity of sitting next to him at dinner; but she had not then realized at what cost the immunity was purchased. John Arment was impossible; but the sting of his impossibility lay in the fact that he made it impossible for those about him to be other than himself. By an unconscious process of elimination he had excluded from the world everything of which he did not feel a personal need: had become, as it were, a climate in which only his own requirements survived. This might seem to imply a deliberate selfishness; but there was nothing deliberate about Arment. He was as instinctive as an animal or a child. It was this childish element in his nature which sometimes for a moment unsettled his wife's estimate of him. Was it possible that he was simply undeveloped, that he had delayed, somewhat longer than is usual, the laborious process of growing up? He had the kind of sporadic shrewdness which causes it to be said of a dull man that he is "no fool"; and it was this quality that his wife found most trying. Even to the naturalist it is annoying to have his deductions disturbed by some unforeseen aberrancy of form or function; and how much more so to the wife whose estimate of herself is inevitably bound up with her judgment of her husband!

Arment's shrewdness did not, indeed, imply any latent intellectual power; it suggested, rather, potentialities of feeling, of suffering, perhaps, in a blind rudimentary way, on which Julia's sensibilities naturally declined to linger. She so fully understood her own reasons for leaving him that she disliked to think they were not as comprehensible to her husband. She was haunted, in her analytic moments, by the look of perplexity, too inarticulate for words, with which he had acquiesced to her explanations.

These moments were rare with her, however. Her marriage had been too concrete a misery to be surveyed philosophically. If she had been unhappy for complex reasons, the unhappiness was as real as though it had been uncomplicated. Soul is more bruisable than flesh, and Julia was wounded in every fibre of her spirit. Her husband's personality seemed to be closing gradually in on her, obscuring the sky and cutting off the air, till she felt herself shut up among the decaying bodies of her starved hopes. A sense of having been decoyed by some world-old conspiracy into this bondage of body and soul filled her with despair. If marriage was the slow life-long acquittal of a debt contracted in ignorance, then marriage was a crime against human nature. She, for one, would have no share in maintaining the pretence of which she had been a victim: the pretence that a man and a woman, forced into the narrowest of personal relations, must remain there till the end, though they may have outgrown the span of each other's natures as the mature tree outgrows the iron brace about the sapling.

It was in the first heat of her moral indignation that she had met Clement Westall. She had seen at once that he was "interested," and had fought off the discovery, dreading any influence that should draw her back into the bondage of conventional relations. To ward off the peril she had, with an almost crude precipitancy, revealed her opinions to him. To her surprise, she found that he shared them. She was attracted by the frankness of a suitor who, while pressing his suit, admitted that he did not believe in marriage. Her worst audacities did not seem to surprise him: he had thought out all that she had felt, and they had reached the same conclusion. People grew at varying rates, and the yoke that was an easy fit for the one might soon become galling to the other. That was what divorce was for: the readjustment of personal relations. As soon as their necessarily transitive nature was recognized they would gain in dignity as well as in harmony. There would be no further need of the ignoble concessions and connivances, the perpetual sacrifice of personal delicacy and moral pride, by means of which imperfect marriages were now held together. Each partner to the contract would be on his mettle, forced to live up to the highest standard of self-development, on pain of losing the other's respect and affection. The low nature could no longer drag the higher down, but must struggle to rise, or remain alone on its inferior level. The only necessary condition to a harmonious marriage was a frank recognition of this truth, and a solemn agreement between the contracting parties to keep faith with themselves, and not to live together for a moment after complete accord had ceased to exist between them. The new adultery was unfaithfulness to self.

It was, as Westall had just reminded her, on this understanding that they had married. The ceremony was an unimportant concession to social prejudice: now that the door of divorce stood open, no marriage need be an imprisonment, and the contract therefore no longer involved any diminution of self-respect. The nature of their attachment placed them so far beyond the reach of such contingencies that it was easy to discuss them with an open mind; and Julia's sense of security made her dwell with a tender insistence on Westall's promise to claim his release when he should cease to love her. The exchange of these vows seemed to make them, in a sense, champions of the new law, pioneers in the forbidden realm of individual freedom: they felt that they had somehow achieved beatitude without martyrdom.

This, as Julia now reviewed the past, she perceived to have been her theoretical attitude toward marriage. It was unconsciously, insidiously, that her ten years of happiness with Westall had developed another conception of the tie; a reversion, rather, to the old instinct of passionate dependency and possessorship that now made her blood revolt at the mere hint of change. Change? Renewal? Was that what they had called it, in their foolish jargon? Destruction, extermination rather — this rending of a myriad fibres interwoven with another's being! Another? But he was not other! He and she were one, one in the mystic sense which alone gave marriage its significance. The new law was not for them, but for the disunited creatures forced into a mockery of union. The gospel she had felt called on to proclaim had no bearing on her own case. . . . She sent for the doctor and told him she was sure she needed a nerve tonic.

She took the nerve tonic diligently, but it failed to act as a sedative to her fears. She did not know what she feared; but that made her anxiety the more pervasive. Her husband had not reverted to the subject of his Saturday talks. He was unusually kind and considerate, with a softening of his quick manner, a touch of shyness in his consideration, that sickened her with new fears. She told herself that it was because she looked badly-because he knew about the doctor and the nerve tonic — that he showed this deference to her wishes, this eagerness to screen her from moral draughts; but the explanation simply cleared the way for fresh inferences.

The week passed slowly, vacantly, like a prolonged Sunday. On Saturday the morning post brought a note from Mrs. Van Sideren. Would dear Julia ask Mr. Westall to come half an hour earlier than usual, as there was to be some music after his "talk"? Westall was just leaving for his office when his wife read the note. She opened the drawing-room door and called him back to deliver the message.

He glanced at the note and tossed it aside. "What a bore! I shall have to cut my game of racquets. Well, I suppose it can't be helped. Will you write and say it's all right?"

Julia hesitated a moment, her hand stiffening on the chair-back against which she leaned.

"You mean to go on with these talks?" she asked.

"I — why not?" he returned; and this time it struck her that his surprise was not quite unfeigned. The discovery helped her to find words.

"You said you had started them with the idea of pleasing me —"

"Well?"

"I told you last week that they didn't please me."

"Last week? Oh —" He seemed to make an effort of memory. "I thought you were nervous then; you sent for the doctor the next day."

"It was not the doctor I needed; it was your assurance —"

"My assurance?"

Suddenly she felt the floor fail under her. She sank into the chair with a choking throat, her words, her reasons slipping away from her like straws down a whirling flood.

"Clement," she cried, "isn't it enough for you to know that I hate it?"

He turned to close the door behind them; then he walked toward her and sat down. "What is it that you hate?" he asked gently.

She had made a desperate effort to rally her routed argument.

"I can't bear to have you speak as if — as if — our marriage — were like the other kind — the wrong kind. When I heard you there, the other afternoon, before all those inquisitive gossiping people, proclaiming that husbands and wives had a right to leave each other whenever they were tired — or had seen some one else —"

Westall sat motionless, his eyes fixed on a pattern of the carpet.

"You have ceased to take this view, then?" he said as she broke off. "You no longer believe that husbands and wives are justified in separating — under such conditions?"

"Under such conditions?" she stammered. "Yes — I still believe that — but how can we judge for others? What can we know of the circumstances — ?"

He interrupted her. "I thought it was a fundamental article of our creed that the special circumstances produced by marriage were not to interfere with the full assertion of individual liberty." He paused a moment. "I thought that was your reason for leaving Arment."

She flushed to the forehead. It was not like him to give a personal turn to the argument.

"It was my reason," she said simply.

"Well, then — why do you refuse to recognize its validity now?"

"I don't — I don't — I only say that one can't judge for others."

He made an impatient movement. "This is mere hair-splitting. What you mean is that, the doctrine having served your purpose when you needed it, you now repudiate it."

"Well," she exclaimed, flushing again, "what if I do? What does it matter to us?"

Westall rose from his chair. He was excessively pale, and stood before his wife with something of the formality of a stranger.

"It matters to me," he said in a low voice, "because I do not repudiate it."

"Well — ?"

"And because I had intended to invoke it as" —

He paused and drew his breath deeply. She sat silent, almost deafened by her heart-beats.

—"as a complete justification of the course I am about to take."

Julia remained motionless. "What course is that?" she asked.

He cleared his throat. "I mean to claim the fulfilment of your promise."

For an instant the room wavered and darkened; then she recovered a torturing acuteness of vision. Every detail of her surroundings pressed upon her: the tick of the clock, the slant of sunlight on the wall, the hardness of the chair-arms that she grasped, were a separate wound to each sense.

"My promise —" she faltered.

"Your part of our mutual agreement to set each other free if one or the other should wish to be released."

She was silent again. He waited a moment, shifting his position nervously; then he said, with a touch of irritability: "You acknowledge the agreement?"

The question went through her like a shock. She lifted her head to it proudly. "I acknowledge the agreement," she said.

"And — you don't mean to repudiate it?"

A log on the hearth fell forward, and mechanically he advanced and pushed it back.

"No," she answered slowly, "I don't mean to repudiate it."

There was a pause. He remained near the hearth, his elbow resting on the mantel-shelf. Close to his hand stood a little cup of jade that he had given her on one of their wedding anniversaries. She wondered vaguely if he noticed it.

"You intend to leave me, then?" she said at length.

His gesture seemed to deprecate the crudeness of the allusion. "To marry some one else?"

Again his eye and hand protested. She rose and stood before him.

"Why should you be afraid to tell me? Is it Una Van Sideren?"

He was silent.

"I wish you good luck," she said.

III

She looked up, finding herself alone. She did not remember when or how he had left the room, or how long afterward she had sat there. The fire still smouldered on the hearth, but the slant of sunlight had left the wall.

Her first conscious thought was that she had not broken her word, that she had fulfilled the very letter of their bargain. There had been no crying out, no vain appeal to the past, no attempt at temporizing or evasion. She had marched straight up to the guns.

Now that it was over, she sickened to find herself alive. She looked about her, trying to recover her hold on reality. Her identity seemed to be slipping from her, as it disappears in a physical swoon. "This is my room — this is my house," she heard herself saying. Her room? Her house? She could almost hear the walls laugh back at her.

She stood up, a dull ache in every bone. The silence of the room frightened her. She remembered, now, having heard the front door close a long time ago: the sound suddenly re-echoed through her brain. Her husband must have left the house, then — her husband? She no longer knew in what terms to think: the simplest phrases had a poisoned edge. She sank back into her chair, overcome by a strange weakness. The clock struck ten — it was only ten o'clock! Suddenly she remembered that she had not ordered dinner . . . or were they dining out that evening? Dinner — Dining Out — the old meaningless phraseology pursued her! She must try to think of herself as she would think of some one else, a some one dissociated from all the familiar routine of the past, whose wants and habits must gradually be learned, as one might spy out the ways of a strange animal. . .

The clock struck another hour — eleven. She stood up again and walked to the door: she thought she would go up stairs to her room. Her room? Again the word derided her. She opened the door, crossed the narrow hall, and walked up the stairs. As she passed, she noticed Westall's sticks and umbrellas: a pair of his gloves lay on the hall table. The same stair-carpet mounted between the same walls; the same old French print, in its narrow black frame, faced her on the landing. This visual continuity was intolerable. Within, a gaping chasm; without, the same untroubled and familiar surface. She must get away from it before she could attempt to think. But, once in her room, she sat down on the lounge, a stupor creeping over her. . .

Gradually her vision cleared. A great deal had happened in the interval — a wild marching and countermarching of emotions, arguments, ideas — a fury of insurgent impulses that fell back spent upon themselves. She had tried, at first, to rally, to organize these chaotic forces. There must be help somewhere, if only she could master the inner tumult. Life could not be broken off short like this, for a whim, a fancy; the law itself would side with her, would defend her. The law? What claim had she upon it? She was the prisoner of her own choice: she had been her own legislator, and she was the predestined victim of the code she had devised. But this was grotesque, intolerable — a mad mistake, for which she could not be held accountable! The law she had despised was still there, might still be invoked . . . invoked, but to what end? Could she ask it to chain Westall to her side? SHE had been allowed to go free when she claimed her freedom — should she show less magnanimity than she had exacted? Magnanimity? The word lashed her with its irony — one does not strike an attitude when one is fighting for life! She would threaten, grovel, cajole . . . she would yield anything to keep her hold on happiness. Ah, but the difficulty lay deeper! The law could not help her — her own apostasy could not help her. She was the victim of the theories she renounced. It was as though some giant machine of her own making had caught her up in its wheels and was grinding her to atoms. . .

It was afternoon when she found herself out-of-doors. She walked with an aimless haste, fearing to meet familiar faces. The day was radiant, metallic: one of those searching American days so calculated to reveal the shortcomings of our street-cleaning and the excesses of our architecture. The streets looked bare and hideous; everything stared and glittered. She called a passing hansom, and gave Mrs. Van Sideren's address. She did not know what had led up to the act; but she found herself suddenly resolved to speak, to cry out a warning. it was too late to save herself — but the girl might still be told. The hansom rattled up Fifth Avenue; she sat with her eyes fixed, avoiding recognition. At the Van Siderens' door she sprang out and rang the bell. Action had cleared her brain, and she felt calm and self-possessed. She knew now exactly what she meant to say.

The ladies were both out . . . the parlor-maid stood waiting for a card. Julia, with a vague murmur, turned away from the door and lingered a moment on the sidewalk. Then she remembered that she had not paid the cab-driver. She drew a dollar from her purse and handed it to him. He touched his hat and drove off, leaving her alone in the long empty street. She wandered away westward, toward strange thoroughfares, where she was not likely to meet acquaintances. The feeling of aimlessness had returned. Once she found herself in the afternoon torrent of Broadway, swept past tawdry shops and flaming theatrical posters, with a succession of meaningless faces gliding by in the opposite direction. . .

A feeling of faintness reminded her that she had not eaten since morning. She turned into a side street of shabby houses, with rows of ash-barrels behind bent area railings. In a basement window she saw the sign LADIES' RESTAURANT: a pie and a dish of doughnuts lay against the dusty pane like petrified food in an ethnological museum. She entered, and a young woman with a weak mouth and a brazen eye cleared a table for her near the window. The table was covered with a red and white cotton cloth and adorned with a bunch of celery in a thick tumbler and a saltcellar full of grayish lumpy salt. Julia ordered tea, and sat a long time waiting for it. She was glad to be away from the noise and confusion of the streets. The low-ceilinged room was empty, and two or three waitresses with thin pert faces lounged in the background staring at her and whispering together. At last the tea was brought in a discolored metal teapot. Julia poured a cup and drank it hastily. It was black and bitter, but it flowed through her veins like an elixir. She was almost dizzy with exhilaration. Oh, how tired, how unutterably tired she had been!

She drank a second cup, blacker and bitterer, and now her mind was once more working clearly. She felt as vigorous, as decisive, as when she had stood on the Van Siderens' door-step-but the wish to return there had subsided. She saw now the futility of such an attempt — the humiliation to which it might have exposed her. . . The pity of it was that she did not know what to do next. The short winter day was fading, and she realized that she could not remain much longer in the restaurant without attracting notice. She paid for her tea and went out into the street. The lamps were alight, and here and there a basement shop cast an oblong of gas-light across the fissured pavement. In the dusk there was something sinister about the aspect of the street, and she hastened back toward Fifth Avenue. She was not used to being out alone at that hour.

At the corner of Fifth Avenue she paused and stood watching the stream of carriages. At last a policeman caught sight of her and signed to her that he would take her across. She had not meant to cross the street, but she obeyed automatically, and presently found herself on the farther corner. There she paused again for a moment; but she fancied the policeman was watching her, and this sent her hastening down the nearest side street. . . After that she walked a long time, vaguely. . . Night had fallen, and now and then, through the windows of a passing carriage, she caught the expanse of an evening waistcoat or the shimmer of an opera cloak. . .

Suddenly she found herself in a familiar street. She stood still a moment, breathing quickly. She had turned the corner without noticing whither it led; but now, a few yards ahead of her, she saw the house in which she had once lived — her first husband's house. The blinds were drawn, and only a faint translucence marked the windows and the transom above the door. As she stood there she heard a step behind her, and a man walked by in the direction of the house. He walked slowly, with a heavy middleaged gait, his head sunk a little between the shoulders, the red crease of his neck visible above the fur collar of his overcoat. He crossed the street, went up the steps of the house, drew forth a latch-key, and let himself in. . .

There was no one else in sight. Julia leaned for a long time against the area-rail at the corner, her eyes fixed on the front of the house. The feeling of physical weariness had returned, but the strong tea still throbbed in her veins and lit her brain with an unnatural clearness. Presently she heard another step draw near, and moving quickly away, she too crossed the street and mounted the steps of the house. The impulse which had carried her there prolonged itself in a quick pressure of the electric bell — then she felt suddenly weak and tremulous, and grasped the balustrade for support. The door opened and a young footman with a fresh inexperienced face stood on the threshold. Julia knew in an instant that he would admit her.

"I saw Mr. Arment going in just now," she said. "Will you ask him to see me for a moment?"

The footman hesitated. "I think Mr. Arment has gone up to dress for dinner, madam."

Julia advanced into the hall. "I am sure he will see me — I will not detain him long," she said. She spoke quietly, authoritatively, in the tone which a good servant does not mistake. The footman had his hand on the drawing-room door.

"I will tell him, madam. What name, please?"

Julia trembled: she had not thought of that. "Merely say a lady," she returned carelessly.

The footman wavered and she fancied herself lost; but at that instant the door opened from within and John Arment stepped into the hall. He drew back sharply as he saw her, his florid face turning sallow with the shock; then the blood poured back to it, swelling the veins on his temples and reddening the lobes of his thick ears.

It was long since Julia had seen him, and she was startled at the change in his appearance. He had thickened, coarsened, settled down into the enclosing flesh. But she noted this insensibly: her one conscious thought was that, now she was face to face with him, she must not let him escape till he had heard her. Every pulse in her body throbbed with the urgency of her message.

She went up to him as he drew back. "I must speak to you," she said.

Arment hesitated, red and stammering. Julia glanced at the footman, and her look acted as a warning. The instinctive shrinking from a "scene" predominated over every other impulse, and Arment said slowly: "Will you come this way?"

He followed her into the drawing-room and closed the door. Julia, as she advanced, was vaguely aware that the room at least was unchanged: time had not mitigated its horrors. The contadina still lurched from the chimney-breast, and the Greek slave obstructed the threshold of the inner room. The place was alive with memories: they started out from every fold of the yellow satin curtains and glided between the angles of the rosewood furniture. But while some subordinate agency was carrying these impressions to her brain, her whole conscious effort was centred in the act of dominating Arment's will. The fear that he would refuse to hear her mounted like fever to her brain. She felt her purpose melt before it, words and arguments running into each other in the heat of her longing. For a moment her voice failed her, and she imagined herself thrust out before she could speak; but as she was struggling for a word, Arment pushed a chair forward, and said quietly: "You are not well."

The sound of his voice steadied her. It was neither kind nor unkind — a voice that suspended judgment, rather, awaiting unforeseen developments. She supported herself against the back of the chair and drew a deep breath. "Shall I send for something?" he continued, with a cold embarrassed politeness.

Julia raised an entreating hand. "No — no — thank you. I am quite well."

He paused midway toward the bell and turned on her. "Then may I ask — ?"

"Yes," she interrupted him. "I came here because I wanted to see you. There is something I must tell you."

Arment continued to scrutinize her. "I am surprised at that," he said. "I should have supposed that any communication you may wish to make could have been made through our lawyers."

"Our lawyers!" She burst into a little laugh. "I don't think they could help me — this time."

Arment's face took on a barricaded look. "If there is any question of help — of course —"

It struck her, whimsically, that she had seen that look when some shabby devil called with a subscription-book. Perhaps he thought she wanted him to put his name down for so much in sympathy — or even in money. . . The thought made her laugh again. She saw his look change slowly to perplexity. All his facial changes were slow, and she remembered, suddenly, how it had once diverted her to shift that lumbering scenery with a word. For the first time it struck her that she had been cruel. "There is a question of help," she said in a softer key: "you can help me; but only by listening. . . I want to tell you something. . ."

Arment's resistance was not yielding. "Would it not be easier to -write?" he suggested.

She shook her head. "There is no time to write . . . and it won't take long." She raised her head and their eyes met. "My husband has left me," she said.

"Westall — ?" he stammered, reddening again.

"Yes. This morning. Just as I left you. Because he was tired of me."

The words, uttered scarcely above a whisper, seemed to dilate to the limit of the room. Arment looked toward the door; then his embarrassed glance returned to Julia.

"I am very sorry," he said awkwardly.

"Thank you," she murmured.

"But I don't see —"

"No — but you will — in a moment. Won't you listen to me? Please!" Instinctively she had shifted her position putting herself between him and the door. "It happened this morning," she went on in short breathless phrases. "I never suspected anything — I thought we were — perfectly happy. . . Suddenly he told me he was tired of me . . . there is a girl he likes better. . . He has gone to her. . ." As she spoke, the lurking anguish rose upon her, possessing her once more to the exclusion of every other emotion. Her eyes ached, her throat swelled with it, and two painful tears burnt a way down her face.

Arment's constraint was increasing visibly. "This — this is very unfortunate," he began. "But I should say the law —"

"The law?" she echoed ironically. "When he asks for his freedom?"

"You are not obliged to give it."

"You were not obliged to give me mine — but you did."

He made a protesting gesture.

"You saw that the law couldn't help you — didn't you?" she went on. "That is what I see now. The law represents material rights — it can't go beyond. If we don't recognize an inner law . . . the obligation that love creates . . . being loved as well as loving . . . there is nothing to prevent our spreading ruin unhindered .

. . is there?" She raised her head plaintively, with the look of a bewildered child. "That is what I see now . . . what I wanted to tell you. He leaves me because he's tired . . . but I was not tired; and I don't understand why he is. That's the dreadful part of it — the not understanding: I hadn't realized what it meant. But I've been thinking of it all day, and things have come back to me — things I hadn't noticed . . . when you and I. . ." She moved closer to him, and fixed her eyes on his with the gaze that tries to reach beyond words. "I see now that you didn't understand -did you?"

Their eyes met in a sudden shock of comprehension: a veil seemed to be lifted between them. Arment's lip trembled.

"No," he said, "I didn't understand."

She gave a little cry, almost of triumph. "I knew it! I knew it! You wondered — you tried to tell me — but no words came. . . You saw your life falling in ruins . . . the world slipping from you . . . and you couldn't speak or move!"

She sank down on the chair against which she had been leaning. "Now I know — now I know," she repeated.

"I am very sorry for you," she heard Arment stammer.

She looked up quickly. "That's not what I came for. I don't want you to be sorry. I came to ask you to forgive me . . . for not understanding that you didn't understand. . . That's all I wanted to say." She rose with a vague sense that the end had come, and put out a groping hand toward the door.

Arment stood motionless. She turned to him with a faint smile.

"You forgive me?"

"There is nothing to forgive —"

"Then will you shake hands for good-by?" She felt his hand in hers: it was nerveless, reluctant.

"Good-by," she repeated. "I understand now."

She opened the door and passed out into the hall. As she did so, Arment took an impulsive step forward; but just then the footman, who was evidently alive to his obligations, advanced from the background to let her out. She heard Arment fall back. The footman threw open the door, and she found herself outside in the darkness.

Forgiveness
Guy de Maupassant

She had been brought up in one of those families who live entirely to themselves, apart from all the rest of the world. Such families know nothing of political events, although they are discussed at table; for changes in the Government take place at such a distance from them that they are spoken of as one speaks of a historical event, such as the death of Louis XVI or the landing of Napoleon.

Customs are modified in course of time, fashions succeed one another, but such variations are taken no account of in the placid family circle where traditional usages prevail year after year. And if some scandalous episode or other occurs in the neighborhood, the disreputable story dies a natural death when it reaches the threshold of the house. The father and mother may, perhaps, exchange a few words on the subject when alone together some evening, but they speak in hushed tones—for even walls have ears. The father says, with bated breath:

"You've heard of that terrible affair in the Rivoil family?"

And the mother answers:

"Who would have dreamed of such a thing? It's dreadful."

The children suspected nothing, and arrive in their turn at years of discretion with eyes and mind blindfolded, ignorant of the real side of life, not knowing that people do not think as they speak, and do not speak as they act; or aware that they should live at war, or at all events, in a state of armed peace, with the rest of mankind; not suspecting the fact that the simple are always deceived, the sincere made sport of, the good maltreated.

Some go on till the day of their death in this blind probity and loyalty and honor, so pure-minded that nothing can open their eyes.

Others, undeceived, but without fully understanding, make mistakes, are dismayed, and become desperate, believing themselves the playthings of a cruel fate, the wretched victims of adverse circumstances, and exceptionally wicked men.

The Savignols married their daughter Bertha at the age of eighteen. She wedded a young Parisian, George Baron by name, who had dealings on the Stock Exchange. He was handsome, well-mannered, and apparently all that could be desired. But in the depths of his heart he somewhat despised his old-fashioned parents-in-law, whom he spoke of among his intimates as "my dear old fossils."

He belonged to a good family, and the girl was rich. They settled down in Paris.

She became one of those provincial Parisians whose name is legion. She remained in complete ignorance of the great city, of its social side, its pleasures and its customs—just as she remained ignorant also of life, its perfidy and its mysteries.

Devoted to her house, she knew scarcely anything beyond her own street; and when she ventured into another part of Paris it seemed to her that she had accomplished a long and arduous journey into some unknown, unexplored city. She would then say to her husband in the evening:

"I have been through the boulevards today."

Two or three times a year her husband took her to the theatre. These were events the remembrance of which never grew dim; they provided subjects of conversation for long afterward.

Sometimes three months afterward she would suddenly burst into laughter, and exclaim:

"Do you remember that actor dressed up as a general, who crowed like a cock?"

Her friends were limited to two families related to her own. She spoke of them as "the Martinets" and "the Michelins."

Her husband lived as he pleased, coming home when it suited him—sometimes not until dawn—alleging business, but not putting himself out overmuch to account for his movements, well aware that no suspicion would ever enter his wife's guileless soul.

But one morning she received an anonymous letter.

She was thunderstruck—too simple-minded to understand the infamy of unsigned information and to despise the letter, the writer of which declared himself inspired by interest in her happiness, hatred of evil, and love of truth.

This missive told her that her husband had had for two years past, a sweetheart, a young widow named Madame Rosset, with whom he spent all his evenings.

Bertha knew neither how to dissemble her grief nor how to spy on her husband. When he came in for lunch she threw the letter down before him, burst into tears, and fled to her room.

He had time to take in the situation and to prepare his reply. He knocked at his wife's door. She opened it at once, but dared not look at him. He smiled, sat down, drew her to his knee, and in a tone of light raillery began:

"My dear child, as a matter of fact, I have a friend named Madame Rosset, whom I have known for the last ten years, and of whom I have a very high opinion. I may add that I know scores of other people whose names I have never mentioned to you, seeing that you do not care for society, or fresh acquaintances, or functions of any sort. But, to make short work of such vile accusations as this, I want you to put on your things after lunch, and we'll go together and call on this lady, who will very soon become a friend of yours, too, I am quite sure."

She embraced her husband warmly, and, moved by that feminine spirit of curiosity which will not be lulled once it is aroused, consented to go and see this unknown widow, of whom she was, in spite of everything, just the least bit jealous. She felt instinctively that to know a danger is to be already armed against it.

She entered a small, tastefully furnished flat on the fourth floor of an attractive house. After waiting five minutes in a drawing-room rendered somewhat dark by its many curtains and hangings, a door opened, and a very dark, short, rather plump young woman appeared, surprised and smiling.

George introduced them:

"My wife—Madame Julie Rosset."

The young widow uttered a half-suppressed cry of astonishment and joy, and ran forward with hands outstretched. She had not hoped, she said, to have this pleasure, knowing that Madame Baron never saw any one, but she was delighted to make her acquaintance. She was so fond of George (she said "George" in a familiar, sisterly sort of way) that, she had been most anxious to know his young wife and to make friends with her, too.

By the end of a month the two new friends were inseparable. They saw each other every day, sometimes twice a day, and dined together every evening, sometimes at one house, sometimes at the other. George no longer deserted his home, no longer talked of pressing business. He adored his own fireside, he said.

When, after a time, a flat in the house where Madame Rosset lived became vacant Madame Baron hastened to take it, in order to be near her friend and spend even more time with her than hitherto.

And for two whole years their friendship was without a cloud, a friendship of heart and mind—absolute, tender, devoted. Bertha could hardly speak without bringing in Julie's name. To her Madame Rosset represented perfection.

She was utterly happy, calm and contented.

But Madame Rosset fell ill. Bertha hardly left her side. She spent her nights with her, distracted with grief; even her husband seemed inconsolable.

One morning the doctor, after leaving the invalid's bedside, took George and his wife aside, and told them that he considered Julie's condition very grave.

As soon as he had gone the grief-stricken husband and wife sat down opposite each other and gave way to tears. That night they both sat up with the patient. Bertha tenderly kissed her friend from time to time, while George stood at the foot of the bed, his eyes gazing steadfastly on the invalid's face.

The next day she was worse.

But toward evening she declared she felt better, and insisted that her friends should go back to their own apartment to dinner.

They were sitting sadly in the dining-room, scarcely even attempting to eat, when the maid gave George a note. He opened it, turned pale as death, and, rising from the table, said to his wife in a constrained voice:

"Wait for me. I must leave you a moment. I shall be back in ten minutes. Don't go away on any account."

And he hurried to his room to get his hat.

Bertha waited for him, a prey to fresh anxiety. But, docile in everything, she would not go back to her friend till he returned.

At length, as he did not reappear, it occurred to her to visit his room and see if he had taken his gloves. This would show whether or not he had had a call to make.

She saw them at the first glance. Beside them lay a crumpled paper, evidently thrown down in haste.

She recognized it at once as the note George had received.

And a burning temptation, the first that had ever assailed her urged her to read it and discover the cause of her husband's abrupt departure. Her rebellious conscience protested but a devouring and fearful curiosity prevailed. She seized the paper, smoothed it out, recognized the tremulous, penciled writing as Julie's, and read:

"Come alone and kiss me, my poor dear. I am dying."

At first she did not understand, the idea of Julie's death being her uppermost thought. But all at once the true meaning of what she read burst in a flash upon her; this penciled note threw a lurid light upon her whole existence, revealed the whole infamous truth, all the treachery and perfidy of which she had been the victim. She understood the long years of deceit, the way in which she had been made their puppet. She saw them again, sitting side by side in the evening, reading by lamplight out of the same book, glancing at each other at the end of each page.

And her poor, indignant, suffering, bleeding heart was cast into the depths of a despair which knew no bounds.

Footsteps drew near; she fled, and shut herself in her own room.

Presently her husband called her:

"Come quickly! Madame Rosset is dying."

Bertha appeared at her door, and with trembling lips replied:

"Go back to her alone; she does not need me."

He looked at her stupidly, dazed with grief, and repeated:

"Come at once! She's dying, I tell you!"

Bertha answered:

"You would rather it were I."

Then at last he understood, and returned alone to the dying woman's bedside.

He mourned her openly, shamelessly, indifferent to the sorrow of the wife who no longer spoke to him, no longer looked at him; who passed her life in solitude, hedged round with disgust, with indignant anger, and praying night and day to God.

They still lived in the same house, however, and sat opposite each other at table, in silence and despair.

Gradually his sorrow grew less acute; but she did not forgive him.

And so their life went on, hard and bitter for them both.

For a whole year they remained as complete strangers to each other as if they had never met. Bertha nearly lost her reason.

At last one morning she went out very early, and returned about eight o'clock bearing in her hands an enormous bouquet of white roses. And she sent word to her husband that she wanted to speak to him. He came-anxious and uneasy.

"We are going out together," she said. "Please carry these flowers; they are too heavy for me."

A carriage took them to the gate of the cemetery, where they alighted. Then, her eyes filling with tears, she said to George:

"Take me to her grave."

He trembled, and could not understand her motive; but he led the way, still carrying the flowers. At last he stopped before a white marble slab, to which he pointed without a word.

She took the bouquet from him, and, kneeling down, placed it on the grave. Then she offered up a silent, heartfelt prayer.

Behind her stood her husband, overcome by recollections of the past.

She rose, and held out her hands to him.

"If you wish it, we will be friends," she said.

Joseph and His Brothers
Genesis 42-45

Joseph's Brothers Go to Egypt

When Jacob learned that there was grain in Egypt, he said to his sons, "Why do you just keep looking at each other?" He continued, "I have heard that there is grain in Egypt. Go down there and buy some for us, so that we may live and not die."

Then ten of Joseph's brothers went down to buy grain from Egypt. But Jacob did not send Benjamin, Joseph's brother, with the others, because he was afraid that harm might come to him. So Israel's sons were among those who went to buy grain, for the famine was in the land of Canaan also.

Now Joseph was the governor of the land, the one who sold grain to all its people. So when Joseph's brothers arrived, they bowed down to him with their faces to the ground. As soon as Joseph saw his brothers, he recognized them, but he pretended to be a stranger and spoke harshly to them. "Where do you come from?" he asked.

"From the land of Canaan," they replied, "to buy food."

Although Joseph recognized his brothers, they did not recognize him. Then he remembered his dreams about them and said to them, "You are spies! You have come to see where our land is unprotected."

"No, my lord," they answered. "Your servants have come to buy food. We are all the sons of one man. Your servants are honest men, not spies."

"No!" he said to them. "You have come to see where our land is unprotected."

But they replied, "Your servants were twelve brothers, the sons of one man, who lives in the land of Canaan. The youngest is now with our father, and one is no more."

Joseph said to them, "It is just as I told you: You are spies! And this is how you will be tested: As surely as Pharaoh lives, you will not leave this place unless your youngest brother comes here. Send one of your number to get your brother; the rest of you will be kept in prison, so that your words may be tested to see if you are telling the truth. If you are not, then as surely as Pharaoh lives, you are spies!" And he put them all in custody for three days.

On the third day, Joseph said to them, "Do this and you will live, for I fear God: If you are honest men, let one of your brothers stay here in prison, while the rest of you go and take grain back for your starving households. But you must bring your youngest brother to me, so that your words may be verified and that you may not die." This they proceeded to do.

They said to one another, "Surely we are being punished because of our brother. We saw how distressed he was when he pleaded with us for his life, but we would not listen; that's why this distress has come upon us."

Reuben replied, "Didn't I tell you not to sin against the boy? But you wouldn't listen! Now we must give an accounting for his blood." They did not realize that Joseph could understand them, since he was using an interpreter.

He turned away from them and began to weep, but then turned back and spoke to them again. He had Simeon taken from them and bound before their eyes.

Joseph gave orders to fill their bags with grain, to put each man's silver back in his sack, and to give them provisions for their journey. After this was done for them, they loaded their grain on their donkeys and left.

At the place where they stopped for the night one of them opened his sack to get feed for his donkey, and he saw his silver in the mouth of his sack. "My silver has been returned," he said to his brothers. "Here it is in my sack."

Their hearts sank and they turned to each other trembling and said, "What is this that God has done to us?"

When they came to their father Jacob in the land of Canaan, they told him all that had happened to them. They said, "The man who is lord over the land spoke harshly to us and treated us as though we were spying on the land. But we said to him, 'We are honest men; we are not spies. We were twelve brothers, sons of one father. One is no more, and the youngest is now with our father in Canaan.'

"Then the man who is lord over the land said to us, 'This is how I will know whether you are honest men: Leave one of your brothers here with me, and take food for your starving households and go. But bring your youngest brother to me so I will know that you are not spies but honest men. Then I will give your brother back to you, and you can trade in the land.'"

As they were emptying their sacks, there in each man's sack was his pouch of silver! When they and their father saw the money pouches, they were frightened. Their father Jacob said to them, "You have deprived me of my children. Joseph is no more and Simeon is no more, and now you want to take Benjamin. Everything is against me!"

Then Reuben said to his father, "You may put both of my sons to death if I do not bring him back to you. Entrust him to my care, and I will bring him back."

But Jacob said, "My son will not go down there with you; his brother is dead and he is the only one left. If harm comes to him on the journey you are taking, you will bring my gray head down to the grave in sorrow."

The Second Journey to Egypt

Now the famine was still severe in the land. So when they had eaten all the grain they had brought from Egypt, their father said to them, "Go back and buy us a little more food."

But Judah said to him, "The man warned us solemnly, 'You will not see my face again unless your brother is with you.' If you will send our brother along with us, we will go down and buy food for you. But if you will not send him, we will not go down, because the man said to us, 'You will not see my face again unless your brother is with you.'"

Israel asked, "Why did you bring this trouble on me by telling the man you had another brother?"

They replied, "The man questioned us closely about ourselves and our family. 'Is your father still living?' he asked us. 'Do you have another brother?' We simply answered his questions. How were we to know he would say, 'Bring your brother down here?'"

Then Judah said to Israel his father, "Send the boy along with me and we will go at once, so that we and you and our children may live and not die. I myself will guarantee his safety; you can hold me personally responsible for him. If I do not bring him back to you and set him here before you, I will bear the blame before you all my life. As it is, if we had not delayed, we could have gone and returned twice."

Then their father Israel said to them, "If it must be, then do this: Put some of the best products of the land in your bags and take them down to the man as a gift—a little balm and a little honey, some spices and myrrh, some pistachio nuts and almonds. Take double the amount of silver with you, for you must return the silver that was put back into the mouths of your sacks. Perhaps it was a mistake. Take your brother also and go back to the man at once. And may God Almighty grant you mercy before the man so that he will let your other brother and Benjamin come back with you. As for me, if I am bereaved, I am bereaved."

So the men took the gifts and double the amount of silver, and Benjamin also. They hurried down to Egypt and presented themselves to Joseph. When Joseph saw Benjamin with them, he said to the steward of his house, "Take these men to my house, slaughter an animal and prepare dinner; they are to eat with me at noon."

The man did as Joseph told him and took the men to Joseph's house. Now the men were frightened when they were taken to his house. They thought, "We were brought here because of the silver that was put back into our sacks the first time. He wants to attack us and overpower us and seize us as slaves and take our donkeys."

So they went up to Joseph's steward and spoke to him at the entrance to the house. "Please, sir," they said, "we came down here the first time to buy food. But at the place where we stopped for the night we opened our sacks and each of us found his silver—the exact weight—in the mouth of his sack. So we have brought it back with us. We have also brought additional silver with us to buy food. We don't know who put our silver in our sacks."

"It's all right," he said. "Don't be afraid. Your God, the God of your father, has given you treasure in your sacks; I received your silver." Then he brought Simeon out to them.

The steward took the men into Joseph's house, gave them water to wash their feet and provided fodder for their donkeys. They prepared their gifts for Joseph's arrival at noon, because they had heard that they were to eat there.

When Joseph came home, they presented to him the gifts they

had brought into the house, and they bowed down before him to the ground. He asked them how they were, and then he said, "How is your aged father you told me about? Is he still living?"

They replied, "Your servant our father is still alive and well." And they bowed low to pay him honor.

As he looked about and saw his brother Benjamin, his own mother's son, he asked, "Is this your youngest brother, the one you told me about?" And he said, "God be gracious to you, my son." Deeply moved at the sight of his brother, Joseph hurried out and looked for a place to weep. He went into his private room and wept there.

After he had washed his face, he came out and, controlling himself, said, "Serve the food."

They served him by himself, the brothers by themselves, and the Egyptians who ate with him by themselves, because Egyptians could not eat with Hebrews, for that is detestable to Egyptians. The men had been seated before him in the order of their ages, from the firstborn to the youngest; and they looked at each other in astonishment. When portions were served to them from Joseph's table, Benjamin's portion was five times as much as anyone else's. So they feasted and drank freely with him.

A Silver Cup in a Sack

Now Joseph gave these instructions to the steward of his house: "Fill the men's sacks with as much food as they can carry, and put each man's silver in the mouth of his sack. Then put my cup, the silver one, in the mouth of the youngest one's sack, along with the silver for his grain." And he did as Joseph said.

As morning dawned, the men were sent on their way with their donkeys. They had not gone far from the city when Joseph said to his steward, "Go after those men at once, and when you catch up with them, say to them, 'Why have you repaid good with evil? Isn't this the cup my master drinks from and also uses for divination? This is a wicked thing you have done.'"

When he caught up with them, he repeated these words to them. But they said to him, "Why does my lord say such things? Far be it from your servants to do anything like that! We even brought back to you from the land of Canaan the silver we found inside the mouths of our sacks. So why would we steal silver or gold from your master's house? If any of your servants is found to have it, he will die; and the rest of us will become my lord's slaves."

"Very well, then," he said, "let it be as you say. Whoever is found to have it will become my slave; the rest of you will be free from blame."

Each of them quickly lowered his sack to the ground and opened it. Then the steward proceeded to search, beginning with the oldest and ending with the youngest. And the cup was found in Benjamin's sack. At this, they tore their clothes. Then they all loaded their donkeys and returned to the city.

Joseph was still in the house when Judah and his brothers came in, and they threw themselves to the ground before him. Joseph said to them, "What is this you have done? Don't you know that a man like me can find things out by divination?"

"What can we say to my lord?" Judah replied. "What can we say? How can we prove our innocence? God has uncovered your servants' guilt. We are now my lord's slaves—we ourselves and the one who was found to have the cup."

But Joseph said, "Far be it from me to do such a thing! Only the man who was found to have the cup will become my slave. The rest of you, go back to your father in peace."

Then Judah went up to him and said: "Please, my lord, let your servant speak a word to my lord. Do not be angry with your servant, though you are equal to Pharaoh himself. My lord asked his servants, 'Do you have a father or a brother?' And we answered, 'We have an aged father, and there is a young son born to him in his old age. His brother is dead, and he is the only one of his mother's sons left, and his father loves him.'

"Then you said to your servants, 'Bring him down to me so I can see him for myself.' And we said to my lord, 'The boy cannot leave his father; if he leaves him, his father will die.' But you told your servants, 'Unless your youngest brother comes down with you, you will not see my face again.' When we went back to your servant my father, we told him what my lord had said.

"Then our father said, 'Go back and buy a little more food.' But we said, 'We cannot go down. Only if our youngest brother is with us will we go. We cannot see the man's face unless our youngest brother is with us.'

"Your servant my father said to us, 'You know that my wife bore me two sons. One of them went away from me, and I said, "He has surely been torn to pieces." And I have not seen him since.

If you take this one from me too and harm comes to him, you will bring my gray head down to the grave in misery.'

"So now, if the boy is not with us when I go back to your servant my father and if my father, whose life is closely bound up with the boy's life, sees that the boy isn't there, he will die. Your servants will bring the gray head of our father down to the grave in sorrow. Your servant guaranteed the boy's safety to my father. I said, 'If I do not bring him back to you, I will bear the blame before you, my father, all my life!'

"Now then, please let your servant remain here as my lord's slave in place of the boy, and let the boy return with his brothers. How can I go back to my father if the boy is not with me? No! Do not let me see the misery that would come upon my father."

Joseph Makes Himself Known

Then Joseph could no longer control himself before all his attendants, and he cried out, "Have everyone leave my presence!" So there was no one with Joseph when he made himself known to his brothers. And he wept so loudly that the Egyptians heard him, and Pharaoh's household heard about it.

Joseph said to his brothers, "I am Joseph! Is my father still living?" But his brothers were not able to answer him, because they were terrified at his presence.

Then Joseph said to his brothers, "Come close to me." When they had done so, he said, "I am your brother Joseph, the one you sold into Egypt! And now, do not be distressed and do not be angry with yourselves for selling me here, because it was to save lives that God sent me ahead of you. For two years now there has been famine in the land, and for the next five years there will not be plowing and reaping. But God sent me ahead of you to preserve for you a remnant on earth and to save your lives by a great deliverance.

"So then, it was not you who sent me here, but God. He made me father to Pharaoh, lord of his entire household and ruler of all Egypt. Now hurry back to my father and say to him, 'This is what your son Joseph says: God has made me lord of all Egypt. Come down to me; don't delay. You shall live in the region of Goshen and be near me—you, your children and grandchildren, your flocks and herds, and all you have. I will provide for you there, because five years of famine are still to come. Otherwise you and your household and all who belong to you will become destitute.'

"You can see for yourselves, and so can my brother Benjamin, that it is really I who am speaking to you. Tell my father about all the honor accorded me in Egypt and about everything you have seen. And bring my father down here quickly."

Then he threw his arms around his brother Benjamin and wept, and Benjamin embraced him, weeping. And he kissed all his brothers and wept over them. Afterward his brothers talked with him.

When the news reached Pharaoh's palace that Joseph's brothers had come, Pharaoh and all his officials were pleased. Pharaoh said to Joseph, "Tell your brothers, 'Do this: Load your animals and return to the land of Canaan, and bring your father and your families back to me. I will give you the best of the land of Egypt and you can enjoy the fat of the land.'

"You are also directed to tell them, 'Do this: Take some carts from Egypt for your children and your wives, and get your father and come. Never mind about your belongings, because the best of all Egypt will be yours.'"

So the sons of Israel did this. Joseph gave them carts, as Pharaoh had commanded, and he also gave them provisions for their journey. To each of them he gave new clothing, but to Benjamin he gave three hundred shekels of silver and five sets of clothes. And this is what he sent to his father: ten donkeys loaded with the best things of Egypt, and ten female donkeys loaded with grain and bread and other provisions for his journey. Then he sent his brothers away, and as they were leaving he said to them, "Don't quarrel on the way!"

So they went up out of Egypt and came to their father Jacob in the land of Canaan. They told him, "Joseph is still alive! In fact, he is ruler of all Egypt." Jacob was stunned; he did not believe them. But when they told him everything Joseph had said to them, and when he saw the carts Joseph had sent to carry him back, the spirit of their father Jacob revived. And Israel said, "I'm convinced! My son Joseph is still alive. I will go and see him before I die."

FRIENDS

The Sexton's Hero
Elizabeth Gaskell

The afternoon sun shed down his glorious rays on the grassy churchyard, making the shadow, cast by the old yew-tree under which we sat, seem deeper and deeper by contrast. The everlasting hum of myriads of summer insects made luxurious lullaby.

Of the view that lay beneath our gaze, I cannot speak adequately. The foreground was the grey-stone wall of the Vicarage garden; rich in the coloring made by innumerable lichens, ferns, ivy of most tender green and most delicate tracery, and the vivid scarlet of the crane's-bill, which found a home in every nook and crevice — and at the summit of that old wall flaunted some unpruned tendrils of the vine, and long flower-laden branches of the climbing rose-tree, trained against the inner side. Beyond, lay meadow green and mountain grey,and the blue dazzle of Morecambe Bay, as it sparkled between us and the more distant view.

For a while we were silent, living in sight and murmuring sound. Then Jeremy took up our conversation where, suddenly feeling weariness, as we saw that deep green shadowy resting-place, we had ceased speaking a quarter of an hour before.

It is one of the luxuries of holiday-time that thoughts are not rudely shaken from us by outward violence of hurry and busy impatience, but fall maturely from our lips in the sunny leisure of our days. The stock may be bad, but the fruit is ripe.

"How would you then define a hero?" I asked.

There was a long pause, and I had almost forgotten my question in watching a cloud-shadow floating over the far-away hills, when Jeremy made answer —

"My idea of a hero is one who acts up to the highest idea of duty he has been able to form, no matter at what sacrifice. I think that by this definition we may include all phases of character, even to the heroes of old, whose sole (and to us, low) idea of duty consisted in personal prowess."

"Then you would even admit the military heroes?" asked I.

"I would; with a certain kind of pity for the circumstances which had given them no higher ideas of duty. Still, if they sacrificed self to do what they sincerely believed to be right. I do not think I could deny them the title of hero."

"A poor, unchristian heroism, whose manifestation consists in injury to others!" I said.

We were both startled by a third voice.

"If I might make so bold, sir" — and then the speaker stopped.

It was the sexton, whom, when we first arrived, we had noticed, as an accessory to the scene, but whom we had forgotten, as much as though he were as inanimate as one of the moss-covered headstones. "If I might be so bold," said he again, waiting leave to speak. Jeremy bowed in deference to his white, uncovered head. And so encouraged, he went on.

"What that gentleman" (alluding to my last speech) "has just now said, brings to my mind one who is dead and gone this many a year ago. I, may be, have not rightly understood your meaning, gentlemen, but as far as I could gather it, I think you'd both have given in to thinking poor Gilbert Dawson a hero. At any rate," said he, heaving a long, quivering sigh, "I have reason to think him so."

"Will you take a seat, sir, and tell us about him?" said Jeremy, standing up until the old man was seated. I confess I felt impatient at the interruption.

"It will be forty-five year come Martinmas," said the Sexton, sitting down on a grassy mound at our feet, "since I finished my 'prenticeship, and settled down at Lindal. You can see Lindal, sir, at evenings and mornings across the bay; a little to the right of Grange; at least, I used to see it, many a time and oft, afore my sight grew so dark: and I have spent many a quarter of an hour a-gazing at it far away, and thinking of the days I lived there, till the tears came so thick to my eyes, I could gaze no longer. I shall never look upon it again, either far off or near, but you may see it, both ways, and a terrible bonny spot it is. In my young days, when I went to settle there, it was full of as wild a set of young fellows as ever were clapped eyes on; all for fighting, poaching, quarrelling, and suchlike work. I were startled myself when I first found what a set I were among, but soon I began to fall into their ways, and I ended by being as rough a chap as any of 'em. I'd been there a matter of two year, and were reckoned by most the cock of the village, when Gilbert Dawson, as I was speaking of, came to Lindal. He were about as strapping a chap as I was (I used to be six feet high, though now I'm so shrunk and doubled up), and, as we were like in the same trade (both used to prepare osiers and wood for the Liverpool coopers, who get a deal of stuff from the copses round the bay, sir), we were thrown together, and took mightily to each other. I put my best leg foremost to be equal with Gilbert, for I'd had some schooling, though since I'd been at Lindal I'd lost a good part of what I'd learnt; and I kept my rough ways out of sight for a time, I felt so ashamed of his getting to know them. But that did not last long. I began to think he fancied a girl I dearly loved, but who had always held off from me. Eh! but she was a pretty one in those days! There's none like her, now. I think I see her going along the road with her dancing tread, and shaking back her long yellow curls, to give me or any other young fellow a saucy word; no wonder Gilbert was taken with her, for all he was grave, and she so merry and light. But I began to think she liked him again; and then my blood was all afire. I got to hate him for everything he did. Aforetime I had stood by, admiring to see him, how he leapt, and what a quoiter and cricketer he was. And now I ground my teeth with hatred whene're he did a thing which caught my Letty's eye. I could read it in her look that she liked him, for all she held herself just as high with him as with all the rest. Lord God forgive me! how I hated that man."

He spoke as if the hatred were a thing of yesterday, so clear within his memory were shown the actions and feelings of his youth. And then he dropped his voice and said —

"Well! I began to look out to pick a quarrel with him, for my blood was up to fight him. If I beat him (and I was a rare boxer in those days), I thought Letty would cool towards him. So one evening at quoits (I'm sure I don't know how or why, but large doings grow out of small words) I fell out with him, and challenged him to fight. I could see he were very wroth by his colour coming and going — and, as I said before, he were a fine active young fellow. But all at once he drew in, and said he would not fight. Such a yell as the Lindal lads, who were watching us, set up! I hear it yet. I could na' help but feel sorry for him, to be so scorned, and I thought he'd not rightly taken my meaning, and I'd give him another chance; so I said it again, and dared him, as plain as words could speak, to fight out the quarrel. He told me then, he had no quarrel against me; that he might have said something to put me up; he did not know that he had, but that if he had, he asked pardon; but that he would not fight no-how.

"I was so full of scorn at his cowardliness, that I was vexed I'd given him the second chance, and I joined in the yell that was set up, twice as bad as before. He stood it out, his teeth set, and looking very white, and when we were silent for want of breath, he said out loud, but in a hoarse voice, quite different from his own —

" "I cannot fight, because I think it is wrong to quarrel, and use violence."

"Then he turned to go away; I were beside myself with scorn and hate, that I called out —

""Tell truth, lad, at least; if thou dare not fight, dunnot go and tell a lie about it. Mother's moppet is afraid of a black eye, pretty dear. It shannot be hurt, but it munnot tell lies."

"Well, they laughed, but I could not laugh. It seemed such a thing for a stout young chap to be a coward, and afraid!

"Before the sun had set, it was talked of all over Lindal, how I had challenged Gilbert to fight, and how he'd denied me; and the folks stood at their doors, and looked at him going up the hill to his home, as if he'd been a monkey or a foreigner — but no one wished him a good e'en. Such a thing as refusing to fight had never been heard of afore at Lindal. Next day, however, they had found voice. The men muttered the word "coward" in his hearing, and kept aloof; the women tittered as he passed, and the little impudent lads and lasses shouted out, "How long is it sin' thou turned Quaker?" "Good-bye, Jonathan Broad-brim," and suchlike jests.

"That evening I met him, with Letty by his side, coming up from the shore. She was almost crying as I came upon them at the turn of the lane; and looking up in his face, as if begging him something. And so she was, she told me after. For she did really like him; and could not abide to hear him scorned by every one for being a coward; and she, coy as she was, all but told him that very night that she loved him, and begged him not to disgrace himself, but fight me as I'd dared him to. When he still stuck to it he could not, for that was wrong, she was so vexed and mad-like at the way she'd spoken, and the feelings she'd let out to coax him, that she said more stinging things about his being a coward than all the rest put together (according to what she told me, sir, afterwards), and ended by saying she'd never speak to him again, as long as she lived; she did once again, though — her blessing was the last human speech that reached his ear in his wild death-struggle.

"But much happened afore that time. From the day I met them walking, Letty turned towards me; I could see a part of it was to spite Gilbert, for she'd be twice as kind when he was near, or likely to hear of it; but by and by she got to like me for my own sake, and it was all settled for our marriage. Gilbert kept aloof from every one, and fell into a sad, careless way. His very gait was changed; his step used to be brisk and sounding, and now his foot lingered heavily on the ground. I used to try and daunt him with my eye, but he would always meet my look in a steady, quiet way, for all so much about him was altered; the lads would not play with him; and as soon as he found he was to be slighted by them whenever he came to quoiting or cricket, he just left off coming.

"The old clerk was the only one he kept company with; or perhaps, rightly to speak, the only one who would keep company with him. They got so thick at last, that old Jonas would say, Gilbert had gospel on his side, and did no more than gospel told him to do; but we none of us gave much credit to what he said, more by token our vicar had a brother, a colonel in the army; and as we threeped it many a time to Jonas, would he set himself up to know the gospel better than the vicar? that would be putting the cart afore the horse, like the French radicals. And if the vicar had thought quarrelling and fighting wicked, and again the Bible, would he have made so much work about all the victories, that were as plenty as blackberries at that time of day, and kept the little bell of Lindal church for ever ringing; or would he have thought so much of "my brother the colonel," as he was always talking on?

"After I was married to Letty I left off hating Gilbert. I even kind of pitied him — he was so scorned and slighted; and for all he'd a bold look about him, as if he were not ashamed, he seemed pining and shrunk. It's a wearying thing to be kept at arm's length by one's kind; and so Gilbert found it, poor fellow. The little children took to him, though; they'd be round about him like a swarm of bees — them as was too young to know what a coward was, and only felt that he was ever ready to love and to help them, and was never loud or cross, however naughty they might be. After a while we had our little one, too; such a blessed darling she was, and dearly did we love her; Letty in especial, who seemed to get all the thought I used to think sometimes she wanted, after she had her baby to care for.

"All my kin lived on this side the bay, up above Kellet. Jane (that's her that lies buried near yon white rose-tree) was to be married, and naught would serve her but that Letty and I must come to the wedding; for all my sisters loved Letty, she had such winning ways with her. Letty did not like to leave her baby, nor yet did I want her to take it: so, after a talk, we fixed to leave it with Letty's mother for the afternoon. I could see her heart ached a bit, for she'd never left it till then, and she seemed to fear all manner of evil, even to the French coming and taking it away. Well! we borrowed a shandry, and harnessed my old grey mare, as I used in th' cart, and set off as grand as King George across the sands about three o'clock, for you see it were high-water about twelve, and we'd to go and come back same tide, as Letty could not leave her baby for long. It were a merry afternoon, were that; last time I ever saw Letty laugh heartily; and, for that matter, last time I ever laughed downright hearty myself. The latest crossing-time fell about nine o'clock, and we were late at starting. Clocks were wrong; and we'd a piece of work chasing a pig father had given Letty to take home; we bagged him at last, and he screeched and screeched in the back part o' th' shandry, and we laughed and they laughed; and in the midst of all the merriment the sun set, and that sobered us a bit, for then we knew what time it was. I whipped the old mare, but she was a deal beener than she was in the morning, and would neither go quick up or down the brows, and they're not a few 'twixt Kellet and the shore. On the sands it were worse. They were very heavy, for the fresh had come down after the rains we'd had. Lord! how I did whip the poor mare, to make the most of the red light as yet lasted. From Bolton side, where we started from, it is better than six mile to Cart Lane, and two channels to cross, let alone holes and quicksands. At the second channel from us the guide waits, all during crossing-time from sunrise to sunset; but for the three hours on each side high-water he's not there, in course. He stays after sunset if he's forespoken, not else. So now you know where we were that awful night. For we'd crossed the first channel about two mile, and it were growing darker and darker above and around us, all but one red line of light above the hills, when we came to a hollow (for all the sands look so flat, there's many a hollow in them where you lose all sight of the shore). We were longer than we should ha' been in crossing the hollow, the sand was so quick; and when we came up again, there, again the blackness, was the white line of the rushing tide coming up the bay! It looked not a mile from us; and when the wind blows up the bay it comes swifter than a galloping horse. "Lord help us" said I; and then I were sorry I'd spoken, to frighten Letty; but the words were crushed out of my heart by the terror. I felt her shiver up by my side, and clutch my coat. And as if the pig (as had screeched himself hoarse some time ago) had found out the danger we were all in, he took to squealing again, enough to bewilder any man. I cursed him between my teeth for his noise; and yet it was God's answer to my prayer, blind sinner as I was. Aye! You may smile, sir, but God can work through many a scornful thing, if need be.

"By this time the mare was all in a lather, and trembling and panting, as if in mortal fright; for though we were on the last bank afore the second channel, the water was gathering up her legs; and she so tired out! When we came close to the channel she stood still, and not all my flogging could get her to stir; she fairly groaned aloud, and shook in a terrible quaking way. Till now Letty had not spoken; only held my coat tightly. I heard her say something, and bent down my head.

"I think, John — I think — I shall never see baby again!"

"And then she sent up such a cry — so loud, and shrill, and pitiful! It fairly maddened me. I pulled out my knife to spur on the old mare, that it might end one way or the other, for the water was stealing sullenly up to the very axle-tree, let alone the white waves that knew no mercy in their steady advance. That one quarter of an hour, sir, seemed as long as all my life since. Thoughts, and fancies, and dreams, and memory ran into each other. The mist, the heavy mist, that was like a ghastly curtain, shutting us in for death, seemed to bring with it the scents of flowers that grew around our own threshold; it might be, for it was falling on them like blessed dew, though to us it was a shroud. Letty told me at after, she heard her baby crying for her, above the gurgling of the rising waters, as plain as ever she heard anything; but the sea-birds were skirling, and the pig shrieking; I never caught it; it was miles away, at any rate.

"Just as I'd gotten my knife out, another sound was close upon us, blending with the gurgle of the near waters, and the roar of the distant (not so distant though); we could hardly see, but we thought we saw something black against the deep lead color of wave, and mist, and sky. It neared and neared: with slow, steady motion, it came across the channel right to where we were.

"Oh, God! it was Gilbert Dawson on his strong bay horse.

"Few words did we speak, and little time had we to say them in. I had no knowledge at that moment of past or future — only of one present thought — how to save Letty, and, if I could, myself. I only remembered afterwards that Gilbert said he had been guided by an animal's shriek of terror; I only heard, when all was over, that he had been uneasy about out return, because of the depth of fresh, and borrowed a pillion, and saddled his horse early in the evening, and ridden down to Cart Lane to watch for us. If all had gone well, we should ne'er have heard of it. As it was, old Jonas told it, the tears down-dropping from his withered cheeks.

"We fastened his horse to the shandry. We lifted Letty to the pillion. The waters rose every instant with sullen sound. They were all but in the shandry. Letty clung to the pillion handles, but drooped her head as if she had yet no hope of life. Swifter than thought (and yet he might have had time for thought and for temptation, sir — if he had ridden off with Letty, he would have been saved, not me), Gilbert was in the shandry by my side.

""Quick!" said he, clear and firm. "You must ride before her, and keep her up. The horse can swim. By God's mercy I will follow. I can cut the traces, and if the mare is not hampered with the shandry, she'll carry me safely through. At any rate, you are a husband and a father. No one cares for me."

"Do not hate me, gentlemen. I often wish that night was a dream. It has haunted my sleep ever since like a dream, and yet it was no dream. I took his place on the saddle, and put Letty's arms around me, and felt her head rest on my shoulder. I trust in God I spoke some word of thanks; but I can't remember. I only recollect Letty raising her head, and calling out —

""God bless you, Gilbert Dawson, for saving my baby from being an orphan this night." And then she fell against me, as if unconscious.

"I bore her through; or, rather, the strong horse swam bravely through the gathering waves. We were dripping wet when we reached the banks in-shore; but we could have but one thought — where was Gilbert? Thick mists and heaving waters compassed us round. Where was he? We shouted. Letty, faint as she was, raised her voice and shouted clear and shrill. No answer came, the sea boomed on with ceaseless sullen beat. I rode to the guide's house. He was a-bed, and would not get up, though I offered him more than I was worth. Perhaps he knew it, the cursed old villain! At any rate, I'd have paid it if I'd toiled my life long. He said I might take his horn and welcome. I did, and blew such a blast through the still, black night, the echoes came back upon the heavy air: but no human voice or sound was heard — that wild blast could not awaken the dead!

"I took Letty home to her baby, over whom she wept the livelong night. I rode back to the shore about Cart Lane; and to and fro, with weary march, did I pace along the brink of the waters, now and then shouting out into the silence a vain cry for Gilbert. The waters went back and left no trace. Two days afterwards he was washed ashore near Flukeborough. The shandry and poor old mare were found half-buried in a heap of sand by Arnside Knot. As far as we could guess, he had dropped his knife trying to cut the traces, and so had lost all chance of life. Any rate, the knife was found in a cleft of the shaft.

"His friends came over from Garstang to his funeral. I wanted to go chief mourner, but it was not my right, and I might not; though I've never done mourning him to this day. When his sister packed up his things, I begged hard for something that had been his. She would give me none of his clothes (she was a right-down having woman), as she had boys of her own, who might grow up into them. But she threw me his Bible, as she said they'd gotten one already, and his were but a poor used-up thing. It was his, and so I cared for it. It were a black leather one, with pockets at the sides, old-fashioned-wise; and in one were a bunch of wild flowers, Letty said she could almost be sure were some she had once given him.

"There were many a text in the Gospel, marked broad with his carpenter's pencil, which more than bore him out in his refusal to fight. Of a surety, sir, there's call enough for bravery in the service of God, and to show love to man, without quarrelling and fighting.

"Thank you, gentlemen, for listening to me. Your words called up the thoughts of him, and my heart was full to speaking. But I must make up; I've to dig a grave for a little child, who is to be buried to-morrow morning, just when his playmates are trooping off to school."

"But tell us of Letty; is she yet alive?" asked Jeremy.

The old man shook his head, and struggled against a choking sigh. After a minute's pause he said —

"She died in less than two year at after that night. She was never like the same again. She would sit thinking, on Gilbert, I guessed: but I could not blame her. We had a boy, and we named it Gilbert Dawson Knipe; he that's stoker on the London railway. Our girl was carried off in teething; and Letty just quietly drooped, and died in less than a six week. They were buried here; so I came to be near them, and away from Lindal, a place and I could never abide after Letty was gone."

He turned to his work, and we, having rested sufficiently, rose up, and came away.

The Count's Apology
Robert Barr

T he fifteen nobles, who formed the Council of State for the Moselle Valley, stood in little groups in the Rittersaal of Winneburg's Castle, situated on a hill-top in the Ender Valley, a league or so from the waters of the Moselle. The nobles spoke in low tones together, for a greater than they were present, no other than their over-lord, the Archbishop of Treves, who, in his stately robes of office, paced up and down the long room, glancing now and then through the narrow windows which gave a view down the Ender Valley.

There was a trace of impatience in his Lordship's bearing, and well there might be, for here was the Council of State in assemblage, yet their chairman was absent, and the nobles stood there helplessly, like a flock of sheep whose shepherd is missing. The chairman was the Count of Winneburg, in whose castle they were now collected, and his lack of punctuality was thus a double discourtesy, for he was host as well as president.

Each in turn had tried to soothe the anger of the Archbishop, for all liked the Count of Winneburg, a bluff and generous-hearted giant, who would stand by his friends against all comers, was the quarrel his own or no. In truth little cared the stalwart Count of Winneburg whose quarrel it was so long as his arm got opportunity of wielding a blow in it. His Lordship of Treves had not taken this championship of the absent man with good grace, and now strode apart from the group, holding himself haughtily; muttering, perhaps prayers, perhaps something else.

When one by one the nobles had arrived at Winneburg's Castle, they were informed that its master had gone hunting that morning, saying he would return in time for the mid-day meal, but nothing had been heard of him since, although mounted messengers had been sent forth, and the great bell in the southern tower had been set ringing when the Archbishop arrived. It was the general opinion that Count Winneburg, becoming interested in the chase, had forgotten all about the Council, for it was well known that the Count's body was better suited for athletic sports or warfare than was his mind for the consideration of questions of State, and the nobles, themselves of similar calibre, probably liked him none the less on that account.

Presently the Archbishop stopped in his walk and faced the assemblage. "My Lords," he said, "we have already waited longer than the utmost stretch of courtesy demands. The esteem in which Count Winneburg holds our deliberations is indicated by his inexcusable neglect of a duty conferred upon him by you, and voluntarily accepted by him. I shall therefore take my place in his chair, and I call upon you to seat yourselves at the Council table."

Saying which the Archbishop strode to the vacant chair, and seated himself in it at the head of the board. The nobles looked one at the other with some dismay, for it was never their intention that the Archbishop should preside over their meeting, the object of which was rather to curb that high prelate's ambition, than to confirm still further the power he already held over them.

When, a year before, these Councils of State had been inaugurated, the Archbishop had opposed them, but, finding that the Emperor was inclined to defer to the wishes of his nobles, the Lord of Treves had insisted upon his right to be present during the deliberations, and this right the Emperor had conceded. He further proposed that the meeting should be held at his own castle of Cochem, as being conveniently situated midway between Coblentz and Treves, but to this the nobles had, with fervent unanimity, objected. Cochem Castle, they remembered, possessed strong walls and deep dungeons, and they had no desire to trust themselves within the lion's jaws, having little faith in his Lordship's benevolent intentions towards them.

The Emperor seemed favorable to the selection of Cochem as a convenient place of meeting, and the nobles were nonplussed, because they could not give their real reason for wishing to avoid it, and the Archbishop continued to press the claims of Cochem as being of equal advantage to all.

"It is not as though I asked them to come to Treves," said the Archbishop, "for that would entail a long journey upon those living near the Rhine, and in going to Cochem I shall myself be called upon to travel as far as those who come from Coblentz."

The Emperor said:

"It seems a most reasonable selection, and, unless some strong objection be urged, I shall confirm the choice of Cochem."

The nobles were all struck with apprehension at these words, and knew not what to say, when suddenly, to their great delight, up spoke the stalwart Count of Winneburg.

"Your Majesty," he said, "my Castle stands but a short league from Cochem, and has a Rittersaal as large as that in the pinnacled palace owned by the Archbishop. It is equally convenient for all concerned, and every gentleman is right welcome to its hospitality. My cellars are well filled with good wine, and my larders are stocked with an abundance of food. All that can be urged in favour of Cochem applies with equal truth to the Schloss Winneburg. If, therefore, the members of the Council will accept of my roof, it is theirs."

The nobles with universal enthusiasm cried:

"Yes, yes; Winneburg is the spot."

The Emperor smiled, for he well knew that his Lordship of Treves was somewhat miserly in the dispensing of his hospitality. He preferred to see his guests drink the wine of a poor vintage rather than tap the cask which contained the yield of a good year. His Majesty smiled, because he imagined his nobles thought of the replenishing of their stomachs, whereas they were concerned for the safety of their necks; but seeing them unanimous in their choice, he nominated Schloss Winneburg as the place of meeting, and so it remained.

When, therefore, the Archbishop of Treves set himself down in the ample chair, to which those present had, without a dissenting vote, elected Count Winneburg, distrust at once took hold of them, for they were ever jealous of the encroachments of their over-lord. The Archbishop glared angrily around him, but no man moved from where he stood.

"I ask you to be seated. The Council is called to order."

Baron Beilstein cleared his throat and spoke, seemingly with some hesitation, but nevertheless with a touch of obstinacy in his voice:

"May we beg a little more time for Count Winneburg? He has doubtless gone farther afield than he intended when he set out. I myself know something of the fascination of the chase, and can easily understand that it wipes out all remembrance of lesser things."

"Call you this Council a lesser thing?" demanded the Archbishop. "We have waited an hour already, and I shall not give the laggard a moment more."

"Indeed, my Lord, then I am sorry to hear it. I would not willingly be the man who sits in Winneburg's chair, should he come suddenly upon us."

"Is that a threat?" asked the Archbishop, frowning.

"It is not a threat, but rather a warning. I am a neighbour of the Count, and know him well, and whatever his virtues may be, calm patience is not one of them. If time hangs heavily, may I venture to suggest that your Lordship remove the prohibition you proclaimed when the Count's servants offered us wine, and allow me to act temporarily as host, ordering the flagons to be filled, which I think will please Winneburg better when he comes, than finding another in his chair."

"This is no drunken revel, but a Council of State," said the Archbishop sternly; "and I drink no wine when the host is not here to proffer it."

"Indeed, my Lord," said Beilstein, with a shrug of the shoulders, "some of us are so thirsty that we care not who makes the offer, so long as the wine be sound."

What reply the Archbishop would have made can only be conjectured, for at that moment the door burst open and in came Count Winneburg, a head and shoulders above any man in that room, and huge in proportion.

"My Lords, my Lords," he cried, his loud voice booming to the rafters, "how can I ask you to excuse such a breach of hospitality. What! Not a single flagon of wine in the room? This makes my deep regret almost unbearable. Surely, Beilstein, you might have amended that, if only for the sake of an old and constant comrade. Truth, gentlemen, until I heard the bell of the castle toll, I had no thought that this was the day of our meeting, and then, to my despair, I found myself an hour away, and have ridden hard to be among you."

Then, noticing there was something ominous in the air, and

an unaccustomed silence to greet his words, he looked from one to the other, and his eye, travelling up the table, finally rested upon the Archbishop in his chair. Count Winneburg drew himself up, his ruddy face coloring like fire. Then, before any person could reach out hand to check him, or move lip in counsel, the Count, with a fierce oath, strode to the usurper, grasped him by the shoulders, whirled his heels high above his head, and flung him like a sack of corn to the smooth floor, where the unfortunate Archbishop, huddled in a helpless heap, slid along the polished surface as if he were on ice. The fifteen nobles stood stock-still, appalled at this unexpected outrage upon their over-lord. Winneburg seated himself in the chair with an emphasis that made even the solid table rattle, and bringing down his huge fist crashing on the board before him, shouted:

"Let no man occupy my chair, unless he has weight enough to remain there."

Baron Beilstein, and one or two others, hurried to the prostrate Archbishop and assisted him to his feet.

"Count Winneburg," said Beilstein, "you can expect no sympathy from us for such an act of violence in your own hall."

"I want none of your sympathy," roared the angry Count. "Bestow it on the man now in your hands who needs it. If you want the Archbishop of Treves to act as your chairman, elect him to that position and welcome. I shall have no usurpation in my Castle. While I am president I sit in the chair, and none other."

There was a murmur of approval at this, for one and all were deeply suspicious of the Archbishop's continued encroachments.

His Lordship of Treves once more on his feet, his lips pallid, and his face colorless, looked with undisguised hatred at his assailant. "Winneburg," he said slowly, "you shall apologize abjectly for this insult, and that in presence of the nobles of this Empire, or I will see to it that not one stone of this castle remains upon another."

"Indeed," said the Count nonchalantly, "I shall apologize to you, my Lord, when you have apologized to me for taking my place. As to the castle, it is said that the devil assisted in the building of it, and it is quite likely that through friendship for you, he may preside over its destruction."

The Archbishop made no reply, but, bowing haughtily to the rest of the company, who looked glum enough, well knowing that the episode they had witnessed meant, in all probability, red war let loose down the smiling valley of the Moselle, left the Rittersaal.

"Now that the Council is duly convened in regular order," said Count Winneburg, when the others had seated themselves round his table, "what questions of state come up for discussion?"

For a moment there was no answer to this query, the delegates looking at one another speechless. But at last Baron Beilstein shrugging his shoulder, said drily:

"Indeed, my Lord Count, I think the time for talk is past, and I suggest that we all look closely to the strengthening of our walls, which are likely to be tested before long by the Lion of Treves. It was perhaps unwise, Winneburg, to have used the Archbishop so roughly, he being unaccustomed to athletic exercise; but, let the consequences be what they may, I, for one, will stand by you."

"And I; and I; and I; and I," cried the others, with the exception of the Knight of Ehrenburg, who, living as he did near the town of Coblentz, was learned in the law, and not so ready as some of his comrades to speak first and think afterwards.

"My good friends," cried their presiding officer, deeply moved by this token of their fealty, "what I have done I have done, be it wise or the reverse, and the results must fall on my head alone. No words of mine can remove the dust of the floor from the Archbishop's cloak, so if he comes, let him come. I will give him as hearty a welcome as it is in my power to render. All I ask is fair play, and those who stand aside shall see a good fight. It is not right that a hasty act of mine should embroil the peaceful country side, so if Treves comes on I shall meet him alone here in my castle. But, nevertheless, I thank you all for your offers of help; that is all, except the Knight of Ehrenburg, whose tender of assistance, if made, has escaped my ear."

The Knight of Ehrenburg had, up to that moment, been studying the texture of the oaken table on which his flagon sat. Now he looked up and spoke slowly.

"I made no proffer of help," he said, "because none will be needed, I believe, so far as the Archbishop of Treves is concerned. The Count a moment ago said that all he wanted was fair play, but that is just what he has no right to expect from his present antagonist. The Archbishop will make no attempt on this castle; he will act much more subtly than that. The Archbishop will lay the redress of his quarrel upon the shoulders of the Emperor, and it is the oncoming of the Imperial troops you have to fear, and not an invasion from Treves. Against the forces of the Emperor we are powerless, united or divided. Indeed, his Majesty may call upon us to invest this castle, whereupon, if we refuse, we are rebels who have broken our oaths."

"What then is there left for me to do?" asked the Count, dismayed at the coil in which he had involved himself.

"Nothing," advised the Knight of Ehrenburg, "except to apologize abjectly to the Archbishop, and that not too soon, for his Lordship may refuse to accept it. But when he formally demands it, I should render it to him on his own terms, and think myself well out of an awkward position."

The Count of Winneburg rose from his seat, and lifting his clinched fist high above his head, shook it at the timbers of the roof.

"That," he cried, "will I never do, while one stone of Winneburg stands upon another."

At this, those present, always with the exception of the Knight of Ehrenburg, sprang to their feet, shouting:

"Imperial troops or no, we stand by the Count of Winneburg!"

Some one flashed forth a sword, and instantly a glitter of blades was in the air, while cheer after cheer rang to the rafters. When the uproar had somewhat subsided, the Knight of Ehrenburg said calmly:

"My castle stands nearest to the capital, and will be the first to fall, but, nevertheless, hoping to do my shouting when the war is ended, I join my forces with those of the rest of you."

And amidst this unanimity, and much emptying of flagons, the assemblage dissolved, each man with his escort taking his way to his own stronghold, perhaps to con more soberly, next day, the problem that confronted him. They were fighters all, and would not flinch when the pinch came, whatever the outcome.

Day followed day with no sign from Treves. Winneburg employed the time in setting his house in order to be ready for whatever chanced, and just as the Count was beginning to congratulate himself that his deed was to be without consequences, there rode up to his castle gates a horseman, accompanied by two lancers, and on the newcomer's breast were emblazoned the Imperial arms. Giving voice to his horn, the gates were at once thrown open to him, and, entering, he demanded instant speech with the Count.

"My Lord, Count Winneburg," he said, when that giant had

presented himself, "His Majesty the Emperor commands me to summon you to the court at Frankfort."

"Do you take me as prisoner, then?" asked the Count.

"Nothing was said to me of arrest. I was merely commissioned to deliver to you the message of the Emperor."

"What are your orders if I refuse to go?"

A hundred armed men stood behind the Count, a thousand more were within call of the castle bell; two lances only were at the back of the messenger; but the strength of the broadcast empire was betokened by the symbol on his breast.

"My orders are to take back your answer to his Imperial Majesty," replied the messenger calmly.

The Count, though hot-headed, was no fool, and he stood for a moment pondering on the words which the Knight of Ehrenburg had spoken on taking his leave:

"Let not the crafty Archbishop embroil you with the Emperor."

This warning had been the cautious warrior's parting advice to him.

"If you will honour my humble roof," said the Count slowly, "by taking refreshment beneath it, I shall be glad of your company afterwards to Frankfort, in obedience to his Majesty's commands."

The messenger bowed low, accepted the hospitality, and together they made way across the Moselle, and along the Roman road to the capital.

Within the walls of Frankfort the Count was lodged in rooms near the palace, to which his conductor guided him, and, although it was still held that he was not a prisoner, an armed man paced to and fro before his door all night. The day following his arrival, Count Winneburg was summoned to the Court, and in a large ante-room found himself one of a numerous throng, conspicuous among them all by reason of his great height and bulk.

The huge hall was hung with tapestry, and at the further end were heavy curtains, at each edge of which stood half-a-dozen armored men, the detachments being under command of two gaily-uniformed officers. Occasionally the curtains were parted by menials who stood there to perform that duty, and high nobles entered, or came out, singly and in groups. Down the sides of the hall were packed some hundreds of people, chattering together for the most part, and gazing at those who passed up and down the open space in the centre.

The Count surmised that the Emperor held his Court in whatever apartment was behind the crimson curtains. He felt the eyes of the multitude upon him, and shifted uneasily from one foot to another, cursing his ungainliness, ashamed of the tingling of the blood in his cheeks. He was out of place in this laughing, talking crowd, experiencing the sensations of an uncouth rustic suddenly thrust into the turmoil of a metropolis, resenting bitterly the supposed sneers that were flung at him. He suspected that the whispering and the giggling were directed towards himself, and burned to draw his sword and let these popinjays know for once what a man could do. As a matter of fact it was a buzz of admiration at his stature which went up when he entered, but the Count had so little of self-conceit in his soul that he never even guessed the truth.

Two nobles passing near him, he heard one of them say distinctly:

"That is the fellow who threw the Archbishop over his head," while the other, glancing at him, said:

"By the Coat, he seems capable of upsetting the three of them, and I, for one, wish more power to his muscle should he attempt it."

The Count shrank against the tapestried walls, hot with anger, wishing himself a dwarf that he might escape the gaze of so many inquiring eyes. Just as the scrutiny was becoming unbearable, his companion touched him on the elbow, and said in a low voice:

"Count Winneburg, follow me."

He held aside the tapestry at the back of the Count, and that noble, nothing loth, disappeared from view behind it.

Entering a narrow passage-way, they traversed it until they came to a closed door, at each lintel of which stood a pikeman, fronted with a shining breastplate of metal. The Count's conductor knocked gently at the closed door, then opened it, holding it so that the Count could pass in, and when he had done so, the door closed softly behind him. To his amazement, Winneburg saw before him, standing at the further end of the small room, the Emperor Rudolph, entirely alone. The Count was about to kneel awkwardly, when his liege strode forward and prevented him.

"Count Winneburg," he said, "from what I hear of you, your elbow-joints are more supple than those of your knees, therefore let us be thankful that on this occasion there is no need to use either. I see you are under the mistaken impression that the Emperor is present. Put that thought from your mind, and regard me simply as Lord Rudolph—one gentleman wishing to have some little conversation with another."

"Your Majesty—" stammered the Count.

"I have but this moment suggested that you forget that title, my Lord. But, leaving aside all question of salutation, let us get to the heart of the matter, for I think we are both direct men. You are summoned to Frankfort because that high and mighty Prince of the Church, the Archbishop of Treves, has made complaint to the Emperor against you alleging what seems to be an unpardonable indignity suffered by him at your hands."

"Your Majesty—my Lord, I mean," faltered the Count. "The indignity was of his own seeking; he sat down in my chair, where he had no right to place himself, and I—I—persuaded him to relinquish his position."

"So I am informed—that is to say, so his Majesty has been informed," replied Rudolph, a slight smile hovering round his finely chiselled lips. "We are not here to comment upon any of the Archbishop's delinquencies, but, granting, for the sake of argument, that he had encroached upon your rights, nevertheless, he was under your roof, and honestly, I fail to see that you were justified in cracking his heels against the same."

"Well, your Majesty—again I beg your Majesty's pardon—"

"Oh, no matter," said the Emperor, "call me what you like; names signify little."

"If then the Emperor," continued the Count, "found an intruder sitting on his throne, would he like it, think you?"

"His feeling, perhaps, would be one of astonishment, my Lord Count, but speaking for the Emperor, I am certain that he would never lay hands on the usurper, or treat him like a sack of corn in a yeoman's barn."

The Count laughed heartily at this, and was relieved to find that this quitted him of the tension which the great presence had at first inspired.

"Truth to tell, your Majesty, I am sorry I touched him. I should have requested him to withdraw, but my arm has always been more prompt in action than my tongue, as you can readily see since I came into this room."

"Indeed, Count, your tongue does you very good service," continued the Emperor, "and I am glad to have from you an expression of regret. I hope, therefore, that you will have no hesitation in repeating that declaration to the Archbishop of Treves."

"Does your Majesty mean that I am to apologize to him?"

"Yes," answered the Emperor.

There was a moment's pause, then the Count said slowly:

"I will surrender to your Majesty my person, my sword, my castle, and my lands. I will, at your word, prostrate myself at your feet, and humbly beg pardon for any offence I have committed against you, but to tell the Archbishop I am sorry when I am not, and to cringe before him and supplicate his grace, well, your Majesty, as between man and man, I'll see him damned first."

Again the Emperor had some difficulty in preserving that rigidity of expression which he had evidently resolved to maintain.

"Have you ever met a ghost, my Lord Count?" he asked.

Winneburg crossed himself devoutly, a sudden pallor sweeping over his face.

"Indeed, your Majesty, I have seen strange things, and things for which there was no accounting; but it has been usually after a contest with the wine flagon, and at the time my head was none of the clearest, so I could not venture to say whether they were ghosts or no."

"Imagine, then, that in one of the corridors of your castle at midnight you met a white-robed transparent figure, through whose form your sword passed scathlessly. What would you do, my Lord?"

"Indeed, your Majesty, I would take to my heels, and bestow myself elsewhere as speedily as possible."

"Most wisely spoken and you, who are no coward, who fear not to face willingly in combat anything natural, would, in certain circumstances, trust to swift flight for your protection. Very well, my Lord, you are now confronted with something against which your stout arm is as unavailing as it would be if an apparition stood in your path. There is before you the spectre of subtlety. Use arm instead of brain, and you are a lost man.

"The Archbishop expects no apology. He looks for a stalwart, stubborn man, defying himself and the Empire combined. You think, perhaps, that the Imperial troops will surround your castle, and that you may stand a siege. Now the Emperor would rather have you fight with him than against him, but in truth there will be no contest. Hold to your refusal, and you will be arrested before you leave the precincts of this palace. You will be thrown into a dungeon, your castle and your lands sequestered; and I call your attention to the fact that your estate adjoins the possessions of the Archbishop at Cochem, and Heaven fend me for hinting that his Lordship casts covetous eyes over his boundary; yet, nevertheless, he will probably not refuse to accept your possessions in reparation for the insult bestowed upon him. Put it this way if you like. Would you rather pleasure me or pleasure the Archbishop of Treves?"

"There is no question as to that," answered the Count.

"Then it will please me well if you promise to apologize to his Lordship the Archbishop of Treves. That his Lordship will be equally pleased, I very much doubt."

"Will your Majesty command me in open Court to apologize?"

"I shall request you to do so. I must uphold the Feudal law."

"Then I beseech your Majesty to command me, for I am a loyal subject, and will obey."

"God give me many such," said the Emperor fervently, "and bestow upon me the wisdom to deserve them!"

He extended his hand to the Count, then touched a bell on the table beside him. The officer who had conducted Winneburg entered silently, and acted as his guide back to the thronged apartment they had left. The Count saw that the great crimson curtains were now looped up, giving a view of the noble interior of the room beyond, thronged with the notables of the Empire. The hall leading to it was almost deserted, and the Count, under convoy of two lancemen, himself nearly as tall as their weapons, passed in to the Throne Room, and found all eyes turned upon him.

He was brought to a stand before an elevated dais, the centre of which was occupied by a lofty throne, which, at the moment, was empty. Near it, on the elevation, stood the three Archbishops of Treves, Cologne, and Mayence, on the other side the Count Palatine of the Rhine with the remaining three Electors. The nobles of the realm occupied places according to their degree.

As the stalwart Count came in, a buzz of conversation swept over the hall like a breeze among the leaves of a forest. A malignant scowl darkened the countenance of the Archbishop of Treves, but the faces of Cologne and Mayence expressed a certain Christian resignation regarding the contumely which had been endured by their colleague. The Count stood stolidly where he was placed, and gazed at the vacant throne, turning his eyes neither to the right nor the left.

Suddenly there was a fanfare of trumpets, and instant silence smote the assembly. First came officers of the Imperial Guard in shining armor, then the immediate advisers and councillors of his Majesty, and last of all, the Emperor himself, a robe of great richness clasped at his throat, and trailing behind him; the crown of the Empire upon his head. His face was pale and stern, and he looked what he was, a monarch, and a man. The Count rubbed his eyes, and could scarcely believe that he stood now in the presence of one who had chatted amiably with him but a few moments before.

The Emperor sat on his throne and one of his councillors whispered for some moments to him; then the Emperor said, in a low, clear voice, that penetrated to the farthest corner of the vast apartment:

"Is the Count of Winneburg here?"

"Yes, your Majesty."

"Let him stand forward."

The Count strode two long steps to the front, and stood there, red-faced and abashed. The officer at his side whispered:

"Kneel, you fool, kneel."

And the Count got himself somewhat clumsily down upon his knees, like an elephant preparing to receive his burden. The face of the Emperor remained impassive, and he said harshly:

"Stand up."

The Count, once more upon his feet, breathed a deep sigh of satisfaction at finding himself again in an upright posture.

"Count of Winneburg," said the Emperor slowly, "it is alleged that upon the occasion of the last meeting of the Council of State for the Moselle valley, you, in presence of the nobles there assembled, cast a slight upon your over-lord, the Archbishop of Treves. Do you question the statement?"

The Count cleared his throat several times, which in the stillness of that vaulted room sounded like the distant booming of cannon.

"If to cast the Archbishop half the distance of this room is to cast a slight upon him, I did so, your Majesty."

There was a simultaneous ripple of laughter at this, instantly suppressed when the searching eye of the Emperor swept the room.

"Sir Count," said the Emperor severely, "the particulars of your outrage are not required of you; only your admission thereof. Hear, then, my commands. Betake yourself to your castle of Winneburg, and hold yourself there in readiness to proceed to Treves on a day appointed by his Lordship the Archbishop, an Elector of this Empire, there to humble yourself before him, and crave his pardon for the offence you have committed. Disobey at your peril."

Once or twice the Count moistened his dry lips, then he said:

"Your Majesty, I will obey any command you place upon me."

"In that case," continued the Emperor, his severity visibly relaxing, "I can promise that your over-lord will not hold this incident against you. Such, I understand, is your intention, my Lord Archbishop?" and the Emperor turned toward the Prince of Treves.

The Archbishop bowed low, and thus veiled the malignant hatred in his eyes. "Yes, your Majesty," he replied, "providing the apology is given as publicly as was the insult, in presence of those who were witnesses of the Count's foolishness."

"That is but a just condition," said the Emperor. "It is my pleasure that the Council be summoned to Treves to hear the Count's apology. And now, Count of Winneburg, you are at liberty to withdraw."

The Count drew his mammoth hand across his brow, and scattered to the floor the moisture that had collected there. He tried to speak, but apparently could not, then turned and walked resolutely towards the door. There was instant outcry at this, the Chamberlain of the Court standing in stupefied amazement at a breach of etiquette which exhibited any man's back to the Emperor; but a smile relaxed the Emperor's lips, and he held up his hand.

"Do not molest him," he said, as the Count disappeared. "He is unused to the artificial manners of a Court. In truth, I take it as a friendly act, for I am sure the valiant Count never turned his back upon a foe," which Imperial witticism was well received, for the sayings of an Emperor rarely lack applause.

The Count, wending his long way home by the route he had come, spent the first half of the journey in cursing the Archbishop, and the latter half in thinking over the situation. By the time he had reached his castle he had formulated a plan, and this plan he proceeded to put into execution on receiving the summons of the Archbishop to come to Treves on the first day of the following month and make his apology, the Archbishop, with characteristic penuriousness, leaving the inviting of the fifteen nobles, who formed the Council, to Winneburg, and thus his Lordship of Treves was saved the expense of sending special messengers to each.

In case Winneburg neglected to summon the whole Council, the Archbishop added to his message, the statement that he would refuse to receive the apology if any of the nobles were absent.

Winneburg sent messengers, first to Beilstein, asking him to attend at Treves on the second day of the month, and bring with him an escort of at least a thousand men. Another he asked for the third, another for the fourth, another for the fifth, and so on, resolved that before a complete quorum was present, half of the month would be gone, and with it most of the Archbishop's provender, for his Lordship, according to the laws of hospitality, was bound to entertain free of all charge to themselves the various nobles and their followings.

On the first day of the month Winneburg entered the northern gate of Treves, accompanied by two hundred horsemen and eight hundred foot soldiers. At first, the officers of the Archbishop thought that an invasion was contemplated, but Winneburg suavely explained that if a thing was worth doing at all, it was worth doing well, and he was not going to make any hole-and-corner affair of his apology. Next day Beilstein came along accompanied by five hundred cavalry, and five hundred foot soldiers.

The Chamberlain of the Archbishop was in despair at having to find quarters for so many, but he did the best he could, while the Archbishop was enraged to observe that the nobles did not assemble in greater haste, but each as he came had a plausible excuse for his delay. Some had to build bridges, sickness had broken out in another camp, while a third expedition had lost its way and wandered in the forest.

The streets of Treves each night resounded with songs of revelry, varied by the clash of swords, when a party of the newcomers fell foul of a squad of the town soldiers, and the officers on either side had much ado to keep the peace among their men. The Archbishop's wine cups were running dry, and the price of provisions had risen, the whole surrounding country being placed under contribution for provender and drink. When a week had elapsed the Archbishop relaxed his dignity and sent for Count Winneburg.

"We will not wait for the others," he said. "I have no desire to humiliate you unnecessarily. Those who are here shall bear witness that you have apologized, and so I shall not insist on the presence of the laggards, but will receive your apology tomorrow at high noon in the great council chamber."

"Ah, there speaks a noble heart, ever thinking generously of those who despitefully use you, my Lord Archbishop," said Count Winneburg. "But no, no, I cannot accept such a sacrifice. The Emperor showed me plainly the enormity of my offence. In the presence of all I insulted you, wretch that I am, and in the presence of all shall I abase myself."

"But I do not seek your abasement," protested the Archbishop, frowning.

"The more honour, then, to your benevolent nature," answered the Count, "and the more shameful would it be of me to take advantage of it. As I stood a short time since on the walls, I saw coming up the river the banners of the Knight of Ehrenburg. His castle is the furthest removed from Treves, and so the others cannot surely delay long. We will wait, my Lord Archbishop, until all are here. But I thank you just as much for your generosity as if I were craven enough to shield myself behind it."

The Knight of Ehrenburg in due time arrived, and behind him his thousand men, many of whom were compelled to sleep in the public buildings, for all the rooms in Treves were occupied. Next day the Archbishop summoned the assembled nobles and said he would hear the apology in their presence. If the others missed it, it was their own fault—they should have been in time.

"I cannot apologize;" said the Count, "until all are here. It was the Emperor's order, and who am I to disobey my Emperor? We must await their coming with patience, and, indeed, Treves is a goodly town, in which all of us find ourselves fully satisfied."

"Then, my blessing on you all," said the Archbishop in a sour tone most unsuited to the benediction he was bestowing. "Return, I beg of you, instantly, to your castles. I forego the apology."

"But I insist on tendering it," cried the Count, his mournful voice giving some indication of the sorrow he felt at his offence if it went unrequited. "It is my duty, not only to you, my Lord Archbishop, but also to his Majesty the Emperor."

"Then, in Heaven's name get on with it and depart. I am willing to accept it on your own terms, as I have said before."

"No, not on my own terms, but on yours. What matters the delay of a week or two? The hunting season does not begin for a fortnight, and we are all as well at Treves as at home. Besides, how could I ever face my Emperor again, knowing I had disobeyed his commands?"

"I will make it right with the Emperor," said the Archbishop.

The Knight of Ehrenburg now spoke up, calmly, as was his custom:

"'Tis a serious matter," he said, "for a man to take another's word touching action of his Majesty the Emperor. You have clerks here with you; perhaps then you will bid them indite a document to be signed by yourself absolving my friend, the Count of Winneburg, from all necessity of apologizing, so that should the Emperor take offence at his disobedience, the parchment may hold him scathless."

"I will do anything to be quit of you," muttered the Archbishop more to himself than to the others.

And so the document was written and signed. With this parchment in his saddle-bags the Count and his comrades quitted the town, drinking in half flagons the health of the Archbishop, because there was not left in Treves enough wine to fill the measures to the brim.

A Spark Neglected
Leo Tolstoy

There once lived in a village a peasant named Ivan Stcherbakof. He was comfortably off, in the prime of life, the best worker in the village, and had three sons all able to work. The eldest was married, the second about to marry, and the third was a big lad who could mind the horses and was already beginning to plow. Ivan's wife was an able and thrifty woman, and they were fortunate in having a quiet, hardworking daughter-in-law. There was nothing to prevent Ivan and his family from living happily. They had only one idle mouth to feed; that was Ivan's old father, who suffered from asthma and had been lying ill on the top of the brick oven for seven years. Ivan had all he needed: three horses and a colt, a cow with a calf, and fifteen sheep. The women made all the clothing for the family, besides helping in the fields, and the men tilled the land. They always had grain enough of their own to last over beyond the next harvest and sold enough oats to pay the taxes and meet their other needs. So Ivan and his children might have lived quite comfortably had it not been for a feud between him and his next door neighbor, Limping Gabriel, the son of Gordey Ivanof.

As long as old Gordey was alive and Ivan's father was still able to manage the household, the peasants lived as neighbors should. If the women of either house happened to want a sieve or a tub, or the men required a sack, or if a cart-wheel got broken and could not be mended at once, they used to send to the other house, and helped each other in neighborly fashion. When a calf strayed into the neighbor's thrashing-ground they would just drive it out, and only say, "Don't let it get in again; our grain is lying there." And such things as locking up the barns and outhouses, hiding things from one another, or backbiting were never thought of in those days.

That was in the fathers' time. When the sons came to be at the head of the families, everything changed.

It all began about a trifle.

Ivan's daughter-in-law had a hen that began laying rather early in the season, and she started collecting its eggs for Easter. Every day she went to the cart shed, and found an egg in the cart; but one day the hen, probably frightened by the children, flew across the fence into the neighbor's yard and laid its egg there. The woman heard the cackling, but said to herself: "I have no time now; I must tidy up for Sunday. I'll fetch the egg later on." In the evening she went to the cart, but found no egg there. She went and asked her mother-in-law and brother-in-law whether they had taken the egg. "No," they had not; but her youngest brother-in-law, Taras, said: "Your Biddy laid its egg in the neighbor's yard. It was there she was cackling, and she flew back across the fence from there."

The woman went and looked at the hen. There she was on the perch with the other birds, her eyes just closing ready to go to sleep. The woman wished she could have asked the hen and got an answer from her.

Then she went to the neighbor's, and Gabriel's mother came out to meet her.

"What do you want, young woman?"

"Why, Granny, you see, my hen flew across this morning. Did she not lay an egg here?"

"We never saw anything of it. The Lord be thanked, our own hens started laying long ago. We collect our own eggs and have no need of other people's! And we don't go looking for eggs in other people's yards, lass!"

The young woman was offended, and said more than she should have done. Her neighbor answered back with interest, and the women began abusing each other. Ivan's wife, who had been to fetch water, happening to pass just then, joined in too. Gabriel's wife rushed out, and began reproaching the young woman with things that had really happened and with other things that never had happened at all. Then a general uproar commenced, all shouting at once, trying to get out two words at a time, and not choice words either.

"You're this!" and "You're that!" "You're a thief!" and "You're a slut!" and "You're starving your old father-in-law to death!" and "You're a good-for-nothing!" and so on.

"And you've made a hole in the sieve I lent you, you jade! And it's our yoke you're carrying your pails on - you just give back our yoke!"

Then they caught hold of the yoke, and spilt the water, snatched off one another's shawls, and began fighting. Gabriel, returning from the fields, stopped to take his wife's part. Out rushed Ivan and his son and joined in with the rest. Ivan was a strong fellow, he scattered the whole lot of them, and pulled a handful of hair out of Gabriel's beard. People came to see what was the matter, and the fighters were separated with difficulty.

That was how it all began.

Gabriel wrapped the hair torn from his beard in a paper, and went to the District Court to have the law on Ivan. "I didn't grow my beard," said he, "for pockmarked Ivan to pull it out!" And his wife went bragging to the neighbors, saying they'd have Ivan condemned and sent to Siberia. And so the feud grew.

The old man, from where he lay on the top of the oven, tried from the very first to persuade them to make peace, but they would not listen. He told them, "It's a stupid thing you are after, children, picking quarrels about such a paltry matter. Just think! The whole thing began about an egg. The children may have taken it — well, what matter? What's the value of one egg? God sends enough for all! And suppose your neighbor did say an unkind word — put it right; show her how to say a better one! If there has been a fight —well, such things will happen; we're all sinners, but make it up, and let there be an end of it! If you nurse your anger it will be worse for you yourselves."

But the younger folk would not listen to the old man. They thought his words were mere senseless dotage. Ivan would not humble himself before his neighbor.

"I never pulled his beard," he said, "he pulled the hair out himself. But his son has burst all the fastenings on my shirt, and torn it...Look at it!"

And Ivan also went to law. They were tried by the Justice of the Peace and by the District Court. While all this was going on, the coupling-pin of Gabriel's cart disappeared. Gabriel's womenfolk accused Ivan's son of having taken it. They said: "We saw him in the night go past our window, towards the cart; and a neighbor says he saw him at the pub, offering the pin to the landlord."

So they went to law about that. And at home not a day passed without a quarrel or even a fight. The children, too, abused one another, having learnt to do so from their elders; and when the women happened to meet by the riverside, where they went to rinse the clothes, their arms did not do as much wringing as their tongues did nagging, and every word was a bad one.

At first the peasants only slandered one another; but afterwards they began in real earnest to snatch anything that lay handy, and the children followed their example. Life became harder and harder for them. Ivan Stcherbakof and Limping Gabriel kept suing one another at the Village Assembly, and at the District Court, and before the Justice of the Peace until all the judges were tired of them. Now Gabriel got Ivan fined or imprisoned; then Ivan did as much to Gabriel; and the more they spited each other the angrier they grew — like dogs that attack one another and get more and more furious the longer they fight. You strike one dog from behind, and it thinks it's the other dog biting him, and gets still fiercer. So these peasants: they went to law, and one or other of them was fined or locked up, but that only made them more and more angry with each other. "Wait a bit," they said, "and I'll make you pay for it." And so it went on for six years. Only the old man lying on the top of the oven kept telling them again and again: "Children, what are you doing? Stop all this paying back; keep to your work, and don't bear malice — it will be better for you. The more you bear malice, the worse it will be."

But they would not listen to him.

In the seventh year, at a wedding, Ivan's daughter-in-law held Gabriel up to shame, accusing him of having been caught horse stealing. Gabriel was tipsy, and unable to contain his anger, gave the woman such a blow that she was laid up for a week; and she was pregnant at the time. Ivan was delighted. He went to the magistrate to lodge a complaint. "Now I'll get rid of my neighbor! He won't escape imprisonment, or exile to Siberia." But Ivan's wish was not fulfilled. The magistrate dismissed the case. The woman was examined, but she was up and about and showed no sign of any injury. Then Ivan went to the Justice of the Peace, but he referred the business to the District Court. Ivan bestirred himself: treated the clerk and the Elder of the District Court to a gallon of liquor and got Gabriel condemned to be flogged. The sentence was read out to Gabriel by the clerk: "The Court decrees that the peasant Gabriel Gordeyef shall receive twenty lashes with a birch rod at the District Court."

Ivan too heard the sentence read, and looked at Gabriel to see how he would take it. Gabriel grew as pale as a sheet, and turned round and went out into the passage. Ivan followed him, meaning to see to the horse, and he overheard Gabriel say, "Very well! He will have my back flogged: that will make it burn; but something of his may burn worse than that!"

Hearing these words, Ivan at once went back into the Court, and said: "Upright judges! He threatens to set my house on fire! Listen: he said it in the presence of witnesses!"

Gabriel was recalled. "Is it true that you said this?"

"I haven't said anything. Flog me, since you have the power. It seems that I alone am to suffer, and all for being in the right, while he is allowed to do as he likes."

Gabriel wished to say something more, but his lips and his cheeks quivered, and he turned towards the wall. Even the officials were frightened by his looks. "He may do some mischief to himself or to his neighbor," thought they.

Then the old Judge said: "Look here, my men; you'd better be reasonable and make it up. Was it right of you, friend Gabriel, to strike a pregnant woman? It was lucky it passed off so well, but think what might have happened! Was it right? You had better confess and beg his pardon, and he will forgive you, and we will alter the sentence."

The clerk heard these words, and remarked: "That's impossible under Statute 117. An agreement between the parties not having been arrived at, a decision of the Court has been pronounced and must be executed."

But the Judge would not listen to the clerk.

"Keep your tongue still, my friend," said he. "The first of all laws is to obey God, who loves peace." And the Judge began again to persuade the peasants, but could not succeed. Gabriel would not listen to him.

"I shall be fifty next year," said he, "and have a married son, and have never been flogged in my life, and now that pockmarked Ivan has had me condemned to be flogged, and am I to go and ask his forgiveness? No; I've borne enough...Ivan shall have cause to remember me!"

Again Gabriel's voice quivered, and he could say no more, but turned round and went out.

It was seven miles from the Court to the village, and it was getting late when Ivan reached home. He unharnessed his horse, put it up for the night, and entered the cottage. No one was there. The women had already gone to drive the cattle in, and the young fellows were not yet back from the fields. Ivan went in, and sat down, thinking. He remembered how Gabriel had listened to the sentence, and how pale he had become, and how he had turned to the wall; and Ivan's heart grew heavy. He thought how he himself would feel if he were sentenced, and he pitied Gabriel. Then he heard his old father up on the oven cough, and saw him sit up, lower his legs, and scramble down. The old man dragged himself slowly to a seat, and sat down. He was quite tired out with the exertion, and coughed a long time till he had cleared his throat. Then, leaning against the table, he said: "Well, has he been condemned?"

"Yes, to twenty strokes with the rods," answered Ivan.

The old man shook his head.

"A bad business," said he. "You are doing wrong, Ivan! Ah! it's very bad — not for him so much as for yourself!...Well, they'll flog him: but will that do you any good?"

"He'll not do it again," said Ivan.

"What is it he'll not do again? What has he done worse than you?"

"Why, think of the harm he has done me!" said Ivan. "He nearly killed my son's wife, and now he's threatening to burn us up. Am I to thank him for it?"

The old man sighed, and said: "You go about the wide world, Ivan, while I am lying on the oven all these years, so you think you see everything, and that I see nothing...Ah, lad! It's you that don't see; malice blinds you. Others' sins are before your eyes, but your own are behind your back. 'He's acted badly!' What a thing to say! If he were the only one to act badly, how could strife exist? Is strife among men ever bred by one alone? Strife is always between two. His badness you see, but your own you don't. If he were bad, but you were good, there would be no strife. Who pulled the hair out of his beard? Who spoilt his haystack? Who dragged him to the law court? Yet you put it all on him! You live a bad life yourself, that's what is wrong! It's not the way I used to live, lad, and it's not the way I taught you. Is that the way his old father and I used to live?

How did we live? Why, as neighbors should! If he happened to run out of flour, one of the women would come across: 'Uncle Trol, we want some flour.' 'Go to the barn, dear,' I'd say: 'take what you need.' If he'd no one to take his horses to pasture, 'Go, Ivan,' I'd say, 'and look after his horses.' And if I was short of anything, I'd go to him. 'Uncle Gordey,' I'd say, 'I want so-and-so!' 'Take it Uncle Trol!' That's how it was between us, and we had an easy time of it. But now?...That soldier the other day was telling us about the fight at Plevna. Why, there's war between you worse than at Plevna! Is that living?...What a sin it is! You are a man and master of the house; it's you who will have to answer. What are you teaching the women and the children? To snarl and snap? Why, the other day your Taraska — that greenhorn — was swearing at neighbor Irena, calling her names; and his mother listened and laughed. Is that right? It is you will have to answer. Think of your soul. Is this all as it should be? You throw a word at me, and I give you two in return; you give me a blow, and I give you two. No, lad! Christ, when He walked on earth, taught us fools something very different...If you get a hard word from any one, keep silent, and his own conscience will accuse him. That is what our Lord taught. If you get a slap, turn the other cheek. 'Here, beat me, if that's what I deserve!' And his own conscience will rebuke him. He will soften, and will listen to you. That's the way He taught us, not to be proud!...Why don't you speak? Isn't it as I say?"

Ivan sat silent and listened.

The old man coughed, and having with difficulty cleared his throat, began again: "You think Christ taught us wrong? Why, it's all for our own good. Just think of your earthly life; are you better off, or worse, since this Plevna began among you? Just reckon up what you've spent on all this law business — what the driving backwards and forwards and your food on the way have cost you! What fine fellows your sons have grown; you might live and get on well; but now your means are lessening. And why? All because of this folly; because of your pride. You ought to be plowing with your lads, and do the sowing yourself; but the fiend carries you off to the judge, or to some pettifogger or other. The plowing is not done in time, nor the sowing, and mother earth can't bear properly. Why did the oats fail this year? When did you sow them? When you came back from town! And what did you gain? A burden for your own shoulders... Eh, lad, think of your own business! Work with your boys in the field and at home, and if someone offends you, forgive him, as God wished you to. Then life will be easy, and your heart will always be light."

Ivan remained silent.

"Ivan, my boy, hear your old father! Go and harness the roan, and go at once to the Government office; put an end to all this affair there; and in the morning go and make it up with Gabriel in God's name, and invite him to your house for tomorrow's holiday (It was the eve of the Virgin's Nativity). Have tea ready, and get a bottle of vodka and put an end to this wicked business, so that there should not be any more of it in future, and tell the women and children to do the same." Ivan sighed, and thought, "What he says is true," and his heart grew lighter. Only he did not know how to begin to put matters right.

But again the old man began, as if he had guessed what was in Ivan's mind.

"Go, Ivan, don't put it off! Put out the fire before it spreads, or it will be too late."

The old man was going to say more, but before he could do so the women came in, chattering like magpies. The news that Gabriel was sentenced to be flogged, and of his threat to set fire to the house, had already reached them. They had heard all about it and added to it something of their own, and had again had a row, in the pasture, with the women of Gabriel's household. They began telling how Gabriel's daughter-in-law threatened a fresh action: Gabriel had got the right side of the examining magistrate, who would now turn the whole affair upside down; and the schoolmaster was writing out another petition, to the Tsar himself this time, about Ivan; and everything was in the petition — all about the coupling-pin and the kitchen garden — so that half of Ivan's homestead would be theirs soon. Ivan heard what they were saying, and his heart grew cold again, and he gave up the thought of making peace with Gabriel.

In a farmstead there is always plenty for the master to do. Ivan did not stop to talk to the women, but went out to the threshing floor and to the barn. By the time he had tidied up there, the sun had set and the young fellows had returned from the field. They had been plowing the field for the winter crops with two horses. Ivan met them, questioned them about their work, helped to put everything in its place, set a torn horse collar aside to be mended, and was going to put away some stakes under the barn, but it had grown quite dusk, so he decided to leave them where they were till next day. Then he gave the cattle their food, opened the gate, let out the horses Taras was to take to pasture for the night, and again closed the gate and barred it. "Now," thought he, "I'll have my supper, and then to bed." He took the horse collar and entered the hut. By this time he had forgotten about Gabriel and about what his old father had been saying to him. But, just as he took hold of the door handle to enter the passage, he heard his neighbor on the other side of the fence cursing somebody in a hoarse voice: "What the devil is he good for?" Gabriel was saying. "He's only fit to be killed!" At these words all Ivan's former bitterness towards his neighbor re-awoke. He stood listening while Gabriel scolded, and, when he stopped, Ivan went into the hut.

There was a light inside; his daughter-in-law sat spinning, his wife was getting supper ready, his eldest son was making straps for bark shoes, his second sat near the table with a book, and Taras was getting ready to go out to pasture the horses for the night. Everything in the hut would have been pleasant and bright, but for that plague — a bad neighbor!

Ivan entered, sullen and cross; threw the cat down from the bench, and scolded the women for putting the slop pail in the wrong place. He felt despondent, and sat down, frowning, to mend the horse collar. Gabriel's words kept ringing in his ears: his threat at the law court, and what he had just been shouting in a hoarse voice about some one who was "only fit to be killed."

His wife gave Taras his supper, and, having eaten it, Taras put on an old sheepskin and another coat, tied a sash round his waist, took some bread with him, and went out to the horses. His eldest brother was going to see him off, but Ivan himself rose instead, and went out into the porch. It had grown quite dark outside, clouds had gathered, and the wind had risen. Ivan went down the steps, helped his boy to mount, started the foal after him, and stood listening while Taras rode down the village and was there joined by other lads with their horses. Ivan waited until they were all out of hearing. As he stood there by the gate he could not get Gabriel's words out of his head: "Mind that something of yours does not burn worse!"

"He is desperate," thought Ivan. "Everything is dry, and it's windy weather besides. He'll come up at the back somewhere, set fire to something, and be off. He'll burn the place and escape scot free, the villain!...There now, if one could but catch him in the act, he'd not get off then!" And the thought fixed itself so firmly in his mind that he did not go up the steps but went out into the street and round the corner. "I'll just walk round the buildings; who can tell what he's after?" And Ivan, stepping softly, passed out of the gate. As soon as he reached the corner, he looked round along the fence, and seemed to see something suddenly move at the opposite corner, as if some one had come out and disappeared again. Ivan stopped, and stood quietly, listening and looking. Everything was still; only the leaves of the willows fluttered in the wind, and the straws of the thatch rustled. At first it seemed pitch dark, but, when his eyes had grown used to the darkness, he could see the far corner, and a plow that lay there, and the eaves. He looked a while, but saw no one.

"I suppose it was a mistake," thought Ivan; "but still I will go round," and Ivan went stealthily along by the shed. Ivan stepped so softly in his bark shoes that he did not hear his own footsteps. As he reached the far corner, something seemed to flare up for a moment near the plow and to vanish again. Ivan felt as if struck to the heart; and he stopped. Hardly had he stopped, when something flared up more brightly in the same place, and he clearly saw a man with a cap on his head, crouching down, with his back towards him, lighting a bunch of straw he held in his hand. Ivan's heart fluttered within him like a bird. Straining every nerve, he approached with great strides, hardly feeling his legs under him. "Ah," thought Ivan, "now he won't escape! I'll catch him in the act!"

Ivan was still some distance off, when suddenly he saw a bright light, but not in the same place as before, and not a small flame. The thatch had flared up at the eaves, the flames were reaching up to the roof, and, standing beneath it, Gabriel's whole figure was clearly visible.

Like a hawk swooping down on a lark, Ivan rushed at Limping Gabriel. "Now I'll have him; he shan't escape me!" thought Ivan. But Gabriel must have heard his steps, and (however he managed it) glancing round, he scuttled away past the barn like a hare.

"You shan't escape!" shouted Ivan, darting after him.

Just as he was going to seize Gabriel, the latter dodged him; but Ivan managed to catch the skirt of Gabriel's coat. It tore right off, and Ivan fell down. He recovered his feet, and shouting, "Help! Seize him! Thieves! Murder!" ran on again. But meanwhile Gabriel had reached his own gate. There Ivan overtook him and was about to seize him, when something struck Ivan a stunning blow, as though a stone had hit his temple, quite deafening him. It was Gabriel who, seizing an oak wedge that lay near the gate, had struck out with all his might.

Ivan was stunned; sparks flew before his eyes, then all grew dark and he staggered. When he came to his senses Gabriel was no longer there: it was as light as day, and from the side where his homestead was something roared and crackled like an engine at work. Ivan turned round and saw that his back shed was all ablaze, and the side shed had also caught fire, and flames and smoke and bits of burning straw mixed with the smoke, were being driven towards his hut.

"What is this, friends?..." cried Ivan, lifting his arms and striking his thighs. "Why, all I had to do was just to snatch it out from under the eaves and trample on it! What is this, friends?..." he kept repeating. He wished to shout, but his breath failed him; his voice was gone. He wanted to run, but his legs would not obey him, and got in each other's way. He moved slowly, but again staggered and again his breath failed. He stood still till he had regained breath, and then went on. Before he had got round the back shed to reach the fire, the side shed was also all ablaze; and the corner of the hut and the covered gateway had caught fire as well. The flames were leaping out of the hut, and it was impossible to get into the yard. A large crowd had collected, but nothing could be done. The neighbors were carrying their belongings out of their own houses, and driving the cattle out of their own sheds. After Ivan's house, Gabriel's also caught fire, then, the wind rising, the flames spread to the other side of the street and half the village was burnt down.

At Ivan's house they barely managed to save his old father; and the family escaped in what they had on; everything else, except the horses that had been driven out to pasture for the night, was lost; all the cattle, the fowls on their perches, the carts, plows, and harrows, the women's trunks with their clothes, and the grain in the granaries — all were burnt up!

At Gabriel's, the cattle were driven out, and a few things saved from his house.

The fire lasted all night. Ivan stood in front of his homestead and kept repeating, "What is this?... Friends!... One need only have pulled it out and trampled on it!" But when the roof fell in, Ivan rushed into the burning place, and seizing a charred beam, tried to drag it out. The women saw him, and called him back; but he pulled out the beam, and was going in again for another when he lost his footing and fell among the flames. Then his son made his way in after him and dragged him out. Ivan had singed his hair and beard and burnt his clothes and scorched his hands, but he felt nothing. "His grief has stupefied him," said the people. The fire was burning itself out, but Ivan still stood repeating: "Friends!... What is this?... One need only have pulled it out!"

In the morning the village Elder's son came to fetch Ivan.

"Daddy Ivan, your father is dying! He has sent for you to say good-bye."

Ivan had forgotten about his father, and did not understand what was being said to him.

"What father?" he said. "Whom has he sent for?"

"He sent for you, to say good-bye; he is dying in our cottage! Come along, daddy Ivan," said the Elder's son, pulling him by the arm; and Ivan followed the lad.

When he was being carried out of the hut, some burning straw had fallen on to the old man and burnt him, and he had been taken to the village Elder's in the farther part of the village, which the fire did not reach.

When Ivan came to his father, there was only the Elder's wife in the hut, besides some little children on the top of the oven. All the rest were still at the fire. The old man, who was lying on a bench holding a wax candle in his hand, kept turning his eyes towards the door. When his son entered, he moved a little. The old woman went up to him and told him that his son had come. He asked to have him brought nearer. Ivan came closer.

"What did I tell you, Ivan?" began the old man. "Who has burnt down the village?"

"It was he, father!" Ivan answered. "I caught him in the act. I saw him shove the firebrand into the thatch. I might have pulled away the burning straw and stamped it out, and then nothing would have happened."

"Ivan," said the old man, "I am dying, and you in your turn will have to face death. Whose is the sin?"

Ivan gazed at his father in silence, unable to utter a word.

"Now, before God, say whose is the sin? What did I tell you?"

Only then Ivan came to his senses and understood it all. He sniffed and said, "Mine, father!" And he fell on his knees before his father, saying, "Forgive me, father; I am guilty before you and before God."

The old man moved his hands, changed the candle from his right hand to his left, and tried to lift his right hand to his forehead to cross himself, but could not do it, and stopped.

"Praise the Lord! Praise the Lord!" said he, and again he turned his eyes towards his son.

"Ivan! I say, Ivan!"

"What, father?"

"What must you do now?"

Ivan was weeping.

"I don't know how we are to live now, father!" he said.

The old man closed his eyes, moved his lips as if to gather strength, and opening his eyes again, said: "You'll manage. If you obey God's will, you'll manage!" He paused, then smiled, and said: "Mind, Ivan! Don't tell who started the fire! Hide another man's sin, and God will forgive two of yours!" And the old man took the candle in both hands and, folding them on his breast, sighed, stretched out, and died.

Ivan did not say anything against Gabriel, and no one knew what had caused the fire.

And Ivan's anger against Gabriel passed away, and Gabriel wondered that Ivan did not tell anybody. At first Gabriel felt afraid, but after a while he got used to it. The men left off quarrelling, and then their families left off also. While rebuilding their huts, both families lived in one house; and when the village was rebuilt and they might have moved farther apart, Ivan and Gabriel built next to each other, and remained neighbors as before.

They lived as good neighbors should. Ivan Stcherbakof remembered his old father's command to obey God's law, and quench a fire at the first spark; and if any one does him an injury he now tries not to revenge himself, but rather to set matters right again; and if any one gives him a bad word, instead of giving a worse in return, he tries to teach the other not to use evil words; and so he teaches his womenfolk and children. And Ivan Stcherbakof has got on his feet again, and now lives better even than he did before.

Forgive And Forget

T S Arthur

Forgive and forget! Why the world would be lonely,
The garden a wilderness left to deform,
If the flowers but remembered the chilling winds only,
And the fields gave no verdure for fear of the storm!

C. SWAIN.

"Forgive and forget, Herbert."

"No, I will neither forgive nor forget. The thing was done wantonly. I never pass by a direct insult."

"Admit that it was done wantonly; but this I doubt. He is an old friend, long tried and long esteemed. He could not have been himself; he must have been carried away by some wrong impulse, when he offended you."

"He acted from something in him, of course."

"We all do so. Nothing external can touch our volition, unless there be that within which corresponds to the impelling agent."

"Very well. This conduct of Marston shows him to be internally unworthy of my regard; shows him to possess a trait of character that unfits him to be my friend. I have been mistaken in him. He now stands revealed in his true light, a mean-spirited fellow."

"Don't use such language towards Marston, my young friend."

"He has no principle. He wished to render me ridiculous and do me harm. A man who could act as he did, cannot possess a spark of honourable feeling. Does a good fountain send forth bitter waters? Is not a tree known by its fruit? When a man seeks wantonly to insult and injure me, I discover that he wants principle, and wish to have no more to do with him."

"Perhaps," said the individual with whom Herbert Arnest was conversing, "it is your wounded self-love, more than your high regard for principle, that speaks so eloquently against Marston."

"Mr. Welford!"

"Nay, my young friend, do not be offended with me. Your years, twice told, would not make mine. I have lived long enough to get a cool head and understand something of the springs of action that lie in the human heart. The best, at best, have little to be proud of, and much to lament over, in the matter of high and honourable impulses. It is a far easier thing to do wrong than right; far easier to be led away by our evil passions than to compel ourselves always to regard justice and judgment in our dealings with others. Test yourself by this rule. Would your feelings for Marston be the same if he had only acted toward another as he has acted toward you? Do not say 'yes' from a hasty impulse. Reflect coolly about it. If not, then it is not so much a regard to principle, as your regard to yourself, that causes you to be so bitterly offended."

This plain language was not relished by the young man. It was touching the very thing in him that Marston had offended—his self-love. He replied, coldly—

"As for that, I am very well satisfied with my own reasons for being displeased with Marston; and am perfectly willing to be responsible for my own action in this case. I will change very much from my present feelings, if I ever have anything more to do with him."

"God give you a better mind then," replied Mr. Welford. "It is the best wish I can express for you."

The two young men who were now at variance with each other had been friends for many years. As they entered the world, the hereditary character of each came more fully into external manifestation, and revealed traits not before seen, and not always the most agreeable to others. Edward Marston had his faults, and so had Herbert Arnest: the latter quite as many as the former. There was a mutual observation of these, and a mutual forbearance towards each other for a considerable time, although each thought more than was necessary about things in the other that ought to be corrected. A fault with Marston was quickness of temper and a disposition to say unpleasant, cutting things, without due reflection. But he had a forgiving disposition, and very many amiable and excellent qualities. Arnest was also quick-tempered. His leading defect of character was self-esteem, which made him exceedingly sensitive in regard to the conduct of others as affecting the general estimation of himself. He could not bear to have any freedom taken with him, in company, even by his best friend. He felt it to be humiliating, if not degrading. He, therefore, was a man of many dislikes, for one and another were every now and then doing or saying something that hurt more or less severely his self-esteem.

Marston had none of this peculiar weakness of his friend. He rarely thought about the estimation in which he was held, and never let the mere opinions of others influence him. But he was careful not to do any thing that violated his own self-respect.

The breach between the young men occurred thus. The two friends were in company with several others, and there was present a young lady in whose eyes Arnest wished to appear in as favorable a light as possible. He was relating an adventure in which he was the principal hero, and, in doing so, exaggerated his own action so far as to amuse Marston, who happened to know all about the circumstances, and provoke from him some remarks that placed the whole affair in rather a ridiculous light, and caused a laugh at Arnest's expense.

The young man's self-esteem was deeply wounded. Even the lady, for whose ears the narrative had been more especially given, laughed heartily, and made one or two light remarks; or, rather, heavy ones for the ears of Arnest. He was deeply disturbed though at the time he managed to conceal almost entirely what he felt.

Marston, however, saw that his thoughtless words had done more (sic) than he had intended them to do, both upon the company and upon the sensitive mind of his friend. He regretted having uttered them and waited only until he should leave the company with Arnest, to express his sorrow for what he had done. But his friend did not give him this opportunity, for he managed to retire alone, thus expressing to Marston the fact that he was seriously offended.

Early the next morning, Marston called at the residence of his friend, in order to make an apology for having offended him; but he happened not to be at home. On arriving at his office, he found a note from Arnest, couched in the most offensive terms. The language was such as to extinguish all desire or intention to apologize.

"Henceforth we are strangers," he said, as he thrust the note aside.

An hour afterward, they met on the street, looked coldly into each other's face, and passed without even a nod. That act sealed the record of estrangement.

Mr. Wellford was an old gentleman who was well acquainted with both of the young men, and esteemed them for the good qualities they possessed. When he heard of the occurrence just related, he was much grieved, and sought to heal the breach that had been made; but without success. Arnest's self-esteem had been sorely wounded, and he would not forgive what he considered a wanton outrage. Marston felt himself deeply insulted by the note he had received, and maintained that he would forfeit his self-respect were he to hold any intercourse whatever with a man who could, on so small a provocation, write such a scandalous letter. Thus the matter stood; wounded self-esteem on one side, and insulted self-respect on the other, not only maintaining the breach, but widening it every day. Mr. Wellford used his utmost influence with his young friends to bend them from their anger, but he argued the matter in vain. The voice of pride was stronger than the voice of reason.

Months were suffered to go by, and even years to elapse, and still they were as strangers. Circumstances threw them constantly together; they met in places of business; they sat in full view of each other in church on the holy Sabbath; they mingled in the same social circles; the friends of one were the friends of the other; but they rarely looked into each other's face, and never spoke. Did this make them happier? No! For, "If ye forgive not men their trespasses, neither will your heavenly Father forgive your trespasses." Did they feel indifferent toward each other? Not by any means! Arnest still dwelt on and magnified the provocation he had received, but thought that the expression of his indignation had not been of a character to give as great offence to Marston as it had done. And Marston, as time passed, thought more and more lightly of the few jesting words he had spoken, and considered them less and less provocation for the insulting note he had received, which he still had, and sometimes turned up and read.

The old friends were forced to think of each other often, for both were rising in the world, and rising into general esteem and respectability. The name of the one was often mentioned with approbation in the presence of the other; and it sometimes happened that they were thrown together in such a way as to render their position toward each other really embarrassing: as, for instance, one was called to preside at a public meeting, and the other chosen secretary. Neither could refuse, and there had to be an official intercourse between them; it was cold and formal in the extreme; and neither could see as he looked into the eyes of the other, a glimmer of the old light of friendship.

Mr. Wellford was present at this meeting, and marked the fact that the intercourse between Arnest and Marston was official only—that they did not unbend to each other in the least. He was grieved to see it, for he knew the good qualities of both, and he had a high respect for them.

"This must not be," said he to himself, as he walked thoughtfully homeward. "They are making themselves unhappy, and preventing a concert of useful efforts for good in society, and all for nothing. I will try again to reconcile them; perhaps I may be more successful than before."

So, on the next day, the old gentleman made it his business to call upon Arnest, who expressed great pleasure in meeting him.

"I noticed," said Mr. Wellford, after he had conversed some time, and finally introduced the subject of the meeting on the previous evening, "that your intercourse with the secretary was exceedingly formal; in fact, hardly courteous."

"I don't like Marston, as you are very well aware," replied Arnest.

"In which feeling you stand nearly alone, friend Arnest. Mr. Marston is highly esteemed by all who know him."

"All don't know him as I do."

"Perhaps others know him better than you do; there may lie the difference."

"If a man knocks me down, I know the weight of his arm much better than those who have never felt it."

"Still nursing your anger, still harbouring unkind thoughts! Forgive and forget, my friend—forgive and forget; no longer let the sun go down upon your wrath."

"I can forgive, Mr. Wellford—I do forgive; for Heaven knows I wish him no harm; but I cannot forget: that is asking too much."

"You do not forget, because you will not forgive," replied the old gentleman. "Forgive, and you will soon forget. I am sure you will both be happier in forgetting than you can be in remembering the past."

But Arnest shook his head, remarking, as he so—"I would

rather let things remain as they are. At least, I cannot stoop to any humiliating overtures for a reconciliation. When Marston outraged my feelings so wantonly, I wrote him a pretty warm expression of my sentiments in regard to his conduct. This gave him mortal offence. I do not now remember what I wrote, but nothing, certainly, to have prevented his coming forward and apologizing for his conduct; but he did not choose to do this, and there the matter rests. I cannot recall the angry rebuke I gave him, for it was no doubt just."

"A man who writes a letter in a passion, and afterwards forgets what he has written," said Mr. Wellford, "may be sure that he has said what his sober reason cannot approve. If you could have the letter you then sent before you now, I imagine that you would no longer wonder that Marston was offended."

"That is impossible; without doubt, he burned my note the moment he received it."

Mr. Wellford tried in vain to induce Arnest to consent to forget what was past; but he affirmed that this was impossible, and that he had no wish to renew an acquaintance with his old friend.

About the same time that this interview took place, Marston was alone, thinking with sad and softened feelings of the past. The letter of Arnest was before him; he had turned it over by accident.

"He could not have been himself when he wrote this," he thought. It was the first time he had permitted himself to think so. "My words must have stung him severely, lightly as I uttered them, and with no intention to wound. This matter ought not to have gone on so long. Friends are not so plentiful that we may carelessly cast those we have tried and proved aside. He has many excellent qualities."

Pride came quickly, with many suggestions about self-respect, and what every man owed to himself.

"He owes it to himself to be just to others," Marston truly thought. "Was I just in failing to apologize to my friend, notwithstanding this offensive letter? No, I was not; for his action did not exonerate me from the responsibility of mine. Ah, me! How passion blinds us!"

After musing for some time, Marston drew towards him a sheet of paper, and, taking up a pen, wrote:

"MY DEAR SIR:—What I ought to have done years ago, I do now, and that is, offer you a sincere apology for light words thoughtlessly spoken, but which I ought not to have used, as they were calculated to wound, and, I am grieved to think, did wound. But for your note, which I enclose, I should have made this apology the moment I had an opportunity. But its peculiar tenor, I then felt, precluded me from doing so. I confess that I erred in letting my feelings blind my cooler judgment.

"Your old friend, MARSTON.

"To Mr. Herbert Arnest."

Enclosing the note alluded to in this letter, Marston sealed, and, ringing for an attendant, despatched it.

"Better to do right late than never," he murmured, as he leaned pensively back in his chair.

"Let what will come of it, I shall feel better, for I will gain my own self-respect, and have an inward assurance that I have done right,—more than I have for a long time had, in regard to this matter at least."

Relieved in mind, Marston commenced looking over some papers in reference to matters of business then on hand, and was soon so much absorbed in them, that the subject which had lately filled his thoughts faded entirely therefrom. Some one opened the door, and he turned to see who was entering. In an instant he was on his feet. It was Arnest.

The face of the latter was pale and agitated, and his lips quivered. He came forward hurriedly, extending his hand, not to grasp that of his old friend, but to hold up his own letter that had been just returned to him.

"Marston," he said, huskily, "did I send you this note?"

"You did," was the firm but mild answer.

"Thus I cancel it!" And he tore it into shreds, and scattered them on the floor. "Would that its contents could be as easily obliterated from your memory!" he added, in a most earnest voice.

"They are no longer there, my friend," returned Marston, with visible emotion, now grasping the hand of Arnest. "You have wiped them out."

Arnest returned the pressure with both hands, his eyes fixed on those of Marston, until they grew so dim that he could no longer read the old familiar lines and forgiving look.

"Let us forgive and forget," said Marston, speaking in a broken voice. "We have wronged each other and ourselves. We have let evil passions rule instead of good affections."

"From my heart do I say 'Amen,'" replied Arnest. "Yes, let us forgive and forget. Would that we had been as wise as we now are, years ago!"

Thus were they reconciled. And now the question is, What did either gain by his indignation against the other? Did Arnest rise higher in his self-esteem, or Marston gain additional self-respect? We think not. Alas! how blinding is selfish passion! How it opens in the mind the door for the influx of multitudes of evil and false suggestions! How it hides the good in others, and magnifies, weakness into crimes! Let us beware of it.

"Reconciled at last," said old Mr. Wellford, when he next saw Arnest and heard the fact from his lips.

"Yes," replied the latter. "I can now forget as well as forgive."

"Rather say you can forget, because you forgive. If you had forgiven truly, you could have ceased to think of what was wrong in your friend long ago. People talk of forgiving and not forgetting, but it isn't so: they do not forget because they do not forgive."

"I believe you are right," said Arnest. "I think, now, as naturally of my friend's good qualities as I ever did before of what was evil. I forget the evil in thinking of the good."

"Because you have forgiven him," returned Mr. Wellford. "Before you forgave him, your thought of evil gave no room for the thought of good."

Mr. Wellford was right. After we have forgiven, we find it no hard matter to forget.

The Things The Play
O. Henry

Being acquainted with a newspaper reporter who had a couple of free passes, I got to see the performance a few nights ago at one of the popular vaudeville houses.

One of the numbers was a violin solo by a striking-looking man not much past forty, but with very gray thick hair. Not being afflicted with a taste for music, I let the system of noises drift past my ears while I regarded the man.

"There was a story about that chap a month or two ago," said the reporter. "They gave me the assignment. It was to run a column and was to be on the extremely light and joking order. The old man seems to like the funny touch I give to local happenings. Oh, yes, I'm working on a farce comedy now. Well, I went down to the house and got all the details; but I certainly fell down on that job. I went back and turned in a comic write-up of an east side funeral instead. Why? Oh, I couldn't seem to get hold of it with my funny hooks, somehow. Maybe you could make a one-act tragedy out of it for a curtain-raiser. I'll give you the details."

After the performance my friend, the reporter, recited to me the facts over Wurzburger.

"I see no reason," said I, when he had concluded, "why that shouldn't make a rattling good funny story. Those three people couldn't have acted in a more absurd and preposterous manner if they had been real actors in a real theatre. I'm really afraid that all the stage is a world, anyhow, and all the players men and women. 'The thing's the play,' is the way I quote Mr. Shakespeare."

"Try it," said the reporter.

"I will," said I; and I did, to show him how he could have made a humorous column of it for his paper.

There stands a house near Abingdon Square. On the ground floor there has been for twenty-five years a little store where toys and notions and stationery are sold.

One night twenty years ago there was a wedding in the rooms above the store. The Widow Mayo owned the house and store. Her daughter Helen was married to Frank Barry. John Delaney was best man. Helen was eighteen, and her picture had been printed in a morning paper next to the headlines of a "Wholesale Female Murderess" story from Butte, Mont. But after your eye and intelligence had rejected the connection, you seized your magnifying glass and read beneath the portrait her description as one of a series of Prominent Beauties and Belles of the lower west side.

Frank Barry and John Delaney were "prominent" young beaux of the same side, and bosom friends, whom you expected to turn upon each other every time the curtain went up. One who pays his money for orchestra seats and fiction expects this. That is the first funny idea that has turned up in the story yet. Both had made a great race for Helen's hand. When Frank won, John shook his hand and congratulated him — honestly, he did.

After the ceremony Helen ran upstairs to put on her hat. She was getting married in a traveling dress. She and Frank were going to Old Point Comfort for a week. Downstairs the usual horde of gibbering cave-dwellers were waiting with their hands full of old Congress gaiters and paper bags of hominy.

Then there was a rattle of the fire-escape, and into her room jumps the mad and infatuated John Delaney, with a damp curl drooping upon his forehead, and made violent and reprehensible love to his lost one, entreating her to flee or fly with him to the Riviera, or the Bronx, or any old place where there are Italian skies and *dolce far niente*.

It would have carried Blaney off his feet to see Helen repulse him. With blazing and scornful eyes she fairly withered him by demanding whatever he meant by speaking to respectable people that way.

In a few moments she had him going. The manliness that had possessed him departed. He bowed low, and said something about "irresistible impulse" and "forever carry in his heart the memory of" — and she suggested that he catch the first fire-escape going down.

"I will away," said John Delaney, "to the furthermost parts of the earth. I cannot remain near you and know that you are another's. I will to Africa, and there amid other scenes strive to for —"

"For goodness sake, get out," said Helen. "Somebody might come in."

He knelt upon one knee, and she extended him one white hand that he might give it a farewell kiss.

Girls, was this choice boon of the great little god Cupid ever vouchsafed you — to have the fellow you want hard and fast, and have the one you don't want come with a damp curl on his forehead and kneel to you and babble of Africa and love which, in spite of everything, shall forever bloom, an amaranth, in his heart? To know your power, and to feel the sweet security of your own happy state; to send the unlucky one, broken-hearted, to foreign climes, while you congratulate yourself as he presses his last kiss upon your knuckles, that your nails are well manicured — say, girls, it's galluptious — don't ever let it get by you.

And then, of course - how did you guess it? — the door opened and in stalked the bridegroom, jealous of slow-tying bonnet strings.

The farewell kiss was imprinted upon Helen's hand, and out of the window and down the fire-escape sprang John Delaney, Africa -bound.

A little slow music, if you please — faint violin, just a breath in the clarinet and a touch of the 'cello. Imagine the scene. Frank, white-hot, with the cry of a man wounded to death bursting from him. Helen, rushing and clinging to him, trying to explain. He catches her wrists and tears them from his shoulders — once, twice, thrice he sways her this way and that - the stage manager will show you how — and throws her from him to the floor a huddled, crushed, moaning thing. Never, he cries, will he look upon her face again, and rushes from the house through the staring groups of astonished guests.

And, now because it is the Thing instead of the Play, the audience must stroll out into the real lobby of the world and marry, die, grow gray, rich, poor, happy or sad during the intermission of twenty years which must precede the rising of the curtain again

Mrs. Barry inherited the shop and the house. At thirty-eight she could have bested many an eighteen-year-old at a beauty show on points and general results. Only a few people remembered her wedding comedy, but she made of it no secret. She did not pack it in lavender or moth balls, nor did she sell it to a magazine.

One day a middle-aged money-making lawyer, who bought his legal cap and ink of her, asked her across the counter to marry him.

"I'm really much obliged to you," said Helen, cheerfully, "but I married another man twenty years ago. He was more a goose than a man, but I think I love him yet. I have never seen him since about half an hour after the ceremony. Was it copying ink that you wanted or just writing fluid?"

The lawyer bowed over the counter with old-time grace and left a respectful kiss on the back of her hand. Helen sighed. Parting salutes, however romantic, may be overdone. Here she was at thirty-eight, beautiful and admired; and all that she seemed to have got from her lovers were approaches and adieus. Worse still, in the last one she had lost a customer, too.

Business languished, and she hung out a Room to Let card. Two large rooms on the third floor were prepared for desirable tenants. Roomers came, and went regretfully, for the house of Mrs. Barry was the abode of neatness, comfort and taste.

One day came Ramonti, the violinist, and engaged the front room above. The discord and clatter uptown offended his nice ear; so a friend had sent him to this oasis in the desert of noise.

Ramonti, with his still youthful face, his dark eyebrows, his short, pointed, foreign, brown beard, his distinguished head of gray hair, and his artist's temperament — revealed in his light, gay and sympathetic manner — was a welcome tenant in the old house near Abingdon Square.

Helen lived on the floor above the store. The architecture of it was singular and quaint. The hall was large and almost square. Up one side of it, and then across the end of it ascended an open stairway to the floor above. This hall space she had furnished as a sitting room and office combined. There she kept her desk and wrote her business letters; and there she sat of evenings by a warm fire and a bright red light and sewed or read. Ramonti found the atmosphere so agreeable that he spent much time there, describing to Mrs. Barry the wonders of Paris, where he had studied with a particularly notorious and noisy fiddler.

Next comes lodger No. 2, a handsome, melancholy man in the early 40s, with a brown, mysterious beard, and strangely pleading, haunting eyes. He, too, found the society of Helen a desirable thing. With the eyes of Romeo and Othello's tongue, he charmed her with tales of distant climes and wooed her by respectful innuendo.

From the first Helen felt a marvelous and compelling thrill in the presence of this man. His voice somehow took her swiftly back to the days of her youth's romance. This feeling grew, and she gave way to it, and it led her to an instinctive belief that he had been a factor in that romance. And then with a woman's reasoning (oh, yes, they do, sometimes) she leaped over common syllogism and theory, and logic, and was sure that her husband had come back to her. For she saw in his eyes love, which no woman can mistake, and a thousand tons of regret and remorse, which aroused pity, which is perilously near to love requited, which is the sine qua non in the house that Jack built.

But she made no sign. A husband who steps around the corner for twenty years and then drops in again should not expect to find his slippers laid out too conveniently near nor a match ready lighted for his cigar. There must be expiation, explanation, and possibly execration. A little purgatory, and then, maybe, if he were properly humble, he might be trusted with a harp and crown. And so she made no sign that she knew or suspected.

And my friend, the reporter, could see nothing funny in this! Sent out on an assignment to write up a roaring, hilarious, brilliant joshing story of — but I will not knock a brother — let us go on with the story.

One evening Ramonti stopped in Helen's hall-office-reception-room and told his love with the tenderness and ardor of the enraptured artist. His words were a bright flame of the divine fire that glows in the heart of a man who is a dreamer and doer combined.

"But before you give me an answer," he went on, before she could accuse him of suddenness, "I must tell you that 'Ramonti' is the only name I have to offer you. My manager gave me that. I do not know who I am or where I came from. My first recollection is of opening my eyes in a hospital. I was a young man, and I had been there for weeks. My life before that is a blank to me. They told me that I was found lying in the street with a wound on my head and was brought there in an ambulance. They thought I must have fallen and struck my head upon the stones. There was nothing to show who I was. I have never been able to remember. After I was discharged from the hospital, I took up the violin. I have had success. Mrs. Barry — I do not know your name except that — I love you; the first time I saw you I realized that you were the one woman in the world for me — and" — oh, a lot of stuff like that

Helen felt young again. First a wave of pride and a sweet little thrill of vanity went all over her; and then she looked Ramonti in the eyes, and a tremendous throb went through her heart. She hadn't expected that throb. It took her by surprise. The musician had become a big factor in her life, and she hadn't been aware of it.

"Mr. Ramonti," she said sorrowfully (this was not on the stage, remember; it was in the old home near Abingdon Square), "I'm awfully sorry, but I'm a married woman."

And then she told him the sad story of her life, as a heroine must do, sooner or later, either to a theatrical manager or to a reporter.

Ramonti took her hand, bowed low and kissed it, and went up to his room.

Helen sat down and looked mournfully at her hand. Well she might. Three suitors had kissed it, mounted their red roan steeds and ridden away.

In an hour entered the mysterious stranger with the haunting eyes. Helen was in the willow rocker, knitting a useless thing in cotton-wool. He ricocheted from the stairs and stopped for a chat. Sitting across the table from her, he also poured out his narrative of love. And then he said: "Helen, do you not remember me? I think I have seen it in your eyes. Can you forgive the past and remember the love that has lasted for twenty years? I wronged you deeply — I was afraid to come back to you — but my love overpowered my reason. Can you, will you, forgive me?"

Helen stood up. The mysterious stranger held one of her hands in a strong and trembling clasp.

There she stood, and I pity the stage that it has not acquired a scene like that and her emotions to portray.

For she stood with a divided heart. The fresh, unforgettable, virginal love for her bridegroom was hers; the treasured, sacred, honored memory of her first choice filled half her soul. She leaned to that pure feeling. Honor and faith and sweet, abiding romance bound her to it. But the other half of her heart and soul was filled with something else - a later, fuller, nearer influence. And so the old fought against the new.

And while she hesitated, from the room above came the soft, racking, petitionary music of a violin. The hag, music, bewitches some of the noblest. The daws may peck upon one's sleeve without injury, but whoever wears his heart upon his tympanum gets it not far from the neck.

This music and the musician called her, and at her side honor and the old love held her back.

"Forgive me," he pleaded.

"Twenty years is a long time to remain away from the one you say you love," she declared, with a purgatorial touch.

"How could I tell?" he begged. "I will conceal nothing from you. That night when he left I followed him. I was mad with jealousy. On a dark street I struck him down. He did not rise. I examined him. His head had struck a stone. I did not intend to kill him. I was mad with love and jealousy. I hid near by and saw an ambulance take him away. Although you married him, Helen —"

"Who are you?" cried the woman, with wide-open eyes, snatching her hand away.

"Don't you remember me, Helen — the one who has always loved you best? I am John Delaney. If you can forgive —"

But she was gone, leaping, stumbling, hurrying, flying up the stairs toward the music and him who had forgotten, but who had known her for his in each of his two existences, and as she climbed up she sobbed, cried and sang: "Frank! Frank! Frank!"

Three mortals thus juggling with years as though they were billiard balls, and my friend, the reporter, couldn't see anything funny in it!

Forgive And Forget
Maria Edgeworth

In the neighborhood of a seaport town in the west of England, there lived a gardener, who had one son, called Maurice, to whom he was very partial. One day his father sent him to the neighboring town to purchase some garden seeds for him. When Maurice got to the seed-shop, it was full of people, who were all impatient to be served: first a great tall man, and next a great fat woman pushed before him; and he stood quietly beside the counter, waiting till somebody should be at leisure to attend to him. At length, when all the other people who were in the shop had got what they wanted, the shopman turned to Maurice—"And what do you want, my patient little fellow?" said he.

"I want all these seeds for my father," said Maurice, putting a list of seeds into the shopman's hand; "and I have brought money to pay for them all."

The seedsman looked out all the seeds that Maurice wanted, and packed them up in paper: he was folding up some painted lady-peas, when, from a door at the back of the shop, there came in a square, rough-faced man, who exclaimed, the moment he came in, "Are the seeds I ordered ready?—

The wind's fair—they ought to have been aboard yesterday. And my china jar, is it packed up and directed? where is it?"

"It is up there on the shelf over your head, sir," answered the seedsman. "It is very safe, you see; but we have not had time to pack it yet. It shall be done to-day; and we will get the seeds ready for you, sir, immediately."

"Immediately! Then stir about it. The seeds will not pack themselves up. Make haste, pray."

"Immediately, sir, as soon as I have done up the parcel for this little boy."

"What signifies the parcel for this little boy? He can wait, and I cannot—wind and tide wait for no man. Here, my good lad, take your parcel, and sheer off," said the impatient man; and, as he spoke, he took up the parcel of seeds from the counter, as the shopman stooped to look for a sheet of thick brown paper and packthread to tie it up.

The parcel was but loosely folded up, and as the impatient man lifted it, the weight of the peas which were withinside of it burst the paper, and all the seeds fell out upon the floor, whilst Maurice in vain held his hands to catch them. The peas rolled to all parts of the shop; the impatient man swore at them, but Maurice, without being out of humor, set about collecting them as fast as possible.

Whilst the boy was busied in this manner, the man got what seeds he wanted; and as he was talking about them, a sailor came into the shop, and said, "Captain, the wind has changed within these five minutes, and it looks as if we should have ugly weather."

"Well, I'm glad of it," replied the rough faced man, who was the captain of a ship. "I am glad to have a day longer to stay ashore, and I've business enough on my hands." The captain pushed forward towards the shop door. Maurice, who was kneeling on the floor, picking up his seeds, saw that the captain's foot was entangled in some packthread which hung down from the shelf on which the china jar stood. Maurice saw that, if the captain took one more step forward, he must pull the string, so that it would throw down the jar, round the bottom of which the packthread was entangled. He immediately caught hold of the captain's leg, and stopped him. "Stay! Stand still, sir!" said he, "or you will break your china jar."

The man stood still, looked, and saw how the packthread had caught in his shoe buckle, and how it was near dragging down his beautiful china jar. "I am really very much obliged to you, my little fellow," said he. "You have saved my jar, which I would not have broken for ten guineas, for it is for my wife, and I've brought it safe from abroad many a league. It would have been a pity if I had broken it just when it was safe landed. I am really much obliged to you, my little fellow, this was returning good for evil. I am sorry I threw down your seeds, as you are such a good natured, forgiving boy. Be so kind," continued he, turning to the shopman, "as to reach down that china jar for me."

The shopman lifted down the jar very carefully, and the captain took off the cover, and pulled out some tulip roots. "You seem, by the quantity of seeds you have got, to belong to a gardener. Are you fond of gardening?" said he to Maurice.

"Yes, sir," replied Maurice, "very fond of it; for my father is a gardener, and he lets me help him at his work, and he has given me a little garden of my own."

"Then here are a couple of tulip-roots for you; and if you take care of them, I'll promise you that you will have the finest tulips in England in your little garden. These tulips were given to me by a Dutch merchant, who told me that they were some of the rarest and finest in Holland. They will prosper with you, I'm sure, wind and weather permitting."

Maurice thanked the gentleman, and returned home, eager to show his precious tulip-roots to his father, and to a companion of his, the son of a nurseryman, who lived near him. Arthur was the name of the nurseryman's son.

The first thing Maurice did, after showing his tulip-roots to his father, was to run to Arthur's garden in search of him. Their gardens were separated only by a low wall of loose stones: "Arthur! Arthur! where are you? Are you in your garden! I want you." But Arthur made no answer, and did not, as usual, come running to meet his friend. "I know where you are," continued Maurice, "and I'm coming to you as fast as the raspberry-bushes will let me. I have good news for you—something you'll be delighted to see, Arthur!—Ha!—but here is something that I am not delighted to see, I am sure," said poor Maurice, who, when he had got through the raspberry-bushes, and had come in sight of his own garden, beheld his bell-glass—his beloved bell-glass, under which his cucumbers were grown so finely—his only bell-glass, broken to pieces!

"I am sorry for it," said Arthur, who stood leaning upon his spade in his own garden; "I am afraid you will be very angry with me."

"Why, was it you, Arthur, broke my bell-glass! Oh, how could you do so?"

"I was throwing weeds and rubbish over the wall, and by accident a great lump of couch-grass, with stones hanging to the roots, fell upon your bell-glass, and broke it, as you see."

Maurice lifted up the lump of couch-grass, which had fallen through the broken glass upon his cucumbers, and he looked at his cucumbers for a moment in silence—"Oh, my poor cucumbers! you must all die now. I shall see all your yellow flowers withered tomorrow; but it is done, and it cannot be helped; so, Arthur, let us say no more about it."

"You are very good; I thought you would have been angry. I am sure I should have been exceedingly angry if you had broken the glass, if it had been mine."

"Oh, forgive and forget, as my father always says; that's the best way. Look what I have got for you." Then he told Arthur the story of the captain of the ship, and the china jar; the seeds having been thrown down, and of the fine tulip-roots which had been given to him; and Maurice concluded by offering one of the precious roots to Arthur, who thanked him with great joy, and repeatedly said, "How good you were not to be angry with me for breaking your bell-glass! I am much more sorry for it than if you had been in a passion with me!"

Arthur now went to plant his tulip-root: and Maurice looked at the beds which his companion had been digging, and at all the things which were coming up in his garden.

"I don't know how it is," said Arthur, "but you always seem as glad to see the things in my garden coming up, and doing well, as if they were all your own. I am much happier since my father came to live here, and since you and I have been allowed to work and to play together, than I ever was before; for you must know, before we came to live here, I had a cousin in the house with me, who used to plague me. He was not nearly so good-natured as you are. He never took pleasure in looking at my garden, or at anything that I did that was well done; and he never gave me a share of anything that he had; and so I did not like him; how could I? But, I believe that hating people makes us unhappy; for I know I never was happy when I was quarrelling with him; and I am always happy with you, Maurice. You know we never quarrel."

It would be well for all the world if they could be convinced, like Arthur, that to live in friendship is better than to quarrel. It would be well for all the world if they followed Maurice's maxim of "Forgive and Forget," when they receive, or when they imagine that they receive, an injury.

Arthur's father, Mr. Oakly, the nurseryman, was apt to take offence at trifles; and when he thought that any of his neighbors disobliged him, he was too proud to ask them to explain their conduct; therefore he was often mistaken in his judgment of them. He thought that it showed SPIRIT, to remember and to resent an injury; and, therefore, though he was not an ill-natured man, he was sometimes led, by this mistaken idea of SPIRIT, to do ill-natured things: "A warm friend and a bitter enemy," was one of his maxims, and he had many more enemies than friends. He was not very rich, but he was proud; and his favorite proverb was, "Better live in spite than in pity."

When first he settled near Mr. Grant, the gardener, he felt inclined to dislike him, because he was told that Mr. Grant was a Scotchman, and he had a prejudice against Scotchmen; all of whom he believed to be cunning and avaricious, because he had once been over-reached by a Scotch peddler. Grant's friendly manners in some degree conquered this prepossession but still he secretly suspected that THIS CIVILITY, as he said, "was all show, and that he was not, nor could not, being a Scotchman, be such a hearty friend as a true-born Englishman."

Grant had some remarkably fine raspberries. The fruit was so large, as to be quite a curiosity. When it was in season, many strangers came from the neighboring town, which was a sea-bathing place, to look at these raspberries, which obtained the name of Brobdingnag raspberries.

"How came you, pray, neighbor Grant, if a man may ask, by these wonderful fine raspberries?" said Mr. Oakly, one evening, to the gardener.

"That's a secret," replied Grant, with an arch smile.

"Oh, in case it's a secret, I've no more to say; for I never meddle with any man's secrets that he does not choose to trust me with. But I wish, neighbor Grant, you would put down that book. You are always poring over some book or another when a man comes to see you, which is not, according to my notions (being a plain, UNLARNED Englishman bred and born), so civil and neighborly as might be."

Mr. Grant hastily shut his book, but remarked, with a shrewd glance at his son, that it was in that book he found his Brobdingnag raspberries.

"You are pleased to be pleasant upon them that have not the luck to be as book-LARNED as yourself, Mr. Grant; but I take it, being only a plain spoken Englishman, as I observed afore, that one is to the full as like to find a raspberry in one's garden as in one's book, Mr. Grant."

Grant, observing that his neighbor spoke rather in a surly tone, did not contradict him; being well versed in the Bible, he knew that "A soft word turneth away wrath," and he answered, in a good humoured voice, "I hear, neighbor Oakly, you are likely to make a great deal of money of your nursery this year. Here's to the health of you and yours, not forgetting the seedling larches, which I see are coming on finely."

"Thank ye, neighbor, kindly; the larches are coming on tolerably well, that's certain; and here's to your good health, Mr. Grant—you and yours, not forgetting your, what d'ye call 'em raspberries"—(drinks)—and, after a pause, resumes, "I'm not apt to be a beggar, neighbor, but if you could give me—"

Here Mr. Oakly was interrupted by the entrance of some strangers, and he did finish making his request—Mr. Oakly was not, as he said of himself, apt to ask favours, and nothing but Grant's cordiality could have conquered his prejudices, so far as to tempt him to ask a favour from a Scotchman. He was going to have asked for some of the Brobdingnag raspberry-plants. The next day the thought of the raspberry-plants recurred to his memory, but being a bashful man, he did not like to go himself on purpose to make his request, and he desired his wife, who was just setting out to market, to call at Grant's gate, and, if he was at work in his garden, to ask him for a few plants of his raspberries.

The answer which Oakly's wife brought to him was that Mr. Grant had not a raspberry-plant in the world to give him, and that if he had ever so many, he would not give one away, except to his own son.

Oakly flew into a passion when he received such a message, declared it was just such a mean, shabby trick as might have been expected from a Scotchman—called himself a booby, a dupe, and a blockhead, for ever having trusted to the civil speeches of a Scotchman—swore that he would die in the parish workhouse before he would ever ask another favour, be it ever so small, from a Scotchman; related to his wife, for the hundredth time, the way in which he had been taken in by the Scotch peddler ten years ago, and concluded by forswearing all further intercourse with Mr. Grant, and all belonging to him.

"Son Arthur," said he, addressing himself to the boy, who just then came in from work—"Son Arthur, do you hear me? let me never again see you with Grant's son."

"With Maurice, father?"

"With Maurice Grant, I say; I forbid you from this day and hour forward to have anything to do with him."

"Oh, why, dear father?"

"Ask no questions but do as I bid you."

Arthur burst out a crying, and only said, "Yes, father, I'll do as you bid me, to be sure."

"Why now, what does the boy cry for? Is there no other boy, simpleton, think you, to play with, but this Scotchman's son! I'll find out another play-fellow for ye, child, if that be all."

"That's not all, father," said Arthur, trying to stop himself from sobbing; "but the thing is, I shall never have such another play-fellow,- -I shall never have such another friend as Maurice Grant."

"Like father like son—you may think yourself well off to have done with him."

"Done with him! Oh, father, and shall I never go again to work in his garden, and may not he come to mine?"

"No," replied Oakly, sturdily; "his father has used me uncivil, and no man shall use me uncivil twice. I say no. Wife, sweep up this hearth. Boy, don't take on like a fool; but eat thy bacon and greens, and let's hear no more of Maurice Grant."

Arthur promised to obey his father. He only begged that he might once more speak to Maurice, and tell him that it was by his father's orders he acted. This request was granted; but when Arthur further begged to know what reason he might give for this separation, his father refused to tell his reasons. The two friends took leave of one another very sorrowfully.

Mr. Grant, when he heard of all this, endeavoured to discover what could have offended his neighbor; but all explanation was prevented by the obstinate silence of Oakly.

Now, the message which Grant really sent about the Brobdingnag raspberries was somewhat different from that which Mr. Oakly received. The message was, that the raspberries were not Mr. Grant's; that therefore he had no right to give them away; that they belonged to his son Maurice, and that this was not the right time of year for planting them. This message had been unluckily misunderstood. Grant gave his answer to his wife; she to a Welsh servant-girl, who did not perfectly comprehend her mistress' broad Scotch; and she in her turn could not make herself intelligible to Mrs. Oakly, who hated the Welsh accent, and whose attention, when the servant-girl delivered the message, was principally engrossed by the management of her own horse. The horse, on which Mrs. Oakly rode this day being ill-broken, would not stand still quietly at the gate, and she was extremely impatient to receive her answer, and to ride on to market.

Oakly, when he had once resolved to dislike his neighbour Grant, could not long remain without finding out fresh causes of complaint. There was in Grant's garden a plum-tree, which was planted close to the loose stone wall that divided the garden from the nursery. The soil in which the plum tree was planted happened not to be quite so good as that which was on the opposite side of the wall, and the plum-tree had forced its way through the wall, and gradually had taken possession of the ground which it liked best.

Oakly thought the plum-tree, as it belonged to Mr. Grant, had no right to make its appearance on his ground: an attorney told him that he might oblige Grant to cut it down; but Mr. Grant refused to cut down his plum- tree at the attorney's desire, and the attorney persuaded Oakly to go to law about the business, and the lawsuit went on for some months.

The attorney, at the end of this time, came to Oakly with a demand for money to carry on his suit, assuring him that, in a short time, it would be determined in his favour. Oakly paid his attorney ten golden guineas, remarked that it was a great sum for him to pay, and that nothing but the love of justice could make him persevere in this lawsuit about a bit of ground, "which, after all," said he, "is not worth twopence. The plum- tree does me little or no damage, but I don't like to be imposed upon by a Scotchman."

The attorney saw and took advantage of Oakly's prejudice against the natives of Scotland; and he persuaded him, that to show the SPIRIT of a true-born Englishman it was necessary, whatever it might cost him, to persist in this law suit.

It was soon after this conversation with the attorney that Mr. Oakly walked, with resolute steps, towards the plum-tree, saying to himself, "If it cost me a hundred pounds I will not let this cunning Scotchman get the better of me."

Arthur interrupted his father's reverie, by pointing to a book and some young plants which lay upon the wall. "I fancy, father," said he, "those things are for you, for there is a little note directed to you, in Maurice's handwriting. Shall I bring it to you?"

"Yes, let me read it, child, since I must." It contained these words:

"DEAR MR. OAKLY,—I don't know why you have quarrelled with us; I am very sorry for it. But though you are angry with me, I am not angry with you. I hope you will not refuse some of my Brobdingnag raspberry-plants, which you asked for a great while ago, when we were all good friends. It was not the right time of the year to plant them, which was the reason they were not sent to you; but it is just the right time to plant them now; and I send you the book, in which you will find the reason why we always put seaweed ashes about their roots; and I have got some seaweed ashes for you. You will find the ashes in the flower-pot upon the wall. I have never spoken to Arthur, nor he to me, since you bid us not. So, wishing your Brobdingnag raspberries may turn out as well as ours, and longing to be all friends again, I am, with love to dear Arthur and self,

"Your affectionate neighbor's son,
"MAURICE GRANT.

"P.S.—It is now about four months since the quarrel began, and that is a very long while."

A great part of the effect of this letter was lost upon Oakly, because he was not very expert in reading writing, and it cost him much trouble to spell it and put it together. However, he seemed affected by it, and said, "I believe this Maurice loves you well enough, Arthur, and he seems a good sort of boy; but as to the raspberries, I believe all that he says about them is but an excuse; and, at anyrate, as I could not get 'em when I asked for them, I'll not have 'em now. Do you hear me, I say, Arthur? What are you reading there?"

Arthur was reading the page that was doubled down in the book, which Maurice had left along with the raspberry-plants upon the wall. Arthur read aloud as follows:—

(Monthly Magazine, Dec. '98, p. 421.)

"There is a sort of strawberry cultivated at Jersey, which is almost covered with seaweed in the winter, in like manner as many plants in England are with litter from the stable. These strawberries are usually of the largeness of a middle-sized apricot, and the flavour is particularly grateful. In Jersey and Guernsey, situate scarcely one degree farther south than Cornwall, all kinds of fruit, pulse, and vegetables are produced in their seasons a fortnight or three weeks sooner than in England, even on the southern shores; and snow will scarcely remain twenty-four hours on the earth. Although this may be attributed to these islands being surrounded with a salt, and consequently a moist atmosphere, yet the ashes (seaweed ashes) made use of as manure, may also have their portion of influence."*

*It is necessary to observe that this experiment has never been actually tried upon raspberry-plants.

"And here," continued Arthur, "is something written with a pencil, on a slip of paper, and it is Maurice's writing. I will read it to you. "'When I read in this book what is said about the strawberries growing as large as apricots, after they had been covered over with seaweed, I thought that perhaps seaweed ashes might be good for my father's raspberries; and I asked him if he would give me leave to try them. He gave me leave, and I went directly and gathered together some seaweed that had been cast on shore; and I dried it, and burned it, and then I manured the raspberries with it, and the year afterwards the raspberries grew to the size that you have seen. Now, the reason I tell you this is, first, that you may know how to manage your raspberries, and next, because I remember you looked very grave, as if you were not pleased with my father, Mr. Grant, when he told you that the way by which he came by his Brobdingnag raspberries was a secret. Perhaps this was the thing that has made you so angry with us all; for you never have come to see father since that evening. Now I have told you all I know; and so I hope you will not be angry with us any longer.'"

Mr. Oakly was much pleased by this openness, and said, "Why now, Arthur, this is something like, this is telling one the thing one wants to know, without fine speeches. This is like an Englishman more than a Scotchman. Pray, Arthur, do you know whether your friend Maurice was born in England or in Scotland?"

"No, indeed, sir, I don't know—I never asked—I did not think it signified. All I know is, that wherever he was born, he is VERY good. Look, papa, my tulip is blowing."

"Upon my word," said his father, "this will be a beautiful tulip!"

"It was given to me by Maurice."

"And did you give him nothing for it?" was the father's inquiry.

"Nothing in the world; and he gave it to me just at the time when he had good cause to be angry with me, just when I had broken his bell-glass."

"I have a great mind to let you play together again," said Arthur's father.

"Oh, if you would," cried Arthur, clapping his hands, "how happy we should be! Do you know, father, I have often sat for an hour at a time up in that crab-tree, looking at Maurice at work in his garden, and wishing that I was at work with him."

Here Arthur was interrupted by the attorney, who came to ask Mr. Oakly some question about the lawsuit concerning the plum-tree. Oakly showed him Maurice's letter; and to Arthur's extreme astonishment, the attorney had no sooner read it, than he exclaimed, "What an artful little gentleman this is! I never, in the course of all my practice, met with anything better. Why, this is the most cunning letter I ever read."

"Where's the cunning?" said Oakly, and he put on his spectacles.

"My good sir, don't you see, that all this stuff about Brobdingnag raspberries is to ward off your suit about the plum-tree? They know— that is, Mr. Grant, who is sharp enough, knows—that he will be worsted in that suit; that he must, in short, pay you a good round sum for damages, if it goes on—"

"Damages!" said Oakly, staring round him at the plum-tree; "but I don't know what you mean. I mean nothing but what's honest. I don't mean to ask for any good round sum; for the plum-tree has done me no great harm by coming into my garden; but only I don't choose it should come there without my leave."

"Well, well," said the attorney, "I understand all that; but what I want to make you, Mr. Oakly, understand, is, that this Grant and his son only want to make up matters with you, and prevent the thing's coming to a fair trial, by sending on, in this underhand sort of way, a bribe of a few raspberries."

"A bribe!" exclaimed Oakly, "I never took a bribe, and I never will"; and, with sudden indignation, he pulled the raspberry plants from the ground in which Arthur was planting them; and he threw them over the wall into Grant's garden.

Maurice had put his tulip, which was beginning to blow, in a flower-pot, on the top of the wall, in hopes that his friend Arthur would see it from day to day. Alas! He knew not in what a dangerous situation he had placed it. One of his own Brobdingnag raspberry-plants, swung by the angry arm of Oakly, struck off the head of his precious tulip! Arthur, who was full of the thought of convincing his father that the attorney was mistaken in his judgment of poor Maurice, did not observe the fall of the tulip.

The next day, when Maurice saw his raspberry-plants scattered upon the ground, and his favorite tulip broken, he was in much astonishment, and, for some moments, angry; but anger, with him, never lasted long. He was convinced that all this must be owing to some accident or mistake. He could not believe that anyone could be so malicious as to injure him on purpose—"And even if they did all this on purpose to vex me," said he to himself, "the best thing I can do, is, not to let it vex me. Forgive and forget." This temper of mind Maurice was more happy in enjoying than he could have been made, without it, by the possession of all the tulips in Holland.

Tulips were, at this time, things of great consequence in the estimation of the country several miles round where Maurice and Arthur lived. There was a florist's feast to be held at the neighboring town, at which a prize of a handsome set of gardening-tools was to be given to the person who could produce the finest flower of its kind. A tulip was the flower which was thought the finest the preceding year, and consequently numbers of people afterwards endeavoured to procure tulip-roots, in hopes of obtaining the prize this year. Arthur's tulip was beautiful. As he examined it from day to day, and every day thought it improving, he longed to thank his friend Maurice for it; and he often mounted into his crab-tree, to look into Maurice's garden, in hopes of seeing his tulip also in full bloom and beauty. He never could see it.

The day of the florist's feast arrived, and Oakly went with his son and the fine tulip to the place of meeting. It was on a spacious bowling- green. All the flowers of various sorts were ranged upon a terrace at the upper end of the bowling-green; and, amongst all this gay variety, the tulip which Maurice had given to Arthur appeared conspicuously beautiful. To the owner of this tulip the prize was adjudged; and, as the handsome garden-tools were delivered to Arthur, he heard a well known voice wish him joy. He turned, looked about him, and saw his friend Maurice.

"But, Maurice, where is your own tulip?" said Mr. Oakly; "I thought, Arthur, you told me that he kept one for himself."

"So I did," said Maurice; "but somebody (I suppose by accident) broke it."

"Somebody! who?" cried Arthur and Mr. Oakly at once.

"Somebody who threw the raspberry-plants back again over the wall," replied Maurice.

"That was me—that somebody was me," said Oakly. "I scorn to deny it; but I did not intend to break your tulip, Maurice."

"Dear Maurice," said Arthur—"you know I may call him dear Maurice—now you are by, papa; here are all the garden-tools; take them, and welcome."

"Not one of them," said Maurice, drawing back.

"Offer them to the father—offer them to Mr. Grant," whispered Oakly; "he'll take them, I'll answer for it."

Mr. Oakly was mistaken: the father would not accept of the tools. Mr. Oakly stood surprised—"Certainly," said he to himself, "this cannot be such a miser as I took him for"; and he walked immediately up to Grant, and bluntly said to him, "Mr. Grant, your son has behaved very handsomely to my son; and you seem to be glad of it."

"To be sure I am," said Grant

"Which," continued Oakly, "gives me a better opinion of you than ever I had before—I mean, than ever I had since the day you sent me the shabby answer about those foolish, what d'ye call em, cursed raspberries."

"What shabby answer?" said Grant, with surprise; and Oakly repeated exactly the message which he received; and Grant declared that he never sent any such message. He repeated exactly the answer which he really sent, and Oakly immediately stretched out his hand to him, saying "I believe you: no more need be said. I'm only sorry I did not ask you about this four months ago; and so I should have done if you had not been a Scotchman. Till now, I never rightly liked a Scotchman. We may thank this good little fellow," continued he, turning to Maurice, "for our coming at last to a right understanding. There was no holding out against his good nature. I'm sure, from the bottom of my heart, I'm sorry I broke his tulip. Shake hands, boys; I'm glad to see you, Arthur, look so happy again, and hope Mr. Grant will forgive—"

"Oh, forgive and forget," said Grant and his son at the same moment. And from this time forward the two families lived in friendship with each other.

Oakly laughed at his own folly, in having been persuaded to go to law about the plum-tree; and he, in process of time, so completely conquered his early prejudice against Scotchmen, that he and Grant became partners in business. Mr. Grant's book-LARNING and knowledge of arithmetic he found highly useful to him; and he, on his side, possessed a great many active, good qualities, which became serviceable to his partner.

The two boys rejoiced in this family union; and Arthur often declared that they owed all their happiness to Maurice's favorite maxim, "Forgive and Forget."

The Penance
Saki

Octavian Ruttle was one of those lively cheerful individuals on whom amiability had set its unmistakable stamp, and, like most of his kind, his soul's peace depended in large measure on the unstinted approval of his fellows. In hunting to death a small tabby cat he had done a thing of which he scarcely approved himself, and he was glad when the gardener had hidden the body in its hastily dug grave under a lone oak-tree in the meadow, the same tree that the hunted quarry had climbed as a last effort towards safety. It had been a distasteful and seemingly ruthless deed, but circumstances had demanded the doing of it. Octavian kept chickens; at least he kept some of them; others vanished from his keeping, leaving only a few bloodstained feathers to mark the manner of their going. The tabby cat from the large grey house that stood with its back to the meadow had been detected in many furtive visits to the hen-coups, and after due negotiation with those in authority at the grey house a sentence of death had been agreed on. "The children will mind, but they need not know," had been the last word on the matter.

The children in question were a standing puzzle to Octavian; in the course of a few months he considered that he should have known their names, ages, the dates of their birthdays, and have been introduced to their favorite toys. They remained however, as non-committal as the long blank wall that shut them off from the meadow, a wall over which their three heads sometimes appeared at odd moments. They had parents in India—that much Octavian had learned in the neighborhood; the children, beyond grouping themselves garment-wise into sexes, a girl and two boys, carried their life story no further on his behoof. And now it seemed he was engaged in something which touched them closely, but must be hidden from their knowledge.

The poor helpless chickens had gone one by one to their doom, so it was meet that their destroyer should come to a violent end; yet Octavian felt some qualms when his share of the violence was ended. The little cat, headed off from its wonted tracks of safety, had raced unfriended from shelter to shelter, and its end had been rather piteous. Octavian walked through the long grass of the meadow with a step less jaunty than usual. And as he passed beneath the shadow of the high blank wall he glanced up and became aware that his hunting had had undesired witnesses. Three white set faces were looking down at him, and if ever an artist wanted a threefold study of cold human hate, impotent yet unyielding, raging yet masked in stillness, he would have found it in the triple gaze that met Octavian's eye.

"I'm sorry, but it had to be done," said Octavian, with genuine apology in his voice.

"Beast!"

The answer came from three throats with startling intensity.

Octavian felt that the blank wall would not be more impervious to his explanations than the bunch of human hostility that peered over its coping; he wisely decided to withhold his peace overtures till a more hopeful occasion.

Two days later he ransacked the best sweet shop in the neighboring market town for a box of chocolates that by its size and contents should fitly atone for the dismal deed done under the oak tree in the meadow. The two first specimens that were shown him he hastily rejected; one had a group of chickens pictured on its lid, the other bore the portrait of a tabby kitten. A third sample was more simply bedecked with a spray of painted poppies, and Octavian hailed the flowers of forgetfulness as a happy omen. He felt distinctly more at ease with his surroundings when the imposing package had been sent across to the grey house, and a message returned to say that it had been duly given to the children. The next morning he sauntered with purposeful steps past the long blank wall on his way to the chicken-run and piggery that stood at the bottom of the meadow. The three children were perched at their accustomed look-out, and their range of sight did not seem to concern itself with Octavian's presence. As he became depressingly aware of the aloofness of their gaze he also noted a strange variegation in the herbage at his feet; the greensward for a considerable space around was strewn and speckled with a chocolate-colored hail, enlivened here and there with gay tinsel-like wrappings or the glistening mauve of crystallized violets. It was as though the fairy paradise of a greedy-minded child had taken shape and substance in the vegetation of the meadow. Octavian's blood-money had been flung back at him in scorn.

To increase his discomfiture the march of events tended to shift the blame of ravaged chicken-coops from the supposed culprit who had already paid full forfeit; the young chicks were still carried off, and it seemed highly probable that the cat had only haunted the chicken-run to prey on the rats which harboured there. Through the flowing channels of servant talk the children learned of this belated revision of verdict, and Octavian one day picked up a sheet of copy-book paper on which was painstakingly written: "Beast. Rats eated your chickens." More ardently than ever did he wish for an opportunity for sloughing off the disgrace that enwrapped him, and earning some happier nickname from his three unsparing judges.

And one day a chance inspiration came to him. Olivia, his two-year- old daughter, was accustomed to spend the hour from high noon till one o'clock with her father while the nursemaid gobbled and digested her dinner and novelette. About the same time the blank wall was usually enlivened by the presence of its three small wardens. Octavian, with seeming carelessness of purpose, brought Olivia well within hail of the watchers and noted with hidden delight the growing interest that dawned in that hitherto sternly hostile quarter. His little Olivia, with her sleepy placid ways, was going to succeed where he, with his anxious well-meant overtures, had so signally failed. He brought her a large yellow dahlia, which she grasped tightly in one hand and regarded with a stare of benevolent boredom, such as one might bestow on amateur classical dancing performed in aid of a deserving charity. Then he turned shyly to the group perched on the wall and asked with affected carelessness, "Do you like flowers?" Three solemn nods rewarded his venture.

"Which sorts do you like best?" he asked, this time with a distinct betrayal of eagerness in his voice.

"Those with all the couloirs, over there." Three chubby arms pointed to a distant tangle of sweetpea. Child-like, they had asked for what lay farthest from hand, but Octavian trotted off gleefully to obey their welcome behest. He pulled and plucked with unsparing hand, and brought every variety of tint that he could see into his bunch that was rapidly becoming a bundle. Then he turned to retrace his steps, and found the blank wall blanker and more deserted than ever, while the foreground was void of all trace of Olivia. Far down the meadow three children were pushing a go-cart at the utmost speed they could muster in the direction of the piggeries; it was Olivia's go-cart and Olivia sat in it, somewhat bumped and shaken by the pace at which she was being driven, but apparently retaining her wonted composure of mind. Octavian stared for a moment at the rapidly moving group, and then started in hot pursuit, shedding as he ran sprays of blossom from the mass of sweet-pea that he still clutched in his hands. Fast as he ran the children had reached the piggery before he could overtake them, and he arrived just in time to see Olivia, wondering but unprotesting, hauled and pushed up to the roof of the nearest sty. They were old buildings in some need of repair, and the rickety roof would certainly not have borne Octavian's weight if he had attempted to follow his daughter and her captors on their new vantage ground.

"What are you going to do with her?" he panted. There was no mistaking the grim trend of mischief in those flushed by sternly composed young faces.

"Hang her in chains over a slow fire," said one of the boys. Evidently they had been reading English history.

"Frow her down the pigs will d'vour her, every bit 'cept the palms of her hands," said the other boy. It was also evident that they had studied Biblical history.

The last proposal was the one which most alarmed Octavian, since it might be carried into effect at a moment's notice; there had been cases, he remembered, of pigs eating babies.

"You surely wouldn't treat my poor little Olivia in that way?" he pleaded.

"You killed our little cat," came in stern reminder from three throats.

"I'm sorry I did," said Octavian, and if there is a standard measurement in truths Octavian's statement was assuredly a large nine.

"We shall be very sorry when we've killed Olivia," said the girl, "but we can't be sorry till we've done it."

The inexorable child-logic rose like an unyielding rampart before Octavian's scared pleadings. Before he could think of any fresh line of appeal his energies were called out in another direction. Olivia had slid off the roof and fallen with a soft, unctuous splash into a morass of muck and decaying straw. Octavian scrambled hastily over the pigsty wall to her rescue, and at once found himself in a quagmire that engulfed his feet. Olivia, after the first shock of surprise at her sudden drop through the air, had been mildly pleased at finding herself in close and unstinted contact with the sticky element that oozed around her, but as she began to sink gently into the bed of slime a feeling dawned on her that she was not after all very happy, and she began to cry in the tentative fashion of the normally good child. Octavian, battling with the quagmire, which seemed to have learned the rare art of giving way at all points without yielding an inch, saw his daughter slowly disappearing in the engulfing slush, her smeared face further distorted with the contortions of whimpering wonder, while from their perch on the pigsty roof the three children looked down with the cold unpitying detachment of the Parcae Sisters.

"I can't reach her in time," gasped Octavian, "she'll be choked in the muck. Won't you help her?"

"No one helped our cat," came the inevitable reminder.

"I'll do anything to show you how sorry I am about that," cried Octavian, with a further desperate flounder, which carried him scarcely two inches forward.

"Will you stand in a white sheet by the grave?"

"Yes," screamed Octavian.

"Holding a candle?"

"An' saying 'I'm a miserable Beast'?"

Octavian agreed to both suggestions.

"For a long, long time?"

"For half an hour," said Octavian. There was an anxious ring in his voice as he named the time-limit; was there not the precedent of a German king who did open-air penance for several days and nights at Christmas-time clad only in his shirt? Fortunately the children did not appear to have read German history, and half an hour seemed long and goodly in their eyes.

"All right," came with threefold solemnity from the roof, and a moment later a short ladder had been laboriously pushed across to Octavian, who lost no time in propping it against the low pigsty wall. Scrambling gingerly along its rungs he was able to lean across the morass that separated him from his slowly foundering offspring and extract her like an unwilling cork from it's slushy embrace. A few minutes later he was listening to the shrill and repeated assurances of the nursemaid that her previous experience of filthy spectacles had been on a notably smaller scale.

That same evening when twilight was deepening into darkness Octavian took up his position as penitent under the lone oak-tree, having first carefully undressed the part. Clad in a zephyr shirt, which on this occasion thoroughly merited its name, he held in one hand a lighted candle and in the other a watch, into which the soul of a dead plumber seemed to have passed. A box of matches lay at his feet and was resorted to on the fairly frequent occasions when the candle succumbed to the night breezes. The house loomed inscrutable in the middle distance, but as Octavian conscientiously repeated the formula of his penance he felt certain that three pairs of solemn eyes were watching his moth-shared vigil.

And the next morning his eyes were gladdened by a sheet of copy-book paper lying beside the blank wall, on which was written the message "Un-Beast."

The Scapegoat
Erckmann-Chatrain

Doesn't everybody at Tubingen know the lamentable history of the quarrel between the Seigneur Kaspar Evig and the young Jew Elias Hirsch? Kaspar Evig was courting Mademoiselle Eva Salomon, the daughter of the old picture-dealer in the Rue de Jericho. One day he found my friend Elias In the broker's shop, and, on what pretext I know not, he boxed his ears soundly three or four times.

Elias Hirsch, who had begun his medical studies only about five months before, was called upon by a council of the students to challenge the Seigneur Kaspar to fight, a step which he took with the greatest repugnance, for it was quite to be expected that a seigneur should be a perfect swordsman.

For all that Elias put himself well on the defensive, and, watching his opportunity, inserted his finely-pointed sword so neatly between the ribs of the above-mentioned seigneur as considerably to affect his breathing, the consequence of which was that he was dead in ten minutes.

The Rector Diemer, being informed of this transaction by credible witnesses, listened coldly and remarked briefly—

"I understand you, gentlemen. He is dead, is he? Very well, then; bury him."

Elias was carried about in triumph, like another Mattathias; but, far from accepting the proffered glory, he drooped under a profound melancholy.

He lost flesh, he sighed, he groaned; his nose, already a pretty long one, seemed to gain in prominence what it lost in solidity, and often in the evening, as he was passing down the Rue des Trois Fontaines, he might be heard murmuring—

"Kaspar Evig, forgive me; I did not mean to take your life. Oh, unhappy Eva! what have you done? By your thoughtless flirting you made two brave men quarrel, and now the shade of the Seigneur Kaspar pursues me everywhere, even in my sleep. Oh, Eva! wretched Eva! why did you behave so?"

So poor Elias moaned in his misery; and he was the more to be pitied because the sons of Israel are not bloodthirsty, and they know it is written in their law, "Whosoever sheddeth man's blood by man shall his blood be shed."

Now one fine day in July, while I was drinking at the Faucon, in walks Elias Hirsch, just as miserable as ever, with hollow cheeks, hair hanging in disorder about his face, and downcast eyes. He laid his hand upon my shoulder, and said —

"Dear Christian, will you do me a pleasure?"

"Of course I will, Elias; only say what."

"Let us go for a walk together in the country; I want to consult you about my grief. You know many things human and divine; perhaps you can point me out a remedy for so much trouble of mind. I can trust in you, Christian, entirely."

As I had already had five or six pints of beer and two or three glasses of schnapps, there was nothing more to detain me, and I consented to go with him. Besides, I felt flattered with his confidence in my wisdom.

So we came through the town, and in twenty minutes we were walking along the little violet-bordered path which winds up to the ancient ruins of Triefels.

Then, feeling alone, passing between hedges balmy with honeysuckle and musical with the song of birds, and slowly climbing up to the lofty pines which crown the Rothalp, Elias breathed more freely; he raised his eyes and cried —

"In all your theological studies, Christian, have you met with a way in which great crimes may be expiated? I know that you have studied this question a good deal. Tell me. Whatever you recommend to put to flight the avenging shade of Kaspar Evig, I will do it."

Hirsch's question made me thoughtful. We walked together, with heads bowed down in thought, in deep silence. He watched me, I could see, out of the corner of his eye, whilst I was endeavouring to collect my thoughts upon this delicate question, but at last I made answer —

"Now, if we were inhabitants of India, Elias, I should tell you to go and bathe in the Ganges, for the waters of that river wash away the pollutions of both body and soul—so, at least, the people of that country think; and they kill, and burn, and steal without fear under the protection of that marvellous river. It is a great comfort for scoundrels! It is a matter of great regret that we have no such river! If we were living in the days of Jason, I should prescribe to you the salt-cakes of Queen Circe, which had the remarkable property of whitening blackened consciences and saving people the trouble of repenting. Finally, if you had the happiness to belong to our holy religion, I would order you to have masses said, and to give up your goods to the Church. But in your state as to locality, time, and belief, I know of only one way to relieve you."

"What is it?" cried Hirsch, already kindling with hope.

We had now reached the Rothalp, and were standing in a lonely place called the Holderloch. It is a deep dark gorge, encircled with gloomy firs; a level rock crowns the abyss, whence fall the dark waters of the Marg with roaring deep and loud.

Our path had brought us there. I sat down upon the mossy turf to breathe the moist air which rises from the gulf, and at that very moment I espied below me a magnificent goat, reaching up to crop the wild cresses that grow on the edge of the cliff.

Let it be remembered that the rocks of the Holderloch rise in the form of successive terraces, each terrace ten feet high perhaps, but not more than a foot wide, and upon these little narrow ledges grow a thousand sweet-smelling plants—thyme and honeysuckle, ivy and convolvulus, and the wild vine, perpetually bedewed with the spray from the falling torrent, and falling over in the loveliest clusters of bloom and foliage.

Now my goat—an animal with a broad brow, garnished with heavy knotted curling horns, with eyes gleaming like a pair of gold buttons, a reddish beard, exhibiting a proud, defiant bearing under those festoons of verdure, and a countenance as bold as that of a prowling satyr—my goat was making a progress upwards towards the very highest of these narrow ledges, and was enjoying a sweet repast of dainty herbs.

"Elias!" I cried, "I feel an inspiration! Just as I was thinking of a scapegoat, there is one! I see it! Look!—behold! There he is! Is not your course plain now? Lay your crime upon that goat, and then forget all about it."

Elias looked at me in stupid ignorance.

"I should like to do that, Christian, but how am I to lay my remorse upon that goat?"

"Nothing can be plainer. What did the Romans do to get rid of their criminals, polluted with every crime? Why they flung them off the Tarpeian rock, to be sure. Well, having laid your imprecations upon that goat, fling him down the Holderloch, and there will be an end of it all."

"But"—replied Elias.

"I know your objections beforehand," I replied. "You are going to say that you see no connection between Kaspar Evig, whose shade follows you, and that goat. But beware! be careful! Where was the connection between the waters of the Ganges, Circe's salt-cakes, and the scapegoat with the crimes to be expiated? None at all. Well, for all that, the expiation was held to be good; therefore lay your curses and imprecations upon that goat, and throw him over! I order you to do that! I feel it my duty to see this thing done. I can see a connection between that goat and your fault, but I cannot explain it because the light of my vast information dazzles me just now!"

Elias did not move a step. I even thought I detected a smile upon his countenance, which irritated me.

"How!" said I; "here am I pointing out to you an infallible method to get rid of the just punishment of your crime, and you doubt—you hesitate—you even smile!"

"No," said he, "but I am not accustomed to walk on the edges of precipices, and I am afraid I should fall into the Holderloch along with the goat."

"Ah, you are a coward! I can see it all. You have just once displayed a little courage to get exemption for the rest of your days. Well, sir, if you refuse to carry out my advice, I will do it myself."

And I rose.

"Christian! Christian!" cried my friend, "don't trust yourself too far. Your foot is not steady—just now."

"My foot not steady! Do you dare to insinuate that I am drunk because I have just had ten or a dozen glasses of beer and three glasses of schnapps this morning? Away with you! Back! back, son of Belial!"

And advancing a few feet above the goat, with my head raised and hands extended, I cried solemnly—

"Azazel! goat destined for misery and expiation, I lay upon

your hairy back the remorse of my friend Elias Hirsch, and I send you down to the spirits of darkness!"

Then, passing round the ledge on which we stood, I descended to the next below to catch the goat and throw him over.

A sacred rage and fury seemed to possess me. I took no notice of the abyss. I stepped along the edge of the precipice like a cat.

The goat, perceiving my approach, eyed me suspiciously, and stepped back a little way.

"Ha!" I cried, "you may flee from me, but you shall not escape from me, accursed beast! I have got you!"

"Oh, Christian, Christian!" Elias kept repeating in a heartrending voice, "do come back. You are risking your life!"

"Silence, unbeliever!" I cried. "You are unworthy of the great sacrifice which I am making for your happiness! But your friend Christian never draws back. Azazel must perish!"

A little farther on the ledge narrowed and ended in a point.

The goat, having a second time examined me with a curious eye, drew back a little farther, but not without some hesitation.

"Aha!" I exclaimed, "you are beginning to understand what is going to happen. Yes, let me get you into that corner, and your doom is sealed!"

And undoubtedly, when he had got to the spot where the ledge came to an end, Azazel seemed puzzled to know what to do next. I edged up to him closer and closer, full of a noble excitement, and laughing in anticipation at the coming descent and the splash in the torrent below.

I now beheld him at four paces from me, and I was grasping tightly a root of holly that was growing out of a rock to launch out a kick at the devoted beast.

"Look, Elias, see the accursed!" I cried.

When, all in a moment, I felt in my stomach a most awful blow, a butt which would have sent *me* into the Holderloch had I not kept hold of that blessed root of holly. The fact was that that miserable goat, seeing himself driven into a corner, had himself commenced the attack.

Oh, what was my astonishment! Before I knew where I was or what had happened, there was the brute standing up again on his hind-legs, and his horns digging into my stomach and my sides with a hollow sound.

What a position to be in! It is impossible to be more astounded than I was at that moment! It was the world upside down. It was a bad dream—a nightmare! The precipice with all its jagged peaks seemed to dance around me, and so did the trees and sky above. At the same moment I heard piercing cries from Elias of "Help! help!" while Azazel's horns were ploughing up my sides.

Then I lost all presence of mind. The goat with his long beard and his hard, sharp horns pounding me, now in my chest, now in my stomach, and then in my shaking limbs, produced a most diabolical effect upon me. My hold on the root slowly relaxed, and I let go. But happily something kept me from falling, something which I could not understand at first. But it was the shepherd Yeri, of the Holderloch, who from the next platform above had caught me by the coat-collar with his crook.

Thanks to his assistance, instead of falling down into the chasm I lay full length along the ledge, and that awful goat walked over my body to get away about his business.

"Come, take firm hold of my crook," cried the shepherd to Elias; "now I will go down for him. Don't let go!"

"You may rely upon me," answered Elias.

I heard all that as if it were a nightmare. I had almost lost consciousness.

When I opened my eyes I saw standing before me that gigantic shepherd, with his grey eyes sunk underneath his bushy eyebrows, his yellow beard, a sheepskin thrown over his shoulders, and I thought I had awoke in the age of Oedipus, which made me wonder a good deal.

"Well," cried the shepherd, in a harsh guttural, "this will teach you not to curse my goat any more!"

Then I saw Azazel rubbing himself comfortably against his master's colossal legs, and looking slyly, and I thought ironically, at me; and then I saw Elias standing behind me, and making the greatest efforts not to laugh.

My scattered senses were beginning to return. I sat myself down with pain and difficulty, for Azazel had bruised me all over, and I felt fearfully stiff and sore.

"Was it you who saved me?" I asked the shepherd.

"Yes, my boy, it was."

"Well, you are a good fellow, and I am much obliged to you. I withdraw the curse I laid upon your goat. Here, take this."

I handed him my purse with sixteen florins in it.

"Thank you, sir," said he, "and now you can begin again if you like on even ground. Down there it was not fair; the goat had all the advantage."

"Thank you very much! But I have had quite enough. Shake hands, old fellow; I'll never forget you. Let us go now."

My comrade and I, arm-in-arm, then descended the hill.

The shepherd, leaning on his crook, watched us till we disappeared. The goat had resumed his walk and his supper on the very edge of the crags. The sky was lovely, the air balmy with a thousand sweet mountain perfumes carried on it with the distant sounds of the shepherd's horn and the booming of the torrent.

We returned to Tubingen with our hearts full.

Since that time my friend Elias has found some comfort for slaying the Seigneur Kaspar, but in an original fashion.

Scarcely had he taken his doctor's degree when he married Mademoiselle Eva Salomon, with the hope of having a numerous family to make up for the loss of that individual who had met with an untimely end at his hand.

Four years ago I was at his wedding as best man, and already there are two fat babies making the pretty little house in Crispin street to rejoice.

This was a promising commencement!

Don't let me be misunderstood. I don't pretend to say that the method I prescribed for making expiation for taking away a life is better than that taught in our holy religion, which, according to the Catholic Church, consists in masses and in giving away your goods to the Church. But I do think it better than the Hindu practice, and I think the theory of the famous scapegoat is not to be compared with that which is taught us by pure religion.

Putting Things Right
Henry Seton Merriman

"Want Berlyng," he seemed to be saying, though it was difficult to catch the words, for we were almost within range, and the fight was a sharp one. It was the old story of India frontier warfare; too small a force, and a foe foolishly underrated.

The man they had just brought in—laying him hurriedly on a bed of pine-needles, in the shade of the conifers where I had halted my little train—poor Charles Noon of the Sikhs, was done for. His right hand was off at the wrist, and the shoulder was almost severed.

I bent my ear to his lips, and heard the words which sounded like "Want Berlyng."

We had a man called Berlyng in the force—a gunner—who was round at the other side of the fort that was to be taken before night, two miles away at least.

"Do you want Berlyng?" I asked slowly and distinctly.

Noon nodded, and his lips moved. I bent my head again till my ear almost touched his lips.

"How long have I?" he was asking.

"Not long, I'm afraid, old chap."

His lips closed with a queer distressed look. He was sorry to die.

"How long?" he asked again.

"About an hour."

But I knew it was less. I attended to others, thinking all the while of poor Noon. His home life was little known, but there was some story about an engagement at Poonah the previous warm weather. Noon was rich, and he cared for the girl; but she did not return the feeling. In fact, there was some one else. It appears that the girl's people were ambitious and poor, and that Noon had promised large settlements. At all events, the engagement was a known affair, and gossips whispered that Noon knew about the some one else, and would not give her up. He was, I know, thought badly of by some, especially by the elders, who had found out the value of money as regards happiness, or rather the complete absence of its value.

However, the end of it all lay on the sheet beneath the pines, and watched me with such persistence that I was at last forced to go to him.

"Have you sent for Berlyng?" he asked, with a breathlessness which I know too well.

Now I had not sent for Berlyng, and it requires more nerve than I possess to tell unnecessary lies to a dying man. The necessary ones are quite different, and I shall not think of them when I go to my account.

"Berlyng could not come if I sent for him," I replied soothingly. "He is two miles away from here trenching the North Wall, and I have nobody to send. The messenger would have to run the gauntlet of the enemy's earthworks."

"I'll give the man a hundred pounds who does it," replied Noon, in his breathless whisper. "Berlyng will come sharp enough if you say it's from me. He hates me too much." He broke off with a laugh which made me feel sick. "Could he get here in time," he asked after a pause, "if you sent for him?"

"Yes," I replied, with my hand inside his soaked tunic.

I found a wounded water-carrier—a fellow with a stray bullet in his hand—who volunteered to find Berlyng, and then I returned to Noon and told him what I had done. I knew that Berlyng could not come.

He nodded, and I think he said, "God bless you."

"I want to put something right," he said, after an effort; "I've been a blackguard."

I waited a little in case Noon wished to repose some confidence in me. Things are so seldom put right that it is wise to facilitate such intentions. But it appeared obvious that what Noon had to say could only be said to Berlyng. They had, it subsequently transpired, not been on speaking terms for some months.

I was turning away when Noon suddenly cried out in his natural voice, "There IS Berlyng."

I turned and saw one of my men, Swearney, carrying in a

gunner. It might be Berlyng, for the uniform was that of a captain, but I could not see his face. Noon, however, seemed to recognize him.

I showed Swearney where to lay his man, close to me alongside Noon, who at that moment required all my attention, for he had fainted.

In a moment Noon recovered, despite the heat, which was tremendous. He lay quite still looking up at the patches of blue sky between the dark motionless tops of the pine trees. His face was livid under the sunburn, and as I wiped the perspiration from his forehead he closed his eyes with the abandon of a child. Some men, I have found, die like children going to sleep.

He slowly recovered, and I gave him a few drops of brandy. I thought he was dying, and decided to let Berlyng wait. I did not even glance at him as he lay, covered with dust and blackened by the smoke of his beloved nine-pounders, a little to the left of Noon, and behind me as I knelt at the latter's side.

After a while his eyes grew brighter, and he began to look about him. He turned his head, painfully, for the muscles of his neck were injured, and caught sight of the gunner's uniform.

"Is that Berlyng?" he asked excitedly.

"Yes."

He dragged himself up and tried to get nearer to Berlyng. And I helped him. They were close alongside each other. Berlyng was lying on his back, staring up at the blue patches between the pine trees.

Noon turned on his left elbow and began whispering into the smoke- grimed ear.

"Berlyng," I heard him say, "I was a blackguard. I am sorry, old man. I played it very low down. It was a dirty trick. It was my money—and her people were anxious for her to marry a rich man. I worked it through her people. I wanted her so badly that I forgot I—was supposed—to be a—gentleman. I found out—that it was you— she cared for. But I couldn't make up my mind to give her up. I kept her—to her word. And now it's all up with me—but you'll pull through and it will all—come right. Give her my—love—old chap. You can now—because I'm—done. I'm glad they brought you in— because I've been able—to tell you—that it is you she cares for. You—Berlyng, old chap, who used to be a chum of mine. She cares for you—God! you're in luck! I don't know whether she's told you— but she told me—and I was—a d—-d blackguard."

His jaw suddenly dropped, and he rolled forward with his face against Berlyng's shoulder.

Berlyng was dead when they brought him in. He had heard nothing. Or perhaps he had heard and understood—everything.

A Jury of her Peers
Susan Glaspell

When Martha Hale opened the storm-door and got a cut of the north wind, she ran back for her big woolen scarf. As she hurriedly wound that round her head her eye made a scandalized sweep of her kitchen. It was no ordinary thing that called her away — it was probably further from ordinary than anything that had ever happened in Dickson County. But what her eye took in was that her kitchen was in no shape for leaving: her bread all ready for mixing, half the flour sifted and half unsifted.

She hated to see things half done; but she had been at that when the team from town stopped to get Mr. Hale, and then the sheriff came running in to say his wife wished Mrs. Hale would come too — adding, with a grin, that he guessed she was getting scared and wanted another woman along. So she had dropped everything right where it was.

"Martha!" now came her husband's impatient voice. "Don't keep folks waiting out here in the cold."

She again opened the storm-door, and this time joined the three men and the one woman waiting for her in the big two-seated buggy.

After she had the robes tucked around her she took another look at the woman who sat beside her on the back seat. She had met Mrs. Peters the year before at the county fair, and the thing she remembered about her was that she didn't seem like a sheriff's wife. She was small and thin and didn't have a strong voice. Mrs. Gorman, sheriff's wife before Gorman went out and Peters came in, had a voice that somehow seemed to be backing up the law with every word. But if Mrs. Peters didn't look like a sheriff's wife, Peters made it up in looking like a sheriff. He was to a dot the kind of man who could get himself elected sheriff—a heavy man with a big voice, who was particularly genial with the law-abiding, as if to make it plain that he knew the difference between criminals and non-criminals. And right there it came into Mrs. Hale's mind, with a stab, that this man who was so pleasant and lively with all of them was going to the Wrights' now as a sheriff.

"The country's not very pleasant this time of year," Mrs. Peters at last ventured, as if she felt they ought to be talking as well as the men.

Mrs. Hale scarcely finished her reply, for they had gone up a little hill and could see the Wright place now, and seeing it did not make her feel like talking. It looked very lonesome this cold March morning. It had always been a lonesome-looking place. It was down in a hollow, and the poplar trees around it were lonesome-looking trees. The men were looking at it and talking about what had happened. The county attorney was bending to one side of the buggy, and kept looking steadily at the place as they drew up to it.

"I'm glad you came with me," Mrs. Peters said nervously, as the two women were about to follow the men in through the kitchen door.

Even after she had her foot on the door-step, her hand on the knob, Martha Hale had a moment of feeling she could not cross that threshold. And the reason it seemed she couldn't cross it now was simply because she hadn't crossed it before. Time and time again it had been in her mind, "I ought to go over and see Minnie Foster"— she still thought of her as Minnie Foster, though for twenty years she had been Mrs. Wright. And then there was always something to do and Minnie Foster would go from her mind. But now she could come.

The men went over to the stove. The women stood close together by the door. Young Henderson, the county attorney, turned around and said, "Come up to the fire, ladies."

Mrs. Peters took a step forward, then stopped. "I'm not—cold," she said.

And so the two women stood by the door, at first not even so much as looking around the kitchen.

The men talked for a minute about what a good thing it was the sheriff had sent his deputy out that morning to make a fire for them, and then Sheriff Peters stepped back from the stove, unbuttoned his outer coat, and leaned his hands on the kitchen table in a way that seemed to mark the beginning of official business. "Now, Mr. Hale," he said in a sort of semi-official voice, "before we move things about, you tell Mr. Henderson just what it was you saw when you came here yesterday morning."

The county attorney was looking around the kitchen.

"By the way," he said, "has anything been moved?" He turned to the sheriff. "Are things just as you left them yesterday?"

Peters looked from cupboard to sink; from that to a small worn rocker a little to one side of the kitchen table.

"It's just the same."

"Somebody should have been left here yesterday," said the county attorney.

"Oh—yesterday," returned the sheriff, with a little gesture as if yesterday having been more than he could bear to think of. "When I had to send Frank to Morris Center for that man who went crazy— let me tell you. I had my hands full yesterday. I knew you could get back from Omaha by today, George, and as long as I went over everything here myself—"

"Well, Mr. Hale," said the county attorney, in a way of letting what was past and gone go, "tell just what happened when you came here yesterday morning."

Mrs. Hale, still leaning against the door, had that sinking feeling of the mother whose child is about to speak a piece. Lewis often wandered along and got things mixed up in a story. She hoped he would tell this straight and plain, and not say unnecessary things that would just make things harder for Minnie Foster. He didn't begin at once, and she noticed that he looked queer—as if standing in that kitchen and having to tell what he had seen there yesterday morning made him almost sick.

"Yes, Mr. Hale?" the county attorney reminded.

"Harry and I had started to town with a load of potatoes," Mrs. Hale's husband began.

Harry was Mrs. Hale's oldest boy. He wasn't with them now, for the very good reason that those potatoes never got to town yesterday and he was taking them this morning, so he hadn't been home when the sheriff stopped to say he wanted Mr. Hale to come over to the Wright place and tell the county attorney his story there, where he could point it all out. With all Mrs. Hale's other emotions came the fear now that maybe Harry wasn't dressed warm enough—they hadn't any of them realized how that north wind did bite.

"We come along this road," Hale was going on, with a motion of his hand to the road over which they had just come, "and as we got in sight of the house I says to Harry, 'I'm goin' to see if I can't get John Wright to take a telephone.' You see," he explained to Henderson, "unless I can get somebody to go in with me they won't come out this branch road except for a price I can't pay. I'd spoke to Wright about it once before; but he put me off, saying folks talked too much anyway, and all he asked was peace and quiet—guess you know about how much he talked himself. But I thought maybe if I went to the house and talked about it before his wife, and said all the women-folks liked the telephones, and that in this lonesome stretch of road it would be a good thing—well, I said to Harry that that was what I was going to say—though I said at the same time that I didn't know as what his wife wanted made much difference to John—"

Now there he was!—saying things he didn't need to say. Mrs. Hale tried to catch her husband's eye, but fortunately the county attorney interrupted with:

"Let's talk about that a little later, Mr. Hale. I do want to talk about that but, I'm anxious now to get along to just what happened when you got here."

When he began this time, it was very deliberately and carefully:

"I didn't see or hear anything. I knocked at the door. And still it was all quiet inside. I knew they must be up—it was past eight o'clock. So I knocked again, louder, and I thought I heard somebody say, 'Come in.' I wasn't sure—I'm not sure yet. But I opened the door—this door," jerking a hand toward the door by which the two women stood. "and there, in that rocker"—pointing to it—"sat Mrs. Wright."

Everyone in the kitchen looked at the rocker. It came into Mrs. Hale's mind that that rocker didn't look in the least like Minnie Foster—the Minnie Foster of twenty years before. It was a dingy red, with wooden rungs up the back, and the middle rung was gone, and the chair sagged to one side.

"How did she—look?" the county attorney was inquiring.

"Well," said Hale, "she looked—queer."

"How do you mean—queer?"

As he asked it he took out a note-book and pencil. Mrs. Hale did not like the sight of that pencil. She kept her eye fixed on her husband, as if to keep him from saying unnecessary things that would go into that note-book and make trouble.

Hale did speak guardedly, as if the pencil had affected him too.

"Well, as if she didn't know what she was going to do next. And kind of—done up."

"How did she seem to feel about your coming?"

"Why, I don't think she minded—one way or other. She didn't pay much attention. I said, 'Ho' do, Mrs. Wright? It's cold, ain't it?' And she said. 'Is it?'—and went on pleatin' at her apron.

"Well, I was surprised. She didn't ask me to come up to the stove, or to sit down, but just set there, not even lookin' at me. And so I said: 'I want to see John.'

"And then she—laughed. I guess you would call it a laugh.

"I thought of Harry and the team outside, so I said, a little sharp, 'Can I see John?' 'No,' says she—kind of dull like. 'Ain't he home?' says I. Then she looked at me. 'Yes,' says she, 'he's home.' 'Then why can't I see him?' I asked her, out of patience with her now. ''Cause he's dead' says she, just as quiet and dull—and fell to pleatin' her apron. 'Dead?' says, I, like you do when you can't take in what you've heard.

"She just nodded her head, not getting a bit excited, but rockin' back and forth.

"'Why—where is he?' says I, not knowing what to say.

"She just pointed upstairs—like this"—pointing to the room above.

"I got up, with the idea of going up there myself. By this time I—didn't know what to do. I walked from there to here; then I says: 'Why, what did he die of?'

"'He died of a rope around his neck,' says she; and just went on pleatin' at her apron."

Hale stopped speaking, and stood staring at the rocker, as if he were still seeing the woman who had sat there the morning before. Nobody spoke; it was as if every one were seeing the woman who had sat there the morning before.

"And what did you do then?" the county attorney at last broke the silence.

"I went out and called Harry. I thought I might—need help. I got Harry in, and we went upstairs." His voice fell almost to a whisper. "There he was—lying over the—"

"I think I'd rather have you go into that upstairs," the county attorney interrupted, "where you can point it all out. Just go on now with the rest of the story."

"Well, my first thought was to get that rope off. It looked—"

He stopped, his face twitching.

"But Harry, he went up to him, and he said. 'No, he's dead all right, and we'd better not touch anything.' So we went downstairs.

"She was still sitting that same way. 'Has anybody been notified?' I asked. 'No, says she, unconcerned.

"'Who did this, Mrs. Wright?' said Harry. He said it businesslike, and she stopped pleatin' at her apron. 'I don't know,' she says. 'You don't know?' says Harry. 'Weren't you sleepin' in the bed with him?' 'Yes,' says she, 'but I was on the inside. 'Somebody slipped a rope round his neck and strangled him, and you didn't wake up?' says Harry. 'I didn't wake up,' she said after him.

"We may have looked as if we didn't see how that could be, for after a minute she said, 'I sleep sound.'

"Harry was going to ask her more questions, but I said maybe that weren't our business; maybe we ought to let her tell her story first to the coroner or the sheriff. So Harry went fast as he could over to High Road—the Rivers' place, where there's a telephone."

"And what did she do when she knew you had gone for the coroner?" The attorney got his pencil in his hand all ready for writing.

"She moved from that chair to this one over here"—Hale pointed to a small chair in the corner—"and just sat there with her hands held together and lookin' down. I got a feeling that I ought to make some conversation, so I said I had come in to see if John wanted to put in a telephone; and at that she started to laugh, and then she stopped and looked at me—scared."

At the sound of a moving pencil the man who was telling the story looked up.

"I dunno—maybe it wasn't scared," he hastened: "I wouldn't like to say it was. Soon Harry got back, and then Dr. Lloyd came, and you, Mr. Peters, and so I guess that's all I know that you don't."

He said that last with relief, and moved a little, as if relaxing. Everyone moved a little. The county attorney walked toward the stair door.

"I guess we'll go upstairs first—then out to the barn and around there."

He paused and looked around the kitchen.

"You're convinced there was nothing important here?" he asked the sheriff. "Nothing that would—point to any motive?"

The sheriff too looked all around, as if to re-convince himself.

"Nothing here but kitchen things," he said, with a little laugh for the insignificance of kitchen things.

The county attorney was looking at the cupboard—a peculiar, ungainly structure, half closet and half cupboard, the upper part of it being built in the wall, and the lower part just the old-fashioned kitchen cupboard. As if its queerness attracted him, he got a chair and opened the upper part and looked in. After a moment he drew his hand away sticky.

"Here's a nice mess," he said resentfully.

The two women had drawn nearer, and now the sheriff's wife spoke.

"Oh—her fruit," she said, looking to Mrs. Hale for sympathetic understanding.

She turned back to the county attorney and explained: "She worried about that when it turned so cold last night. She said the fire would go out and her jars might burst."

Mrs. Peters' husband broke into a laugh.

"Well, can you beat the women! Held for murder, and worrying about her preserves!"

The young attorney set his lips.

"I guess before we're through with her she may have something more serious than preserves to worry about."

"Oh, well," said Mrs. Hale's husband, with good-natured superiority, "women are used to worrying over trifles."

The two women moved a little closer together. Neither of them spoke. The county attorney seemed suddenly to remember his manners—and think of his future.

"And yet," said he, with the gallantry of a young politician. "for all their worries, what would we do without the ladies?"

The women did not speak, did not unbend. He went to the sink and began washing his hands. He turned to wipe them on the roller towel—whirled it for a cleaner place.

"Dirty towels! Not much of a housekeeper, would you say, ladies?"

He kicked his foot against some dirty pans under the sink.

"There's a great deal of work to be done on a farm," said Mrs. Hale stiffly.

"To be sure. And yet" —with a little bow to her—'I know there are some Dickson County farm-houses that do not have such roller towels." He gave it a pull to expose its full length again.

"Those towels get dirty awful quick. Men's hands aren't always as clean as they might be.

"Ah, loyal to your sex, I see," he laughed. He stopped and gave her a keen look, "But you and Mrs. Wright were neighbors. I suppose you were friends, too."

Martha Hale shook her head.

"I've seen little enough of her of late years. I've not been in this house—it's more than a year."

"And why was that? You didn't like her?"

"I liked her well enough," she replied with spirit. "Farmers' wives have their hands full, Mr. Henderson. And then—" She looked around the kitchen.

"Yes?" he encouraged.

"It never seemed a very cheerful place," said she, more to herself than to him.

"No," he agreed; "I don't think anyone would call it cheerful. I shouldn't say she had the home-making instinct."

"Well, I don't know as Wright had, either," she muttered.

"You mean they didn't get on very well?" he was quick to ask.

"No; I don't mean anything," she answered, with decision. As she turned a little away from him, she added: "But I don't think a place would be any the cheerfuller for John Wright's bein' in it."

"I'd like to talk to you about that a little later, Mrs. Hale," he said. "I'm anxious to get the lay of things upstairs now."

He moved toward the stair door, followed by the two men.

"I suppose anything Mrs. Peters does'll be all right?" the sheriff inquired. "She was to take in some clothes for her, you know—and a few little things. We left in such a hurry yesterday."

The county attorney looked at the two women they were leaving alone there among the kitchen things.

"Yes—Mrs. Peters," he said, his glance resting on the woman who was not Mrs. Peters, the big farmer woman who stood behind the sheriff's wife. "Of course Mrs. Peters is one of us," he said, in a manner of entrusting responsibility. "And keep your eye out, Mrs. Peters, for anything that might be of use. No telling; you women might come upon a clue to the motive—and that's the thing we need."

Mr. Hale rubbed his face after the fashion of a showman getting ready for a pleasantry.

"But would the women know a clue if they did come upon it?" he said; and, having delivered himself of this, he followed the others through the stair door.

The women stood motionless and silent, listening to the footsteps, first upon the stairs, then in the room above them.

Then, as if releasing herself from something strange. Mrs. Hale began to arrange the dirty pans under the sink, which the county attorney's disdainful push of the foot had deranged.

"I'd hate to have men comin' into my kitchen," she said testily—"snoopin' round and criticizin'."

"Of course it's no more than their duty," said the sheriff's wife, in her manner of timid acquiescence.

"Duty's all right," replied Mrs. Hale bluffly; "but I guess that deputy sheriff that come out to make the fire might have got a little of this on." She gave the roller towel a pull. 'Wish I'd thought of that sooner! Seems mean to talk about her for not having things slicked up, when she had to come away in such a hurry."

She looked around the kitchen. Certainly it was not "slicked up." Her eye was held by a bucket of sugar on a low shelf. The cover was off the wooden bucket, and beside it was a paper bag—half full.

Mrs. Hale moved toward it.

"She was putting this in there," she said to herself—slowly.

She thought of the flour in her kitchen at home—half sifted, half not sifted. She had been interrupted, and had left things half done. What had interrupted Minnie Foster? Why had that work been left half done? She made a move as if to finish it,—unfinished things always bothered her,—and then she glanced around and saw that Mrs. Peters was watching her—and she didn't want Mrs. Peters to get that feeling she had got of work begun and then—for some reason—not finished.

"It's a shame about her fruit," she said, and walked toward the cupboard that the county attorney had opened, and got on the chair, murmuring: "I wonder if it's all gone."

It was a sorry enough looking sight, but "Here's one that's all right," she said at last. She held it toward the light. "This is cherries, too." She looked again. "I declare I believe that's the only one."

With a sigh, she got down from the chair, went to the sink, and wiped off the bottle.

"She'll feel awful bad, after all her hard work in the hot weather. I remember the afternoon I put up my cherries last summer.

She set the bottle on the table, and, with another sigh, started to sit down in the rocker. But she did not sit down. Something kept her from sitting down in that chair. She straightened—stepped back, and, half turned away, stood looking at it, seeing the woman who had sat there "pleatin' at her apron."

The thin voice of the sheriff's wife broke in upon her: "I must be getting those things from the front-room closet." She opened the door into the other room, started in, stepped back. "You coming with me, Mrs. Hale?" she asked nervously. "You—you could help me get them."

They were soon back—the stark coldness of that shut-up room was not a thing to linger in.

"My!" said Mrs. Peters, dropping the things on the table and hurrying to the stove.

Mrs. Hale stood examining the clothes the woman who was being detained in town had said she wanted.

"Wright was close!" she exclaimed, holding up a shabby black skirt that bore the marks of much making over. "I think maybe that's why she kept so much to herself. I s'pose she felt she couldn't do her part; and then, you don't enjoy things when you feel shabby. She used to wear pretty clothes and be lively—when she was Minnie Foster, one of the town girls, singing in the choir. But that—oh, that was twenty years ago."

With a carefulness in which there was something tender, she folded the shabby clothes and piled them at one corner of the table. She looked up at Mrs. Peters, and there was something in the other woman's look that irritated her.

"She don't care," she said to herself. "Much difference it makes to her whether Minnie Foster had pretty clothes when she was a girl."

Then she looked again, and she wasn't so sure; in fact, she hadn't at any time been perfectly sure about Mrs. Peters. She had that shrinking manner, and yet her eyes looked as if they could see a long way into things.

"This all you was to take in?" asked Mrs. Hale.

"No," said the sheriffs wife; "she said she wanted an apron. Funny thing to want, " she ventured in her nervous little way, "for there's not much to get you dirty in jail, goodness knows.

But I suppose just to make her feel more natural. If you're used to wearing an apron—. She said they were in the bottom drawer of this cupboard. Yes—here they are. And then her little shawl that always hung on the stair door."

She took the small gray shawl from behind the door leading upstairs, and stood a minute looking at it.

Suddenly Mrs. Hale took a quick step toward the other woman, "Mrs. Peters!"

"Yes, Mrs. Hale?"

"Do you think she—did it?'

A frightened look blurred the other thing in Mrs. Peters' eyes.

"Oh, I don't know," she said, in a voice that seemed to shink away from the subject.

"Well, I don't think she did," affirmed Mrs. Hale stoutly. "Asking for an apron, and her little shawl. Worryin' about her fruit."

"Mr. Peters says—." Footsteps were heard in the room above; she stopped, looked up, then went on in a lowered voice: "Mr. Peters says—it looks bad for her. Mr. Henderson is awful sarcastic in a speech, and he's going to make fun of her saying she didn't— wake up."

For a moment Mrs. Hale had no answer. Then, "Well, I guess John Wright didn't wake up—when they was slippin' that rope under his neck," she muttered.

"No, it's strange," breathed Mrs. Peters. "They think it was such a—funny way to kill a man."

She began to laugh; at sound of the laugh, abruptly stopped.

"That's just what Mr. Hale said," said Mrs. Hale, in a resolutely natural voice. "There was a gun in the house. He says that's what he can't understand."

"Mr. Henderson said, coming out, that what was needed for the case was a motive. Something to show anger—or sudden feeling."

'Well, I don't see any signs of anger around here," said Mrs. Hale, "I don't—" She stopped. It was as if her mind tripped on something. Her eye was caught by a dish-towel in the middle of the kitchen table. Slowly she moved toward the table. One half of it was wiped clean, the other half messy. Her eyes made a slow, almost unwilling turn to the bucket of sugar and the half empty bag beside it. Things begun—and not finished.

After a moment she stepped back, and said, in that manner of releasing herself:

"Wonder how they're finding things upstairs? I hope she had it a little more red up up there. You know," — she paused, and feeling gathered, — "it seems kind of sneaking: locking her up in town and coming out here to get her own house to turn against her!"

"But, Mrs. Hale," said the sheriff's wife, "the law is the law."

"I s'pose 'tis," answered Mrs. Hale shortly.

She turned to the stove, saying something about that fire not being much to brag of. She worked with it a minute, and when she straightened up she said aggressively:

"The law is the law — and a bad stove is a bad stove. How'd you like to cook on this?" — pointing with the poker to the broken lining. She opened the oven door and started to express her opinion of the oven; but she was swept into her own thoughts, thinking of what it would mean, year after year, to have that stove to wrestle with. The thought of Minnie Foster trying to bake in that oven — and the thought of her never going over to see Minnie Foster — .

She was startled by hearing Mrs. Peters say: "A person gets discouraged — and loses heart."

The sheriff's wife had looked from the stove to the sink — to the pail of water which had been carried in from outside. The two women stood there silent, above them the footsteps of the men who were looking for evidence against the woman who had worked in that kitchen. That look of seeing into things, of seeing through a thing to something else, was in the eyes of the sheriff's wife now. When Mrs. Hale next spoke to her, it was gently:

"Better loosen up your things, Mrs. Peters. We'll not feel them when we go out."

Mrs. Peters went to the back of the room to hang up the fur tippet she was wearing. A moment later she exclaimed, "Why, she was piecing a quilt," and held up a large sewing basket piled high with quilt pieces.

Mrs. Hale spread some of the blocks on the table.

"It's log-cabin pattern," she said, putting several of them together, "Pretty, isn't it?"

They were so engaged with the quilt that they did not hear the footsteps on the stairs. Just as the stair door opened Mrs. Hale was saying:

"Do you suppose she was going to quilt it or just knot it?"

The sheriff threw up his hands.

"They wonder whether she was going to quilt it or just knot it!"

There was a laugh for the ways of women, a warming of hands over the stove, and then the county attorney said briskly:

"Well, let's go right out to the barn and get that cleared up."

"I don't see as there's anything so strange," Mrs. Hale said resentfully, after the outside door had closed on the three men — "our taking up our time with little things while we're waiting for them to get the evidence. I don't see as it's anything to laugh about."

"Of course they've got awful important things on their minds," said the sheriff's wife apologetically.

They returned to an inspection of the block for the quilt. Mrs. Hale was looking at the fine, even sewing, and preoccupied with thoughts of the woman who had done that sewing, when she heard the sheriff's wife say, in a queer tone:

"Why, look at this one."

She turned to take the block held out to her.

"The sewing," said Mrs. Peters, in a troubled way, "All the rest of them have been so nice and even — but — this one. Why, it looks as if she didn't know what she was about!"

Their eyes met — something flashed to life, passed between them; then, as if with an effort, they seemed to pull away from each other. A moment Mrs. Hale sat there, her hands folded over that sewing which was so unlike all the rest of the sewing. Then she had pulled a knot and drawn the threads.

"Oh, what are you doing, Mrs. Hale?" asked the sheriff's wife, startled.

"Just pulling out a stitch or two that's not sewed very good," said Mrs. Hale mildly.

"I don't think we ought to touch things," Mrs. Peters said, a little helplessly.

"I'll just finish up this end," answered Mrs. Hale, still in that mild, matter-of-fact fashion.

She threaded a needle and started to replace bad sewing with good. For a little while she sewed in silence. Then, in that thin, timid voice, she heard:

"Mrs. Hale!"

"Yes, Mrs. Peters?"

'What do you suppose she was so — nervous about?"

"Oh, I don't know," said Mrs. Hale, as if dismissing a thing not important enough to spend much time on. "I don't know as she was — nervous. I sew awful queer sometimes when I'm just tired."

She cut a thread, and out of the corner of her eye looked up at Mrs. Peters. The small, lean face of the sheriff's wife seemed to have tightened up. Her eyes had that look of peering into something. But next moment she moved, and said in her thin, indecisive way:

'Well, I must get those clothes wrapped. They may be through sooner than we think. I wonder where I could find a piece of paper—and string."

"In that cupboard, maybe," suggested to Mrs. Hale, after a glance around.

One piece of the crazy sewing remained unripped. Mrs. Peter's back turned, Martha Hale now scrutinized that piece, compared it with the dainty, accurate sewing of the other blocks. The difference was startling. Holding this block made her feel queer, as if the distracted thoughts of the woman who had perhaps turned to it to try and quiet herself were communicating themselves to her.

Mrs. Peters' voice roused her.

"Here's a bird-cage," she said. "Did she have a bird, Mrs. Hale?"

'Why, I don't know whether she did or not." She turned to look at the cage Mrs. Peters was holding up. "I've not been here in so long." She sighed. "There was a man round last year selling canaries cheap—but I don't know as she took one. Maybe she did. She used to sing real pretty herself."

Mrs. Peters looked around the kitchen.

"Seems kind of funny to think of a bird here." She half laughed—an attempt to put up a barrier. "But she must have had one—or why would she have a cage? I wonder what happened to it."

"I suppose maybe the cat got it," suggested Mrs. Hale, resuming her sewing.

"No; she didn't have a cat. She's got that feeling some people have about cats—being afraid of them. When they brought her to our house yesterday, my cat got in the room, and she was real upset and asked me to take it out."

"My sister Bessie was like that," laughed Mrs. Hale.

The sheriff's wife did not reply. The silence made Mrs. Hale turn round. Mrs. Peters was examining the bird-cage.

"Look at this door," she said slowly. "It's broke. One hinge has been pulled apart."

Mrs. Hale came nearer.

"Looks as if someone must have been—rough with it."

Again their eyes met—startled, questioning, apprehensive. For a moment neither spoke nor stirred. Then Mrs. Hale, turning away, said brusquely:

"If they're going to find any evidence, I wish they'd be about it. I don't like this place."

"But I'm awful glad you came with me, Mrs. Hale." Mrs. Peters put the bird-cage on the table and sat down. "It would be lonesome for me—sitting here alone."

"Yes, it would, wouldn't it?" agreed Mrs. Hale, a certain determined naturalness in her voice. She had picked up the sewing, but now it dropped in her lap, and she murmured in a different voice: "But I tell you what I do wish, Mrs. Peters. I wish I had come over sometimes when she was here. I wish—I had."

"But of course you were awful busy, Mrs. Hale. Your house— and your children."

"I could've come," retorted Mrs. Hale shortly. "I stayed away because it weren't cheerful—and that's why I ought to have come. I"—she looked around—"I've never liked this place. Maybe because it's down in a hollow and you don't see the road. I don't know what it is, but it's a lonesome place, and always was. I wish I had come over to see Minnie Foster sometimes. I can see now—" She did not put it into words.

"Well, you mustn't reproach yourself," counseled Mrs. Peters. "Somehow, we just don't see how it is with other folks till— something comes up."

"Not having children makes less work," mused Mrs. Hale, after a silence, "but it makes a quiet house—and Wright out to work all day—and no company when he did come in. Did you know John Wright, Mrs. Peters?"

"Not to know him. I've seen him in town. They say he was a good man."

"Yes—good," conceded John Wright's neighbor grimly. "He didn't drink, and kept his word as well as most, I guess, and paid his debts. But he was a hard man, Mrs. Peters. Just to pass the time of day with him—." She stopped, shivered a little. "Like a raw wind that gets to the bone." Her eye fell upon the cage on the table before her, and she added, almost bitterly: "I should think she would've wanted a bird!"

Suddenly she leaned forward, looking intently at the cage.

"But what do you s'pose went wrong with it?"

"I don't know," returned Mrs. Peters; "unless it got sick and died."

But after she said it she reached over and swung the broken door. Both women watched it as if somehow held by it.

"You didn't know—her?" Mrs. Hale asked, a gentler note in her voice.

"Not till they brought her yesterday," said the sheriff's wife.

"She—come to think of it, she was kind of like a bird herself. Real sweet and pretty, but kind of timid and—fluttery. How—she—did—change."

That held her for a long time. Finally, as if struck with a happy thought and relieved to get back to everyday things, she exclaimed:

"Tell you what, Mrs. Peters, why don't you take the quilt in with you? It might take up her mind."

"Why, I think that's a real nice idea, Mrs. Hale," agreed the sheriff's wife, as if she too were glad to come into the atmosphere of a simple kindness. "There couldn't possibly be any objection to that, could there? Now, just what will I take? I wonder if her patches are in here—and her things?"

They turned to the sewing basket.

"Here's some red," said Mrs. Hale, bringing out a roll of cloth. Underneath that was a box. "Here, maybe her scissors are in here—and her things." She held it up. "What a pretty box! I'll warrant that was something she had a long time ago—when she was a girl."

She held it in her hand a moment; then, with a little sigh, opened it.

Instantly her hand went to her nose.

"Why—!"

Mrs. Peters drew nearer—then turned away.

"There's something wrapped up in this piece of silk," faltered Mrs. Hale.

"This isn't her scissors," said Mrs. Peters, in a shrinking voice.

Her hand not steady, Mrs. Hale raised the piece of silk. "Oh, Mrs. Peters!" she cried. "It's—"

Mrs. Peters bent closer.

"It's the bird," she whispered.

"But, Mrs. Peters!" cried Mrs. Hale. "Look at it! Its neck—look at its neck! It's all—other side to."

She held the box away from her.

The sheriff's wife again bent closer.

"Somebody wrung its neck," said she, in a voice that was slow and deep.

And then again the eyes of the two women met—this time clung together in a look of dawning comprehension, of growing horror. Mrs. Peters looked from the dead bird to the broken door of the cage. Again their eyes met. And just then there was a sound at the outside door. Mrs. Hale slipped the box under the quilt pieces in the basket, and sank into the chair before it. Mrs. Peters stood holding to the table. The county attorney and the sheriff came in from outside.

"Well, ladies," said the county attorney, as one turning from serious things to little pleasantries, "have you decided whether she was going to quilt it or knot it?"

"We think," began the sheriff's wife in a flurried voice, "that she was going to—knot it."

He was too preoccupied to notice the change that came in her voice on that last.

"Well, that's very interesting, I'm sure," he said tolerantly. He caught sight of the bird-cage.

"Has the bird flown?"

"We think the cat got it," said Mrs. Hale in a voice curiously even.

He was walking up and down, as if thinking something out.

"Is there a cat?" he asked absently.

Mrs. Hale shot a look up at the sheriff's wife.

"Well, not now," said Mrs. Peters. "They're superstitious, you know; they leave."

She sank into her chair.

The county attorney did not heed her. "No sign at all of anyone having come in from the outside," he said to Peters, in the manner of continuing an interrupted conversation. "Their own rope. Now let's go upstairs again and go over it, piece by piece. It would have to have been someone who knew just the—"

The stair door closed behind them and their voices were lost.

The two women sat motionless, not looking at each other, but as if peering into something and at the same time holding back. When they spoke now it was as if they were afraid of what they were saying, but as if they could not help saying it.

"She liked the bird," said Martha Hale, low and slowly. "She was going to bury it in that pretty box."

When I was a girl," said Mrs. Peters, under her breath, "my kitten—there was a boy took a hatchet, and before my eyes—before I could get there—" She covered her face an instant. "If they hadn't held me back I would have"—she caught herself, looked upstairs where footsteps were heard, and finished weakly—"hurt him."

Then they sat without speaking or moving.

"I wonder how it would seem," Mrs. Hale at last began, as if feeling her way over strange ground—"never to have had any children around?" Her eyes made a slow sweep of the kitchen, as if seeing what that kitchen had meant through all the years "No, Wright wouldn't like the bird," she said after that—"a thing that sang. She used to sing. He killed that too." Her voice tightened.

Mrs. Peters moved uneasily.

"Of course we don't know who killed the bird."

"I knew John Wright," was Mrs. Hale's answer.

"It was an awful thing was done in this house that night, Mrs. Hale," said the sheriff's wife. "Killing a man while he slept—slipping a thing round his neck that choked the life out of him."

Mrs. Hale's hand went out to the bird cage.

"We don't know who killed him," whispered Mrs. Peters wildly. "We don't know."

Mrs. Hale had not moved. "If there had been years and years of—nothing, then a bird to sing to you, it would be awful—still—after the bird was still."

It was as if something within her not herself had spoken, and it found in Mrs. Peters something she did not know as herself.

"I know what stillness is," she said, in a queer, monotonous voice. "When we homesteaded in Dakota, and my first baby died—after he was two years old—and me with no other then—"

Mrs. Hale stirred.

"How soon do you suppose they'll be through looking for the evidence?"

"I know what stillness is," repeated Mrs. Peters, in just that same way. Then she too pulled back. "The law has got to punish crime, Mrs. Hale," she said in her tight little way.

"I wish you'd seen Minnie Foster," was the answer, "when she wore a white dress with blue ribbons, and stood up there in the choir and sang."

The picture of that girl, the fact that she had lived neighbor to that girl for twenty years, and had let her die for lack of life, was suddenly more than she could bear.

"Oh, I wish I'd come over here once in a while!" she cried. "That was a crime! Who's going to punish that?"

"We mustn't take on," said Mrs. Peters, with a frightened look toward the stairs.

"I might 'a' known she needed help! I tell you, it's queer, Mrs. Peters. We live close together, and we live far apart. We all go through the same things—it's all just a different kind of the same thing! If it weren't—why do you and I understand? Why do we know—what we know this minute?"

She dashed her hand across her eyes. Then, seeing the jar of fruit on the table she reached for it and choked out:

"If I was you I wouldn't tell her her fruit was gone! Tell her it ain't. Tell her it's all right—all of it. Here—take this in to prove it to her! She—she may never know whether it was broke or not."

She turned away.

Mrs. Peters reached out for the bottle of fruit as if she were glad to take it—as if touching a familiar thing, having something to do, could keep her from something else. She got up, looked about for something to wrap the fruit in, took a petticoat from the pile of clothes she had brought from the front room, and nervously started winding that round the bottle.

"My!" she began, in a high, false voice, "it's a good thing the men couldn't hear us! Getting all stirred up over a little thing like a—dead canary." She hurried over that. "As if that could have anything to do with—with—My, wouldn't they laugh?"

Footsteps were heard on the stairs.

"Maybe they would," muttered Mrs. Hale—"maybe they wouldn't."

"No, Peters," said the county attorney incisively; "it's all perfectly clear, except the reason for doing it. But you know juries when it comes to women. If there was some definite thing—something to show. Something to make a story about. A thing that would connect up with this clumsy way of doing it."

In a covert way Mrs. Hale looked at Mrs. Peters. Mrs. Peters was looking at her. Quickly they looked away from each other. The outer door opened and Mr. Hale came in.

"I've got the team round now," he said. "Pretty cold out there."

"I'm going to stay here awhile by myself," the county attorney suddenly announced. "You can send Frank out for me, can't you?" he asked the sheriff. "I want to go over everything. I'm not satisfied we can't do better."

Again, for one brief moment, the two women's eyes found one another.

The sheriff came up to the table.

"Did you want to see what Mrs. Peters was going to take in?"

The county attorney picked up the apron. He laughed.

"Oh, I guess they're not very dangerous things the ladies have picked out."

Mrs. Hale's hand was on the sewing basket in which the box was concealed. She felt that she ought to take her hand off the basket. She did not seem able to. He picked up one of the quilt blocks which she had piled on to cover the box. Her eyes felt like fire. She had a feeling that if he took up the basket she would snatch it from him.

But he did not take it up. With another little laugh, he turned away, saying:

"No; Mrs. Peters doesn't need supervising. For that matter, a sheriff's wife is married to the law. Ever think of it that way, Mrs. Peters?"

Mrs. Peters was standing beside the table. Mrs. Hale shot a look up at her; but she could not see her face. Mrs. Peters had turned away. When she spoke, her voice was muffled.

"Not—just that way," she said.

"Married to the law!" chuckled Mrs. Peters' husband. He moved toward the door into the front room, and said to the county attorney:

"I just want you to come in here a minute, George. We ought to take a look at these windows."

"Oh—windows," said the county attorney scoffingly.

"We'll be right out, Mr. Hale," said the sheriff to the farmer, who was still waiting by the door.

Hale went to look after the horses. The sheriff followed the county attorney into the other room. Again—for one final moment—the two women were alone in that kitchen.

Martha Hale sprang up, her hands tight together, looking at that other woman, with whom it rested. At first she could not see her eyes, for the sheriff's wife had not turned back since she turned away at that suggestion of being married to the law. But now Mrs. Hale made her turn back. Her eyes made her turn back. Slowly, unwillingly, Mrs. Peters turned her head until her eyes met the eyes of the other woman. There was a moment when they held each other in a steady, burning look in which there was no evasion or flinching. Then Martha Hale's eyes pointed the way to the basket in which was hidden the thing that would make certain the conviction of the other woman—that woman who was not there and yet who had been there with them all through that hour.

For a moment Mrs. Peters did not move. And then she did it. With a rush forward, she threw back the quilt pieces, got the box, tried to put it in her handbag. It was too big. Desperately she opened it, started to take the bird out. But there she broke—she could not touch the bird. She stood there helpless, foolish.

There was the sound of a knob turning in the inner door. Martha Hale snatched the box from the sheriff's wife, and got it in the pocket of her big coat just as the sheriff and the county attorney came back into the kitchen.

"Well, Henry," said the county attorney facetiously, "at least we found out that she was not going to quilt it. She was going to—what is it you call it, ladies?"

Mrs. Hale's hand was against the pocket of her coat.

"We call it—knot it, Mr. Henderson."

Forgiveness
Rev. Joseph Alden

"I will never forgive her, if I live a thousand years!"

"Don't say so, Julia; you don't mean what you say."

"Yes I do mean what I say; I will never forgive her, if I live a thousand years."

Agnes was silent, for she saw that Julia was not in a state of mind to be reasoned with. There are times when it is unwise to make appeals to the hearts and consciences of our friends.

You will wish to know what led Julia to make the fearful expression above recorded, fearful in view of the words of the Saviour, "For if ye forgive not men their trespasses, neither will your Father who is in heaven forgive your trespasses."

Mary's father had taken a house very near Julia's residence, and hence the girls were near neighbors. Mary was of a social, lively disposition, and Julia soon became warmly attached to her.

Julia was a very sincere and unsuspicious girl. She never said what she did not feel; and she never suspected others of doing so.

Mary was not a sincere girl. She was pleasant and good natured, but her professions were not always in accordance with truth. She would profess great affection for a person she cared little about. She would praise you to your face, and ridicule you in your absence.

Julia, I said, was unsuspicious, and did not see the faults of her friend. She thought, indeed, that she spoke of others rather too freely, but then she had no idea that she could ever do so with respect to herself.

The other girls saw Mary's character in its true light, and gave Julia many hints to be on her guard; but it was not according to her ideas of friendship to listen to anything to the disadvantage of a friend.

Julia was accustomed to tell Mary all her secrets, all her plans and wishes, and to ask and to follow her advice on all occasions. It is well to ask advice of the wise, but we should never implicitly follow the advice of any one ; we must follow our advisers only as they follow Christ.

Mary would listen with eagerness to all that Julia had to say, and then would repeat it, not always accurately, to such as were mean enough to listen to her. If there were no listeners there would be no slanderers.

Julia always consulted Mary respecting her dress. Mary would praise whatever she wore, and by this means Julia was led to think more of her dress than was proper, and sometimes to act in a manner which gave her friends surprise and pain.

One morning Julia's brother happened to overhear Mary ridiculing his sister's simplicity, and especially her want of taste in regard to dress, which was not in truth very good, but then it was of Mary's formation. His testimony Julia could not refuse to hear, and with a sorrowful heart she went to see her treacherous friend. She could not condemn her unheard, a safe and wise rule for us all to adopt.

Mary was at first disposed to deny the charge, but she soon saw that it would be useless; so she put a bold face on the matter, and declared she had a right to say what she pleased: "My tongue is my own, and I can do what I please with it, I suppose."

"O, Mary! how could you be so cruel?"

" What have I done that is so bad? If you chose to be such a fool as to believe all I said to you, I'm not to blame."

"Not to blame!"

"No; nobody of common sense would have thought I was in earnest."

Julia by this time was very angry, and expressed her sense of wrong in pretty strong terms, to which Mary listened with a scornful smile.

It was when coming from this interview, that she made the expression recorded at the commencement of this tale.

Perhaps the reader will say, "She had a right to be angry. If I had been treated so, I should have been angry."

I think it is very likely you would; but that does not prove that you would have had a right to be angry. No man has a right to sin. The only passage of Scripture I ever heard quoted in excuse of anger, is, "Be ye angry and sin not." If you can be angry without sinning, very well; but if you cannot be angry without feeling or saying something wrong, then you have no right to be angry. But there is a "more excellent way" than to get angry, however great the provocation.

When Julia went to her chamber for the purpose of going to bed, she read a chapter in her little Bible, and kneeled down to pray. She found it rather hard work. She was accustomed to end with the Lord's prayer. She began to repeat it, and got along well enough till she came to the expression, "forgive us our trespasses as we forgive those who trespass against us." This arrested her attention, and she paused. She saw that we are allowed to ask God's forgiveness only so far as we give it to others. With her present feelings, if she were to offer that petition, she would ask God not to forgive her sins, a dreadful prayer! She recollected the solemn declaration of the Savior, "For if ye forgive not men their trespasses, neither will your Father who is in heaven forgive your trespasses." She arose from her knees and sat down to meditate; she remembered her intercourse with Mary, to see if she could find some excuse for Mary's conduct, that she might forgive her; but she could find none. She could not accuse herself of ever treating Mary with the least unkindness. What should she do? She ought to forgive Mary; but how could she? At length this expression occurred to her, "even as God for Christ's sake hath forgiven you." In this passage she saw was contained the idea needed; she prayed for a forgiving spirit, that she might be enabled to forgive Mary for Christ's sake. And she thought of the treatment which he received, and how he forgave it all.

She did not compose herself to rest till she could say, "forgive us our trespasses as we forgive those who trespass against us." The next day she arose in a calm state of mind. When she thought of Mary's unkindness she felt sad, but not unhappy, as she had the day before.

Agnes called on her at an early hour, that she might talk with her about the affair of Mary, and lead her to a better state of mind than was exhibited the day before. But she soon saw that her efforts were unnecessary, that Julia had already repented of the fearful expression, "I will never forgive her."

Proclaim Liberty Throughout The Land
Leviticus 25

The LORD said to Moses on Mount Sinai, "Speak to the Israelites and say to them: 'When you enter the land I am going to give you, the land itself must observe a sabbath to the LORD. For six years sow your fields, and for six years prune your vineyards and gather their crops. But in the seventh year the land is to have a sabbath of rest, a sabbath to the LORD. Do not sow your fields or prune your vineyards. Do not reap what grows of itself or harvest the grapes of your untended vines. The land is to have a year of rest. Whatever the land yields during the sabbath year will be food for you—for yourself, your manservant and maidservant, and the hired worker and temporary resident who live among you, as well as for your livestock and the wild animals in your land. Whatever the land produces may be eaten.

"'Count off seven sabbaths of years—seven times seven years—so that the seven sabbaths of years amount to a period of forty-nine years. Then have the trumpet sounded everywhere on the tenth day of the seventh month; on the Day of Atonement sound the trumpet throughout your land. Consecrate the fiftieth year and proclaim liberty throughout the land to all its inhabitants. It shall be a jubilee for you; each one of you is to return to his family property and each to his own clan. The fiftieth year shall be a jubilee for you; do not sow and do not reap what grows of itself or harvest the untended vines. For it is a jubilee and is to be holy for you; eat only what is taken directly from the fields.

"'In this Year of Jubilee everyone is to return to his own property.

"'If you sell land to one of your countrymen or buy any from him, do not take advantage of each other. You are to buy from your countryman on the basis of the number of years since the Jubilee. And he is to sell to you on the basis of the number of years left for harvesting crops. When the years are many, you are to increase the price, and when the years are few, you are to decrease the price, because what he is really selling you is the number of crops. Do not take advantage of each other, but fear your God. I am the LORD your God.

"'Follow my decrees and be careful to obey my laws, and you will live safely in the land. Then the land will yield its fruit, and you will eat your fill and live there in safety. You may ask, "What will we eat in the seventh year if we do not plant or harvest our crops?" I will send you such a blessing in the sixth year that the land will yield enough for three years. While you plant during the eighth year, you will eat from the old crop and will continue to eat from it until the harvest of the ninth year comes in.

"'The land must not be sold permanently, because the land is mine and you are but aliens and my tenants. Throughout the country that you hold as a possession, you must provide for the redemption of the land.

"'If one of your countrymen becomes poor and sells some of his property, his nearest relative is to come and redeem what his countryman has sold. If, however, a man has no one to redeem it for him but he himself prospers and acquires sufficient means to redeem it, he is to determine the value for the years since he sold it and refund the balance to the man to whom he sold it; he can then go back to his own property. But if he does not acquire the means to repay him, what he sold will remain in the possession of the buyer until the Year of Jubilee. It will be returned in the Jubilee, and he can then go back to his property.

"'If a man sells a house in a walled city, he retains the right of redemption a full year after its sale. During that time he may redeem it. If it is not redeemed before a full year has passed, the house in the walled city shall belong permanently to the buyer and his descendants. It is not to be returned in the Jubilee. But houses in villages without walls around them are to be considered as open country. They can be redeemed, and they are to be returned in the Jubilee.

"'The Levites always have the right to redeem their houses in the Levitical towns, which they possess. So the property of the Levites is redeemable—that is, a house sold in any town they hold—and is to be returned in the Jubilee, because the houses in the towns of the Levites are their property among the Israelites. But the pastureland belonging to their towns must not be sold; it is their permanent possession.

"'If one of your countrymen becomes poor and is unable to support himself among you, help him as you would an alien or a temporary resident, so he can continue to live among you. Do not take interest of any kind from him, but fear your God, so that your countryman may continue to live among you. You must not lend him money at interest or sell him food at a profit. I am the LORD your God, who brought you out of Egypt to give you the land of Canaan and to be your God.

"'If one of your countrymen becomes poor among you and sells himself to you, do not make him work as a slave. He is to be treated as a hired worker or a temporary resident among you; he is to work for you until the Year of Jubilee. Then he and his children are to be released, and he will go back to his own clan and to the property of his forefathers. Because the Israelites are my servants, whom I brought out of Egypt, they must not be sold as slaves. Do not rule over them ruthlessly, but fear your God.

"'Your male and female slaves are to come from the nations around you; from them you may buy slaves. You may also buy some of the temporary residents living among you and members of their clans born in your country, and they will become your property. You can will them to your children as inherited property and can make them slaves for life, but you must not rule over your fellow Israelites ruthlessly.

"'If an alien or a temporary resident among you becomes rich and one of your countrymen becomes poor and sells himself to the alien living among you or to a member of the alien's clan, he retains the right of redemption after he has sold himself. One of his relatives may redeem him: An uncle or a cousin or any blood relative in his clan may redeem him. Or if he prospers, he may redeem himself. He and his buyer are to count the time from the year he sold himself up to the Year of Jubilee. The price for his release is to be based on the rate paid to a hired man for that number of years. If many years remain, he must pay for his redemption a larger share of the price paid for him. If only a few years remain until the Year of Jubilee, he is to compute that and pay for his redemption accordingly. He is to be treated as a man hired from year to year; you must see to it that his owner does not rule over him ruthlessly.

"'Even if he is not redeemed in any of these ways, he and his children are to be released in the Year of Jubilee, for the Israelites belong to me as servants. They are my servants, whom I brought out of Egypt. I am the LORD your God.

Jerusalem

"Let's be the same wound if we must bleed.
Let's fight side by side, even if the enemy
is ourselves: I am yours, you are mine."
-Tommy Olofsson, Sweden

I'm not interested in
Who suffered the most.
I'm interested in
People getting over it.

Once when my father was a boy
A stone hit him on the head.
Hair would never grow there.
Our fingers found the tender spot
and its riddle: the boy who has fallen
stands up. A bucket of pears
in his mother's doorway welcomes him home.
The pears are not crying.
Later his friend who threw the stone
says he was aiming at a bird.
And my father starts growing wings.

Each carries a tender spot:
something our lives forgot to give us.
A man builds a house and says,
"I am native now."
A woman speaks to a tree in place
of her son. And olives come.
A child's poem says,
"I don't like wars,
they end up with monuments."
He's painting a bird with wings
wide enough to cover two roofs at once.

Why are we so monumentally slow?
Soldiers stalk a pharmacy:
big guns, little pills.
If you tilt your head just slightly
it's ridiculous.

There's a place in my brain
Where hate won't grow.
I touch its riddle: wind, and seeds.
Something pokes us as we sleep.

It's late but everything comes next.

                              Naomi Shihab Nye

FILMS

"F" Word Films

Reading stories can be personally entertaining and if by chance someone else has read the same story, you can share your insights about it. Watching stories can be solitary, but it really lends itself to a communal bowl of fresh popcorn and shared insights about what we have just experienced together. At the peaceCENTER we call this *Popcorn Peacemaking*. Watching a film together as a family or with friends and sharing not only the Milk Duds, but also how the movie affects each person, adds to the richness of the experience.

With this in mind I have selected some of my favorite "F" word films that have helped me to travel to different places and to remember that we are all a part of the human family and express our shared feelings in different languages and customs. Forgiveness is an affair of the heart, remembering what makes us more human can only increase the good will that seems to be in such short supply. So silence your cell phones and enjoy the film...together.

Atonement
2008, Keira Knightly & James McAvoy

When Briony Tallis, 13 years old and an aspiring writer, sees her older sister Cecilia and Robbie Turner at the fountain in front of the family estate she misinterprets what is happening thus setting into motion a series of misunderstandings and a childish pique that will have lasting repercussions for all of them.

Babette's Feast
1988, Stephan Audan

In 19th century Denmark, two beautiful sisters live in an isolated village with their father, who is the honored pastor of a strict, small Protestant church. Although they are each presented with a real opportunity to leave the tiny village, the sisters choose to stay with their father, to serve to him and their church. Some years after his death, a French Catholic refugee, Babette, arrives at their door, begs them to take her in, and commits herself to work for them as maid/housekeeper/cook. After many years the sisters decide to hold a dinner to commemorate the 100th anniversary of their father's birth. Babette experiences unexpected good fortune and implores the sisters to allow her to take charge of the preparation of the celebration. From the novel by Karen Blixen, the exotic meal transforms the members of the tiny church just as this gorgeous film transforms all who partake of Babette's Feast.

Beaches
1988, Bette Midler & Barbara Hershey

When the New York child performer CC Bloom and San Francisco rich kid Hillary meet in a holiday resort in Atlantic City, it marks the start of a lifetime friendship between them. The two keep in touch through letters for a number of years until Hillary, now a successful lawyer, moves to New York to stay with struggling singer CC. The movie shows the various stages of their friendship and their romances, including their love for the same man.

Blow Dry
2001, Alan Rickman

When the tiny burgh of Keighley lands the rights to host the annual British hairdressing championships, practically every city in the United Kingdom is represented in the competition — except Keighley itself. It seems the event is team-oriented, and the only suitable local contestants had a huge falling out a decade ago. For Brian, the son of two hairdressers, that falling out had personal consequences: His mother, Shelley, left his father, Phil, to take up with Phil's hair model, Sandra, former styling champ. Phil has settled for training Brian to help run his lowly barber shop, while Shelley and Sandra have opened a salon of their own. But when Shelley learns that she has terminal cancer, she reaches out to her family in hopes that a reunion for the hairdressing contest might help them all find some sense of closure.

Chocolat
1997, Juliette Binoche & Judi Dench

Vianne Rocher and her young daughter are strangers who are met with skepticism and resistance when they move to a conservative village in rural France and open a chocolate shop during Lent. As Vianne begins to work her magic and help those around her, the townspeople are soon won over by her exuberance and her delicious chocolates - except for the mayor, who is determined to shut her down. When a group of river drifters visit the town, Vianne teaches the townspeople something about acceptance and finds love along the way.

Cinema Paradiso
1990, Phillipe Noiret

A boy who grew up in a Sicilian Village returns home as a famous director after receiving news about the death of his old friend, Alfredo. Told in a flashback, Salvatore reminiscences about his childhood and his relationship with Alfredo, the projectionist at Cinema Paradiso. Under the fatherly influence of Alfredo, Salvatore fell in love with film making, with the duo spending many hours discussing films and Alfredo painstakingly teaching Salvatore the skills that became a stepping stone for the young boy into the world of film making. Cinema Paradiso brings the audience through the changes in cinema and the dying trade of traditional film making, editing and screening. It also explores a young boy's dream of leaving his little town to foray into the world outside.

The Color Purple
1985, Danny Glover & Oprah Winfrey

The Color Purple follows the life of Celie Johnson as she struggles through life in the early 1900s. The film begins with Celie, about 17 years old, giving birth to her second child, sired by her father. Her father takes the second child away from her and tells her never to tell anyone about it. Time passes and a local farmer, "Mister", comes by to marry Celie's younger, prettier sister, Nettie. Her father refuses to let Nettie marry and gives the man Celie instead. Meanwhile, Mister's lover comes to visit and befriends Celie, helping her to understand that she is more than

Mister's servant. The movie culminates in Celie leaving Mister with the threat that everything he touches will fall apart until he does right by her. Mister finds compassion and goes to the INS to help Celie's sister Nettie prove that she is a US citizen and return from Africa where she has been living with Celie's two children. Celie is reunited with Nettie and her two children in a heartfelt ending to an extraordinary film.

Crimes and Misdemeanors
1989, Woody Allen, Martin Landau, Claire Bloom, Alan Alda, Anjelica Huston, Sam Waterston, Jerry Orbach & Mia Farrow

An ophthalmologist's mistress threatens to reveal their affair to his wife; his brother suggests a solution to his problem. Meanwhile an unhappily married documentary filmmaker is attracted to another woman in the midst of making a film about a philosopher who he admires. This interesting philosophical exploration of good and evil ends in a moral dilemma.

Dead Man Walking
1997, Susan Sarandon & Sean Penn

Based on the memoir of Sister Helen Prejean, who visited with the convicted murderer, Matthew Poncelet, during the final week before his state-ordered execution. Though inexperienced in criminal chaplaincy, Sister Helen becomes Poncelet's spiritual counselor and connects him with a lawyer, who helps him appeal his conviction with the State Board of Capital Punishment, the Governor of Louisiana, and the State of Louisiana Supreme Court without success. Sister Helen visits the victims' families and listens to their stories of pain, suffering, and anguish. With a tidal wave of opposition and criticism, she helps Matthew come to terms with the responsibility of the murders and rape he has committed.

Enchanted April
1992, Josie Lawrence & Miranda Richardson

Imagine a month in paradise with nothing to do but everything you dreamed of...Lottie and Rose, two married women living in a 1920s London, share the misery of empty relationships with their spouses and decide to rent an Italian villa for the month of April to get away. In order to save money, they advertise for two other women to join them. Mrs. Fisher, an elderly widow who knew many famous authors in her youth and Lady Caroline Dester who is a gorgeous, young widow who only wants to be left alone... or so she thinks...

The four arrive at Villa San Salvatore on the Italian seaside drenched in wisteria and sunshine, they find themselves in a beauty so enchanting that they experience transformations in themselves they never thought possible. The film is gorgeous, the scenery is breathtaking... no doubt you will want to visit the Italian coast after seeing this film.

The Fourth Wise Man
1985, Alan Arkin & Martin Sheen

Artaban is a young Magus who desires to follow the star to the birthplace of the coming King, against the counsel of his friends and family. Carrying three precious jewels to give to the Messiah, Artaban and his reluctant servant Orontes set off to join the caravan of the three other wise men. They miss the caravan, but Artaban continues his search, always one step behind. Artaban spends much of his remaining wealth and all of his energy helping the poor and unfortunate people he meets, until at the end of his life he finally finds his Messiah.

The Great Debaters
2007, Denzel Washington & Forest Whitaker

Marshall, Texas, described by James Farmer, Jr. as "the last city to surrender after the Civil War," is home to Wiley College, where, in 1935-36, inspired by the Harlem Renaissance and his clandestine work as a union organizer, Professor Melvin Tolson coaches the debate team to a nearly-undefeated season that sees the first debate between U.S. students from white and Negro colleges and ends with an invitation to face Harvard University's national champions. The team of four, which includes a female student and a very young James Farmer, is tested in a crucible heated by Jim Crow, sexism, a lynch mob, an arrest and near riot, a love affair, jealousy, and a national radio audience. Based on actual events.

Invictus
2009, Morgan Freeman & Matt Damon

The film tells the inspiring true story of how Nelson Mandela joined forces with the captain of South Africa's rugby team to help unite their country. Newly elected President Mandela knows his nation remains racially and economically divided in the wake of apartheid. Believing he can bring his people together through the universal language of sports, Mandela rallies South Africa's rugby team as they make their historic run to the 1995 Rugby World Cup Championship match.

It's a Wonderful Life
1939, James Stewart & Donna Reed

On the Christmas Eve in Bedford Falls, the guardian angel Clarence is assigned to convince the desperate George Bailey not to commit suicide. George is a good man who sacrificed his dreams and his youth on behalf of the citizens of his small town. He inherited the loan business from his father and he gave up traveling the world and going to university as scheduled. Later he resisted the proposals of the evil banker, Mr. Potter, and never sold his business in order to protect the less fortunate of Bedford Falls, offering them a means to afford to buy their own house. When Clarence sees that he is not able to persuade George to give up his intention to commit suicide, he shows George how life in Bedford Falls would have been if George had never existed.

I've Loved You So Long
2007, Kristin Scott Thomas

This powerful story of familial struggles and redemption follows a shell-shocked Juliette, who returns to live with her young sister Lea after being banished from the family for 15 years. An enormous critical and box office success in France, Scott-Thomas' phenomenal performance has already been singled out by critics for end-of-year award consideration

Jean de Florette
1986, Yves Montand & Gerard Depardieu

In a rural French village an old man and his only remaining relative cast their covetous eyes on an adjoining vacant property. They need its spring water for growing their flowers, so are dismayed to hear that the man who has inherited it is moving in. They block up the spring and watch as their new neighbor tries to keep his crops watered from wells far afield through the hot summer. Though they see his desperate efforts are breaking his health and his wife and daughter's hearts they think only of themselves. Part 1 is followed by...

Mannon of the Spring
1986, Yves Montand & Emmanuelle Beart

In this, the sequel to Jean de Florette, Mannon has grown into a beautiful young shepherdess living in the idyllic Provencal countryside. She is determined to take revenge upon the men responsible for the death of her father in the first film, Jean de Florette, but a miraculous event changes her heart.

Joshua
2002, Tony Goldwyn, F. Murray Abraham & Giancarlo Gianinni

One day a stranger named Joshua comes to the small town of Auburn and begins to help out in small, but miraculous ways. As Joshua's reputation and popularity grow, a local, embittered clergyman believes that Joshua is a false prophet trying to cheat the people and reports him to the Vatican for condemnation. The conflicts build, but the people of Auburn are forever changed by this unknown stranger.

Joyeux Noel
2005, Diane Kruger & Benno Furman

On the Christmas Eve of 1914, along the Eastern border of Alsace Lorrain in France during World War I, the Scottish, German and French troops share a moment of truce and friendship. A famous soprano succeeds in convincing the Prussian Prince to join her tenor husband to sing for the German high command. She goes to the trenches to sing for the soldiers. A Scottish Lieutenant and a French Lieutenant have an informal and unauthorized meeting with a German Lieutenant and the three negotiate a truce for that night, and an impromptu Christmas Eve mass is celebrated for all the soldiers. When their superiors become aware of the event, they are punished for fraternizing with the enemy. Based on true events.

The King of Masks
2003, Chinese

Wang Bianlian is an aging street performer known as the King of Masks for his mastery of Sichuan Change Art. More than thirty years ago his wife left him with an infant son. The boy died from illness at age ten, leaving Wang a melancholy loner aching for a male descendent to learn his rare and dying art. A famous master performer of the Sichuan Opera offers to bring him into his act, thus giving Wang fame and possible fortune, but Wang opts for living the life of a simple street performer. Then, one night after a performance he buys a young boy from a slave trader who is posing as the boy's father. "Grandpa" finds new joy in life as he plans to teach "Doggie" (an affectionate term often used for young children in China) his family secret of Change Art. Doggie's unconditional love transforms their mutual destinies.

Ladies in Lavender
2004, Judi Dench & Maggie Smith

The story takes place in pre-war England, where aging sisters Ursula and Janet live peacefully in their cottage on the shore of Cornwall. One morning following a violent storm, the sisters spot from their garden a nearly-drowned man lying on the beach. They nurse him back to health, and discover that he is Polish. Communicating in broken German while they teach him English, they learn his name is Andrea and that he is a particularly gifted violinist. His boat was on its way to America, where he was headed to look for a better life. It doesn't take long for them to become attached to Andrea.

Malèna
2001, Monica Bellucci

On the day in 1940 that Italy enters the war, two things happen to the 12-year-old Renato: he gets his first bike, and he gets his first look at Malèna. She is a beautiful, silent outsider who's moved to this Sicilian town to be with her husband, Nico. He promptly goes off to war, leaving her to the lustful eyes of the men and the sharp tongues of the women. During the next few years, as Renato grows toward manhood, he watches Malèna suffer and prove her mettle. He sees her loneliness, then grief when Nico is reported dead, the effects of slander on her relationship with her father, her poverty, her humiliating search for survival, and her final transformation.

The Reader
2008, Ralph Fiennes & Kate Winslet

In post-WWII Germany, after a summer affair with a mysterious older woman, the youthful barrister Michael Berg loses contact with her. Ten years later he encounters his former lover as she defends herself in a war crimes trial and wrestles with a secret. This is a beautifully interpreted tale of truth and reconciliation: how one generation comes to terms with the crimes of another.

Remember the Titans
2000, Denzel Washington

Suburban Virginia schools had been segregated for generations, in sight of the Washington Monument over the river in the nation's capital. One black and one white high school are closed and the students are sent to Williams High School under federal mandate to integrate. The year is seen through the eyes of the football team where the man hired to coach the black school is made head coach over the highly successful white coach. Based on actual events of 1971, the team becomes the unifying symbol for the community as the boys and the adults learn to depend on and trust each other.

The Scent of a Woman
1992, Al Pacino & Chris O'Donnell

Retired colonel Frank Slade has a secret plan for a special Thanksgiving weekend in New York City. Charlie Simms, a prep school student, needs some money and agrees to care for the blind veteran for the weekend. The two enter an event-filled, life-changing experience when their code of honor collides with one's past and the other's present. Based on the 1974 Italian film *Profumo di Donna*.

Shadrach
1998, Harvey Keitel

In 1935, 99-year-old former slave Shadrach asks to be buried on the soil where he was born to slavery. That land is owned by the large Dabney family — Vernon, Trixie and their seven children — who defy law and tradition to do what is right.

Shirley Valentine
1989, Pauline Collins & Tom Conti

Shirley is a middle-aged Liverpool housewife, who finds herself talking to the wall while she prepares her husband's chip'n'egg, wondering what happened to her life. She compares scenes in her current life with what she used to be like and feels that she and her life have stagnated. But when her best friend wins an all-expenses-paid vacation to Greece for two, Shirley begins to see the world, and herself, in a different light.

The Straight Story
1999, Sissy Spacek

This film chronicles a trip made by 73-year-old Alvin Straight from Laurens, Iowa, to Mt. Zion, Wis., in 1994 on a riding lawn mower. The man undertook this strange journey in order to mend his relationship with his estranged, 75-year-old brother Lyle. Based on a true story.

The Way Home
2003, Korean

Seven-year-old Sang-woo is left with his grandmother in a remote village while his mother looks for work. Born and raised in the city, Sang-woo quickly comes into conflict with his old-fashioned, mute grandmother and his new rural surroundings. Disrespectful and selfish, Sang-woo lashes out in anger, perceiving that he has been abandoned. He trades his grandmother's only treasure for a video game; he throws his food and he throws tantrums. When Sang-woo's mother finds work and finally returns for him, Sang-woo has become a different boy. Through his grandmother's boundless patience, love and devotion, he learns to embrace empathy, humility and family.

Whale Rider
2002, Keisha Castle-Hughes

On the east coast of New Zealand, the Whangara people believe their presence there dates back a thousand years or more to a single ancestor, Paikea, who escaped death when his canoe capsized by riding to shore on the back of a whale. From then on, Whangara chiefs, always the first-born, always male, have been considered Paikea's direct descendants. Pai, an 11-year-old girl in a patriarchal New Zealand tribe, believes she is destined to be the new chief. But her grandfather Koro is bound by tradition to pick a male leader. Pai loves Koro more than anyone in the world, but she must fight him and a thousand years of tradition to fulfill her destiny.

The White Countess
Ralph Fiennes & Natasha Richardson

Russian Countess Sofia Belinskya remembers old times of opulence and fancy parties, while she and her husband's family are living in exile in Shanghai, during the 1930s. Now, she has a poor life with her daughter Katya. The Countess works as a hostess and companion lady in a dance club, where she entertains all kinds of men, dancing with them and having a chat. There, she makes the acquaintance of a blind American diplomat, Todd Jackson, a kind man with whom she begins a friendship. Years later, Jackson sets up a glamorous club, called "The White Countess", taking Sofia with him to work there as a companion lady. But Sofia doesn't want Katya to find out about her real work, protecting the girl from following in her foot steps in the future. Between Jackson and Sofia there exists a special attraction, which could turn into love at any moment. The Japanese invasion begins, threatening their dreams and longings.

William Shakespeare's Romeo and Juliet
1968, Leonard Whiting and Olivia Hussey

Shakespeare's classic tale of romance, tragedy and reconciliation. In the last scene the feuding Montagues and Capulets, looking in horror upon the bodies of their dead children, lay aside their hatred and vow to make peace. No need to say more: this exquisitely beautiful film classic by Franco Zeffirelli says it all.

Wit;
2001, Emma Thompson

Based on the Margaret Edson play, Vivian Bearing, a demanding and uncompromising professor of 17th century English poetry specializing in the holy sonnets of John Donne, is diagnosed with advanced (stage 4) metastatic ovarian cancer. Being an academic, she treats the news with a certain matter-of-factness much like she would her own research. Indeed, her medical team treat her like a research experiment, with a "live at all cost" mentality. The doctors recommend an experimental treatment of aggressive chemotherapy, to which she agrees. As her treatment progresses, she wishes she had some more truly caring human interaction from people who see her as a person and not just a research experiment.

Authors, Stories & Notes

The Rev. Joseph Alden

Joseph Alden (1807–1885) was an American academic, prolific writer and Presbyterian pastor. *Forgiveness* is from *The Lost Lamb and Other Tales* (1863).

T.S. Arthur

Timothy Shay Arthur (1809–1885) was a popular nineteenth-century American author. Although now largely forgotten, his 1854 temperance novel, *Ten Nights in a Bar-Room, and What I Saw There*, rivaled *Uncle Tom's Cabin* in popularity. The selection in this anthology, *Forgive And Forget*, is from his 1851 book *Lessons in Life for All Who Will Read Them*.

Maurice Baring

Maurice Baring (1874–1945) was an English dramatist, poet, novelist, translator, essayist, travel writer and war correspondent. *Jean Francois* was included in his collection *Orpheus in Mayfair* in 1909.

Robert Barr

Robert Barr (1849-1912) was a Scottish-born Canadian editor, journalist and writer who spent most of his life in England. He and Jerome K. Jerome founded the humor magazine, *The Idler*. A great friend of Arthur Conan Doyle, he was best known for his "Sherlaw Kombs" parodies of the Sherlock Holmes stories which he wrote under the pen name Luke Sharp. *The Count's Apology* was taken from *The Strong Arm* (1899).

L. Adams Beck

Lily Adams Beck (1862-1931) was a pen name of Elizabeth Louisa Moresby, the first prolific female fantasy writer of Canada. She was a Buddhist, a strict vegetarian and critic of the materialism of the West. *The Hatred of the Queen; A Story of Burma* is taken from *The Ninth Vibration and Other Stories* (1922).

Algernon Blackwood

Algernon Henry Blackwood (1869–1951) was an English writer of supernatural fiction. *Cain's Atonement* is from *Day and Night Stories* (1917).

Anton Chekhov

Anton Pavlovich Chekhov (1860–1904) was a Russian short story writer, playwright and physician, considered to be one of the greatest short story writers in world literature. *The Requiem* was first published in Russian in 1886 and first appeared in English in *The Schoolmistress and Other Stories* (1921). *A Problem* is taken from *The Party and Other Stories* (1917). Both were translated by Constance Garnett.

Maria Edgeworth

Maria Edgeworth (1767–1849) was an Anglo-Irish novelist. She and her father, R.L. Edgeworth, wrote a series of well-regarded lesson plans for teaching children. *Forgive and Forget* is from the 1865 American edition of her short story collection, *The Parent's Assistant*.

Erckmann-Chatrain

Erckmann-Chatrian was the name used by French authors Émile Erckmann (1822-1899) and Alexandre Chatrian (1826-1890), nearly all of whose works were jointly written. *The Scapegoat* was published in *The Man-Wolf and Other Stories* (1876). The translator is identified as "F.M."

Edna Ferber

Edna Ferber (1885–1968) was an American novelist, author and playwright. Several theater and film productions have been made based on her works, including *Show Boat* and *Giant*. *The Woman Who Tried to Be Good* was first published in *The Saturday Evening Post* on June 14, 1913.

F. Scott Fitzgerald

Francis Scott Key Fitzgerald (1896–1940) was an American author of novels and short stories. *The Fiend* was originally published in *Esquire Magazine* in 1935 and was anthologized in *Taps at Reveille* that same year.

Elizabeth Gaskell

Elizabeth Cleghorn Gaskell (1810–1865) was an English novelist and short story writer. The daughter and wife of Unitarian ministers, her rounds among her Manchester parishioners gave her unusual access to the lives of the poor and working class, which she wrote about in novels such as *Mary Barton* and *North and South. The Heart of John Middleton* was originally published in Charles Dickens' *Household Words* magazine in 1850. *The Sexton's Hero* originally appeared in *Howitt's Journal* in 1847.

Susan Glaspell

Susan Keating Glaspell (1876–1948) was a Pulitzer Prize-winning playwright, actress, director, bestselling novelist and a founding member of the Provincetown Players. *A Jury of Her Peers*, loosely based on the murder of John Hossack, which Glaspell covered while working as a journalist, was originally written as a one-act play entitled *Trifles* for the Provincetown Players in 1916 and was published as a short story in *Every Week* magazine the following year.

Thomas Hardy

Thomas Hardy (1840 –1928) was an English novelist and poet. Most of his fictional works, including *Tess of the D'Ubervilles, Far From the Madding Crowd* and *Jude the Obscure,* were set in the semi-fictional land of Wessex (based on the Dorchester region where he grew up.) *For Conscience' Sake* is from *Life's Little Ironies: A Set Of Tales, With Some Colloquial Sketches* (1894).

Jerome K. Jerome

Jerome Klapka Jerome (1859–1927) was an English writer, best known for the humorous travelogue *Three Men in a Boat. The Cost of Kindness* was published in 1908.

Guy de Maupassant

Henri René Albert Guy de Maupassant (1850–1893) was a popular 19th Century French writer, considered one of the fathers of the modern short story. *Forgiveness (Le Pardon)* was first published in 1882 and *A Sister's Confession (La Confession)* in 1883.

Henry Seton Merriman

Hugh Stowell Scott (1863–1903) was an insurance underwriter at Lloyd's who wrote under the pseudonym of Henry Seton Merriman. *Putting Things Right* was published posthumously in *Tomaso's Forturne and Other Stories* in 1904.

Miss Mitford

Mary Russell Mitford (1787–1855), was an English novelist and dramatist best known as the author of *Our Village*, a series of sketches of village scenes. We found the story in this collection, *Tajima*, in *Stories by English Writers: The Orient* (Scribner's, 1896).

Yei Theodora Ozaki

Yei Theodora Ozaki The daughter of one of the first Japanese men to study in the west, and an English woman, was an early 20th century translator of Japanese short stories and fairy tales. *The Mirror Of Matsuyama* was published in *Japanese Fairy Tales* (1908), translated from modern versions written by Sadanami Sanjin.

Thomas Nelson Page

Thomas Nelson Page (1853–1922) was a Virginia lawyer and writer who also served as the U.S. ambassador to Italy during World War I. *The Christmas Peace* was published in *Scribner's Magazine* in 1891.

O. Henry

William Sydney Porter (1862-1910), who wrote under the name O. Henry, was a prolific American short story writer, who published ten collections and more than 600 stories in his lifetime. In 1884 he started a humorous weekly, *The Rolling Stone*. When it failed, he joined the *Houston Post* as a reporter and columnist. In 1897 he was convicted of embezzling money; while in prison he started to write short stories. *The Things the Play* was anthologized in his book *Strictly Business: More Tales of the Four Million* (1910).

Saki

Hector Hugh Munro (1870–1916), better known by the pen name Saki, was a British writer. *The Penance* was anthologized in *The Toys of Peace, and other papers*, published in 1919.

Leo Tolstoy

Count Lev Nikolayevich Tolstoy (1828–1910) was a Russian writer widely regarded as among the greatest of novelists. His masterpieces are *War and Peace* and *Anna Karenina*. *A Spark Neglected* (sometimes translated as *Quench the Spark)* was first published in 1885. *God Sees the Truth, But Waits* was first published in 1872.

Edith Wharton

Edith Wharton (1862–1937) was an American novelist and short story writer. She was the first woman to win the Pulitzer Prize for Literature, in 1921, for *Age of Innocence*. *The Reckoning* first appeared in *Harper's Monthly* in 1902 and was anthologized in *The Descent of Man and Other Stories* in 1904.

Oscar Wilde

Oscar Fingal O'Flahertie Wills Wilde (1854–1900) was an Irish playwright, poet and author of numerous short stories and one novel. Known for his biting wit, he was one of the greatest "celebrities" of his day. *The Star Child* is from *A House of Pomegranates* (1892).

Israel Zangwill

Israel Zangwill (1864-1926) was an English humorist and writer. The use of the metaphorical phrase "melting pot" to describe American absorption of immigrants was popularized by Zangwill's play *The Melting Pot*; his short novel *The Big Bow Mystery* was the first locked room murder mystery. *The Silent Sister* was taken from *The Grey Wig* (1903), a collection of short stories that Zangwill described as "mainly a study of women" in his dedication to his mother and sisters.

Rosalyn Falcón Collier

Rosalyn Falcón Collier is the cofounder of the San Antonio peaceCENTER. A native of San Antonio, Texas, she has led local meditation groups in Catholic parishes since 1997. Through Oblate School of Theology Rosalyn is currently co-facilitating the Called Back to the Well Spiritual Renewal Program. She is a spiritual director and mediator and facilitates skillshops on nonviolence and transformative mediation. Rosalyn was a mediator with the Victim Offender Mediation Program through the Texas Department of Criminal Justice from 1999 to 2003.

Rosalyn is the author of *Working it Out: Managing and Mediating Everyday Conflicts* (2008) and co-author of *Walking Jesus' Path of Peace: Living Faithfully in a Violent World* (Augsburg, 2001); *Peace Is Our BirthRight* (2008) and *Shall We Ever Rise? A Holy Walk* (2009).

Marietta Jaeger-Lane

Marietta Jaeger-Lane was a founding board member of Murder Victim Families for Reconciliation and Murder Victim Families for Human Rights and is cofounder and board member of the Journey of Hope...From Violence to Healing. Marietta speaks about the death penalty in numerous venues throughout the United States, participates in the Journey of Hope's annual speaking tour, and has given two interviews to Vatican Radio, testified before the UN Commission on Human Rights in Geneva, and spoken for Amnesty International's Worldwide Campaign to Abolish the Death Penalty. She lives in Montana.

Naomi Shihab Nye

Naomi Shihab Nye, daughter of a Palestinian father and an American mother, lived as a teenager in Ramallah, the Old City in Jerusalem, and San Antonio, Texas, where she later received her B.A. in English and world religions from Trinity University.

Naomi is the author of numerous books of poems, including *You and Yours* (BOA Editions, 2005), which received the Isabella Gardner Poetry Award, and *19 Varieties of Gazelle: Poems of the Middle East* (2002), a collection of new and selected poems about the Middle East, the collection in which the poem *Jerusalem* appeared. She lives in San Antonio.

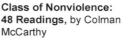

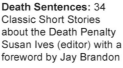